Also by Robin Kaye

The Bad Boys of Red Hook Series

Hometown Girl
(A Penguin Special)
Back to You

YOU'RE THE ONE

BAD BOYS OF RED HOOK

ROBIN KAYE

A SIGNET ECLIPSE BOOK

SIGNET ECLIPSE
Published by the Penguin Group
Penguin Group (USA) Inc., 375 Hudson Street,
New York, New York 10014, USA

USA | Canada | UK | Ireland | Australia | New Zealand | India | South Africa | China

Penguin Books Ltd., Registered Offices: 80 Strand, London WC2R 0RL, England
For more information about the Penguin Group visit penguin.com.

First published by Signet Eclipse, an imprint of New American Library,
a division of Penguin Group (USA) Inc.

First Printing, June 2012

SIGNET ECLIPSE and logo are trademarks of Penguin Group (USA) Inc.

ISBN: 978-0-451-41356-7

Printed in the United States of America
10 9 8 7 6 5 4 3 2 1

ALWAYS LEARNING   **PEARSON**

To all the booksellers who support their favorite authors, put great novels in the hands of their customers, and share the gifts that can be found only in a good book. Thanks for loving books and sharing that love with your customers. Especially Dena Russ at B & L Books in Altamonte Springs, Florida, and Kaori Fischer and all my friends at the Barnes & Noble in Melbourne, Florida.

Lord! When you sell a man a book you don't sell just twelve ounces of paper and ink and glue—you sell him a whole new life. Love and friendship and humour and ships at sea by night—there's all heaven and earth in a book, a real book.

—Christopher Morley

ACKNOWLEDGMENTS

I'd love to say I wrote this book all on my own but, as with most things, it takes a village to make a book. Here are some of the people who have helped me:

I'd like to thank chef Jeff Eng and pastry chef Maura Radmanesh of Clydes Tower Oaks Lodge in Rockville, Maryland. They invited me to spend a day in their kitchen, allowed me to ask all the questions I could think of, no matter how stupid, and fed me some of the best food I've had in the state of Maryland. Chef Eng even helped me come up with a few menu items. If there are mistakes, they are all on me.

I'm lucky to have the love and support of my incredible family. My husband, Stephen, who after twenty-three years of marriage is still the man of my dreams and best friend. My children, Tony, Anna, and Isabelle, who in spite of being teenagers are my favorite people to hang out with. Alex Henderson and Jessye and Dylan Green, whom I love like my own kids. All of them make me laugh, amaze me with their intelligence and generosity, and make me proud every day.

My parents, Richard Williams and Ann Feiler, and my stepfather, George Feiler, who always encouraged me, and continue to do so.

My wonderful critique partners Laura Becraft and Deborah Villegas. They shortened my sentences, corrected my grammar, and put commas where they needed to be. They listened to me whine when my muse took a vacation, gave me great ideas when I was stuck, and answered that all-important question: Does this suck? They helped me plot, loved my characters almost as much as I did, and challenged me to be a better writer. They are my friends, my confidantes, and my bullshit meters.

I owe a debt of gratitude to their families, who so graciously let me borrow them during my deadline crunch. So, to Robert, Joe, Elisabeth, and Ben Becraft, and Ruben, Alexander, Donovan, and Cristian Villegas, you have my thanks and eternal gratitude.

I'd also like to thank my writing friends who are always there when I need a fresh eye or a sounding board—Grace Burrowes, Hope Ramsay, Susan Donovan, Mary Freeman, R. R. Smythe, Margie Lawson, Michael Hauge, and Christie Craig.

I wrote most of this book at the Mt. Airy, Maryland, Starbucks, and I have to thank all my baristas for keeping me in laughter and coffee while I camped out in their store. I also need to thank my fellow customers who have become wonderful friends: Cory, Melissa, Liz, Barbara, Cheryl, Kelly, Mike, Doug, Jerry, Jennifer, and Phil.

As always, I want to thank my incredible agent, Kevan Lyon, for all she does, and my team at NAL—the cover artists for the beautiful job they did, and my editors, Kerry Donovan and Jesse Feldman, for all their insight, direction, and enthusiasm. Working with you has been a real pleasure.

CHAPTER 1

Logan Blaise pulled Breanna Collins—no, make that the new Mrs. Storm Decker—into a tight turn and twirled her around the dance floor. As he drew her closer, her floor-length white wedding gown swirled against his legs.

Bree's hand relaxed on his shoulder. "Are you and Payton planning to have your wedding reception here too?"

The thought of Payton and her family at his family's restaurant in Brooklyn, the Crow's Nest, was enough to make his ass twitch. Her idea of slumming it was staying at the Plaza without an en suite butler. "The Crow's Nest is a nice place by Red Hook standards, but by Payton's standards . . . not so much."

"I thought California girls were laid-back. How'd you two hook up anyway?"

A question he'd been asking himself for some time. He and Payton were one hell of an unlikely pair, the princess and the pauper. He wasn't a pauper now, but he had been when they got together—not that he publicized the fact. He did his best to never talk about his life before college.

He said he was from New York, and if they thought it was Park Avenue instead of Red Hook—all the better. Most people at Stanford didn't know Red Hook, Brooklyn, even existed. "We've been together since college. After graduation, I did an internship at her family's vineyard and I've been working for her dad ever since. You know how it goes on the relationship train. I was just riding along and one day I realized we'd gone from dating to living together. It was comfortable and it worked. Marriage just seems like the next stop on the line."

Bree raised one of her very expressive eyebrows at that. "Wow, that sounds so romantic—not."

"Bree, Payton's a nice woman. I like being with her. She's beautiful, classy, we work well together, and we get along well. Her dad is great and he's grooming me to take over the vineyard. Since Payton never had much interest in the business, it all makes a weird kind of sense."

"Love isn't supposed to make sense, Logan. Love just is. But then, you know that already—after all, you and Payton have been together a lot longer than Storm and me. You must be doing something right."

He'd never really thought about it. "It's . . . comfortable." And there was nothing wrong with comfort, was there?

"So, what's with the dark, broody look?"

Shit, he must have been frowning again. He pasted on a smile. Pop had always teased him about his dour expression whenever he studied or contemplated some new idea. The gears were always turning, only his gears revolved around compounds, elements, and chemistry. Normally the chemistry was blowing something up or perfecting the bouquet of a fine wine. This was the first time it had to do with the L word. "I'm happy for you, Bree. Really, I am. You're my favorite sister-in-law."

"I'm your only sister-in-law."

"I just don't understand why you had to get married now. How can you in good conscience leave me with a convalescing crotchety old fart like Pop?"

"Pete's not old and he's getting stronger every day. He's been out of the hospital for weeks. He's not going to die on you."

Logan looked over. Pop was holding up the bar, surrounded by his cronies—the guys from when they'd all been cops in the neighborhood. Pop wasn't supposed to be drinking yet. He sipped something that did not look like soda. "No, he'll sneak stogies and beer. Shit, he's probably already hidden a bottle of scotch under his pillow."

For the special occasion, Pop had slicked back what was left of his white hair. He still wore his jacket, but his tie was history. No surprise there. "He needs a babysitter more than Nicki, and she's only ten."

"Exaggerate much? Pete's well enough to work a few hours a day. Just don't let him overdo it."

"Right. But you don't get it. No matter how old I am, I'm still his son—he tells *me* what to do. He'll never take orders from me."

Pop slapped one of his friends on the back and let out a shotgun laugh. "Look at him, Bree." He turned her toward Pop.

"Don't worry—nothing keeps Pete Calahan down. Not a bullet, not a major heart attack, not a quad bypass."

"That's what I'm afraid of. I've already threatened him, but, unlike you, I'm not scary."

Bree's hold on his shoulder tightened midspin. "If I had known that hitting Storm over the head with a cast-iron frying pan would make every man afraid of me, I would have done it years ago. Just a clue, Logan: I'm not the only one who can wield a mean skillet."

"No, but you're the only one who can get away with it. Face it—I'm screwed here. Even you—Wonder Woman with the frying pan of truth—have a hard time controlling Pop."

"I'm not worried. You'll manage."

"What about Nicki? What do I know about taking care of a ten-year-old girl? Women—no problem. Preteen girls—shit—I didn't even know anything about them when I was that age."

"It's common sense, Logan. Just don't ever let her forget that you're the adult."

"Bree, it's like Nicki's just getting settled into the canoe. You and Storm leaving is rockin' it. Leaving me in charge is enough to make it flip. We hardly know each other."

"Don't you think it's about time you changed that?" Bree's green eyes reminded him of an experiment with potassium nitrate gone awry. She had a short fuse and could emit a big bang.

"Hey, it's not as if I don't want to know Nicki." He leaned in closer. "I want to know her, but I just met her. We're practically strangers."

"As hard as it seems, it's good you'll have one-on-one time to bond with Nicki."

"Bree, I had a dozen foster fathers in nine years and they could be standing next to me and I wouldn't recognize them. Bonding is not my strong suit. I didn't get a real dad until Pop took me in when I was twelve."

"Pete's the best dad I've ever known. You, Storm, and Slater turned out great. You're a warm, loving, giving, successful man."

Someone cleared his throat right behind him. Logan turned to find Storm, his foster brother, wearing a glare that would have made a lesser man want to sleep with one eye open. "I'm just borrowing her, bro. I'll give her back real soon—if you're lucky and the lady's accommodating."

Storm was just shy of Logan's six foot three, with the same dark hair, but that's where the resemblance ended. Logan had a darker complexion, where Storm had the light skin and eyes of the Black Irish.

"Breezy, we've been married less than four hours and you're already flirting with my brother?"

Logan stepped away. He wasn't about to push his luck. It hadn't ever been that good.

"I'm surprised you even noticed. You were too busy dancing with Patrice." Bree feigned jealousy, but she would never make it onstage. Not even off-off-Broadway.

Storm rolled his eyes and pulled her into his arms. They came together as if they'd rehearsed it a million times.

Compared to Storm and Bree, Logan and Payton's relationship looked about as genuine as a ring at the bottom of a Cracker Jack box. He shook his head. First Pop's heart attack, then Nicki's appearance in his life, now the whirlwind marriage of his brother to a girl they had known practically forever. No wonder Logan couldn't get his balance—his world had been thrown on a psychedelic Tilt-A-Whirl. It was a wonder he was still sane.

Storm and Bree's connection was palpable. It was

something that he'd never had with Payton. It was something he'd never had with anyone, really. It was something, until now, he never knew existed.

Logan fought the urge to back away into obscurity and reinserted himself. He kissed Bree on the cheek— "Be happy, Bree"—and tugged Storm into a guy hug, smacking his back harder than necessary. "Take good care of her. You're one lucky son of a bitch."

"Don't I know it?" Storm pulled away but held on to Logan's shoulders—too close to his neck for his peace of mind. "Take care of everything here and if you run into problems, don't call us. Just work it out. We're outta here, big brother."

Nicki ran toward them in a cloud of teal taffeta.

"Incoming." Logan motioned toward the running Crayola. "Word on the street is that you had to bribe Nicki to wear a dress and play bridesmaid."

Nicki's dark hair, the same color as his, was falling out of the once-artful pile on her head, and her long spindly legs ate up the distance. "Wait!"

Logan caught her before she could take out the bride. "Slow down, Nicki. You need to adjust your stopping distance. Those dress shoes aren't like your trusty Vans."

Nicki ignored him. "Bree, Storm, you can't leave until you throw the bouquet and garter."

Logan figured that if anything good came out of marriage, it would be that he'd never have to stand like an ass with all the other single dudes dodging the garter. It was a dumb tradition—almost as dumb as the bride tossing the bouquet to all the desperate single females. Marriage was nothing more than a sensible decision—well, except for people like Storm and Bree. For them, it was something he would never have believed existed if he hadn't seen it with his own eyes—it was a love match.

Logan knelt, and the drumroll started. He slid the garter up Rocki O'Sullivan's Rockette-worthy, drool-inducing, smoothly sinful long, long, long leg.

Rocki's short, choppy platinum blond hair had a fluorescent pink streak bisecting the sideswept bangs obscuring one of her brilliant blue eyes. She shot him a sexy smirk and slid her pointed foot up the inside of his thigh. "You know, it's a real shame you're not single. I'd take you in a Brooklyn minute."

He knew better than to ask, but he couldn't help himself. "A Brooklyn minute?"

"Yeah, it's a little longer than a New York minute." She trailed her toe right up to his family jewels. "Let's face it—there are just some things that shouldn't be rushed."

He grabbed her ankle and pushed it away from his crotch.

Patrice—amateur videographer, busybody, and the first girl Logan had ever pictured naked—drew nearer for a close-up.

Logan's gaze darted over the crowd, looking for a lifeline, a friend, anyone who would help him out of this clusterfuck. Pop stood in his line of vision and seemed to be enjoying Logan's situation.

Rocki ate it up and judging by the smile on her face, she was enjoying the hell out of making a spectacle of him. "Smile, Logan. You're on *Candid Camera*."

Great. He could see this going viral in less than ten minutes, knowing Patrice—the woman was better connected than John Gotti's successor. Logan was so fucked, and Rocki knew there wasn't a damn thing he could do about it. When he got the garter over her knee, he stilled.

Rocki grabbed his arm and played to the camera. "Oh, come on, big boy, give the crowd a show. Slide it all the way up."

"Shit." The drumroll picked up speed and the crowd egged him on. His hands disappeared beneath her emerald dress and slid the garter to the top of her thigh-high silk stockings and released it with a stinging snap. He took great pleasure in Rocki's wince—served her right. He held her mile-high heel out to her, partially so she could slide her small foot into it, and partially to protect his manhood. When Cinderella donned her heels, he offered her a hand, and pulled her up.

The chair she'd sat on in the middle of the dance floor disappeared and the band struck the first chords of the song they were to dance to. Of course Rocki had chosen a song about sex. "Insatiable" was a great song if you were looking to get lucky—unfortunately Logan was feeling anything but. He tugged Rocki into his arms praying she wouldn't make a scene.

"So, handsome, how come your fiancée isn't here with you?"

"She's home planning the wedding."

"When's the big day?"

"New Year's Eve."

"Going for the tax break, huh?"

"Excuse me?"

"If you marry before January first, you can file your taxes jointly. It'll save you a chunk of change. Isn't that why you're doing it?"

"No, Payton thought it would be romantic, and it's a

good time for me to be away from the vineyard for the honeymoon." He didn't mention the fact that his future in-laws wanted to have the mother of all New Year's Eve bashes to get plenty of free publicity. What started out as a small family wedding at the vineyard had quickly turned into something better held under a big top.

"Sounds about as romantic as getting hitched to save on your taxes."

He didn't say anything. It wasn't very chivalrous to agree.

"Do you love her, Logan?"

He didn't publicize his love life or lack thereof. Especially not to Rocki. The first thing she'd do would be to tell Patrice—fewer people would hear about it if he took out a full-page ad in the *Post*. The skin on the back of his neck felt as if it were being used as a pincushion.

"Hey." Rocki pushed away from him. "I'm not coming on to you, but if you don't know if you love your fiancée— the woman you're supposed to spend the rest of your life with—then, I'm sorry to say, the answer is no. So why, pray tell, are you marrying her?"

"Payton is nice, beautiful, she's well connected, we get along well, and we're good together. It's a smart decision."

"Sounds like a match made in hell. Sorry." She patted his chest. "But without love, you got nothin'. Just ask Storm and Bree—they've got the real deal."

He was used to nothin'. He was comfortable with nothin'. He'd never known anything but. "Love doesn't happen to people like me."

Rocki looked as if she was fighting tears.

"What did I say?"

She blinked her blue eyes and sniffed. "Just the saddest thing I've ever heard."

"It's not sad—it's just the way it is. Some people are not meant to love or be loved. I'm one of them."

"Love happens to everyone if you let it. Pete loves you. Storm and Slater do too. And Bree, hell, Bree loves everyone. But the kind of love we're talking about, the kind that grabs you by the balls and won't let go, that doesn't happen if you go around marrying people you don't love because it's a good business decision. I never thought I'd say this, but I feel sorry for you."

Rocki dropped his hand, turned, and left him standing alone in the middle of the dance floor, staring after her.

"You made Rocki sad."

He blinked and cursed his luck. "Nicki, I thought you'd gone to bed. Aren't ten-year-olds supposed to be asleep by now?" He looked at his watch and wondered if Bree had recorded Nicki's bedtime in the annals of her handwritten encyclopedia of child rearing. "What's your bedtime?"

Nicki planted her hands on what would someday be her hips and dug her foot into the wood floor. "I don't have one. I'm not a baby."

That was a lie. "In Bree's book, everyone has a bedtime."

"Ten o'clock?"

"Is that a question or a statement?"

"Fine, it's nine, but I don't want to go to bed until after Storm and Bree leave. Please, Logan, let me stay up. I want to say good-bye. They're going away for, like, forever."

"Only if you don't tell Bree I let you. If she finds out I'm screwing up already, she might never leave. On second thought, maybe she'll rethink this whole honeymoon thing."

"Yeah, nice try. Believe me, it's not gonna work. I've done everything I can to make them want to stay. I even got into trouble at school."

"You did?"

Nicki shrugged. "Bree didn't fall for it. She saw right through me. She always does."

"Is the thought of staying with me and Pop that much of a nightmare?" Damn, he'd done it again. Nicki had that same sad look on her face Rocki did moments before, and she blinked too frequently for it to be anything but something in her eye or the onset of tears. He patted her shoulder. "It'll be okay." He lied through his teeth. "I'm not so bad. You'll see." Logan scanned the restaurant searching for Bree's telltale white dress. A little girl's tears were enough to unman him. He didn't know how to handle them. What the hell was Bree thinking leaving him in charge of Nicki and Pop?

Nicki rested her cheek against the back of his hand and slid her arm around his waist. "That's what Bree said. That and she'll only be gone a month. We even made a calendar to cross off the days. She said she'd send me postcards and everything."

Something trickled against his hand. Damn, either Nicki was crying or she spit on him. He'd been hoping for the latter but no such luck—the angle was all wrong. What the hell was he supposed to do now?

"Logan?"

"Yeah, kid?"

"Who's gonna tuck me in after Storm and Bree leave?"

"I guess I will. But you'll have to tell me what to do."

"Do you give kisses too?"

"Is it part of the whole bedtime routine?"

"Uh-huh."

"Then I guess I'd better start, huh?" He turned her to face him and crouched down low. She was definitely losing a battle with tears. He took out his handkerchief and wiped her face. "I don't know a damn thing about kids, Nicki, but I'll learn. I promise. Just don't cry any more, okay?"

Nicki sniffed and a few more tears fell. "I'm not crying."

"Glad to hear it. Now, come on, let's go and say goodbye to Storm and Bree and you can tell me all about this bedtime thing." He took her hand in his and was floored by how small the kid was. He couldn't remember ever being that small. His neck felt like a pincushion again— but this time, the pins were on fire.

When he'd shown up a few weeks earlier to help take care of his dad and the bar, he'd not only met Nicki for the first time; he'd found out that there was a darn good chance that Nicki might be his daughter. It was a shock to say the least, and he hadn't a clue what to do with her. All he knew was he'd give away everything he'd ever owned, even his '56 Jag, never to see her cry again.

CHAPTER 2

Skye Maxwell sat in the main dining room of the country club, looked at the presents scattered around the large table amid the crumbs of what was once a decadent chocolate fudge birthday cake, and tried not to let her disappointment show. Sure, she had known her family wouldn't be handing her the keys to the new Maxwell's restaurant's kitchen that she would run, but she'd expected at least preliminary architectural drawings. After all, that's what each of her four brothers received on his thirtieth birthday. And as with their gifts, she had expected to see hers encased in a cardboard tube and wrapped like a big Tootsie Roll. Not one of the gifts on the table was in the shape of a tube; none of her gifts were wrapped like a Tootsie Roll. They were square or round, and in no way looked as though any would be large enough to contain blueprints.

Her mother, Mary Margaret Maxwell, patted her dark brown, almost black shoulder-length hair, which had to be dyed. A woman of her age must have at least a few gray hairs after raising four rambunctious boys and Skye, who was no shrinking violet herself. Mary Margaret gave her an assessing look and must have kicked Skye's father, Jack, under the table. Either that or she'd goosed him, because he jumped and shot her mother a what-the-hell-is-wrong-with-you glare. "Is everything okay, Skye?" her mother asked.

Skye could hardly hear beyond the noise in her head—it was as if she went swimming in a pool-sized bowl of Rice Krispies. She reminded herself to breathe and gave the question some real thought. Was everything okay?

Seriously?

Not only no, but hell no! Things were so far from okay, they weren't even in the same hemisphere, but if her own family couldn't figure that out, she wasn't about to tell them. "Yes, of course. Why do you ask?"

"I don't know. You look a little down."

Just a little? Damn—she deserved an Academy Award for her performance. "Not at all. I'm just stuffed—I can't believe we've completely destroyed that whole cake."

Patrick, her eldest brother, clapped his hands. "Okay, start opening your presents. I need to get back to the restaurant."

Of course he did—Paddy was the first to get his restaurant and he was married to the darn place. The only time he let Skye in his kitchen was when he wanted her to come up with the monthly specials for their upscale family-run line of restaurants. Other than that, he loved to stick her back in the business office to handle the books, the human resources, and insurances—something she dreaded. She might be good at it, but it wasn't where she wanted to be. She wanted her own kitchen, and from the looks of the presents, she wasn't going to get it.

She opened each package—all thoughtful gifts she would normally love, but not after working her butt off for years to earn her own kitchen. She thanked her parents and each of her brothers in turn.

Patrick had saved his gift for last. He held out a long, flat box. "I had this made specially for you. I hope you like it."

She eyed it like she would a snake. He held it out to her and she had no choice but to take it. She ripped off the paper, opened the box, and found an engraved name-plate with her name on it above the words MAXWELL'S BUSINESS MANAGER.

He took his glass of wine and held it up to toast. "Here's to you, Skye, and your new partnership position. Congratulations. You're finally a full-fledged owner."

Kier, Colin, Reilly, and her parents raised their glasses, and her heart sank. She'd worked to earn her own kitchen, and now she was made the business manager? She swallowed hard. "Don't you think you should have asked how I felt about this before promoting me to business manager?"

Paddy smirked his I'm-the-oldest-bad-boy-in-the-family smirk. "I didn't think we needed to. We all know you like to play chef, but let's face it, Skye. You're going to want to marry, have kids—all us guys are married to our restaurants. We don't want that for you. This way you get to play in our kitchens, you can do the monthly specials, and still have a partnership role. It's the perfect compromise."

Not for her it wasn't. But then if she blew off her head of steam here, she'd just come off looking like a brat. She'd be damned if she'd give Paddy the satisfaction of calling her one. No, she'd get through her damn birthday dinner; then she'd figure out where to go from here. The last thing she wanted was to be stuck in the business office for the rest of her life and coming up with amazing specials for her father's and brothers' restaurants—and watch them take full credit for all her hard work. No, she was going to do something—she just wouldn't do it in a fit of rage. She was a thirty-year-old woman, not some snotty teenager.

Skye looked from one family member to the next, stopping at her mother, who appeared to be fighting a smile. When she stared into her mother's eyes, she was surprised to see a look that could only be called encouragement. She seemed to be waiting to see Skye's reaction. She'd have a while to wait. Skye had a lot to think about. Hell, she owned one-seventh of the company—it wasn't something she could just shrug off. No, whatever she did, she had to protect the investment she'd made. Well, that was if she didn't let her temper get the best of her. She figured the chances of that happening were about fifty-fifty. Not great, and the odds would only get worse if she didn't make a hasty escape. She hated pulling the sentimental, gushy woman card. It was so not her, but even the hint of happy tears would have the men in her family scattering like roaches at the flick of a kitchen light.

"Well played, dear," her mother whispered when she hugged her good-bye. "You are a formidable Maxwell."

Skye wasn't sure where her mother was coming from, but chose to abandon any further conversation with the final bite of chocolate cake on her plate. Strong enough to leave the last bite but knowing she would regret it later. She gathered her gifts and made like a mixer and beat it.

*   *   *

"Patrick Maxwell, you're the world's biggest asshole." Skye had held on to her temper through payroll and end-of-the-month financials, but this was the final straw. She pulled a knife through the dish towel and then stuffed it in the sheath. "I quit." Her brother wore a chef's hat, probably to make himself look taller, the jerk. As if his six-foot-two frame didn't tower over her enough.

"You're not an employee—you're an owner and you're family. You can't quit."

"Wanna bet? Watch me." She rolled up the carrying case where she stored her prized knives, and ripped the apron from around her waist before throwing it at his face.

Of course Paddy caught it.

"Have a nice life."

"I'm calling Dad."

"Wow, that's real mature. Go ahead—cry to Daddy. And after you're finished with your whine fest, tell him I quit. I've had enough of you and the rest of the testosterone-charged idiots I'm related to, and Dad's the ringleader."

"Stop behaving like a brat. You're just mad because Dad didn't give you a restaurant for your thirtieth birthday like he did the rest of us. Someone in the family has to run the business side of the restaurants, and while you like to play in the kitchens, you're better suited to working in the office—we discussed this. There's more to being an executive chef than just dreaming up specials."

"Because you don't know a balance sheet from a supply list, I'm relegated to the back office? I don't think so." Skye shoved the Incredible Hulk impersonator she called a brother as hard as she could.

He didn't move. The man even had the nerve to laugh.

"Never laugh at a woman carrying knives, Paddy. Now get out of my way before I take one out and practice my carving technique."

"Fine, go. You'll just come crawling back after you get over your snit."

"Don't hold your breath." She turned and then smiled. "You know, on second thought, do." She imagined him passing out due to lack of oxygen. A minor bump on the head would do the trick. Maybe he'd hit something on the way down that would leave him looking like he lost a fight with George Foreman before he started hawking electric grills. That would be sweet. She pictured him with birdies flying in cartoon formation around his head and a huge rainbow-striped goose egg popping out of his thinning hair. She'd noticed him checking it out the other day in his reflection in the stainless steel. Skye made a mental note to send him a bottle of Rogaine for his next birthday. She was thirty years old and what did she have to show for all her hard work? Not a damn thing and the only reason was that she was born without a penis.

Paddy's laughter followed her through the doors and into the alley, spurring her anger. She was finished. She was going home to pack a bag and then catch the first plane out. She'd show them all. She was going to do what none of her brothers ever did—make it in the food world on her own. She didn't need her father to give her a restaurant to become a success. She didn't need to use the Maxwell family name. She already had everything she'd ever need, her talent, her taste buds, and her experience. She'd show them and everyone else interested that she was good for a lot more than managing the business part-time and then spending the rest of her life planning a benefit, a wedding, or whatever the hell they expected her to do at the country club while her nonexistent husband took over her birthright and added another link to their chain of restaurants. "When hell starts taking reservations."

"Did you say something, Skye?"

She jumped when the dishwasher stepped out of the shadows, reeking of smoke. "No, Bobby. I'm just talking to myself." And not paying attention to her surroundings, which was stupid. San Francisco wasn't the safest place in the world—especially the alley behind the restaurant.

"Do you want me to walk you to your car?"

"Thanks, but no. I'll be fine." After all, she was armed and dangerous—not to mention pissed.

Skye's mad-on lasted until she dragged herself out of bed on her first morning in New York. She sat in her Times Square hotel room eating bad room service oatmeal while she went over the want ads. She smacked her forehead and dialed her best friend.

"Do you have any idea what time it is? Did someone die?"

"No. I'm sorry, Kelly. I forgot about the time change. I've been up all night."

"Time change? What are you talking about? And for your information, it's still the middle of the night."

"Not in New York, it's not."

"Did you say New York? What does the time in New York have to do with the price of tea in Chinatown?"

Skye stabbed her spoon into the glutinous mess they called oatmeal, walked over to the floor-to-ceiling windows, and looked down from her suite on the fortieth floor. Times Square was already teeming with people dressed in suits and carrying briefcases, all walking briskly like rats through a maze. "Kelly, I screwed up. Big-time." Skye heard someone in the background. "Oh God, you're not alone."

"Not now, Ted. Just go back to sleep." There was a rustle of sheets and the sound of a slap followed by a giggle.

Skye sucked in a shocked breath and felt her cheeks heat. She'd never heard her best friend since seventh grade giggle. Ever. "Who the hell is Ted?"

"What's this about a big screwup?"

"You first. It seems I'm not the only one who's getting screwed, but I bet you're enjoying the experience with Ted, whereas I definitely am not. Mine doesn't involve a slap and tickle."

"Very funny. Now are you going to tell me what's going on or do I have to get out my trusty crystal ball?"

"I quit."

"It's about time. You should have done it five years ago."

"And I left town."

"What?"

"You heard me."

"You're in New York? Seriously?"

"I'm looking at the Jumbotron in Times Square right now."

"Holy shit!"

"That's what I said when I realized the flaw in my plan."

"You had a plan? What plan?"

"Of course I had a plan—however flawed. I thought I'd come to New York and make a splash in the food world all on my own. I'm not using my credit cards—I've always had the bills sent to my office. It would be too easy for Paddy to steam the envelopes open and figure out where I am."

"Don't you have to give them a credit card to get a room?"

"Sure, I gave the guy my card when I registered, but asked him not to run the charge through. It's amazing what a wink and a smile can get you in this town."

"And how dare you leave San Francisco without so much as a good-bye?"

"I didn't say good-bye because I was afraid you'd talk me out of it or do something insane like tell Paddy."

"I would never rat you out to your lout of a brother."

"Which lout are you talking about?"

"Any of the four. Take your pick. It goes against the code of sisterhood."

"So did dating one and you had no problem doing that."

"Patrick and I are ancient history."

"So you keep saying. Can we get back to the topic at hand?"

"Fine with me. I'm not the one sticking my nose in someone's past mistakes. So you flew to New York and you're using only cash—it sounds very *CSI*-ish but completely understandable knowing your family."

"Intimately as you do."

Kelly let out an exasperated huff that traveled through space and sounded so clear, Skye felt air movement. "Again, ancient history. Go on."

"I just realized that if I got a chef's position at any of the top restaurants here, word would get back to my family."

"And it took you how long to figure that out?"

"I was mad. You know I don't think straight when I'm mad. Just a hint, Kell—this would not be a good time to say 'duh.' Work with me here."

"I'm trying, but you're not giving me much to go on."

The tapping of fingernails against teeth filled Skye's ear. "Stop that. You know it drives me nuts."

"For you that's just a slow roll down a low hill in neutral, my dear. Okay, I think I have it."

"What?"

"An answer to your problem. Don't get a job in Manhattan."

Skye rolled her eyes. "Don't you see, I'd have the same problem in any major city."

"Duh. Sorry, but I couldn't help myself."

"Try."

"Even though your family seems to be unaware of it, there are five boroughs in New York—Manhattan just happens to be the only one they acknowledge. I'm sure there are nice restaurants in all the rest and if you stay out of Manhattan, your family will never be the wiser. Choose one. I hear Brooklyn is Manhattan light. Jump on the ferry or the subway and see what's across the bay. Brooklyn Heights is upscale and beautiful. Same with Park Slope."

"You're a genius. I take back every nasty thought I had about you."

"Right."

"Okay, not every one, but most of them. Thanks. You can go back to bed with Ted now."

"Are you going to be okay?"

"I'm fine. I'll call you in a few days. And remember, not a word."

"I'm sworn to secrecy. I got it."

"Not even a hint to Paddy. You know you're the first person he's going to try to weasel information out of."

"Why would he even bother? You just gave him what he wanted. He's no longer competing with you in the kitchen. Anyway, if he shows his face, I won't be able to tell him a thing. I really have no idea where you are— well, not specifically."

"Good. But even if you did, it wouldn't matter. I'm going to have to find a less expensive place to stay. I don't keep that much cash in my personal account and I didn't have time to liquidate funds. I'm going to have to live really cheap between now and my first payday, especially if I have to rent an apartment."

"I can wire you cash."

"No, but thanks. I want to prove to myself I can make it without my family's money. Now is as good a time as any to start. I'll be fine." But she'd have to get a job pretty darn quick and move out of the four-hundred-dollar-a-night hotel room. "I'm going to get dressed and head to Brooklyn."

"Be careful, and let me know how things go. I worry about you."

"I love you too, Kelly. And I expect a full report on Ted. You're not getting off the hook that easily. I'll call you when I have time for a nice long chat." Skye ended the call with a smile on her face. It was good to finally get the last word.

CHAPTER 3

"Rex, the head cook, just quit." Logan leaned against the bar and looked from Rocki to Francis DeBruscio, waiting for their promised help.

Francis was a cross between a walk-in refrigerator and Shrek's Sicilian cousin, Guido the Ogre. He'd been a fixture at the Crow's Nest since he'd beaten the spit out of Logan back when they were in high school. Pete had told Frankie either he could work off the emergency room bill washing dishes or he'd call the cops.

Under Pete's tutelage and watchful eye, Francis had turned his life around, and became a paramedic and an all-around good guy. It was hard to believe that the man upstairs acting like a cantankerous old fart had changed so many lives and single-handedly turned them all into men of whom he could be proud. Logan shook his head at the irony.

Francis did a double take. "Rex would never just up and quit."

Logan rubbed his forehead where the mother of all headaches was forming. "He's an only child and his mother just had a stroke. She's paralyzed on the left side—and she lives in Florida. It's not as if he really had a choice."

Rocki tapped her foot. "Bummer."

Logan couldn't believe this. "Come on, guys, you're supposed to help me out. Can either of you cook?"

The two of them looked like a pair of bobblehead dolls in a crosswind.

"Neither can I. This is just great. What am I supposed to do now?"

Rocki shrugged one shoulder. "I suggest you start looking for a cook."

"It's Sunday. How the hell am I going to find a cook by opening on Tuesday?"

A grin split Francis's face. "You can put a Help Wanted sign in the window."

"What does Pop do if Rex gets sick, Francis?"

"It's never happened as long as I've known Rex—but Harrison the sous chef might be able to take over for a day or two, I think. Bree knew what was what in the kitchen. I'm sure she could step in if necessary."

"Not a big help since Bree's halfway to New Zealand."

Rocki went around the bar and poured herself a soda, missing the glass and making a mess of the bar Logan just scrubbed. "Have you asked Pete?"

"No, I didn't want him to have another coronary."

Both Rocki and Francis shot him matching glares.

"Bad joke. He's had a rough morning. I caught him smoking his cigar on the roof and we had words." Logan was definitely not ready for the role-reversal situation he'd found himself in since he returned. "All I need to do is tell Pop his cook just quit."

Rocki took a long sip of her soda and watched him

over the rim of the glass. "It's not as if you're going to be able to hide it from him for long. He'll notice on Tuesday. Maybe he has a backup chef."

Francis shook his head. "I doubt it. He's never needed one before."

Logan's phone vibrated. He didn't have to check to know it was Payton; she'd been calling constantly, crying desertion. He let it go to voice mail. "Fine, I'll tell Pop, but first I'm going to put a Help Wanted sign in the window. Maybe an incredible cook will walk by and want the job."

Francis laughed. "Yeah, and maybe I'll win the lottery."

He got busy with the sign while they made fun of him. He had nothing to lose, and other than putting an ad in the paper, he didn't have a plan B.

Logan taped the sign up in the front window and wondered if temp services had cooks—it was worth a try.

He was still running his finger over the tape when a beautiful dark-haired woman dragging a suitcase shouldered the door open. She was a little thing with black shoulder-length hair, pale, almost translucent skin, and the darkest blue eyes he'd ever seen.

"You're hiring a cook?"

Logan shot a glance at Rocki and Francis, who stood beside the bar with their mouths hanging open.

"That's what the sign says. Can you cook?"

"Honey, there's nothing I can't do in a kitchen." She had a deep, smoky voice that made him think of tangled sheets and sleepy sex.

Between her voice and her comment, Logan's mind spun directly into the gutter. What was wrong with him?

Not only was she not his type, but he was engaged. He cleared his throat, temporarily rendered speechless.

"Lucky for you, I'm looking for a job. Can I see the kitchen?"

"Why?"

"I won't work in a dirty or unsafe kitchen."

"Where have you worked?"

"Here and there. You know how it is in the restaurant business." She pulled a menu out of the rack on the side of the hostess stand and paged through it. "There's nothing on here I can't handle. How many people do you seat in a night?"

Logan looked at Rocki and Francis. The two of them shrugged.

"I don't know. I just took over the place last night—I'm filling in for the month. It was a really bad time for the cook to quit."

She smiled and she went from beautiful in a girl-next-door kind of way to simply stunning. "It's a good thing I walked by, then." She looked around. "I assume the kitchen is through there?" She pointed at the swinging double doors.

"Yes, it is."

"Okay then, let's take a look." She set her backpack and suitcase on the bench of a booth and he found himself following her to the kitchen.

"Did you close today because you lost your cook?"

"No, we're only open Tuesday through Saturday."

She shot him another heart-stopping grin. Nope, he hadn't imagined it. She was absolutely staggering. Her lips were full, rose-colored, and bare. She wasn't wearing all that lip crap Payton was always applying—most of which tasted bad enough to put him off kissing for life. If this woman wore makeup, he couldn't detect it—not that she needed it. Her eyelashes were coal black, full enough to create shadows on her pale cheeks, and as long as Payton's fake ones.

"So I'll only have to work five days a week? It'll seem like a vacation."

The way she spoke, he'd think he'd given her the job. He hadn't. Still, he followed her into the kitchen and couldn't help but notice that her back was as attractive as her front—not that he was looking. His cell phone vibrated. He snuck a peek—Payton—and shoved his phone into his pocket as the woman inspected the kitchen like a general inspecting her troops. She even ran her finger under the hood. "Your cook kept a clean kitchen. I like that." She took a turn through the walk-through refrigerator, stepped out, and closed the door behind her. "Okay, I'll take the job."

"You will?" He shook his head. "Hold on, I haven't even offered it yet. Hell, I don't even know your name."

She stepped toward him and held out her hand. "Skye. Skye Sinclair."

He took it—her hand was small, warm, and as calloused as his. Her shake was surprisingly firm considering she barely came up to his shoulder, and her touch sent a shock wave through him that had him holding on to see if it would continue. It did.

Once he tasted her cooking, Skye was sure she'd get the job. There was no question that he'd hire her on the spot. The kitchen was first-class, and the dining room was large enough to keep the menu interesting, but still small enough to cook everything to order.

Since the man seemed completely clueless when it came to running a restaurant, she'd have total control of the kitchen for at least the month he was scheduled to work. That was the one thing she'd always longed for—her very own kitchen.

She'd always had to borrow her brothers' kitchens. And they made it sound as if she should be grateful they'd let her run the business side of the family-owned line of restaurants. But all she wanted was to cook. She wanted to live in the kitchen. She wanted to create.

Here at the Crow's Nest she'd be able to do that—on a much smaller scale than she was used to, but then that wasn't necessarily a bad thing. None of her family would ever think of looking for her in Red Hook. Besides, she had to start somewhere. Without the use of her family name, she was lucky to get a job at all. Yes—she fingered the four-leaf clover charm she wore around her neck—this was a real lucky break.

When Skye entered the restaurant and spotted the manager—he'd looked familiar. Tall, really tall, he was at least a foot taller than her five feet two. Sometimes it really sucked being short. He had dark brown, almost black hair, a narrow nose, a square jaw, and high cheek-bones sharp enough to fillet meat. His eyes were the color of rich caramel—her favorite indulgence other than chocolate. He was tan and lean, and hotter than a desert afternoon during a heat wave. He looked like one of the models she'd seen while paging through the stack of magazines she'd picked up to read on the plane—the man was gorgeous. But the more she watched him, the more he reminded her of someone specific. She just couldn't put her finger on it.

When he took her hand in his to shake, she wasn't

sure whether the shock she felt running through her arm straight to her breasts was because he touched her, or whether it was God's way of zapping her for lying about her name.

Then it hit her; he reminded her of that vintner who was engaged to Payton Billingsly—Logan something. She'd never met him in person, but she'd seen him once at her parents' country club from a distance. She took a closer look and laughed at her ridiculousness. A woman like Payton Billingsly would never stoop so low to be engaged to a man who would step foot in Brooklyn—not this section of Brooklyn anyway. She'd done a little research and found one of the foodie blogs talking about all the great restaurants in Red Hook—it sounded as if the neighborhood was in the midst of gentrification. Obviously it was just beginning, because the neighborhood she just walked through was still pretty rough. Besides, according to the society pages, Payton's fiancé was on the other side of the country, running Billingsly Vineyards and helping the ice princess to plan their New Year's Eve wedding. As if Payton would ever lower herself to marry someone who hadn't come out of a penthouse on Park Avenue.

"It's nice to meet you, Skye. I'm Logan Blaise."

Oh God, no! It *was* him. She did her best to smile through the shock, but the way his smile flattened told her she failed.

"About the job—"

She did a mental eye roll. Her patience slipped another notch, so she decided to just go with it. "Yes, about the job. How much are you paying me?"

His mouth dropped open.

"And is there a reason you're still holding my hand?"

"What?" Logan looked down, seemingly stunned to see their joined hands, and broke the connection.

Thank God—she checked to see if he was using one of those shocking hand buzzers. No such luck. What the hell?

"I'm sorry. Um . . . I don't know how much the job pays. I'm going to have to figure it out. But I haven't offered it to you yet."

Good thing he'd said "yet." If he hadn't, she'd have walked, which was still a distinct possibility. "From where I'm standing, I don't see that you have much of a choice. What are you going to do, call Rent-a-Chef?"

His brows drew together—she'd shocked him. Good.

"Do they have rent-a-chefs?"

"If they did, I'd be the last person to tell you."

"I have to discuss this with my dad. He owns the place."

"Then why isn't he interviewing me?" She'd much rather deal with the man in charge than Payton's plaything.

"He had a heart attack and bypass surgery a few months ago, so my brothers and I are taking turns coming home to help out. The manager just ran off and married one of them, which is why I'm here. She'll be back in a month and then I'll return to my life."

"Good to know." She let out a relieved breath. She could work with anyone for a month. After all, she'd put up with her brothers for years. "I can wait if you want to discuss this with your father. Are you hungry? Do you want me to throw together lunch while you ferret out the paperwork and talk to him?"

"Um . . ."

"Think of it as a working interview. You wouldn't hire a band without hearing them play, would you?"

"No."

"I'll even clean up after myself. What are you and your friends in the mood for? Or would you rather me go off the menu?"

"You want to cook?"

She shrugged. "It's what I do. Besides, I haven't cooked in two days and not cooking makes me antsy."

"Okay. It'll get me out of having to cook lunch. If you could make something heart healthy that doesn't taste it, it would be great. Pop's on a pretty strict diet, and he's not happy about it. Oh, and try to make it something a kid wouldn't mind eating."

"You have a child?"

Was it her imagination or did he just blanch? "Nicki is my dad's foster child. She's ten." He headed out the swinging doors toward the bar, so she followed. "Hey, Rocki, Francis, this is Skye Sinclair. She's going to cook for us as part of her job interview. Are you staying for lunch?"

Skye looked toward the ceiling and cursed silently. God was having a good ol' time at her expense. This had to be some kind of cosmic joke. Leave it to her to get a job working for the future Mr. Payton Billingsly. Then she remembered, she *had* seen his picture on the plane—*Food & Wine* did a spread on their upcoming nuptials.

She'd never met Logan Blaise, probably because she avoided people like Payton and this guy was engaged to her.

She smiled through Logan's introductions to Rocki, the lead singer of the house band, and Francis, who looked more like a bouncer than a bartender. All the while her mind spun. If she'd traded her brothers only to work for a carbon copy, she'd have to quit her second job in two days. No matter how badly she needed the money.

He even sounded like her brothers—not a hint of the Brooklyn accent his friends had. He was gorgeous, polished, shallow, and fake. Skye couldn't help but wonder whether when he and Payton married, he'd take the Billingsly family name. After all, anyone who married Payton had to have a set of balls the size of Mexican jumping beans if he had any at all.

At least Logan hadn't recognized her—not that they traveled in the same circles. She'd always avoided his circles. Still, it was a darn good thing she'd thought to use her mother's maiden name and since it was also her middle name, it wasn't much of a lie, was it? "So it's five for lunch, right?"

Logan raised his brows. "Six including you. You do eat your own food, don't you?"

"Not usually with the people for whom I'm cooking."

"Make an exception today. I'm sure Pop would like to talk to you."

"Fine. Any food allergies I should know about?"

They all shook their heads. "Okay, I'll go see what there is to make. Give me about forty-five minutes. I have to start everything from scratch."

"No problem, take your time and holler if you need any help."

"You know your way around the kitchen?"

Rocki and Francis laughed, and then Francis stepped forward and threw his arm over her shoulder. "My man Logan knows a lot about a lot of things. He knows his way around a lab, a distillery, a brewery, and a vineyard definitely. But the kitchen is one place he has little or no experience. I'm Italian, so I'm no stranger to the kitchen. If you need anything, just call my name."

Skye took a relieved breath. She liked Francis immediately, even if he could bench-press her using only his pinkies. Rocki seemed nice too. She just wasn't sure what they were doing with a guy like Logan Blaise.

Logan watched Skye saunter to the kitchen. "Is it my imagination or does it seem like she doesn't like me?"

Rocki smiled. "Nope, not your imagination. I think she likes Francis and me just fine. What'd you do?"

"Nothing." Nothing except hold her hand way too long. Not that he'd ever tell Rocki.

Francis raised his eyebrows. "Maybe it's the way you undress her with your eyes."

"I do not."

"Hey"—Francis held up his hands—"she's a cute girl. There's no reason not to look—after all, you're not married yet. Next time try not to make it so obvious."

"I'm not looking."

Francis smiled. "Okay, chief. Whatever you say." He let out a laugh. "Are you going to tell Pete he's expected to have a lunch with us prepared by our new cook?"

"I guess I'd better." He took a deep breath and shook his head at Rocki and Francis, who were obviously enjoying his discomfort. "Wish me luck."

Rocki gave him a pat on the back. "You're definitely going to need it. We'll stay here and hold down the fort. Call us if you need reinforcements, and I'll be sure to send Francis." She blew him a kiss. "Go get 'em, tiger."

Logan dragged ass up the steps to the apartment. He stepped inside and Nicki's big mutt, who looked like a weird mixture of German shepherd and golden retriever, planted both paws on his chest. "Get down, D.O.G." He wondered, not for the first time, how Nicki had managed to get a dog of her own. He and his brothers were never that lucky. Maybe Pop had mellowed in his old age. He spotted his father sitting in the recliner in his usual outfit, Dockers and a white T-shirt. "Hey, Pop. When's Nicki coming home?"

"Soon. She has a playdate with a friend from school."

"Good. Look, we have a situation. Rex called earlier today. His mom had a stroke and he has to go down to Florida and take care of her. It sounds as if he's moving down there indefinitely."

Pete rubbed his chest and then ran his hands through what was left of his white hair. "Hell, I don't even have a backup—Harrison could cover for a night or two, maybe. Shit. I've never needed a backup before. I've always had Bree here. What the hell are we going to do? Rex does all the food orders. I don't think Harrison even knows how to."

"It's okay. I think I found us a new cook."

Pop's stunned look almost made him smile. He always liked surprising the old man.

"And just how the hell did you do that?"

"The usual way. I put a Help Wanted sign in the window. She's downstairs now whipping us up something for lunch."

"She?" Pete rose slowly from his chair. He'd always thought that Pop was indestructible, but all it took was a heart attack and bypass surgery to change that. Logan had been there almost a month. His boss had come out of semiretirement so he could swing it. And after all that time he was still shocked by the difference in his father.

"Yes, her name is Skye Sinclair and she's offered to

cook as part of her job interview. She's ours if we want her."

"Skye is a good Irish name. Unfortunately, the Irish aren't known for their cooking. What's she making?"

"I don't know. I gave her free rein. I asked that she prepare something heart healthy a kid wouldn't mind eating. Why don't you throw a shirt on and come down for lunch?"

Pete shot him a look of either disgust or disbelief. Maybe both. He hadn't been happy with his new diet.

"What's the worst that could happen?"

"She could start a kitchen fire."

"With Rex gone, we might have had to close the kitchen. If there's a fire, at least we're insured, so we could recoup the loss of business." Logan followed his dad to his bedroom and leaned against the doorjamb while Pop carefully pulled a sweater over his T-shirt. He obviously was still feeling the effects of his surgery. "Face it, Pop. It's a win-win situation. You won't have to eat my cooking and I have a good feeling about this woman. I think she knows what she's doing."

"Where has she worked?"

Logan shrugged. "Here and there. You know the restaurant business. Maybe you can get the particulars—she doesn't seem to like me much."

A smile broke over Pop's face and Logan caught a glimpse of the old Pete Calahan. "At least the girl shows intelligence. Why the mystery, is she running from someone? If she is, that could lead to trouble."

He didn't like the idea of her running from anyone, but if she was hiding out, he'd prefer she do it in the safety of the Crow's Nest. "If she is on the run, who's going to see her if she's in the kitchen cooking?"

"Good point. Okay, let's go down and meet this beautiful woman." He headed toward the stairway leading to the bar.

"Hey, I never said she was beautiful."

"You didn't have to. You have that look about you — the same one you always wore when you got shot down by a knockout. But then you always went for the knockouts."

Logan followed him down the steps and stood beside him when they reached the floor of the restaurant. He glanced toward the kitchen. "You make it sound as if I got shot down often."

Pop slapped him on the back. "Often enough. It's good to see it's still happening. I wouldn't want you to get too big for your britches."

"Skye didn't shoot me down. For that to happen, I would have had to ask her out." He probably would have, had he been single, but he wasn't. "I'm engaged, remember?"

"That's right. You're engaged to a girl I've never met. For all I know, she's a figment of your imagination. I'll believe it when I see her."

"Pop, your faith in me is humbling."

"It has nothing to do with faith. It has to do with the fact that you've known this girl for years and you've never once brought her home. That tells me something."

Logan shrugged and wished he knew what that something was. There were countless reasons he'd never brought Payton home. If he had, she'd be filled with questions he had no way to answer or had no interest in answering. It was better to avoid the situation altogether.

Rocki, Francis, and Francis's wife, Patrice, waited at the bar. Damn, the last thing he needed was Patrice and

Rocki—the dynamic duo—ganging up on him in front of his new hire. "Patrice, when did you get here?" He gave her a kiss, much to Francis's chagrin.

Logan found out a long time ago that Patrice had been the reason Francis had beat the crap out of him and Storm both when they were kids. Still, neither of them had ever really gotten hurt until Francis somehow had gotten the insane idea that Patrice had a crush on him—which was news to Logan. Patrice didn't know he existed, but that didn't stop Frankie the bruiser. Nicki once told him that Patrice reminded her of an African-American Barbie doll—and the kid was right. Patrice was the beauty queen type and everyone knew beauty queens didn't go for geeks—and at the time, he was a major geek.

Patrice tossed her long hair over her shoulder. "Francis told me about your new cook, so I thought I'd drop by and meet her."

"Right." The woman was a veritable Wikipedia of who's who and what's what in her little corner of the world. Not in a bad way—she never struck him as a gossip, but she definitely had her finger on the pulse of the community.

Francis stood behind her and wrapped his arms around her middle. "I told Skye we'd have one more at lunch. I didn't think you'd mind."

"I don't."

Pete went around the bar and poured himself a beer and Rocki gave Logan the you-better-do-something look.

Great. "Hey, Pop, thanks for pouring one for me. It's thoughtful, since you're off the juice until the doctors give you the go-ahead." Logan reached across the bar and took the beer from him and smiled at the grimace Pop shot back.

Nicki burst through the door, her sneakers slapping against the hardwood floor. "I'm home." She ran right past him, not even giving him a second glance before she scooted under the pass-through right into Pop's open arms.

"How was your day?" Pop gave her a noogie and poured her a soda.

"It was good. We watched movies and did arts and crafts."

Logan groaned when Rocki's elbow made contact with his ribs. "What the heck was that for?"

Rocki crossed her arms, before closing her eyes and shaking her head. "I don't know. You're supposed to act fatherly. Standing there doing nothing is not fatherly."

Nicki's mother, Marisa, had dumped Nicki on Pop's doorstep six months ago and told Pop that Nicki was his granddaughter. Up until a few weeks ago, everyone had been convinced Storm was Nicki's father—that is, until they asked him. Apparently he'd been so hung up on Bree even eleven years ago, he'd never slept with Marisa. The same couldn't be said for Logan. He'd done a whole lot more than just sleep with her, but he'd always used protection. Still, nothing was one hundred percent effective. Marisa was no paragon of virtue at the time, nor did it seem as if she was now—after all, she'd left a great kid like Nicki with a virtual stranger. Logan might be Nicki's father, but then, it could have all been a big lie. No one knew, which was why they were waiting on the paternity test before they said anything. He'd thought that meant they wouldn't say anything to anyone—obviously he'd thought wrong. From the look on Patrice's and Francis's faces, the only one who didn't know was Nicki. Shit. "Things take time, Rocki. Give me a break." What did they expect? No matter how much he wished he and Nicki were close, things like that didn't happen overnight.

The doors to the kitchen banged open, saving him from having to try to make conversation. Skye walked out with her arms filled with plates. "Lunch is served."

CHAPTER 4

Skye waited for everyone to come to the table they'd set before she placed a plate in front of the little girl's seat.

Nicki wore a confused frown and looked at Skye as if she'd just stolen her candy. "Hi, Nicki. I'm Skye." She placed the next plate in front of Pete—at least she assumed it was Pete, since no one had introduced them. Still, he was the only one old enough to be Logan's father. "I hope you enjoy it, sir."

His face split in a smile. "I'm sure I will. And the name's Pete. No one's called me sir since I left the force. It's nice to meet you, Skye." He took the two plates and handed them around and then shook her hand.

Francis sat Patrice before heading to the kitchen. "I'll just get the rest of the plates for you."

"Thanks."

Pete pulled out the chair next to his. "Have a seat. What can I get you to drink?"

"No, I'll get it." She started to rise when Pete's firm hand came down on her shoulder and squeezed.

"Sit. Logan, open up a couple bottles of that wine you're so damn proud of. And Rocki, run and get us all water glasses and a pitcher." He scooted Skye's chair in, and brought his head close to hers. "Rocki's a disaster behind the bar," he whispered, "but she should be able to handle water without making much of a mess."

Francis placed the rest of the plates around the table and groaned when he noticed Rocki behind the bar.

Pete smiled at him. "Calm down. It's only water."

"Oh, thank God. It took me three hours to clean up after Rocki's last bartending adventure and I have a shift at my other job later today. I don't have time to clean up after her again."

Skye felt Nicki's eyes on her. She met them and then Nicki looked at the plate in front of her and smiled. "Look, Pop. Skye made me a happy face."

Skye blew out a slow breath. "It's braised chicken with mushrooms, artichokes, and peppers in a white wine sauce." She shrugged. "I make it a lot for my younger clientele and they like smiley faces. I left the pepperoncini peppers off yours, Nicki—they can be a little hot." She had pounded out chicken breasts, cooked the meal, and saved the roundest breast especially for Nicki. She covered the plate with sauce, plated the chicken breast, cut the mushrooms to look like eyes and a nose, and used the artichoke hearts for brows and eyelashes, and turned the red peppers into lips before artfully arranging the rice to look like hair. It had worked—Skye fingered the four-leaf clover, thankful for the luck of the Irish, and held her breath.

Pete cut into his chicken, piled on peppers, took a bite, and groaned. "I haven't had anything this good since before my heart attack. It's wonderful."

Logan placed a glass of wine in front of her, and she smiled her thanks.

Pete continued, but this time he was watching Logan. "See, I knew heart healthy wasn't synonymous with tasteless." He looked over at Nicki. "Try it. It's good. Really good."

Rocki passed around glasses of water and finally took a seat on the other side of Skye, next to Patrice.

Logan sat across from her, next to Nicki, and tucked into his meal. Silence reigned—always a good sign. She figured with this bunch, it would be quiet only while they were eating; they looked like a boisterous crowd.

"Skye"—Pete took a sip of his water while he eyed her wineglass—"if this group hasn't scared you away, and you're still interested in the job, I can call a meeting of the kitchen staff. Are you free to meet with them tomorrow morning?"

"Yes. I'll make time to meet the staff. I don't have any plans as of yet. I'm new in town, so all I have on my agenda is finding a place to stay." She sat back and sipped her wine. She had to admit Logan knew what he was doing when it came to wine—this bottle was fabulous.

Patrice sat forward and wiped her mouth with a napkin. "You're looking for an apartment?"

"Yes, I spent last night in Manhattan, but it's kind of pricey. I thought I'd find something more affordable here in Brooklyn."

Patrice smiled. "Really? How do you feel about dogs?"

"Dogs?"

"Rex, the cook you're replacing, has a puggle—she's fifty percent pug, fifty percent beagle, and one hundred percent adorable. She's just a little thing and she comes with a fabulous apartment."

"What?"

"Rex asked me to sublet his place and find a home for Pepperoni—that's her name. It fits—believe me. He can't bring the dog to his mom's and he has no idea how long he'll be away. He hates the thought of it, but the way things look right now, he'll have to move there permanently." Patrice shook her head. "Rex has a great one-bedroom just down the street on the other side of the alley. It's furnished, clean, safe, and, well, Pepperoni is just a love bug. I'd take her, but my daughter Callie is allergic."

"I've never had a dog. Not because I don't like them, but it wasn't conducive to my hours. I've always worked six or seven days a week."

Pete leaned forward. "That won't happen here. I think it's important to have a life, so we're only open Tuesdays through Saturdays. Rex trained the kitchen staff well. He's usually out the door right after the dinner rush. He orders all the food and does the schedule and specials, so he comes in for a little while on Mondays. Harrison, the sous chef, checks in deliveries, and takes over for him once the mad dinner rush is over. Harrison could probably handle a night or two alone if you need to take time off, but he's only been with us for six months. I don't think he's ready to fill Rex's shoes just yet. That's something we can discuss in my office after lunch. If you're interested in meeting Pepperoni and checking out Rex's place, I'm sure Patrice will run you over there when we're through, won't you, Patrice?"

"Sure, the girls are at a friend's house, so I'm free for the afternoon."

"Good, it's settled, then. Skye, eat your meal. It's great."

"I'm glad you think so." Her head was spinning. A

furnished apartment, a job, and a dog—something she'd always wanted—just fell into her lap. How lucky was that? She rubbed her four-leaf clover again.

Logan reached across the table and refilled her wine.

Skye took another sip and found him watching her. "The wine is wonderful. What is it?"

"It's Billingsly Special Reserve Chardonnay 2006. It's my first vintage."

"You should have saved it for a special occasion."

"I did."

The sound of his voice slid over her like silk and the look in his eyes made her breath catch.

"It looks like you passed Pop's taste test."

"I told you there was nothing I couldn't do in a kitchen."

"Touché."

The way he looked at her was enough to make a girl blush, and damned if she didn't. Her heart sped up and her throat went dry, while other parts of her did just the opposite. Damn, of all the times for her hormones to come out of hiding. The last thing she needed was to be attracted to her new boss. At least he'd only be there for a month.

Pete took a seat in his office and watched Skye Sinclair over the application she'd filled out. There were more holes in it than a lead suspect's alibi. She hadn't even filled out her last place of employment.

"I've been working in restaurants all my life. I trained at the California Culinary Academy and have been employed steadily for the last seven years."

"So why did you leave?"

"Personal reasons."

He gave her a look that had made grown men cry for their mamas. "You don't want me to call for references?" The girl was nervous and he wasn't sure why. After eating her cooking, he knew Skye could get a job at a fine restaurant. That much was obvious. The Crow's Nest was a great place, but it wasn't Jean-Georges. So why was she sweating the interview for a restaurant she could probably run with one hand tied behind her back?

He tossed her application down. "What's the deal, Skye?"

"The deal?"

"We both know this application isn't worth the paper it's printed on. Let's cut to the chase. Are you in some kind of trouble?"

"No. I'm just not interested in my past employer knowing my whereabouts."

"You do realize I used to be a cop, right? I can have a background check run on you faster than you can say 'Bob's your uncle.'"

"You won't find anything if you were to do that."

"Then why the secrecy? You didn't even fill out the emergency contact information."

"You can call Kelly in case of emergency. I used her as a reference." She leaned forward and pointed out Kelly's information.

"Did you work with her?"

"Yes, a few years ago. She's since left the business."

Pete raised an eyebrow. "Why don't you just come clean with me? Is some guy giving you a hard time?"

"I left for personal reasons. There was nothing dangerous, just . . . well, personal."

"Is trouble going to follow you here, Skye?"

"No. There's no danger. I just needed to escape. I

might have a problem with them, but you won't. It's personal."

Them. He sat back and watched her. There was more than one of them. That cut out the psycho ex-boyfriend scenario. He wasn't sure he believed her problems wouldn't follow her, but she certainly did. "Is that the only reason you left?"

"No. It became clear to me that I had no future there. I want a fresh start, a chance to make my own way in a new town. Pete, I'm honest and a really hard worker. I promise I won't disappoint you. I'm more than capable of running your kitchen. I just need a chance to prove myself."

She was nervous, sure, but she wasn't lying to him. A man didn't spend twenty-five years on the force without knowing when someone was lying. She didn't fear whoever she ran from, but she was pissed as hell. Damn, what was with him and fiery Irish women? He just hoped when Bree got back, she and Skye got along. If not, he'd be up shit's creek.

"I'll start you out at forty-five thousand a year and you'll be on probation for three months."

She nodded with what looked like relief. Good, she didn't blink at the salary, which meant it was enough. It also meant she wasn't in any big financial trouble.

"After your probationary period, you'll get a raise, benefits, and two weeks' vacation a year, three weeks after five years." He tossed an employee handbook on the top of his desk. "Read it and sign the last page. Get it back to me with your withholding and other tax information in the morning. You can start tomorrow."

Skye smiled and Pete saw why Logan had been tripping over his own tongue for the last few hours. There was something special about her, something that ran deeper than just beauty—although there was plenty of that too. Logan was going to have his hands full with this one. It was going to be fun to watch.

"Thank you so much. You won't regret it."

"Just promise me one thing. If you have trouble with whoever or whatever you're running from, you'll come to me."

She looked down at her feet for a long moment, raised her eyes to his, and nodded.

"I want a promise, Skye. I can help you out, but not if I don't know what is going on."

"I promise. It's just—"

"I know, personal." He watched her for another second, waiting for her to spill her guts, but the girl had whatever it was locked up so tight, it would take a crowbar to pry it loose. He'd give it time; she'd come around. Eventually, they all did or they didn't last. "How are you on cash? Do you need an advance on your first paycheck?" He pulled out his billfold and counted out three hundred bucks.

Skye turned bright red, and put up her hand to stop him. "No, thank you for the offer, but I'm fine. I just need to find a place to stay, and Patrice thinks Rex's apartment will work for me, so I'm going to take a look at it."

Pete couldn't help but smile. "You'll like the little piglet."

Skye's face formed its own version of a question mark. "Patrice said it was a dog."

"It is. She just sounds a little like a piglet. Pepperoni and D.O.G., Nicki's dog, are best buddies—kinda like Mutt and Jeff." He shook his head. "Rex and Nicki used to walk them together and take them to the dog park.

You'll have to bring Pepperoni over to play. They're quite a pair."

"I can't believe that anyone would just hand his apartment and his dog over to a complete stranger. Heck, I'm not sure I can even afford the place."

"I know Rex, and unless you are in a hell of a lot of debt and have massive bills to pay, I don't foresee a problem when it comes to affording his apartment. As for the dog, Patrice is known for her ability to read people. If she trusts you, Rex will too. Let me know if you need some cash to hold you over; we'll work something out."

"Thanks again for the offer, but I want to do this on my own."

"God save me from independent women. I'm here if you change your mind." He walked around his desk. Skye was already on her feet. He cleared his throat and she turned to face him. "Welcome to the family, Skye. That's what we are here at the Crow's Nest—one big, usually happy family. You just got yourself one hell of a job. Congratulations."

Skye's face lit up. "Thanks for the opportunity. I promise I won't let you down."

"I know you won't. Just don't forget that other promise you made me and we'll be fine."

She nodded and dashed out the door. His instincts had kept him alive the entire twenty-five years he'd been on the force and gave him what he needed to remain one step ahead while raising three boys; he just hoped they were still as sharp as ever. He had no reason to, but he trusted Skye—maybe not to tell the whole truth, but he trusted that she was a good person.

*   *   *

Patrice unlocked the apartment that turned out to be over an art gallery and almost next door to the Crow's Nest. "Rex is kind of a clean freak, but you probably knew that as soon as you saw the kitchen. I swear he's the only man alive who could pack up his stuff with an hour's notice and be prepared to sublet his place. I spent the morning packing the rest of his clothes, his CDs, and such." She placed the keys on a table next to the door. "The TV, DVR, and everything else stays. You'll have to call Rex and talk about the rent, although I'm sure he'll work with you. I haven't had a chance to even go there yet with him, but I don't imagine he'll charge much. He's been here forever and I think the apartment is rent-controlled."

The door swung open and a little fawn-colored dog with a short nose, wrinkled forehead, and sausagelike body danced on her hind legs around Patrice's ankles. Patrice leaned over and picked up the puggle, curling her tail under and holding her in the crook of her arm. "And this is Pepperoni." Patrice handed the dog to Skye.

Skye stared into the big, slightly bugged-out brown eyes. "Aren't you just the cutest little thing ever?" Pepperoni gave her face a bath with the longest tongue she'd ever seen come out of a dog so small. "Is she going to get any bigger?"

Patrice scrunched up her nose. "I don't think so. She'll be a year old in February. When Rex took her to the vet last, they said she was pretty much full-grown. She's only about eighteen pounds, small for a puggle, but she was the runt of the litter. I brought her home with me last night, but my daughter Callie isn't handling it well. Her eyes are already itchy and red. I was hoping with Pepperoni's short hair it would be okay, but I just can't see keeping Callie on allergy medicine for the duration."

"I understand completely." Skye set down the squirming pup and followed Patrice through the roomy apartment. It was an airy space with big windows and lots of light. There was a nice kitchen with all the bells and whistles—granite countertops, a small commercial stove, and tons of light. The furnishings were comfortable, leather couches, mission-style tables, and the bedroom was big enough to handle the king-sized bed and double dressers. The apartment had hardwood floors throughout, throw rugs, and a nice homey feel.

When Patrice caught her staring at the huge bed, she stopped beside her. "It's a sleep-number bed." She motioned to the controllers lying on the bedside table. "Rex got a king because he's a big guy."

Skye found herself smiling. "That's something I realized when I cooked in his kitchen. I had to get a chair to reach some of the pans he had hanging above the workstation."

"The bathroom is through here." Patrice opened the door.

Skye peeked in. The bathroom was big and gorgeous. The apartment was perfect. "I'm just not sure I'm going to be able to afford it—especially if Rex wants the first and last months' rent up front."

Patrice waved her hand as if a little thing like money was nothing to get excited about. "Rex is more concerned about his renter taking care of his things and his dog than making money."

"He's not going to have a problem with you leaving his dog with a total stranger?"

Patrice smiled. "No, that's why he asked me to handle it. He knows I'm a great judge of character and I have a really good feeling about you, Skye."

She couldn't believe this. First Pete hired her even though she refused to list her previous experience, and now Patrice was all but handing her the keys to an incredible apartment. She'd been shown more blind trust in the past twenty-four hours than in her entire life. Maybe people from New York just got a bad rap.

Pepperoni sat on Skye's foot, looking up at her and holding what looked like a stuffed version of the puppet Lamb Chop in her little mouth.

"It looks as if Pepperoni has a good feeling about you too. Let's give Rex a call and tell him you're interested. I'm sure you two can work something out. It will be a real relief for him to know that you're taking over for him at the Crow's Nest. It's killed him to leave Pete without a cook, not to mention leaving Pepperoni. If there were any way he could take her, he would have. He loves his little girl."

Skye had to admit, Pepperoni was adorable.

After a conversation with Rex, they'd made a deal they could both live with. He was going to send a lease agreement out in a few days. He told her about caring for Pepperoni and she was surprised to find out the dog was used to sleeping with him. He gave her the lowdown on the kitchen staff, told her about the specials he'd planned for next week, filled her in on where the orders were in his desk, gave her his cell number in case she had any questions Harrison or Pete couldn't answer, and wished her luck, thanking her for stepping into his shoes.

She had a smile on her face when she hung up. Pepperoni slept on her lap and Patrice sipped a diet soda she'd found in the fridge. "The place and the puppy are mine—for now at least."

"Great. Now, are you going to use Rex's towels and sheets, or do we need to take a run to Ikea? I have my car if you want to go."

"Maybe after payday. For now, I'll make do with Rex's if it's all the same to you."

"Sure. I already washed his sheets and towels and changed the bedding. There's a washer and dryer in the closet next to the bathroom."

"Great. I guess all I need are the keys, and then I have to go back to the Crow's Nest to get my things."

"No, you don't. The boys will be here—"

A knock at the door interrupted Patrice. "I texted Francis during your conversation with Rex." She unlocked the door and opened it to Francis, Logan, Nicki, and a huge dog—an oversized puppy of questionable lineage. One ear stood up and the other flopped over.

Pepperoni jumped from Skye's lap to the back of the couch and leaped off it like a cat, landing next to the dog that was easily five times her size. She planted her paws on his neck and nipped the bigger dog's floppy ear, pulling it down to her height. The two danced around, licking each other and playing.

Nicki ran and grabbed the leash that hung on a hook by the door. "Francis said we can take Pepperoni and D.O.G. for a walk. Is that okay with you, Skye?"

"Sure, I guess." Before she knew what was happening, they had Pepperoni in a harness. Francis, Patrice, and Nicki ushered the dogs out the door and left her alone with Logan.

"I brought your suitcase and a bottle of champagne to celebrate your new job and apartment."

"Thanks, you didn't have to do that." She took the bottle from him. "Maybe we should wait until Francis and Patrice get back to open it."

"They'll probably be gone for a while. But we can wait if you'd like." He sat on the couch and crossed one of his legs over the other like he was planning on a nice long visit.

She checked the label, another Billingsly vintage. It was an expensive bottle. She should know—she ordered the wine for all the Maxwell's restaurants and they carried the full line of Billingsly wines. "I don't even know if I have champagne glasses."

"You do. They're in the cupboard over the dishwasher."

She went around the bar that separated the kitchen from the living area and sure enough, there were champagne glasses; of course she'd need a chair to reach them.

Skye stepped back to get one and ran into a solid wall of man. Logan had snuck up behind and reached over her, taking down four glasses.

He didn't touch her, but his heat seared her back. What was it with this guy? She slid to the left and stepped back to get away from him. Unfortunately, he did too. His arm wrapped around her was the only thing that kept her from falling over his gigantic feet. "Easy." He placed the glasses on the counter before he released her.

She looked at him, sure that her face was the color of a fire engine. "Thanks."

"I didn't do that on purpose."

"I didn't say you did."

"True. Look, I came over because I'm concerned we started off on the wrong foot. I got the distinct impression that you don't like me much. Since we're going to be working together, I thought that maybe we could start over. If I did anything to offend you—"

"You didn't. I have no problem with you, Logan. And I'm sorry if I gave you that impression."

"There's no need to apologize. I just want us to be able to work together."

"I don't have a problem if you don't. I can work with anyone for a month." That had been her mantra since she found out when he was leaving.

His piercing brown eyes stared into hers. One brow slowly winged its way up toward his hairline.

Her heartbeat sped up and the blood rushing through her ears drowned out the hum of the refrigerator, the ticking of the clock, and the drone of traffic on Van Brunt Street. They were at an impasse. She'd probably said too much already, and it seemed as if he was waiting for her to continue. It would be a long, long wait. She knew when to keep her mouth shut, and this was one of those times.

Logan stared at Skye waiting for her to say or do something. He was clearly incapable, since it was all he could do to punch down the urge to kiss her. He wasn't sure what that was all about—he was a grown man, not a horny teenager.

He held her gaze as if they were in an adolescent staring contest, while he reminded himself again of the numerous reasons she wasn't his type. First of all, he was engaged to Payton, which made Skye and every other woman on the planet off-limits. It was something that had never bothered him before, but then he'd never been tempted by another woman until he'd met Skye. It was crazy—temptation certainly wasn't on her agenda.

Payton and Skye were polar opposites in every way imaginable. Payton was tall, runway-model thin, blond, and, well, flexible—both physically and mentally. She was easygoing as long as his decisions didn't affect Payton's world. Until he'd packed his bags to come home and help out his dad, his plans hadn't. Now that they had, Payton proved she wasn't quite as flexible as he'd thought.

Skye was short and curvaceous—a real beauty. She was a dark-haired, fair-skinned, blue-eyed version of Botticelli's Venus. She had more than enough heavenly goddess in her to arouse mere mortals to physical love. And probably enough to inspire intellectual love too—in anyone capable of it, anyone but him.

"It's not going to work."

"Why's that?"

Payton was also never one to argue, question, or even have an independent thought or idea—at least none she voiced. He wondered for the first time whether he'd just never bothered to ask.

With Skye, there'd be no reason to wonder. She'd made it known from the first moment he'd met her that she had so many thoughts and ideas, they would eventually form a flash mob in that quick-working mind of hers, drowning out all other stimuli.

"I'm not easily ignored."

"I'm not planning to ignore you. I'm simply saying our working relationship is temporary. We don't know each other." She put the bottle of champagne in the refrigerator and poked her head in while she did a quick inventory of its contents. "Sure, everyone has preconceived notions." She shut the door and headed toward the living area.

He followed.

"But when it comes down to it, we're strangers." She turned toward him as soon as she put a huge leather club chair between them. "I need this job and I'm used to working with minimal input from anyone not directly involved in my kitchen."

"That's going to change, Skye, because like it or not, I'm intimately involved with everything that goes on in the restaurant, at least until my work here is done, and the kitchen is part of the restaurant."

She shook her head. "You don't know the first thing about the workings of a restaurant, no less a busy kitchen." A sardonic smile played about her full lips. "You didn't even know how many people you typically serve a night."

"I'm a quick study."

"That's great, but do it on someone else's watch. I'll do my job, you do yours, and we'll get along fine."

"If we're going to work together, we need to be able to communicate effectively."

"I've never had a problem communicating and I have no problem telling you exactly what I think. Let me demonstrate. Since I'm not on the clock, I think you should leave. Thank you for bringing my suitcase and for the champagne." She walked him to the door and opened it before meeting his eyes with what could only be described as a steely blue glare. "I'll see you tomorrow morning at the restaurant. At that time, we can communicate about whatever you'd like as long as it relates to my work."

Logan knew she was deadly serious but had a difficult time keeping a look of total male appreciation off his face. It wasn't what she was going for—just the opposite in fact. He'd have to rethink the whole Venus thing.

Right now, she was more like a modern-day Irish Lady Godiva, only fully clothed, which was a damn shame.

He took a deep breath, trying to calm his racing heart. It was a mistake—her scent surrounded him: pure female with a hint of garlic, peppers, the wine they drank, and something so subtle, something so spicy, he wanted to move closer until he could categorize it.

The woman was magnificent and could give lessons on controlled businesslike evisceration of the enemy. She might be a handful, but he had no doubt she'd be able to successfully lead the kitchen staff into a good protest or even war if necessary.

Logan held up his hands in supplication and nodded. "Fair enough, Skye. I'll see you in the morning. Enjoy your evening. I'm sure Francis and Patrice will be back shortly with your new dog." He was halfway down the steps before he let himself smile. When the door shut and locked behind him, he let out a relieved laugh, thankful she didn't see the physical effect she had on him.

CHAPTER 5

The door to her new apartment jiggled against Skye's back, as if someone had tried to walk in only to find it locked. She wasn't sure how long she'd stood leaning against the only thing she thought would hold her up the moment Logan left. She'd never been the kind of woman who was bowled over by a man—especially a man who was engaged—no matter how good-looking he was or how great he smelled, or how good he felt against her.

She shook her head. She was proud of herself; she'd been forceful—something she'd been working on for some time—and she'd gotten her point across. She had to admit, Logan took it like a man. Still, the entire episode left her feeling as shaky as a sailor after a yearlong voyage, fighting to find his land legs.

She took a deep breath, stepped aside, threw the dead bolt, and pasted on a smile. "Hey, you're back."

Patrice carried Pepperoni in and was followed by a limping, tearstained Nicki, and Francis wearing a grim expression, holding D.O.G.'s leash tight against his thigh.

"What happened?" One look at the ripped knees of Nicki's jeans told the story.

"D.O.G. pulled too hard and I fell."

Skye took Nicki's hand. "Come on in and let's get you cleaned up. I have a first aid kit in my bag. Go on into the bathroom and I'll be there in a second."

Patrice put Pepperoni down and unhooked her leash. "You don't have to do that. I can take Nicki back to the bar and clean her up there."

"Nonsense. I have everything we'll need in my bag. When you're a chef, you need a good first aid kit in every kitchen, even your kitchen at home. Once we get it cleaned out, it'll stop stinging. It's not a problem."

"Okay." Patrice lifted her perfectly arched eyebrows in what looked like surprise.

"Francis"—Skye turned to him—"there's beer, soda, or a bottle of champagne that Logan brought over in the fridge. Help yourself to whatever you want." She dragged her suitcase into the bedroom, tossed it on the foot of the bed, and rooted through it until she found her first aid kit. By the time she made it to the bathroom, Patrice had Nicki's pants rolled above her knees and was washing them with a soapy washcloth. She looked over Patrice's shoulder at the scraped knees, and then to Nicki, who was blinking back tears and showing a brave face. "That hurts, huh? I have a spray that will numb it and finish cleaning it at the same time. Then all we have to do is put some antibacterial cream on it and cover it with Band-Aids."

Patrice rinsed off Nicki's wounds, patted them dry, and then cleaned up the sink.

Skye knelt and then sprayed the abrasions.

Nicki sucked in a breath through her teeth.

Skye blew on the abrasions to relieve the sting. "There. It's better now, isn't it?" She waited for Nicki's nod before squeezing antibiotic ointment onto the wound. "I'm just going to put a little bit on the scrapes and you won't feel a thing. Promise."

"Really?" Nicki didn't look too sure.

"Believe me, I grew up with four brothers and I was always the one getting hurt."

"Okay." Nicki stilled, her eyes locked on Skye. "I have three brothers—Storm, Logan, and Slater."

She had the Band-Aids on before Nicki even noticed. "There you go. You'll be all better in no time." Sitting back on her heels, Skye helped Nicki roll down her tattered jeans.

"Thanks for taking care of me."

"Anytime, Nicki."

Nicki followed her out and Skye tugged on one of her pigtails. They found Patrice and Francis curled on the couch sipping sodas.

Francis pulled himself to his feet. "All better, Nicki?"

Nicki nodded.

"Good girl." He checked his watch. "I've got to get to work. Want me to walk D.O.G. home for you?"

Nicki looked at her knees and then to the dog that was as big as she was. "Sure."

He leaned over to Patrice and gave her a kiss. "I'll see you in the morning, Patty. Behave."

"Don't I always?"

"I wish." He grabbed D.O.G.'s leash. "Come on, big guy. Let's get you home before I'm late for my shift."

Pepperoni jumped around until Skye picked her up— the little thing was a handful when she wasn't interested in being held. "Thanks for all the help, guys."

Patrice laughed and waved away Francis, who was already pulling D.O.G. out the door. "Oh, Nicki and I

aren't leaving. We thought we'd stay, help you get un-
packed, and get to know each other."

Skye was not against making friends, but she had the
distinct feeling that Patrice was on more of a fact-finding
mission than anything else. The light shining in Patrice's
eyes made her nervous and she instinctively knew Patrice wouldn't be as easily derailed as Logan.

Patrice took the remote control for the TV and turned
on the Disney Channel. "Here you go, Nicki. I'll be right
in the bedroom with Skye."

Nicki wrapped her arm around Pepperoni, who had
jumped onto the couch and leaned against her side.
"Okay."

Patrice threaded her arm through Skye's and steered
her into the bedroom before flopping down on the bed.
"What's up with you and Logan?"

"Nothing."

Patrice's face made it clear she didn't believe her.

Maybe it was time to break out that champagne after
all.

Skye pulled the chicken stock from the walk-in refrigerator, dragged a stool over to reach one of the sauce-
pans hanging off the rack, and then banged it down on
the stove. "Maybe I should just get a stick with a hook on
the end of it, or rearrange the entire kitchen for those of
us who are vertically challenged."

She ladled a few cups of the broth into the saucepan
and turned the heat on to simmer, wanting to make sure
it was worthy of saving. The only way to know that was
to try it.

Rubbing her tired eyes, she cursed jet lag—labeling
the cause of her insomnia, since she refused to believe it

was the grilling Patrice had given her while she "helped" her unpack her belongings. The woman must have been an inquisitor of the Spanish variety in a past life.

Okay, maybe Skye had been a little hard on Logan. It wasn't his fault she was incapable of not drooling while in his presence. And it wasn't as if he'd made a pass at her—if he'd tried, she'd have taken a spatula to him. And it wasn't as if it bothered her that he hadn't made a pass. Okay, maybe a little, but he was engaged. "Let's face it, the guy can't win. You just need to get your hormones under control."

It wasn't his fault that when he shook her hand, there seemed to be an electric current that ran straight to her breasts and other body parts that hadn't seen any action in, well, way too long. "Maybe if I didn't have four goons for brothers who scared every human with a Y chromosome I came into contact with, I'd actually have a sex life."

She grabbed a spoon and stirred the stock, drawing the scent toward her, wanting to know what spices were used. It smelled good so far.

Since it would be a few minutes before it was at a full simmer, she went to the storeroom with a clipboard in hand to do a quick inventory. She'd read Rex's order and wanted to double-check a few things before she called it in. Dragging the stool behind her, she took one look at the shelves and cursed—a lot. She really hated feeling like a midget in the land of giants. Climbing onto the wobbly stool, she grabbed the shelves to steady herself, and cranked her neck back to see what the heck was up there. "What makes tall people put heavy things on the top shelves?"

"Problem?"

Skye's heart tripped into triple time. She had a big problem—Logan—and he was standing in the doorway. He'd caught her talking to herself. Skye closed her eyes and took a deep breath, hearing her mother's voice in her head. *Breathe, Skye. In through the nose, out through the mouth.* All the deep-breathing and relaxation techniques she'd learned in the yoga classes her mother dragged her to weren't helping. Of course, she'd always scoffed at them. Maybe she needed to start meditating like her mother said she should. "Logan." The stool teetered.

He stepped closer and offered her a hand. "That's dangerous."

Not as dangerous as touching him was to her mental health.

"If you need the storeroom rearranged, you should ask Harrison to take care of it."

She looked at his hand, and then at his face, not really wanting to get the electric shock she knew would assault her if she touched him.

In one swift move, Logan lifted her off the stool as if she were a child, and set her on the tiled floor.

She really needed to be grounded around this guy. Even through clothing, Logan's touch was like sucking on a live wire.

"No more climbing on wobbly stools. I can't afford to lose another cook. Harrison's still out front with the rest of the kitchen staff—I'll send him in. Let him help you rearrange things."

"I was trying to keep a lid on the overtime."

"I'd rather pay overtime than a hospital bill."

Skye bit her tongue. This wasn't one of her obnoxious brothers; this was her boss. She never realized what a big difference that made. "Thank you—that would be great. I need to be able to reach things. Maybe I can get a step stool in here too. I don't want to pull someone away from their work just because I'm short."

He laughed at that, showing off his white even teeth. Wow, the man had a great smile. She reminded herself not to drool and did the deep-breathing thing again. Still not helping. Neither was being in a small room with Logan—especially since he seemed to fill the space. She slid past him into the kitchen. "I also need to pull the pots off that rack." She turned in a full circle, trying to figure out where to store them that would be out of the way and yet easily accessible. "I guess it's going to take some time to figure out a new setup that will work for all of us."

Logan tilted his head and stared.

"What is it?" She walked around him to stir the simmering broth.

"Nothing."

Still, he stared at her as if he'd never seen her before. She took a spoon and tasted the broth and turned off the heat. It was good. Hers was better, but if she added a bouquet garni and let it simmer for a half hour or so, it would do.

"Are you cooking?"

"No. I'm just testing the chicken broth. I'm picky and wanted to make sure it was something I wanted to use. Why, are you hungry?"

There was that smile again. "I'm a guy. I'm always hungry."

"I can throw together a quick Stracciatella."

"A what?"

"It's chicken broth, with strands of egg with spinach,

and lots of Parmesan cheese. The broth needs a few more spices, but it will be a quick fix. And then, since I'm in an Italian mood, how about linguini with clam sauce?"

"We have clams?"

"I stopped at the fish market before I came over. I was going to cook myself dinner later, but I can easily fix it here."

He slid a stool from beneath the worktable and sat. "You have enough?"

"For two? Of course."

"That sounds great on one condition."

Deep breath, here it comes. "What's that?"

"Let me reimburse you for the food you bought."

She pulled the clams out of the walk-in, trying to keep busy. "It's not necessary. You supply the wine and we'll call it good."

"It's not negotiable."

"Fine." She smiled to herself. "Just for that, I'm not going to let you have any of my dessert."

He leaned forward, resting his elbows on bent knees. "What's for dessert?"

"I have a tray of chocolate tiramisu chilling in my refrigerator at home."

"When did you make that?"

"Last night. I couldn't sleep—jet lag."

"Lucky me." He leaned back against the worktable. "I just happen to have an incredible port I've been saving. It goes great with chocolate."

"Okay, since you have the port, and I was thinking of using it for a dessert special, I guess you can have a taste. I'll start cooking. Send Harrison in to help rearrange the shelves and then if you wouldn't mind, run over to my place and bring back the tiramisu." She tossed him her key ring.

"Deal." He turned and made his way to the doors. "I'll be back in a flash. And Skye, no more climbing on stools."

"Right." She looked at the pot rack above her head. "But if you expect that to happen, you'd better put a step stool or a ladder on your list of things to buy. I'm pretty sure I'm not going to get any taller."

He shot her another killer smile and slipped through the doors.

"Damn, the man is lethal." She took a deep breath. "In through the nose, out through the mouth." She gave it a few tries, each time hearing her mother's high-pitched voice. Amazingly enough, after about five deep breaths, it started working. She wondered if it would have worked as well while dealing with her brothers. She shook her head and put some water on to boil. No, probably not. After all, her brothers seemed to enjoy tormenting her.

Logan stepped up to the bar where Harrison, a blond guy with a goatee and gauges in his ears, was gesturing wildly, ending with what looked like a description of a woman's breasts.

He had obviously interrupted one of the sous chef's comedy routines—a crude one from the looks of it. "Harrison, could you spend some time with Skye rearranging the storeroom? She's having a hard time reaching things."

"Sure." He shot a cocky grin at the rest of the kitchen staff.

Logan realized what he'd interrupted. It wasn't Harrison's skit; it was Harrison talking about Skye. Shit. He tamped down the urge to pick him up by his collar and bang him into the wall a few times. "Wipe that smile off your face, Bubba—I'm not sending you in there to play spin the bottle. Skye's your boss, and although she might not look it, she's tough as nails."

Harrison's smile vanished. "I wasn't—"

Logan's eyes locked on his.

The man took a giant step back and nodded.

"Good. See that you don't." He pulled out his wallet and withdrew a hundred-dollar bill. "And on your way home, pick up a sturdy step stool so she doesn't kill herself climbing around back there. Make sure you bring me the receipt and change."

"Will do." Harrison took the cash, shoved it in his pocket, and stepped out of Logan's reach, double-timing it to the kitchen.

Logan stared at each one of the crew in turn. "That goes for all of you."

Every one of them nodded and slid off his stool, heading for the door as if someone just lit a fire under his ass. Okay, maybe he was being a little heavy-handed when it came to Skye and the opposite sex. It wasn't as if she couldn't take care of herself. She'd had no problem giving him the brush-off. Still, he felt territorial when it came to Skye. If he were a cat, Pop would have him neutered. No, she wasn't his and he wasn't even available. He was just being a good manager; there'd be no sexual harassment under his watch—and he'd be watching.

He was tempted to follow Harrison into the kitchen to make sure he behaved. Yet he knew he should give her some room and let her handle Harrison. After what he'd seen of her, Harrison was nothing Skye couldn't manage.

He followed the crew out, shaking his head. Was it Skye he didn't understand or women in general? He was almost glad Payton was a low-maintenance kind of woman. She didn't expect much from him, he didn't expect much from her, and neither of them seemed to mind. He'd bet his left nut Skye would be just the opposite.

Skye probably wasn't used to the way things were done at the Crow's Nest. Pop thought of everyone involved as family, and Logan had fallen back into the fold over the last month. Going to one of the crew's apartments wasn't unusual. Hell, he'd already made friends with most of the staff. It was pretty obvious that Skye had never worked in a family-run restaurant. It had taken him a while to cool down enough to look at the situation from her point of view. She hadn't been rude—just cautious. She was alone in an unfamiliar city—maybe for the first time—and was in a new apartment with a strange man who was twice her size. That would make any woman a little nervous.

That morning he'd been determined to respect her boundaries, and was relieved when at the meeting with the kitchen staff she was relaxed, in charge, and friendly. Within a few minutes, she'd put everyone at ease. She talked about her style of cooking and her expectations. She seemed tough but fair, and spent more time smiling than not. He'd been impressed.

Pepperoni met him at the door with the remnants of a light pink lacy bra in her mouth. Logan bent to pet the little scrap of a dog and swiped the bra. "What have you gotten into?" The apartment was strewn with shoes and clothing. He doubted Skye left the mess. "Why didn't she put you in your crate, you little monster?" He tossed one of Pepperoni's bones into the crate and locked the puppy in as soon as her butt crossed the threshold. "There you go."

He picked up a shoe the dog had gnawed the heel off. "Damn, Skye's not going to be happy with you when she finds this." He turned the slingback over and blew out a breath when he saw they were Manolo Blahniks. He didn't know much about women's shoes, but these were the kind of shoes Payton wore, and she didn't wear anything on her feet that cost less than a grand. What was a woman making forty-five thousand a year doing wearing that kind of footwear? He looked at the puppy, then stared at the shoe. "You'll be lucky if Skye doesn't turn you into next week's special. It's a good thing she's already taken her knives to work."

He picked up Skye's slightly wet, mostly gnawed, and barely there unmentionables and placed them on the bed, noting that her taste in lingerie was as expensive as her shoes. Shit, she'd been there less than twenty-four hours and the room already smelled like her—he'd recognize whatever her scent was anywhere. It wasn't something out of a bottle. It was a little sweet, a little earthy, and a whole lot sexy with a hint of puppy.

He backed out of her bedroom and grabbed the tiramisu, wondering how he was going to break the news of the mess to Skye. Maybe he'd tell her after a full bottle of wine and the port.

CHAPTER 6

Skye ran through the dining room on her way to the kitchen after her lunch break. She had taken her first paycheck from the Crow's Nest out for a spin and had found great buys at the local thrift store. Unfortunately, the only place she'd been able to afford to shop wasn't her usual haunt—Nordstrom. Heck, she didn't even know if they had Nordies in New York, but then she'd never found a pair of Jones New York slacks for a dollar before either.

She held her bags in front of her and wove her way through the tables, smiling at some of the customers she recognized.

Her first week and a half at her new job had been a success. She and her kitchen staff were getting into the swing of working together. Harrison had finally realized his X-ray vision was on the fritz and stopped staring at her boobs, and Randy and Travis stopped fighting over the waitress they both wanted to date. Of course, all it took to keep Randy and Travis from a fight in the back alley was a look from Logan. She'd been about to jump into the fray when he appeared out of nowhere and, with one well-placed sexy-as-sin raised eyebrow, had the boys cowering.

Think of the devil. Logan stepped in front of her and eyed her packages. "Do you have a moment?"

She checked her watch. The answer was no, but she mentally restructured her to-do list to make one—something she never would have done had one of her brothers asked the same question in their kitchens. "Sure."

He motioned toward the office and followed her back.

Skye placed her bags on the chair instead of sitting, so he'd know she didn't have all day without her having to tell him. Tact—that was something else her mother had kept hoping she'd discover. The woman finally got her wish—sort of, as Skye was now practicing on her new boss.

He closed the door, slid by her to take a seat at his desk, and nodded toward her packages. "Pepperoni get more of your things?"

"No." Her face flamed remembering her first day of work. After a leisurely lunch and a full bottle of wine Logan had told her about Pepperoni's penchant for destruction when left alone outside her crate. Of course he hadn't mentioned exactly what he'd found, something she was eternally grateful for once she'd seen the pile of bras and undies he must have gathered and placed neatly in a pile on her unmade bed. "I didn't bring much in the way of clothes with me—just one suitcase. I'm filling the gaps in my wardrobe. So you wanted me?"

His eyebrows rose, and she probably turned even redder. "Yes. I got a call from someone at Foods of New York Tours. They have food tours through Chelsea Market, No-lita, Greenwich Village, Chinatown, and the like. They're looking into starting a tour in Brooklyn and requested a private tasting. They heard we had a new chef and someone in-house raved about the food."

"When?"

"Monday afternoon. Do you have plans?"

"My social calendar is all filled up."

He did that sexy eyebrow thing again.

"Kidding." She tossed her bags on the floor and took a seat. "This is great. How often do they have them?"

He leaned back in his chair and laced his fingers behind his neck. "I don't know."

"How many restaurants are on a tour?"

"Another good question. I bought two tickets to a tour this Sunday of Central Greenwich Village and SoHo. I thought you could join me if you were free. Think of it as a working lunch."

"Okay. That doesn't leave me much time for planning, but it's nothing I can't handle."

"Good." He sat forward and twirled a pencil through his fingers—the man even had nice hands. "I think this will be a great way to attract new customers. Pop's never been much for marketing, and Bree's had her hands full for the last few months. I'm trying to pick up the slack. You're doing a great job, Skye. It's thanks to you we have this opportunity."

She didn't know what to say, having never been in this particular position before. *Thanks for noticing*? *You're welcome*? She just nodded and smiled, grabbed her bags, and rushed out the door, almost running over one of the servers.

"Sorry, Wendy. I didn't see you there."

"Is Logan in the office? There's some high-society chick demanding to speak to him."

"Huh?" Skye peeked around the corner and swore. Payton Billingsly stood beside the bar glaring at everyone and holding her oversized Fendi bag under her arm as if she were about to be swarmed by thieves. Skye slid back to safety. "Someone had better tell Logan that his fiancée is here and she's looking none too pleased."

"That's her?"

"Yes. I saw the article about them in *Food & Wine*." Good save. Now all she had to do was get her ass into the kitchen and stay there for the duration of Payton's visit, which, from the look on Payton's face, wouldn't be long. Skye eyed the door she'd just shut. "Go keep her busy. I'll tell Logan."

"Do I have to?"

"Yes. And whatever you do, don't let her come back here."

She knocked on the door, let herself in without waiting for a response, and closed it quickly behind her, pressing her back against the cool wood. Logan looked up from whatever he was working on and smiled before he leaned back in his chair. "Are you hiding from someone?"

"Um . . . no." If he only knew. "I just ran into Wendy."

"Did it hurt?"

"No. I wasn't being literal."

"Okay." He lowered his head to sign a check. "Did you come back to tell me that?" He eyed her, ripped out the check, and stuffed it into an envelope, concentrating on making sure the address showed through the cellophane panel. "I don't know why my dad doesn't just bite the bullet and do his bill paying online like a normal person. It's the twenty-first century, for God's sake."

"There's someone out front to see you."

He was still fooling with the envelope.

"Your fiancée is out front, and she doesn't look happy."

Logan's head reared up so quickly, he might have given himself whiplash.

"Excuse me?"

"Your fiancée—tall, blond, and as skinny as a swizzle stick. Ring a bell?"

His face drained of all color, and if she wasn't mistaken, he was sweating even though the room always felt like a freezer. "How did she find me?"

"I wasn't aware you were hiding." But she could certainly see why. She'd been avoiding Payton Billingsly for years.

Logan stood and his expressionless face looked as if he wore a mask. Gone was the easy smile—it was replaced by emptiness. His expression went blank, and his once beautiful eyes seemed dull and lifeless. "I'm not hiding. I just wasn't expecting her." He rolled down his sleeves, buttoned his cuffs with a weird kind of military precision she'd never seen in him before, cursed under his breath, and then ran his hands through his hair.

Obviously not a happy reunion.

Logan nodded at her as if she were some kind of servant and then stepped around his desk. His whole bearing had changed. He looked like an actor stepping into the role of a man headed for the gallows.

The man standing before her now was not the man she'd spent the last week and a half getting to know. Before her very eyes, he'd turned back into the man she'd thought he'd been at their first meeting.

She took a deep breath, in through the nose, out through the mouth. At least she no longer had the drooling problem she'd had a minute ago. Her mouth had suddenly gone as dry as a desert martini.

Logan wondered what the hell had happened. Skye stared at him wearing the same expression he'd seen that first day they'd met—one full of derision. He'd thought they'd made progress. He'd thought they'd become friends. Apparently he'd thought wrong.

He shook his head. It didn't matter; he had bigger problems to deal with than Skye's personality disorder.

Payton.

Fuck.

He was finally going to have to come clean—about everything. On the bright side, at least the problem he'd had the entire time Skye had been in the office deflated quicker than a helium balloon at a frat party. "Is Pop on the floor or behind the bar?"

Skye blinked at him with her mouth hanging open. She shut it and shook her head. "I don't know. I didn't see him when I came in, but I wasn't exactly looking for him either."

"Okay. If you'll excuse me, I have to get out there." He wished she'd give him a smile, something. She just nodded and stepped aside to let him pass. He felt her eyes on him and went to meet his fate.

Women.

Straightening his shoulders, he took a deep breath, and did his best to smile.

Payton stood beside the bar like a queen among peasants. She was tall and beautiful—in an unnaturally perfect way. Her lips were enhanced with collagen, her breasts enhanced with silicone or whatever they used these days, and her body was sculpted by a personal trainer. Her makeup was perfect, her clothing designer, and her jewelry twenty-four karat or platinum.

Payton's eyes locked on his. She was pissed. She didn't have to say a word; her anger slapped his face as hard as a hand.

"You should have told me you were coming."

She tossed a length of blond hair over her shoulder. "How was I supposed to do that? You never answer your phone or return my calls."

"I'm sorry. I've been busy." Every eye in the house was glued on Payton. He leaned over and kissed her cheek.

She stepped away and drew her lips back in a fake smile. "You said you were from New York." She spoke through clenched teeth.

"I am. Brooklyn, New York. It's one of the five boroughs."

She waved a hand to encompass the restaurant. "This was not what I expected. You lied to me."

"I never lied. You just never asked. Let's go upstairs where we can talk without the entire neighborhood listening in." He placed his hand on the small of her back and applied pressure.

She didn't move. "Upstairs? This place has a second floor?"

"Yes, our apartment."

"You can't be serious. You're actually living above this dump?"

Logan thought he'd feel embarrassment, but no. All he felt was the hot, sharp edge of rage. "Come with me." He grabbed her wrist, and dragged her through the throng of gawkers to his office before slamming the door.

Payton took one look at him and stepped back so far, she hit the desk. In heels, she was only a few inches shorter than him, almost eye to eye, and hers were blazing. "Don't you dare drag me around like some kind of unruly child ever again."

"If you want me to stop treating you like a brat, then stop acting like one. Now, what the hell are you doing here, Payton? I doubt your intention in coming was to insult me and piss me off, both of which you could have done over the phone."

"Oh really? How? You never answer your phone. It was as if you just dropped off the face of the earth."

"I called you last week. Unlike you, I have a job to do. I've been busy. Believe it or not, a bar and restaurant don't run themselves."

She looked around his office as if she expected to find a dead rodent somewhere. "I came to bring you home."

He rubbed his eyes. "I told you. I can't leave until Slater gets here to relieve me. Bree and Storm are still on their honeymoon."

"If you don't come home now, we may never have a honeymoon."

He held on to his temper by a thread. "Is that a threat? Think about what you're saying."

"Logan." She stepped forward as if someone had instantly deflated her anger like popping a balloon. She slid her hand up his chest, leaning in. "Honey, I've missed you," she whispered, her lips brushing his ear. Her other hand slid lower and toyed with the waistband of his jeans before she kissed him.

Payton tasted like waxy lipstick, the cigarette she must have snuck before she came in, and Altoids—her cover-up of choice. He waited to feel the rush. He had a beautiful woman in his arms, her tongue in his mouth, and she was practically dry-humping him. But he felt nothing. Not a fucking thing. He tried to set aside his anger, his embarrassment, and the feeling of being caught in a lie of his own making and concentrated on her. They'd always worked well together, in bed and out of it. He slid his hand under her jacket and reached her breast. Nope, that wasn't cutting it either—at least not for him. Her hand moved lower and stilled over his fly, which, for the first time in recent memory, was not bulging. Damn.

She dragged her mouth away from his and stared into his eyes. Hers were wide with shock. "What's wrong?"

Logan shook his head and wiped his mouth with the back of his hand. Lipstick. Shit. "Nothing's wrong. I'm in my office. Anyone can walk in."

She reached around him and locked the door. "Now"—she nuzzled his neck—"where were we?"

The doorknob rattled and then he heard the jingle of keys.

"Shit. This is not a good time." He stepped away from her and opened the door. "Pop." Could this day get any worse? The answer was hell yes, but only if he'd been sporting a hard-on. He wasn't sure which was more embarrassing, getting caught with a woody by his dad, or getting caught without one by his fiancée. Neither was something he'd experienced.

"Why the hell are you locking the—" Pop stopped and stared at Payton. "Oh, sorry. I didn't mean to interrupt."

"Payton, this is my father, Pete Calahan. Pop, this is my fiancée, Payton Billingsly."

Pop's bushy white eyebrows rose and he grinned like

a used-car salesman. He took her hand and pulled her into a hug. "Welcome to the family, Payton. I was beginning to think you were a figment of Logan's imagination."

Payton was not a hugger. She stiffened and awkwardly patted Pop's back.

Pop either didn't notice her discomfort or didn't care. "When did you get in? Logan never even mentioned you were coming."

Logan threw Payton a lifeline. He took her hand and pulled her toward him. "That's because I didn't know. She's just full of surprises. Aren't you, Payton?"

She looked from him to Pop and probably saw no resemblance because there was none. "It's nice to meet you, Mr. Calahan. But I don't understand. Logan's last name is Blaise. . . ."

Pop shot him a what-the-fuck look and then turned the full wattage of his smile on Payton. "Mr. Calahan was my father. Call me Pete or Pop. Whatever you like." He looked around the office. "Where are your bags?"

"At the hotel. I'm staying at the Plaza."

"Nonsense, you're staying with us." He reached over the desk, slipped his hand into the top drawer, and took out a cigar.

Logan snatched it before Pop could pocket it and then broke it in half. He tossed it in the trash.

Pop looked as if he bit back a curse. "What the hell did you do that for?"

"You're not allowed to smoke."

"I'll just buy more, you know."

"Then I guess I'll just break more."

Pop turned to Payton. "Is he always this bossy?"

She had a strange look on her face. "No, never."

Pop shrugged. "Look, Payton. There's no reason to waste your money. We have plenty of room. You two can stay at Bree's place if you'd like to have some privacy." He tossed his arm around her shoulder. "So, tell me, do you have a nickname or something?"

"No, why?"

"Your name is kind of a mouthful, isn't it? It's not easy to shorten either. What would they call you? Pay?" He shook his head and rubbed his chin. "Nah, that doesn't work. Ton? That doesn't fit either. You're way too skinny for that. What's Logan's pet name for you?"

"He doesn't have one. He calls me Payton."

"Oh." He shot her one of his X-rated smiles with an eyebrow waggle. "So it's one of *those* names. I understand."

"Logan?" Payton's frown lines were so defined, if she kept it up, the next thing he knew she'd be running out for Botox injections. "What is he talking about?"

"Don't worry about it. Pop, Payton and I were just talking."

"Right. That's why you locked the door. I wasn't born yesterday, son."

"Pop."

"I'll go. Let's have dinner. I'll have Skye fix something special and have Wendy serve it upstairs." Pop didn't wait for an answer; he opened the door and before he had the chance to leave, Nicki ran in.

"Logan, I got an A on my math test! Do you believe it?" She shoved the paper at him, wrapped her skinny arms around his waist, and looked up, resting her chin on his chest.

He held the test paper in one hand and he slid his arm around Nicki and her backpack. "Of course you got an A. You're a smart kid and you've been working hard."

"I only got an A 'cause you've been helping me with my homework every night."

"I just explained it a different way. You did the hard part yourself."

Nicki's eyes slid to Payton and then back to him. "Who's that lady staring at us?" she whispered into his chest.

Logan gave her a squeeze and a smile before turning her to face Payton. "Nicki, this is my fiancée, Payton. Payton, this is Nicki."

"I'm his little sister. Right, Logan?" She looked at him with so much trust it was frightening.

"Right." At least for now.

Pop slid Nicki's backpack off her bony shoulders and caught the sweatshirt she shrugged off and was about to toss on the floor. "Can I go to the kitchen and get a snack from Skye?"

Logan thanked God she didn't ask any more questions. "Sure, kiddo. But only if she's not too busy."

Nicki pulled the door open. He was just about to tell her to mind her manners when she stopped, and grinned. "It was nice to meet you, Payton."

"Nice to meet you too."

Nicki headed out and then looked back over her shoulder. "Logan, you got lipstick on you."

"Great." He wiped his mouth again and cursed under his breath.

Payton stepped closer. "You never told me you had a sister."

"I know. Look, Payton, we need to talk." He took her

hands in his and when his father didn't move, he glared at him. "Pop?"

"I'm leaving. You two take as long as you need. Do you want me to have Simon send in something to drink?"

Payton smiled at him like she would a waiter. "Yes. A Chambord and champagne would be lovely."

Pop nodded and then shot Logan his trademark do-you-believe-this-shit look. "I'll get right on that."

"No." Logan dropped Payton's hand. "Pop, you keep an eye on Nicki. I'll get the drinks." He pinned Payton with his gaze. "I'll be right back. Wait here."

She inspected the chair and brushed off the seat before she sat, crossing her long legs.

He followed his father out.

Once Pop cleared the hallway, he scowled. "She looks awfully fake to me. And what the hell does she have on her eyes?"

"False eyelashes."

"Why?"

A vision of Skye with her thick dark lashes popped into his head. "Beats the hell out of me."

"I think a figment of your imagination would have been an improvement over the real thing—that's if anything on her is real. She looks like one of those blow-up dolls you find in the back of those nudie magazines you and Storm collected."

He tried to dredge up some righteous indignation. "Pop, that's not fair." The look of disbelief he got in return told him his well of righteous indignation was running dry. He stopped speaking. The last thing he wanted to do was catalog Payton's enhanced parts.

"You haven't brought her here all these years because you're ashamed of where you come from."

"Not true. I didn't bring Payton here because I knew she wouldn't fit in. I'm not ashamed of a damn thing."

"Are you sure about that?"

"Yes, I am. Payton . . . she's, well—"

"As cold as the Jane Doe I found in that psycho's freezer?"

"I was going to say cultured. She's never seen how the other half live."

"The other half? Try the other ninety-nine percent."

"Whatever. She's a nice woman, so give her a break. Okay, Pop?"

"Fine, you're going to do what you want, but you'd better think long and hard before handcuffing yourself to a woman you don't love."

Pop walked away before Logan could ask how he knew. What, was it written all over his face or something? Yeah, probably in Payton's lipstick.

Logan slid under the pass-through behind the bar. "Simon, I need a split of our best champagne."

Simon laughed and reached into the cooler. "It's easy to pick out." He handed Logan the bottle. "We only stock one kind."

"Right." Logan looked at the vintage and grimaced. He really needed to take over the wine order. He reached up to grab the Chambord and then popped the cork on the champagne.

"So, that blonde is your fiancée?"

"Payton? Yes. She surprised me."

"You're not the only one. She said something to Rocki. Must have pissed her off, because she's been playing Shostakovich and Prokofiev ever since."

"What'd Payton say?"

"I don't know but it must have been something bad. Rocki doesn't often pull out the pissed-off Russian composers, you know?"

No, he didn't. He hadn't spent enough time at the bar to know what Rocki played. He was surprised she knew classical music. She didn't seem the type.

Logan poured Payton's drink, going heavy on the Chambord hoping to cover the taste of the less-than-stellar champagne. It didn't have a prayer of working. She'd grown up tasting wines; even with the damage her closet smoking did to her taste buds, she'd know the difference.

He grabbed a bottle of tequila, poured a shot, threw it back, and then poured another.

"Looks like Rocki's not the only one your fiancée pissed off. But then if you love her, you'll get through it. It's amazing what love can overcome."

Logan downed the second shot. "I guess you would know." He checked the end of the bar and found Simon's girlfriend, Elyse, working over a beer and a plate of chicken wings. Simon and Elyse were almost as bad as Storm and Bree.

The song "Fools in Love" played on his mental soundtrack, drowning out the angry Russian sonata. "Pour me a Guinness, will you?" He put the tequila and the Chambord back on the top shelf. "I have to face the music."

Simon took a chilled mug from the cooler and poured the dark brew, sliding it down the bar to him. "Better you than me. Good luck."

"Thanks." He grabbed the two drinks. "I have a feeling I'm going to need it."

*   *   *

Nicki ran through the kitchen door and stopped short. "Did you see her, Skye?"

"Hi, Nicki." Skye tossed a fryer full of wings in her special sauce, and plated them before turning to her little friend. "How was school?" The last thing she wanted to talk about was Payton Billingsly.

"Great. I got an A on my math test. Logan helped me."

"Good for you."

"He said I can have a snack if you have time."

Skye looked over her orders. "Harrison, can you take over? I'm going to take a break with Nicki."

"Sure, Skye."

"Come on, Nicki." She reached into the walk-in and grabbed the snack she'd put together earlier. "I thought you'd be hungry, so I made us a snack to share."

Nicki wrinkled her nose. "Is it healthy?"

"Yes. It's very healthy. Why would I serve you something unhealthy?"

"'Cause it tastes good?"

"I made us my favorite and I can attest to the fact that it tastes great."

Nicki harrumphed and dug the heel of her sneaker into the tile floor. "You sound just like Bree."

Skye had a feeling she'd like Bree when she finally met her. "You miss her a lot, don't you?"

"Yeah, but she's coming back. She promised."

"Of course she is." Skye placed the plate of celery sticks filled with peanut butter and topped with raisins, and apple slices with cheddar cheese, on the worktable, and then pulled out a stool. "Come on, at least try it before you talk Harrison into making you fries and gravy."

Harrison ducked his head. "Hey, I just cook the orders; I don't okay them."

Nicki sat beside Skye and picked up a piece of celery before licking the peanut butter and raisins off it.

"You're supposed to eat them together."

"I don't like green food."

"Try it. It's good—really."

Nicki took a bite and her eyebrows rose with apparent shock.

"Told ya."

Nicki covered her mouth with her hand. "Have you met Logan's girlfriend yet?" She spoke around a mouthful of celery.

"No, I haven't had the pleasure." And if she stayed behind closed doors, she hoped to avoid the woman altogether. That was her plan anyway.

Harrison put out a plate of potato skins. "I didn't meet her, but I saw her. She's hot with a capital H."

Nicki finally swallowed her food and shrugged. "I guess she's pretty, but she doesn't look very nice."

Smart kid. Still, it wouldn't help for her to agree with Nicki. "Looks can be deceiving. You should give her a chance."

"Pop doesn't like her."

"How do you know?"

"From the look on his face. And I can tell Rocki doesn't like her either."

"Really?"

"Yeah, she's playing angry music. You know the old-fashioned stuff without words."

"Classical?" She tried to hear over the hip-hop Harrison favored.

Nicki nodded and bit into a piece of apple.

"Try it with the cheese. The flavors work well together."

Nicki took a tentative bite and must have agreed because she stuffed the rest of the piece of cheese into her overfilled mouth. Her table manners were horrendous.

"Slow down, Nicki. You're going to choke."

Nicki looked down at the plate and then back up to Skye. "Sometimes I forget that now I can eat whenever I want. Logan says I'll start rememberin', but it takes a while."

Harrison grabbed a celery stick off the plate. "Nicki's only been with Pete for four or five months. She's his new foster kid."

"That's how I got brothers. Storm, Logan, and Slater are Pop's foster kids too—they're just like me 'cept they're boys, and they're really old."

"You're all foster kids?"

"Uh-huh. Storm says we're the lucky ones because Pop is a forever kinda guy."

Skye nodded and swallowed the lump in her throat.

"Do you want a piece of apple, Skye?"

"No thanks, I've had enough. You go ahead; just take smaller bites."

Pete pushed his way through the kitchen doors. "There you are, Nicki." He put his hands on the little girl's shoulders. "You left your sweatshirt and backpack in the office." He dropped them on the table and smiled at Skye. "Thanks for getting Nicki a snack."

"It's not a problem. I always enjoy our visits."

"I was wondering if you could make us a special dinner tonight. Logan's fiancée is here. I asked Wendy, and she said she wouldn't mind running it upstairs."

"I'd be happy to. Just let me know what and when."

Nicki bounced on the stool. "Hey Pop, can we have dessert too?"

"Sure. Whatever you want." He kissed the top of her head. "Let's get you out of Skye and Harrison's hair. We can take the rest of that snack upstairs. You can eat and do your homework at the same time."

"But, Pop—"

"No buts. You need to get your homework done before dinner. We're having company, so you better be on your best behavior."

"I know, I know." She slid off the stool and shouldered the backpack that looked almost as big as she was. "Bye, Skye. Thanks for the snack."

Skye wasn't prepared for it, but Nicki threw her arms around her and gave her a big hug. "I like you way better than that Payton lady."

Skye hugged Nicki back—it had been so long since anyone hugged her, she'd forgotten how nice it was. "You don't know her. Give her a chance. She might surprise you."

The look on Pete's face told her it wasn't likely, and she had to agree. If Logan really loved Payton, she hoped she was wrong. In the last week and a half, she realized she'd misjudged him. He didn't fit the stereotype—at least not until Payton appeared.

Her chest tightened at the thought. She wasn't sure why—she hadn't had any of Harrison's fries and gravy, so she knew it wasn't heartburn. She didn't have time to examine what else it could be. Nicki released her. "Okay, I'll give Payton a chance, but I'm not gonna like it."

Skye shook her head trying to remember what they'd been talking about. Her mind kept circling back to Logan's weird transformation she'd witnessed earlier. Giving Payton a chance. She did her best not to laugh at her own wayward thoughts. "Get used to it, Nicki. There are a lot of things you're going to do that you're not going to like. Just try to keep an open mind. Do it for Logan. They're engaged, so he must really love her." Skye found Pete shaking his head. He gave her a whatcha-gonna-do shrug.

Nicki gave her a final squeeze and ran out of the kitchen.

Pete grabbed Nicki's sweatshirt, threw it over his shoulder, and took the plate. "Nicki thinks a lot of you, Skye. Thanks for being so good to her. She's really missing Bree. It's good she has women like you and Rocki to talk to."

"No thanks necessary. If it's okay with you, I was thinking of inviting Nicki and D.O.G. over to play this weekend. I thought we could take the dogs to the park for a while, and then come back and make a batch of dog cookies."

Pete's smile probably sent hearts pitter-pattering in his younger days. "Only if you promise to make a batch of human cookies too."

"I think I can manage that. What kind do you want?"

"Whatever kind you want to make. Just make sure they're not heart healthy. This diet is going to kill me. Oh, and you have to keep them our little secret, okay? Logan's turning into a regular food Nazi."

Skye watched Pete leave and found Harrison doing the same thing. "What?"

Harrison took an order off the computer and shrugged. "Pete's a hell of a guy. I heard he caught Storm stealing a boat before he fostered him, and Logan was into building pipe bombs when Pete took him in. Just look at them now: Storm's designing multimillion-dollar yachts, and Logan's making wine instead of bombs. Pete has a real way with kids."

"What's Slater's story?"

"He's one of those computer geniuses who made hacking into secure systems look like tiddlywinks. If there was security involved, it was like waving a Red Bull in front of a caffeine addict. He's almost done getting his master's in computer science at one of the top computer-programming schools in the country. I think he's finishing up an internship with Microsoft now."

"Amazing."

Harrison handed her an order. "Pretty much."

Logan gave Payton her drink and took a long draw of his beer. He set it on the desk, not ready to meet Payton's questioning eyes. "I hope you don't mind having dinner with the family."

"No. I mean, I don't mind." Payton shook her head, confusion wrinkling her brow. "Logan, I don't understand what's going on."

He sat on the edge of the desk. "What's to understand, Payton? This is where I grew up. Well, actually I grew up upstairs in a three-bedroom apartment you could probably fit in our living room. I have two foster brothers, Storm and Slater. Pop took us all in within a few months of each other. I was about twelve, I think."

"You don't remember?"

"No." He took her hand in his and watched the diamond she'd picked out for her engagement ring catch the light. "Not everyone grew up like you did. You had everything you could ever want. I was the kid on the other end of the spectrum."

He straightened and looked out the window trying to remember. He didn't know why he bothered; it had never worked before. He'd spent a lifetime trying to remember. "I was the kid who got dumped off at a police station or a hospital when I was about three, the nearest they could tell. I wasn't talking. Either I couldn't or wouldn't tell them a thing. I was put into the foster system and bounced from one foster home to another until I landed here." He blew out a breath and turned to look at her.

A tear ran down the side of her face and she brushed it away with a shaking, perfectly manicured hand. Her false eyelashes looked as if they should be running for the ark.

He handed her his handkerchief. God, he'd dreaded doing this for years, and it sucked as badly as he thought it would. "The only thing I have from my life before Pete Calahan is a memory book filled with faded photographs of foster parents and kids I hardly recognize. All I have of my life before I moved here is a fucking book. I left it here when I left Red Hook. I buried that kid."

"Your parents gave you up willingly?"

"I never saw my picture on the back of a milk carton, if that's what you're asking." And he had looked. At least Storm and Slater knew who the hell they were. But then that knowledge came with its own problems. "Let me spell it out for you. My parents dumped me. I was a foundling. I was a three-year-old kid no one wanted."

"Didn't you look for them? I mean, it's not as if Blaise is a common name."

"No one knew my name. My name and birth date were given to me by my case manager. I don't even know how she came up with them."

Pity clouded Payton's eyes. "Why didn't you ever tell me?"

"Because I knew if I had, you'd look at me the way you are now. I'm fine. Where I came from doesn't make me the man I am. I made myself who I am. Lord knows, Pop helped, but when it comes right down to it, I decided who I wanted to be, what I wanted to do, and I made it happen. I went to Stanford on a full scholarship. I took a bus to California and never looked back."

"You lied to me and everyone we know." Her voice rose like an air-raid siren.

"I never lied to you. I don't lie."

"You might not have out-and-out lied, but you weren't honest with me. What else don't I know about you?"

"Nothing important."

"Nothing important? My God, Logan, I don't even know who you are. How is that not important? I'm marrying a stranger. How could I have lived with you for two years and not have known?"

"There wasn't anything to know. You assumed I grew up on Park Avenue. I didn't. I grew up in Brooklyn, living over a bar. It's not that big a deal."

"Not a big deal? You know everything about me. You know my parents—"

"And you met Pop. He's the closest thing to a father I have. You know about Storm and Slater."

"I never knew about Nicki."

"That makes two of us. I didn't know Nicki existed until Storm came to take care of Pop after his heart attack."

Logan looked at his watch. He didn't think this was a good time to get into the whole Nicki thing.

"Our whole relationship has been nothing but an illusion."

"If it's an illusion, it's the way you wanted it. You only saw what you wanted to see."

"No, I only saw what you showed me. What you allowed me to see. You had me fooled until I walked in the door. You're all smoke and mirrors."

"You seemed happy enough with it until now."

She stood and walked to him, staring at his face as if she'd never seen him before. "What were you like when you were a boy?"

"I was always in trouble." He tried to smile, but it didn't work. He wasn't proud of what he'd been. "I liked to blow things up and by all accounts, I was pretty good at it. I was the youngest member of the Latin Kings, a gang around here. I got caught with a few pipe bombs and was handed over to Pop the next day."

"You what?" All the color drained from her face and she sat back down.

He shrugged. "I liked to see things blow up. It was something to do. Then Pop took me in. He brought me home, introduced me to Storm, and told me exactly what I had to do to stay."

Logan couldn't look at her. Hell, maybe he was ashamed after all, but not of Pop, not of where he came from, but of who he was. "Pop was a real hard-ass ex-cop back then. Less than a week after I came here, I hooked up with my gang and took off. I wasn't counting on Pop coming after me. I didn't think anyone cared until Pop found me. The next day he took me to a prison. He dragged me by the collar through a cellblock and showed me what I had to look forward to. Then he took me to the high school and showed me the chem lab. He said the choice was mine. I chose school and the rest is history. Pop saved my life."

"You have a record?"

"Had. It's been sealed and from what I hear, after Slater hacked into the NYPD's computer system, maybe deleted. I don't know. It doesn't matter."

"It doesn't matter?" She looked shell-shocked.

"Payton, I've left all of that stuff behind. It only matters now if you want it to."

CHAPTER 7

Logan slid Payton's room key into the reader of her suite at the Plaza Hotel. She hadn't said a word the entire trip from Red Hook. He followed her in, tossed the key card on the table in the entryway, and wondered how to broach the subject of Nicki's paternity. He hadn't a fucking clue how one did something like that, but he had to. It was time—past time. It couldn't be avoided any longer. If there was a way to salvage this relationship, she had to know the whole truth.

A couple of months ago he wouldn't have noticed the furnishings in the suite, but tonight when he switched on the lights, he noticed everything. This place made the apartment they'd just left look like a dump.

If he'd looked at his childhood home through Payton's eyes, he'd have seen a shabby little space with scarred furniture, canned art, and people who had never even dreamed of stepping foot in the palatial suite Payton took for granted. Hell, he'd been living large for so long, he'd done the same thing until he'd come home.

Payton kicked off her shoes and tossed the cape she'd bought on their trip to Paris over the back of a chair. She made a beeline to the bar and handed him a bottle of chilled champagne to open—the same champagne he'd given to Skye. Payton wasn't finished drinking, but then he couldn't really blame her—she'd had a lot to take in today, and the day wasn't over.

She slipped out of her blouse and did a striptease on the way to the bedroom. "Are you staying?" Her voice was low and deep and false. The way she'd asked made it impossible to know if she even wanted him to stay. It didn't sound as if she gave a shit.

"No, I have to get back. I can't leave Pop and Nicki overnight. Pop's still on the mend. God forbid anything happens, I need to be there. He's probably up on the roof smokin' a stogie right now. I'll stay for a while, though."

She let out a long, pained sigh. As long and pain-filled as a root canal with a dull drill and no painkiller. This told him a multitude of things. First of which was that she was severely put out that he hadn't dropped everything—including his responsibilities—to spend the night with her. She'd always had a way of testing him and this time he'd failed. It also told him she was still mad as hell. Maybe she had a right to be. He honestly didn't know.

He'd thought their relationship was the way she wanted it. No fuss, no muss. There was no depth of feeling, but that worked for him. They got along, they were assets to each other, and they didn't make each other miserable—until today.

He poured her a champagne and Chambord, wondering how she could drink as much as she did of the stuff and not end up with the hangover from hell. He pulled a beer out of the fridge for himself and took a long draw.

Payton returned wearing one of her sexy-as-hell nightgowns and it didn't escape his notice that she looked amazing in it. He'd never seen this one before and there was no way he'd ever have forgotten it if he had. If Payton had gone on another of her infamous shopping sprees, whatever town she chose to shop in was definitely happy.

He couldn't keep his eyes off her in the sheer, black lace gown, artistically covering certain body parts and not others. She was beautiful—her long blond hair played peekaboo with her breasts; a side slit showed off her long length of tan, toned leg, and the fact that she wore absolutely nothing under the gown. He remembered a day he'd had to wipe his mouth after getting a load of Payton on her Killer Attraction setting. Unfortunately, today, he was completely immune.

She lowered herself onto the couch and went right into her practiced pose. It was like déjà vu. She'd done the same thing the night they'd decided to get married. Then, like tonight, she'd had just enough come-hither to make a man drool, but not enough to look too obvious. Together with the lingerie, any man would be toast. She was good, but for some reason, now it didn't work on him.

He felt nothing. He handed her the drink and sat in the chair opposite.

She pouted. He wasn't sure if she was pouting about him not sitting beside her or about the situation.

"Your family, such as it is, doesn't like me."

"My family, such as it is?" She was trying and failing to manipulate him and she didn't have a clue. She also had no idea how insulting she was; either that or she didn't care. "Let's cut to the chase. What exactly are you getting at here, Payton?"

"Even you must admit they leave a little to be desired." She ran the tip of her pointer finger from her full bottom lip southward to her perfectly displayed cleavage, and she tilted her head. "Would you feel comfortable bringing them to the country club for dinner?"

"No, but then I didn't feel comfortable bringing you, such as you are, to the Crow's Nest. That doesn't mean you're not a good person. It just means that you don't fit in there."

"And neither do you."

He took a long draw from his beer, thinking about what she said. "The funny thing is, I do. I fit there fine." He leaned back and crossed his legs. "I slid back into my old life as easily as my favorite pair of worn jeans. It's relaxed and comfortable, and something I hadn't realized I'd missed until I came home." He had half a mind to put his feet up on the coffee table just to see her reaction.

"That place is not your home. Your home is with me. I'm not putting your family down, Logan. I'm sure they're the salt of the earth and all that, but a man in your position can't afford to be seen in that kind of an establishment or with those kinds of people. Not everyone will be as understanding as I am and overlook your humble beginnings."

Was she serious? He expected the embarrassment he'd carried his whole life to crash over him like shards of broken glass—cutting him to ribbons—but it didn't come. All he felt was anger. Hot, hard, settling in his chest just this side of rage. He set his beer on the coffee table, and squeezed the arms of the leather chair, leaning forward. "You're willing to overlook my humble beginnings?"

She shot that practiced look of superior magnanimity right at him. "Yes, I see no reason to hold that against you. After all, it's not as if you had much of a choice about your childhood, but you certainly have a choice of what to do now."

"You better hold off on that until you get all the information."

"There's more?"

There was no easy way to give her the news about Nicki, so he figured it would be like pulling off a Band-Aid. In his experience, faster was less painful. "Yes. There's a hell of a lot more. Payton, it's about Nicki. She might be my daughter. I'm waiting for the results of the paternity test."

Her face went ghostly pale, even under all that makeup. "You have a ten-year-old daughter and you're just mentioning this to me?" She looked off—like a sick person trying to hide a terminal condition.

"I only found out after I arrived, and it wasn't something I wanted to discuss over the phone. Besides, I'm still not sure of anything yet. I'm waiting for the results of the paternity test—they take a while. I saw no need to upset you before knowing all the facts."

"No need to upset me?" Payton sank into the cushions. "She looks just like you." Her voice was flat, emotionless. Her pale face might be blank, but he knew that look. Her mind was spinning.

"Nicki's mother looks as if she's of Hispanic descent too. Actually, Nicki's a carbon copy of Marisa."

"And where exactly is this Marisa woman?"

"I don't know. We got together when she worked at the Crow's Nest. No one had seen her in years until the day about four or five months ago—she dropped Nicki off at Pop's and told him Nicki was his granddaughter."

"Did she name you as the father?"

"No." He shrugged and threaded his fingers together. "I slept with Marisa. I used protection, but there are warning labels all over the packaging for a reason."

"And your other brothers?"

"Storm never slept with her. I'm not sure about Slater, but I highly doubt it. I have no idea if what Marisa said is even the truth. Even though Marisa might have lied, it doesn't change the fact that Nicki needs a family."

"She has a family. She has your father."

"Pop can't handle a girl her age on his own. What if something happened to him? He had a bypass surgery and he's no spring chicken. Nicki is only ten."

She threw her legs over the edge of the couch and leaned toward him. "Are you suggesting we take her?" Her expression made it clear how she felt about that idea.

He looked at Payton, really looked at her. He hadn't thought about it before, maybe because in his mind, there was no other option. Nicki was part of him. And even if she wasn't his biological child, he loved her. How could Payton know Nicki—even a little bit—and not see how incredible his little girl was? How could Payton know him and think that he would ever leave Nicki? How could Payton even entertain the idea? What kind of person would do that?

If Nicki was his child, he would never give her up. He'd never do what his parents did to him—he'd sooner cut off his arm than hurt Nicki. Parents were supposed to take care of their kids. Real parents. He might not have realized it until this very second, but he wanted to be a real parent. He wanted to be Nicki's dad.

He tried to imagine his life without Nicki. Without tucking her into bed, without helping her with her homework, without hearing about the kids who teased her in school. He couldn't—it was just too painful. Somehow, over the last month, Nicki had become one of the best parts of his life. He never wanted to lose whatever it was they shared. He wanted to watch her grow up into the incredible young woman he knew she would be. He wanted to scare her boyfriends and wait up for her when she was out on dates. He wanted to know where she was and who she was with every moment of the day. He wanted them to be a family. Hell, they were a family. "Yes, that's exactly what I'm suggesting. I want her with us. Nicki and I are a package deal."

"Absolutely not." Payton had obviously forgotten her agenda, and stomped to the bar for a refill.

Logan waited for her tirade to finish. She was worked up and nowhere near done.

Payton yanked the cork from the champagne, refilled her glass, and pointed the bottle at him, shaking her head. "Logan, I will not raise your bastard daughter."

It was as if she'd kicked him in the diaphragm—all the air left his body, and blood roared through his ears like a riptide. He grabbed the back of the chair to anchor himself.

"I'm willing to overlook your shortcomings, but I will not spend the rest of my life paying for your mistakes."

"That's enough. Nicki is not a mistake. She's a wonderful, smart, amazing little girl. I haven't known her long and I already love her. I don't know if she's mine or not, but she deserves a family. She deserves a father. She deserves everything I never had. We can adopt her, Payton. We can be her parents. We can give her brothers and sisters and a happy family. We have so much to offer."

"You can't expect me to consider raising her with our

future children. It wouldn't be fair to them, and she most certainly will never be a part of the vineyard; she won't get one red cent of my inheritance."

Logan took a step toward her and stopped. He set the beer bottle carefully on the table and then stuffed his hands in his pockets, afraid of the rage he felt. Years of slurs and teasing, and a lifetime of self-hate caused by the cruel, thoughtless comments of people like Payton, coalesced into a boulder crushing his chest. He fought to draw breath, and then another. "Fine. It's over."

"What's over?" Her voice rose an octave—gone was that sexy controlled woman. Her mouth tightened and if he wasn't mistaken, he saw fear in her eyes.

"Everything. You, me, the wedding—every fucking thing we ever had between us is finished. Dead. Gone."

She set the champagne bottle on the bar and slid her shaking hands down her sides. He wasn't sure if she was trying to calm herself or look sexy—whatever she was going for wasn't working.

Logan looked around the opulent suite and shook his head. It looked as cold as Payton. He needed to leave before he said something he'd regret. He started toward the door.

Her eyes widened—she must have realized he was serious. "Logan, you can't do this."

"I just did."

"That girl means more to you than I do? She might not even be yours."

"Nicki means the world to me." He wasn't sure what Payton meant to him, but it was definitely not enough anymore. He'd always known she was far from perfect—he'd known she was a little on the superficial side—but he'd never known her to be cruel and hateful. Right now, looking at her, he wondered if she'd been this way the whole time and he'd never noticed.

"Do you actually think you'll still have a job without me?"

"Payton, I don't care. Nicki means more to me than any job. I know what it feels like to be unwanted, to be tossed aside like day-old garbage, and I'd never do that to Nicki, nor will I be with someone who could."

She stared at him with a stunned expression, her mouth hanging open.

He headed to the door, opened it, and took one last look at her. "Have a nice life, Payton."

"Looks like the chocolate fairies haven't visited, which is a damn shame." Skye needed a chocolate fix—bad. She shut the cabinet door. She might not have any on hand, but there was plenty at the restaurant. Still, that would mean she'd have to put shoes on and go out after already changing for bed. She wore sweatpants and the huge Pratt sweatshirt she'd picked up at the thrift store and cut the neck out of. Not very attractive but comfy, and right now that counted for a lot.

She'd been in a bad mood ever since Logan had taken Payton back to the hotel. Wendy said dinner had been a clusterfuck. Fortunately for Skye, it had nothing to do with the food. Still, she wondered what was going on. Wendy had said the tension in Pete's apartment was so thick, it was like breathing in pea soup. Poor Nicki. The kid had enough problems without having to deal with an uncomfortable situation like that.

Skye put the sleeping puppy in her crate, grabbed her keys, and headed to the Crow's Nest. Less than a minute later, she let herself into the restaurant's dark kitchen.

She switched on the lights and opened the walk-in to grab a piece of the double-chocolate cake. The only thing that would make it better was whipped cream, but she wasn't in the mood to make it.

A smile crossed her face. They had to have some Reddi-wip behind the bar. She just needed a squirt. She grabbed the embarrassingly large slab of cake and kicked open the swinging kitchen doors only to have them slap back. The cake splattered against her chest, some of it falling down the front. She looked up to find Logan staring at her.

"Are you okay? I saw the lights and thought someone had broken in."

"I'm fine except I think the chocolate gods are against me. I'm a mess." She leaned over and peeled her shirt off the squished cake. There was no polite way to grab the hunk that was now plastered to her chest and firmly lodged between her breasts. "What are you doing here?"

He motioned to the bottle of tequila and the glass on the bar. "Just thinking and drinking. You?"

"Chocolate fix." She grabbed a piece of cake hanging off her sweatshirt and, with a shrug, popped it in her mouth. "I was just coming out for whipped cream."

He motioned her over to the bar. "Are you willing to share?"

"Smashed cake?" She held the plate toward him. "Sure, why not?"

"Let's get that whipped cream." He put his hand on the small of her back and led her to the bar. "Take a seat." He went around and grabbed the can of Reddi-wip, and then took a seat beside her.

"So what are you thinking about?"

"Life. Payton and I called it quits tonight."

"Oh, I'm sorry." She really wasn't, but then she could hardly say "yippee," could she?

"I'm not." He stared at the now-empty tequila glass, rolling it between his palms. "Payton was willing to overlook my humble beginnings and Nicki. I'm not willing to overlook Nicki."

"Nicki?"

His gaze met hers. "You don't know?"

"I guess not, since I haven't a clue what you're talking about."

"That's surprising. I thought by now Patrice or Rocki would have filled you in on all the gossip."

"I don't encourage gossip."

"Nicki might be my daughter. And before you say anything, I didn't know Nicki even existed until Storm came back to Red Hook after Pop got sick. I didn't find out that she could be mine until I got here. I guess Pop figured that would be an awkward phone conversation. Nicki doesn't know anything about any of this yet. I'm waiting for the paternity test before I tell her."

"And Payton wasn't happy to have a ready-made family?"

"Not happy would be an understatement. I called off the engagement and told her to have a nice life."

"How do you feel about that?"

"Would it be rude to say I feel relieved as hell?"

"Not rude—just honest."

"It's crazy. In one fell swoop my life has veered off course. A month ago I had a job I loved, an incredible home, a fiancée who I thought was the perfect partner. It was fine until I got home." He shook his head wondering what the hell it all meant. "I should feel something."

He looked into her eyes for a long time, as if she held all the answers. "I don't know, Skye. I guess coming home made me look at my life and I realized I've just been going through the motions."

"How much have you had to drink?"

"Just one. Why?"

"No reason."

He raised an eyebrow.

"Fine." She rested her forearms on the bar and turned her head to look at him. "I wondered if you were sober enough to know what you feel."

"It's been a long time since I felt much of anything. I came home over a month ago and in that time I've realized that what Payton and I had wasn't what it should be."

"How so?"

"I don't love her. I never have. I really thought I was incapable of love. But I love Nicki. I love Pop and my brothers—"

"You were going to marry someone you don't love?"

"Yes, I was." He ran his hand through his hair. "It was stupid, but we worked well together. I figured that made us a good match. I worked for her family. We'd been going out since we were in college and we didn't make each other miserable. It made a weird kind of sense. I never knew I could feel . . . I thought I was incapable of feeling."

"What happened?"

"Other than Nicki?"

She nodded.

"I was at my brother's wedding, and it hit me. Payton and I didn't have the connection that Bree and Storm do. Not even close. Hell, I'd been here for weeks and I didn't even miss her. That's not right."

"Did you ever have that kind of connection with her?"

He shook his head.

"Have you ever had that kind of connection with anyone else?"

"Yes, I think so, but I never acted on it."

"Why not?"

"Because until a few hours ago, I was engaged to someone else, and I don't cheat."

She couldn't help but wonder who the lucky woman was. "You're not engaged now. You're free to do whatever you want." She reached across the bar for the can of Reddi-wip and gave it a good shake. She squirted it all over what was left of her cake and then thought the hell with it—she tipped her head back, opened her mouth, and filled it with whipped cream.

"You think I should do whatever I want?"

Shit, all the whipped cream in the world wasn't going to satisfy the craving his voice alone sparked within her. She swallowed and licked her lips. "Sure, it isn't like you're hung up on Payton, right?"

"No, definitely not."

She took another shot of Reddi-wip to keep from asking who he was hung up on.

"I thought you were going to share." He spun the stool around midshot and before she even knew what was happening, he kissed her.

The taste of Reddi-wip exploded on his tongue as it slid over Skye's lips. Her eyes widened, but she didn't pull away. She didn't move closer either.

His hand slipped under the fall of her hair, caressing

the back of her neck, and he felt her swallow. He teased her lips, nibbling, asking for permission to enter.

Her mouth opened under his—cold and then, God, oh so hot.

Something hit the bar, probably the can of whipped cream. Her hand grabbed his shoulder and their tongues tangled. She tasted like chocolate and whipped cream and something else that was quintessentially her. He could kiss her all day.

He pulled away and her eyes opened. Her dark lashes created shadows on her cheeks from the overhead lights, her lips berry red and slightly swollen, her face flushed.

"I've wanted to taste you since the first moment I saw you." He slid one finger from the top of her cleavage, scooping up double-chocolate icing, and brought it to his mouth, sucking the icing off. "You taste really good."

"It's the chocolate."

"I don't think so." He nuzzled her ear, drinking in her scent—no smoke, no cosmetics, no perfume—just the scent of chocolate, Reddi-wip, and Skye. He nipped her earlobe, and then sucked. "Nope, I was right. It's you. You taste sweet, hot, and sinful."

He continued to kiss his way down her neck. Her fingers scissored though his hair and over his scalp, sending sparks of need right to his dick. Her pulse pounded beneath his lips. He raked his teeth over it and licked his way to the chocolate between her breasts, cleaning off all remnants of cake and frosting. Her back arched over his arm, allowing him access to whatever he wanted.

Logan tugged her against him, chest to chest, and her legs slid around his, opening herself to him. His need rioted against his better sense. All he wanted to do was toss her onto the bar, peel off her clothing, and create a Reddi-wip bikini so he could spend the rest of the night licking it off. He settled for another kiss, taking her mouth the way he wanted to take her body—hot, hard, and relentless. His hand tucked into the waistband of her baggy sweatpants, pulling her against him, swallowing her groan when she came into contact with his erection.

Her arms wrapped around his neck, her legs around his waist, and he slid his hands under her ass when the sound of squirting whipped cream broke through their heavy breathing.

Skye pushed him away so hard, he hit the stool beside him. "Oh God. I'm sorry. I . . ." She pulled the neck of her sweatshirt up, covering her cleavage, while he did his best to protect her modesty and the family jewels. Skye was strong, embarrassed, and, from the way her dark blue eyes shone, pissed as hell.

He didn't need to look to know who was standing on the other side of the bar. He did anyway. "Pop."

The old man let out a shotgun laugh. "Oh, don't mind me. I just came down for some cake. It needed whipped cream." He kept his eyes on the plate of smashed cake and wilted whipped cream on the bar. "Looks like you two had the same idea—initially at least."

Skye slid off the stool and ran into the kitchen.

Logan took off after her.

"Logan. Let her go."

He stopped and spun around. "What the hell were you thinking sneaking up on us like that?"

"What the hell were you thinking taking advantage of Skye?"

"I wasn't taking advantage of her."

"Weren't you?"

"Hell, no."

"I take it you eighty-sixed the blow-up doll?"

"Of course I did. I'm no cheater."

Pop looked him square in the eye and Logan cursed his luck. He was in for another one of Pop's talks when all he wanted to do was make sure Skye was all right.

"I gotta admit whipped cream looks better on you than lipstick, but damn, Logan, Skye is my cook. I like her and I don't want to lose her. Don't forget she has problems of her own. She might be keeping them in her pocket, but that doesn't mean they're not there. The last thing she needs is to be your rebound girl."

"You said yourself I never loved Payton."

"Just because you never loved her doesn't change the fact that you've been with her for years. No matter what, you don't go from being engaged to single without some kind of emotional backlash."

"The only backlash I'm having is a profound sense of relief."

"So you thought you'd celebrate by making Skye your very own hot fudge sundae? Ever hear the old saying 'Don't shit where you eat'?"

"That doesn't apply. I'm only working here until Bree comes home."

"And what are you going to do then?"

"Hell, I don't know." He sat, rubbed the back of his neck and then poured another tequila. "I just lost my job, my home, and everything I've worked for since I left school."

"Another reason this is not the time to jump Skye."

"I wasn't jumping her."

"You were about to."

And he still wanted to. "It's not as if I'm leaving. I

have Nicki to think of now. I can't just uproot her after everything she's been through."

"Don't go counting your chick before the paternity test comes back."

He took a sip and looked over the rim of his glass to his father. "Nicki needs a father. She needs a family."

"Logan, if you're not her father, we'll have to reevaluate. For all we know, she could be anyone's daughter—even Slater's."

Logan laughed at that. "Unless Marisa had a motherboard and a USB port I didn't discover, Slater wouldn't have looked twice at her."

"Come on, Slater might have been the ultimate computer geek, but he was still a boy. Every boy will look and touch if presented with the opportunity. Besides, I thought before that Nicki was Storm's, which taught me not to jump to conclusions when it comes to you boys. You always end up surprising me. Until we find out differently, Nicki's nothing more than your little sister."

"She feels like more."

"She feels like more to Bree and Storm too. That don't make Nicki their daughter."

"I'm not going to say anything to Nicki until I have confirmation."

"Good." Pop took another bite of his whipped-cream-covered cake. "Since you've lost your job, have you thought about what you're going to do with yourself?"

"No."

"I suggest you spend some time thinking about your future with or without Nicki before you start something with Skye."

"I like her, Pop." A lot more than he cared to admit. With Skye, he felt things he'd never felt before. Possessiveness, protectiveness, and intense pleasure, well, until his father had shown up.

"And it doesn't hurt that she's gorgeous."

"No, that certainly doesn't hurt."

"I'm not telling you to back off completely. I'm just suggesting you take it slow. Make sure what you are doing with Skye is an action and not a reaction to your newfound freedom."

He refilled his tequila, took a big gulp, and felt the burn all the way down. "It's not. But fine. I'll take things slow—that is, if she ever speaks to me again."

Pop nodded and headed back to the apartment, leaving him alone in the darkened bar with his bottle of tequila—a poor substitute for chocolate, Reddi-wip, and Skye.

Skye ran into her apartment, past the puppy's crate, and headed straight for the shower to wash off the scent of Logan.

She pulled off her sweatshirt and tossed it on the floor along with her chocolate-stained bra—not that he hadn't done his best to clean it off.

Her face was the color of a cherry tomato; she wasn't sure if it was from embarrassment or residual sexual frustration. How could she have been so stupid? God, she'd gone to the restaurant for a chocolate fix, and ended up with a fix of a totally different kind, with a man who, though now thankfully disengaged, was still on the do-not-touch list.

She adjusted the water, stepped into the shower, and was tempted to thunk her head against the tile. How the hell was she going to get out of this situation? She'd put her job and her fresh start on the line for a hot, chocolate-induced make-out session with her boss, only to get caught by the owner of the restaurant.

The last thing she needed was people wondering if she had slept her way into the job. Besides, she loved working at the Crow's Nest, she loved her apartment, she loved Pepperoni, and she felt appreciated for her talent for the first time in her life. She wasn't willing to give that up and go home a failure. She scrubbed every inch of her body and turned off the water. Unfortunately, she couldn't scrub out the memories of the way Logan kissed her, his scent, his taste, or the feel of him against her.

She wrapped herself in a towel, threw her clothes in the washer, grabbed her phone, and speed-dialed Kelly.

"It's about time you got in touch with me. I was just about to send out a search party."

"Sorry." She sat on the edge of her bed and slid on her panties. "I got a job, an apartment, and a puppy."

"Wow, you do work fast. I didn't know you wanted a puppy."

"I didn't. The job kinda came with the apartment and puppy. It's a long story." She pulled her only other sweatshirt over her head and curled up under the down comforter.

"So you have your own kitchen—other than the one in your apartment?"

"Yes, and although the pay isn't great, it's a wonderful spot. I'm appreciated—or I was until tonight."

"What happened?"

"That's an even longer story. Suffice it to say the owner caught me making out with his son, who is, temporarily at least, my boss."

"Is he hot?"

"Kelly!"

"Okay, he must be off the charts hot for you to put your job on the line like that."

She groaned and ran a towel over her still wet hair. "God, my job isn't even the worst part."

"It's not?"

"My boss is Logan Blaise. Ring a bell?"

"Not really. Care to fill me in?"

"Logan Blaise was, until earlier this evening, engaged to Payton Billingsly."

"The Payton Billingsly?"

"See why I'm freaking out?"

"Oh, man. You're kidding me. You got caught canoodling with Payton's fiancé?"

"Ex-fiancé."

"What the hell is Payton's fiancé doing in ... where the hell are you, anyway?"

"Red Hook, Brooklyn."

"Red Hook? Seriously?"

"Yes. Red Hook is really changing. The community has banded together to clean up the streets and revitalize the neighborhood. It's becoming known as a place for great restaurants and art galleries. It's still a little gritty, and believe me, Payton was not pleased when she found out where Logan came from, but you're missing the point here."

"And that is?"

"Kelly, I got caught by the owner of my restaurant making out with his son—my temporary boss. Shit, he could be my permanent boss now that he and Payton are disengaged. When he dumped her, he lost his job and his home too."

"I just googled Logan Blaise. My God, the man is gorgeous."

"Kelly—"

"So, how was it?"

"What?"

"The make-out session, of course. Man, is Payton ever going to be pissed when she finds out Logan dumped her for you."

"He didn't dump Payton for me. He dumped her for a lot of other reasons I can't get into, but it had nothing to do with me."

"Are you sure about that? He certainly wasted no time sticking his tongue down your throat, did he?"

"He didn't come after me, if that's what you're asking. We ran into each other—literally."

"It's sure going to be interesting to see how Payton spins this one. You know they were planning a New Year's Eve wedding, don't you?"

"I read the article in *Food & Wine*."

"What happens if she tells your family?"

"She doesn't even know I'm here. She has nothing to tell them."

"How did you pull that off?"

"I hid."

"I guess all those years we played hide-and-seek came in handy after all. Speaking of which, your brothers are worried about you. They told your mother that you're on vacation. She's been keeping the office up and running, but she thinks you're coming back. Paddy's been calling me on a daily basis. He didn't even do that when we were together. He's beginning to sound desperate, which I have to say is enjoyable. "

"I'm sorry he's bothering you. What have you told him?"

"That I had no idea where you were, which, until now,

was the truth. So, back to your dilemma. What are you going to do?"

"I'm going to tell Logan it was a mistake."

"Are you nuts? What? Did he have a teeny weenie or something?"

"No."

"So you checked out his size?"

"Has anyone ever told you you're evil?"

"Yes. Where did you run into Logan Blaise?"

"I went to the restaurant for a chocolate fix and ran into him when I walked through the doors to get to the front. I went in search of whipped cream; he slammed into me and smashed double-chocolate fudge cake all over my chest."

"Sounds kinky."

"It was. He licked the chocolate fudge off my chest and then his father interrupted us. I wanted to die."

"Wow."

"It was horrible. And you know what the worst part is?"

"Getting caught?"

"Besides that. The worst part is I never even got my chocolate fix. Not only am I jones'n' for chocolate—"

"You're jones'n' for Logan Blaise."

"Big-time." She threw herself back onto the fluffy pillows on the bed. "And now I have to tell him it was all a big mistake and hope he'll pretend it never happened."

"Good luck with that. I give it three days tops."

"Your support is overwhelming."

"I support you, but let's face it: Logan Blaise is like a Bugatti and you have the keys. You're not gonna be happy until you take that boy out for a spin. It's been forever since anyone has made you want to even put him in first gear, and from what you said, you came in close contact with Logan's instruments."

"That's it—no more *Top Gear* for you. You're cut off, young lady."

"No way. It's my favorite show. The British one. What can I say? I have a real thing for Jeremy Clarkson."

"He's married."

"And on another continent—therefore he's safe to dream about. That's the way I want my men—completely out of reach."

"I take it things didn't go well with Ted?"

"It went fine until I found out he's as married as Jeremy."

"Damn, are all men pigs?"

"I don't know; you tell me. If I had a single man who looked like Logan Blaise licking chocolate off of me, I certainly wouldn't tell him it was a mistake."

"I need this job."

"You also need to get laid. And it isn't as if things like this never work out."

"When do they work out, Kelly? Name one person who dated her boss and it didn't turn ugly." She waited a moment—Kelly didn't say anything. "See, I have to tell him it was a mistake. I have no choice."

"Fine. At least I know what to get you for Christmas."

"What's that?"

"A pound of Godiva and a vibrator—a large one from the looks of Logan Blaise. Sweet dreams, Skye."

CHAPTER 8

Logan's alarm rang and he groaned and smashed his hand against the phone. His head was ready to split in two. Damn, he should know better than to drink tequila. When he pried his eyes open, he found D.O.G. and Nicki staring at him.

"D.O.G.'s gotta go, and I can't walk him alone."

His mouth felt as if an army had tromped through it and left cotton in its wake. "Okay, give me a minute and I'll get up. Do me a favor, Nicki. Press the brew button on the coffeemaker, will ya?"

"I already did." She pointed to a cup on his bedside table.

"Thanks, kiddo." He sat up and took a sip of the brew. Maybe after another five cups he'd feel as if he might live. He sat farther up, glad that he'd started wearing sleep pants to bed.

"Logan?" Nicki stood with her arm around D.O.G.'s neck, and her sneakered foot digging into the worn carpet of his bedroom. "What's gonna happen when you marry Payton?"

He ran his hand through his hair, which was standing

straight up from the feel of it. Shit, even his hair hurt. He didn't know what the hell to say to her. Still, she looked at him with those big brown eyes full of worry; he had to say something. He patted the edge of the bed and D.O.G. took it as an invitation to jump up. Logan narrowly missed being unmanned by the eighty-pound puppy.

Nicki wasn't nearly as enthusiastic. She leaned her hip against the mattress, her hand holding D.O.G.'s paw. "Nicki, Payton and I had a long talk last night and decided that we really didn't want to get married."

Her eyes got wide and she sucked in a deep breath. "Did she dump you because of me? I don't think she liked me and Pop very much."

"First of all, she didn't dump me, and secondly, it had absolutely nothing to do with you. It was about us— Payton and me. We realized we were making a mistake. When you marry someone, you have to love them a whole lot, and we just didn't love each other enough."

"Did she cry when you told her?"

He shook his head—a big mistake. "No."

"Did you stay and make sure she was okay?"

He shook his head again. Evidently, he was a slow learner. He probably should have stayed with Payton a little while, but damn, he'd been so pissed at what she'd said, he didn't give a shit if she cried. He tried to dredge up some remorse.... Nope, it wasn't happening. "No, I didn't stay."

"What if she was really upset? She's here all alone. You should call her, Logan. You should make sure she's okay."

He was stunned. All through dinner, Payton had acted as if Nicki didn't exist and now Nicki was worried about her. She was one hell of a kid. "I'll call Payton later and make sure she's okay, but if she's anything like me, she's relieved it's over."

"I don't know. Wendy said you're quite a catch."

He wasn't going to touch that one. "Nicki, getting engaged to Payton was a mistake. I just didn't see it until I came home. Storm and Bree love each other enough to get married and stay married. Payton and I didn't love each other that way. It wasn't anyone's fault—you can't make yourself love someone no matter how hard you try."

Nicki nodded and looked way older than her ten years. "I know."

"How do you know?"

"I tried to love some of my mom's boyfriends when I was little. It didn't work either." She shrugged her little shoulders. "They didn't want me around."

"That's not a problem anymore. You love Pop, and Storm, and Bree—"

Nicki nodded. "And D.O.G., Ms. Patrice and Mr. Francis, and you."

He let out a relieved breath. "That's good, because I love you too, Nicki." He wrapped her in a big hug. "And I'll always want you around."

"You promise? Even if I do something bad?"

"Even then. No matter what."

D.O.G. whined as if he didn't like being left out.

Logan patted the big dog's head. "You too, boy. Now both of you get outta here so I can throw on some clothes and take this monster for a walk. Nicki, you finish getting ready for school. When I get back, I'll fix you a quick breakfast."

"Okay. Come on, D.O.G., let's go put my books in my backpack."

Logan watched her bounce out of his room before getting out of bed. He threw on a pair of jeans and a sweatshirt. The weather was getting cooler, which reminded him that he needed to take Nicki out and buy her some heavier clothes. Maybe Skye would help him out on that front—that is, if she was still speaking to him after last night's fiasco.

He could ask Patrice or Rocki for help—and Lord knew he needed help. He had no idea how to buy little girls' clothes, but he had a feeling that shopping with Patrice or Rocki would be a fate worse than death. Skye seemed like a woman who shopped because it was a necessity—not a vocation. For Patrice and Rocki shopping was a religious experience—heck, it was a calling. Just thinking about it sent chills down his spine. No, he'd do just about anything to avoid shopping with them. He'd beg Skye if necessary.

He took care of business, brushed his teeth, and then slogged his way to the kitchen to fill a to-go cup with more coffee.

Nicki and D.O.G. waited by the door. "I'm all ready for school, so I have time to go with you guys on your walk, okay?"

"Sure." He checked his watch and snapped the leash on the dog's collar. "Let's go."

Nicki skipped down the steps wearing her backpack. He wasn't sure why she brought her backpack, but it wasn't worth asking. It was all he could do to get down the steps in one piece with D.O.G. tugging like a one-dog sled team. Logan opened the door for the three of them and headed toward the park. He took a sip of hot coffee just as they turned the corner.

D.O.G. lunged.

Coffee spilled.

Logan sidestepped Nicki to avoid knocking her over and ran right into Skye and Pepperoni. "D.O.G., down."

The big mutt had his paws on Skye's shoulders, while Pepperoni jumped all over D.O.G. and Nicki.

Logan grabbed D.O.G.'s collar and pulled him to the ground. "Sorry." Skye looked completely edible . . . again. She wore another pair of sweats and a baseball cap with her hair pulled through the back. He remembered how soft her skin was, the way her hair felt like silk slipping through his fingers, and the taste of her. He remembered everything. "We have to stop running into each other like this."

Skye's face flamed. "It isn't as if I planned it."

"Hey, I'm not complaining. I imagine it's much more fun wearing chocolate than hot coffee, though. Want a taste?" If Skye's face was red before, it was crimson now.

Nicki picked up Pepperoni and gave her a hug. "Hey, Skye, can you come to the dog park with us? If we stop at the bagel shop for breakfast, we'll have a whole half hour to play and then you can walk me to school. I have my backpack with me. It'll be fun."

Skye didn't look thrilled with the idea. "Sure, Nicki."

He winked at Skye. "You don't mind hanging around with us for a while, do you, Skye?"

Skye completely ignored him and kept her eyes on Nicki. "I'd love to hang out with you and D.O.G."

Ouch, that stung.

Nicki bounced up and down like he supposed little girls did when they got excited. "Good. Can I walk Pepperoni? She pulls, but not hard."

Skye nodded and handed her the leash. "Make sure

you put your hand through the loop so we don't lose her if you should drop the leash."

"No problem." Nicki grabbed Skye's hand like she'd done it a thousand times before, and tugged her toward the park. "Come on, Skye. Wait till you see the tricks I'm teaching D.O.G. I taught him to jump over the benches."

"Hmm ..." Skye quirked her eyebrow. "Maybe encouraging D.O.G. to jump isn't the best thing."

Nicki laughed, something she didn't do often enough. Her pigtails bounced in time with her steps. "Maybe not, but it sure is fun watching him fly."

Logan and D.O.G. hung back, letting the girls set the pace and chat. When they arrived at the dog park, he held the gate for them, and then let D.O.G. off the leash.

The dog flew and Nicki and Pepperoni ran after him. "Watch us, Skye!"

Logan stopped beside Skye. She still hadn't looked at him. He knew he should say something, but what? *I had a great time last night until Pop showed up.* No, he didn't think that would go over well. He didn't want to apologize, because that would be a lie, and he didn't lie. "I was worried about you last night. You took off so fast, I didn't get a chance to—"

"What?" She finally looked at him and he almost wished she hadn't. Until that moment he still had some hope that they could get past this. Sure, it had been embarrassing, but it wasn't the end of the world.

"Hell, I don't know, Skye. I'm sorry Pop showed up."

"I'm not. I don't know what I was thinking. It was a mistake. Let's just forget it ever happened."

"Not likely."

Her face flushed and her mouth tightened. He was

waiting for her to snarl. She tugged the sleeve of his sweatshirt. "You have to."

"No, I don't. I had a great time and so did you. I spent the rest of the night remembering it over and over again."

She blew out a breath of exasperation and he couldn't help but chuckle. She was sexy as hell when she was pissed. "Well, stop."

"Make me. I can't wait for a repeat performance, but next time we'll do it behind locked doors. I'm not normally an exhibitionist."

Skye's mouth opened, closed; then she sputtered.

He had to laugh. He couldn't help it. She was so hot, if he didn't laugh, he'd have to kiss her, and she looked mad enough to bite. Not that he would mind.

"Logan, damn it. Don't you dare laugh at me."

"I'll stop just as soon as you stop talking nonsense. 'Forget it ever happened.' You gotta admit that's funny as hell." He stepped closer so she had to crane her neck to look him in the eye. "If Nicki wasn't here with us, I'd drag you behind the bushes and show you just how much I remember. Then I'd spend the rest of the morning reminding you of how good it felt. I'd tell you how great you taste, and all the things I plan to do with you."

"Logan Blaise, listen to me."

"Sure, sugar."

"Sugar? That sounds weird coming from a Brooklyn bad boy. What are you trying to do? Channel your inner Mark Twain?"

"No, but the nickname suits."

"I can't do this."

He grinned even bigger. God, he hadn't had this much

fun fighting in . . . well, ever. "You sure had no problem doing it last night. You did great."

"It will never happen again."

"And why's that?"

"Because I won't fool around with my boss."

He tugged on her ponytail. He couldn't resist; he had to touch her. "I'm glad to hear it. I don't think Pop's heart is strong enough to handle the likes of you. Besides, you're young enough to be his daughter."

"Logan." She crossed her arms, which only highlighted her perfect breasts.

"Yeah, sugar?"

"Would you stop calling me that?"

"Why? You taste like sugar, and Lord knows, I have a hell of a sweet tooth."

"You need to stop this. I can't . . . we can't—"

"Sure we can. Hell, we did. And if Pop hadn't interrupted, we'd have done a hell of a lot more."

"I don't sleep with people I work with."

"Skye. I'm working here temporarily. Pop's your boss—"

"Yes, and he caught me making out at the bar with you. God, he probably thinks I'm trying to sleep my way to the top."

"Sugar, you're already at the top. If anyone's taking the heat for last night, it's me. Pop's worried about you."

"He's not the only one."

Logan was just about to ask what she meant by that when she tugged on his shirt again.

"Look, it was fine, but it's over. It takes two to tango, and I just flushed my dance card."

"It was fine?" Hell, that was possibly the hottest make-out session he'd ever had. It was a damn sight better than fine.

"Yes, it was nice, but it's over."

"Nice? Fine? Sugar, them's fightin' words. You don't tell a man who licked chocolate frosting and whipped cream off your hot little body that it was fine and nice."

"What do you want, a medal?"

"No, I want another dessert."

"Tough. I don't have relationships with people I work with."

"I'm only working with you temporarily."

"Temporarily, huh? So once Bree comes back, what are you going to do?"

"I have no idea."

"I'm not gonna be your little piece on the side while you try to figure it out. I'm not temporary. I want to build a life on my own. I don't need people wondering how I got my job."

"Everyone at the Crow's Nest knows you're an asset to the team. You've earned their respect. Our seeing each other isn't going to change that."

"It changes everything, so I choose not to. Don't fight me on this, Logan."

"Fine."

Nicki ran up and skidded, kicking up a cloud of dust. "Did you see us, Skye?"

"Sure did, Nicki. You guys are amazing. Come on, I'm hungry. Let's go get a bagel and then eat it on the way to your school."

Logan bought the girls breakfast and walked both dogs so they could eat, since he'd mysteriously lost his appetite back in the dog park.

What was it with him? He couldn't win for trying. Skye was freaking out, and Pop thought he was moving too fast. Unfortunately, ever since he saw Skye being mauled by D.O.G., all he wanted to do was pull her into his arms and kiss her—everywhere. And he wasn't blind; he saw the look on her face when he told her all the things he wanted to do to her. She still wanted him all right; she just didn't think it was a good idea. Fine. She'd come around. He wasn't the only one with a sweet tooth. There were a lot more desserts on the menu and he planned to try every single one of them—on her.

Skye waved to Nicki and watched her run up the steps and through the doors. Nicki had hugged her good-bye and said she'd stop in the kitchen for a snack after school. Now, if Logan would only disappear. She wasn't beneath taking her dog and running all the way home, but since Logan had Pepperoni, she had to at least look at him.

She took a deep breath and held out her hand. "May I please have Pepperoni's leash?"

"So you can run home and not finish our discussion?"

"That was the plan."

"Then I guess I'll have to hold Pepperoni hostage. Besides, the little beast is too tired to walk. Look at her."

The puppy was lying beside them half-asleep. "I can carry her."

"She's almost twenty pounds, Skye, and it's a long way home." He bent and picked the puppy up, leaned her against his shoulder, and held her like he would a baby.

Damn the man. How was she supposed to stay mad at him when he did something sweet like that? "Fine."

"Is that your new favorite word?"

"Don't push me, Logan."

"Why not?"

"Because I'll retaliate."

"I look forward to it. It's better than you pretending I don't exist."

"Oh . . . Did I hurt your feelings?"

"No." He shook his head and frowned. "Hell, I don't know, Skye. I understand why you're upset, but come on, give me a break. It wasn't my fault Pop caught us."

"No, it wasn't your fault. It was mine. It never should have happened in the first place and it can only end badly. And I need my job. I like it. I don't want to do anything to jeopardize it. I'm sorry to say this, but you're just not worth it."

"Ouch." He actually flinched and rubbed his chest. "I'll let that one slide because I know how you feel. Believe me. You need to get it through that thick head of yours that I'm not going to do anything to jeopardize your career. What happens between you and me has nothing to do with work."

"How can you say that when it was your father, my boss, who caught us?"

"Pop was afraid I was taking advantage of you and thought that I should slow down. And just for clarification, he didn't tell me to back off, just slow down and make sure I wasn't on the rebound."

Skye sucked in a not-so-silent breath and hoped Logan didn't notice her flinch. "Which is yet another reason this isn't a good situation. You are on the rebound."

"I am not."

She rolled her eyes. "Isn't that convenient?"

"Sugar, if it was convenient, I wouldn't be fighting with you. You knew where I was coming from before I ever kissed you. And just in case you've forgotten, since it was only nice, or fine, or whatever, you kissed me back, really, really well." He threw his free arm around her—

okay, so it wasn't really free, since he was holding D.O.G.'s leash with it — and tilted his head toward hers — as close as he could get without bending over. "So this is when you come clean. Why'd you pull a disappearing act and end up here with me in Red Hook?"

Skye swallowed. How did he know she was on the run? She wasn't sure how to answer because she sure as hell wasn't going to tell him about her family.

They stopped at a crosswalk and waited for the light. "Were you dating someone you worked with and it went south? Is that why this has you so freaked-out?"

Thank God the light changed, so she could step away from him without being obvious. "No. I've never dated anyone I've worked with. And for your information, I'm not in Red Hook *with* you and I'm not freaked-out. You just can't believe you're resistible, can you?"

"Who, me?" He smiled, and damned if her heart didn't kick into a conga beat. "Sugar, I am irresistible, at least to you."

Her jaw dropped. She didn't even have words. He had an ego as big as her brothers. Logan Blaise was conceited, narcissistic, dangerous, and way out of her league.

"So since you're not freaked about a past experience, why'd you run?"

"I didn't run. I left. It was personal. And since you're not my boss, stop questioning me."

"Fine. But you know that whatever you tell me stays between us."

"That's a lie."

"No, it's not."

"What if I told you I was running from the law? Don't tell me you wouldn't say anything."

"I guess it depends on how interesting the charges are." He waggled his eyebrows at her.

Clearly he wasn't worried. Smart man. "Don't look at me like that. I'm not running from the law. But it's one more reason why we're not going to—"

"Date?"

"Continue with this farce. Do us both a favor, and drop it."

She saw the door to her apartment up ahead. It wasn't close enough.

He slowed. "It's not gonna help, you know. I'm irresistible, remember?"

She put her key in the door. "I guess it's something I'm going to have to live with." She turned to take the puppy from him and he crowded her against the brick building, forcing her to look up at him.

"I'm not going to make it easy." His voice was all low, gravelly, and sexy as chocolate fudge and whipped cream, damn it.

"Really? What are you going to do?"

"Nothing, I'll just be my irresistible self. When you change your mind, let me know." He passed her the sleepy puppy, his hand brushing against her breast, but the way he held the puppy didn't give him much of an option. Still, it didn't help that after he pulled his hand away, he winked. "Don't worry, when you change your mind, I'll bring the chocolate fudge and whipped cream."

He left her to watch him walk away, and damn the man, he even had a sexy walk. She was toast.

Logan grabbed his keys and slid into his favorite leather jacket and looked out the window for any sign of Skye. When he'd called her to arrange a time to leave for the food tour, she said she'd meet him there—as if they weren't coming from the same place. He never should have given her the tour ticket.

Skye had successfully avoided spending any time alone with him for the last three days. Maybe he wasn't as irresistible as he'd thought.

"What are you doing?" Nicki hopped up and down in front of him, craning her neck back and forth out the window, which had a good shot of the door to Skye's apartment.

He winced. He couldn't very well tell Nicki he was stalking Skye.

"Just checking the weather." The look on Nicki's face told him she wasn't buying it. Shit, it was pretty bad that a ten-year-old could get the make on him.

"Skye left early this morning. She said she had stuff to do in the city."

"On a Sunday?"

Nicki shrugged. "I don't know. Maybe she was going to church."

Or maybe she was avoiding him. At least she couldn't hold out forever. He checked his watch. "I'd better get out of here or I'll be late."

"Okay, tell Skye that D.O.G. loves the dog cookies we made him. We had to cut Pepperoni's in half, 'cause, you know, she's like half the size."

"More like a quarter."

She giggled and it took him by surprise. He didn't think he'd ever heard Nicki giggle. It was infectious. "What's so funny?"

"Skye had to cut the big dog bones in half for Pepperoni. You know what they looked like?"

"No."

"Butts and boobs."

"What?"

Nicki looked at him as if he were too stupid to live. "Picture a dog cookie, cut it in half. . . ."

He rolled his eyes and gave her a noogie. "Very funny, little girl."

"Sheesh, you sound like Pop. Skye is cool—she thought it was funny when I pointed it out to her."

"No talk of butts and boobs. You're growing up way too fast." He'd missed the first ten years of her life and he'd be damned if he was going to miss any more.

"How come grown-ups can talk about butts and boobs and kids can't?"

"Because."

"That's what Pop said too."

Great, now he sounded like his father. "Ms. Patrice is going to pick you up for a playdate in a little while. And don't you dare mention the butt and boob dog biscuits to the girls. They're not as grown-up as you. Got it?"

"Duh. I'm not an idiot, Logan."

"I know that. Now give me a hug good-bye."

She wrapped her arms around him and buried her face in his chest. He leaned down and kissed the top of her head. "You smell good."

"Thanks. I'll be by to pick you up tonight. Have fun and behave yourself." He stepped out the door and took one more look at Nicki.

"Yeah, you too. Tell Skye I said hi. Don't do anything I wouldn't do, and if you do, don't name it after me."

He just shook his head. Nicki was growing up way too fast all right, and she was too observant for her own good.

Logan took the subway from Carroll Gardens to

Sixth Avenue and then walked the few blocks to Bleecker and MacDougal. He was half a block away when he spotted Skye talking to a group of people. Perfect. He had the element of surprise on his side, and the advantage of height. He used both when he wrapped his arms around her from behind. "Hey, sugar. Sorry I'm late," and went in for the kiss. For a second he wondered if she was going to slug him.

Her gasp of surprise opened her mouth beneath his, and he took it as an invitation.

Her taste slid over him like a fine wine, soft, subtle, with a hint of chocolate and a kick of something spicy.

She grabbed both sides of his open jacket, and instead of pushing him away like he'd expected her to do, she tugged him closer. He drew away and watched her eyes blink open, widen, and then focus. She released the leather she'd gathered in her fists, licked her lips, and stared up at him. "What's your angle, Logan?"

He wished he could read her busy mind like a ticker tape. "Right now, due to the differences in our height, my angle is bent. But I don't mind in the least. You taste decadent, even without the whipped cream." He straightened, and then smiled at the people around them who stared.

Skye had that look in her eye—the one that came right before she shot him down.

He put his finger over her lips. "Before you say anything, remember, we're not at work. Let's just have a good time. No pressure, just you, me, fresh air, and great food. What do you say?"

"I still have to decide what to make for the tasting tomorrow."

"We'll talk about work later." Much later if he had

anything to say about it. "We have all day." And night, but he didn't mention that.

Thankfully, the guide gathered everyone on the tour for introductions. Most of the people were tourons; there were only three locals besides them, and from the conversation he'd overheard, the ladies were relatively new to the area.

The first stop was a few blocks away. An outdoor tasting at an Italian bistro. He was surprised when Skye stayed close. It might have been because the three ladies, Mary, Cheryl, and Sophia, seemed to surround them wanting to find out about the city from a native.

He took a bite of the focaccia, prosciutto, and fresh mozzarella sandwich, wiped his mouth, and had to bend over to hear Sophia when she asked something about the local nightlife.

"My family has a bar and restaurant in Red Hook, so most weekends I'm home, I'm there."

"Really?" Cheryl, a blonde who did amazing things to a Coldplay sweatshirt, piped up and moved closer. "I hear Red Hook is the next Park Slope. What's your place called?"

Skye stepped under his free arm. "The Crow's Nest. It's a great little restaurant and bar. I'm the chef and Logan is helping out his dad while the manager's away." She turned and smiled up at him. "You missed a spot."

He was trying to figure out how to manage the sandwich and the bottle of water he'd just opened when she reached up and ran her finger over the corner of his mouth. "There, I got it."

She turned back to the women. "We're closed on Sundays and Mondays, so Logan thought it would be fun to spend the day together. He surprised me with tickets for the tour and promised to show me around SoHo. We don't get to see each other outside of work much. Do we, Logan?"

"Not as much as I'd like, that's for sure."

It must have been the right answer, because the smile she wore as she slid her arm inside his jacket and around his waist had his temperature rising.

"Are you cold?"

"A little. I need to buy a coat."

He popped the rest of his sandwich in his mouth, capped his water, and set it on the newspaper vending machine. "Here—wear mine." He took off his jacket and held it open for her.

"Are you sure?"

He helped her into it. It hung almost to her knees. Damn, she was a tiny thing. He rolled up the sleeves and stopped when he saw her fingertips poking out. "That's as far as the jacket sleeves can roll, sugar."

"Thanks." She pulled it around her and took a deep breath. "Mmm . . . It smells like you."

"I hope that's a good thing."

"Definitely."

The tour moved on to an Indian place, then to an Italian trattoria, where they were seated. They ordered some wine with their hot appetizers. A short time later they were off to a Cuban place for some black bean soup and sangria.

The ladies left them to themselves after Skye's little show—not that he'd minded her staking her claim, as long as he was it.

Logan couldn't remember a better time. Away from the restaurant, Skye seemed to relax and enjoy the day. They didn't talk about work, just about food, music, and whatever else came to mind. The tour hit a cheese shop on the way back, and then a French bakery for dessert and coffee. Before he knew it, their three-hour tour was over and he didn't want the day to end. Skye didn't look as if she was in a rush to go home either.

"Come on—let's go to Fanelli's Café. It's just over on Prince Street. You're going to love it—it's a bar, but they changed the name to a café during Prohibition. Legend has it there's a working still behind a false wall."

They chatted about what to do for the tasting while cuddled in a booth. She pulled a big notebook out and he had a great time talking about that and the idea of a five-course meal and wine pairing. He could have stayed all night, but he figured he'd better get her back. Poor Pepperoni probably had her little legs crossed.

They took the subway back to Brooklyn and he hailed a cab to Skye's place. "Let me take the dog out. You're still cold."

Her nose was red. "You don't mind?"

"Not at all." Francis had already called and offered to drop off Nicki and take D.O.G. out for him. "Pop's taking care of tucking Nicki in tonight."

"Okay, if you don't mind. I want to jump into a hot shower and warm up."

He followed her into the apartment and grabbed the leash and the puppy.

"Don't forget your jacket."

He put it on and headed out.

"Oh, and take my keys. I could be a while."

"Sure." He was going to have to take Pepperoni for a long walk to cool off after the thought of her all wet and soapy.

CHAPTER 9

Skye spent a good twenty minutes in the shower lecturing herself about the dangers of getting too close to Logan. She'd told herself the same thing she'd been saying since she'd come home after the chocolate cake fiasco, but suddenly her reasons sounded more lame than sensible.

The problem was that she liked him—a lot. She could listen to him talk for hours and never get bored—a first for her. With most of her dates, she was hiding yawns after an hour. Not with Logan. He was a fascinating mix of chemistry geek and hot gentleman winemaker with a bit of bad boy tossed in for effect. And what an effect—she'd spent the day in a near constant state of arousal, except for the time the three bimbos were sizing him up. Another first—she'd never been the jealous type. Until today.

She found everything about him attractive and he never let up. She kept waiting for the deal-breaking fault. They all had one—that one thing that was such a turnoff she would cross him off her list no matter how good he smelled, or sexy he sounded, or how incredibly he kissed. It wasn't as if she hadn't looked for it. She had—to no avail.

After spending the day in Logan's jacket, surrounded

by his scent, his warmth, and his own brand of geeky, bad-boy humor, for her own sanity, she'd planned to get rid of him at the door. Then he went and did something so thoughtful, she caved. Who else would think to walk her dog because she was cold?

She stepped out of the shower and dried off. She wanted him. What could it hurt? He was only going to be working with her for a few more weeks, and it wasn't as if they hadn't proved they could work together even after the chocolate cake and whipped cream incident.

She rushed into her bedroom and grabbed the phone. "Kelly, what do I wear?"

"When?"

"Now. I just got out of the shower, and Logan took Pepperoni for a walk. He'll be back any minute."

"And what are we dressing for?"

"Sex?"

"So I guess I won the bet. How long has it been? Oh yeah, three days."

"Would you mind gloating later? Help me out, would you?"

"What time is it out there?"

"Seven thirty. Why?"

"Too early to put on a naughty nightie, huh?"

"I don't have any of those."

"What do you have?"

"Not a lot."

"Yoga pants?"

"Yes."

"With nothing underneath."

"Really?"

"Definitely. Do you have a low-cut sweater, maybe something fuzzy?"

"Yes."

"Put that on with a sexy bra."

"Why no panties?"

"Just trust me on this. They'll only get in the way or get ripped and your panties are too expensive to replace on your budget."

Skye tossed the phone on the bed. "Hold on a sec." She pulled on a racy little bra with a lace strip that would peek out of the sweater when she leaned forward. Hot but not slutty. She picked up the phone and pulled her black yoga pants up her legs. "Any other advice?"

"Dry your hair or you'll get bed head."

"You really do think of everything."

"Do you have protection?"

"No."

"Skye, what am I going to do with you? You got close enough to take Logan's measure and you didn't go out and buy condoms in his size?"

"I wasn't going to sleep with him until about twenty minutes ago."

"What happened to change your mind?"

"He took my puppy, Pepperoni, out."

"Okay. It's not a sin to be easy; just don't be cheap."

"Kelly, I've spent the last three days looking for his one big fault. I haven't found it yet."

"Amazing."

"He's interesting and funny and hot. He even smells good. God, if he hadn't been engaged to Payton, he'd be perfect."

The door slammed and she heard Pepperoni's nails race across the hardwood floor.

"Skye, we're back. Did you get warmed up yet?"

Just thinking about Logan while she showered got her downright hot. "He's back. I gotta go," she whispered.

"Okay, have fun, but be safe and call me when he leaves."

"Yes. I just have to dry my hair." She tossed her phone on the table and pulled her sleeves down over her hands.

"Are you hungry?"

Not for food. "Not really. Go ahead and raid the fridge if you want. There are a ton of leftovers."

"You cook at home too?"

She stepped out of the bedroom and the way he looked at her made her think that having bed head wouldn't be such a bad thing.

"God, you're beautiful."

She ran her hand through her hair, not sure of what to say. "What are you in the mood for?" She made her way to the kitchen—the one place she felt comfortable—and opened the refrigerator.

Behind her, he rubbed his hands together as if he was trying to warm them, and then leaned against the counter.

She felt his eyes on her ass. Damn, she should never have listened to Kelly about going commando. "I have chicken scaparelli—it's chicken with mushrooms, Italian sausage, and enough garlic to keep the vampires away for the next year."

"Only if you're going to eat with me. It's the garlic— we both have to eat it so we'll cancel each other out."

"I have some leftover roast. I can make you a French dip sandwich on ciabatta bread with provolone and au jus."

He pulled her away from the refrigerator and slid his

hands under her sweater, covering her stomach. He kissed the side of her neck. "I think I lost my appetite for food."

She closed the door and leaned back against him. "We can always raid the refrigerator later."

"My thoughts exactly." His kissed his way to the spot where her neck met her shoulder. "I couldn't get the taste of you out of my head. I had almost talked myself into believing it was my imagination. It wasn't."

If she didn't know better, she'd think the man wrote romances in his spare time. "Logan? Do you have protection? I don't—"

"I stopped just in case." He pulled a bag out of his jacket pocket and tossed it on the counter.

"Thank God." She blew out a breath, and sucked in another as his hand toyed with the rolled waistband of her yoga pants. Her stomach tightened and heat rushed everywhere. She felt as if she were on fire and he hadn't even really done anything yet. She turned in his arms and reached up to kiss him. She was on her tiptoes, her mouth pressed against his, and she groaned as he lifted her off her feet and then set her on the counter like she weighed nothing. It wasn't as if she was fat or anything, but the man didn't even grunt.

She stared into his eyes. "Have I ever told you that your eyes are the color of a rich caramel?"

"No."

"Caramel is my favorite—it can be even better than chocolate if it's made right."

He pulled her to the edge of the counter and slid between her legs.

"Don't tell anyone—I don't want to be forced to turn in my Chocoholics Anonymous Bar. But then it's not as if I don't love chocolate. Sometimes you just have to have it, you know?"

"Is that what you want, Skye? Chocolate?"

"No." She swallowed and felt as if she were drowning in caramel. "I want you to kiss me."

"That I can do." He smiled—even his teeth were perfect.

She was expecting a full frontal assault. Okay, maybe she was hoping for one. If he'd move things along, she wouldn't have much time to think, and thinking at times like this was highly overrated. But then she really didn't remember—she'd been quite a bit younger and more than a few pounds lighter the last time she was anywhere near this position. Instead of putting her out of her misery and kissing her, Logan took his sweet time.

He stared into her eyes until she swore he could read her thoughts, before brushing his nose against hers like she used to do with her dad when she was little. Then his hand slid from her hip up her back and cupped her neck.

Damn, at this rate she was going to go gray or chicken out before he actually followed through—and she really didn't want to chicken out. The one thing she always wanted and never got was good sex. She had a feeling that whatever Logan was willing to give her would be a far cry better than her past experiences. Not that she had that many—she had been with only three men.

"What are you thinking?"

"Do you really want to know?"

"I wouldn't have asked if I didn't."

"I'm wondering what's taking you so long to kiss me. Then I started thinking about how I'd wish you'd hurry up because I don't want to think. Thinking right now would not be kind to either of us—"

"I guess the theory that nine-tenths of the seduction of a woman is between her ears is a fallacy. At least for you. Personally, I've always compared women to a fine red wine. You have to let them breathe."

"Logan, I've been breathing all day." She slid the jacket off his shoulders, folded it, and laid it beside her on the counter—out of Pepperoni's reach. "You're not going to need this for a while. The sweater needs to go too."

He reached behind him and yanked the dark brown turtleneck over his head—it was so soft, it had to be merino wool, maybe cashmere. It was one of those sweaters girls stole from their boyfriends and guarded with their lives when they broke up with the guy.

He tossed it on the counter and stood between her thighs wearing a plain white T-shirt and slim-fitting jeans that on most men would make her question their sexual orientation—but not him.

She lifted the T-shirt's hem and he sucked in a breath that tightened already-tight abs. She kissed the center of his chest as he tugged off the shirt and tossed it. She didn't care if the T-shirt ended up as Pepperoni's plaything, as long as Logan ended up as hers.

He stepped back and blew out a breath. Under the fluorescent lights every muscle in his arms, his chest, his neck, even his face, stood out in stark relief. "Skye, are you sure this is what you want?"

"Yes. I want you."

Logan grabbed the bag and hauled Skye off the counter so fast, she yelped. Pepperoni jumped against his legs as he carried her to the bedroom. There was no way their first time was going to be kitchen-counter sex. No, he needed room to maneuver, and a hard, cold, granite counter was fine for a quickie, but this wasn't going to be quick. He hoped.

He'd spent weeks wanting her, weeks thinking about exactly what he'd do if he was ever lucky enough to find himself in this position. He didn't have weeks, but he'd take a night to start with.

He laid her on the bed, kicked off his shoes, and climbed up beside her, pulling her over him. "We have all night. I plan to make the most of it."

He kissed the sexy little smile right off her face. The kiss went from sweet and shy on her part to down and dirty on his. Her taste was seductive like the finest merlot—velvety smooth—as smooth as her skin. Her scent was overwhelming—vanilla and blueberries and musk—her touch, electric. He wanted to climb inside her and take up residence. He wanted to consume her, control her, brand her—he wasn't sure where these strange feelings came from, but he was too far gone to contemplate it.

He needed Skye and he'd never needed anyone.

Her nails dug into his shoulders and she sucked on his tongue, drawing a groan from deep within him.

He grabbed hold of her ass and surged against her. Skye's soft sweater brushed his chest, her scent surrounded him, and he threaded his hand through her hair, holding the back of her head, anchoring her mouth to his.

Her heat penetrated his jeans. If he didn't slow down and get a grip, he'd take her like an animal. That wasn't him. He was a gentle lover, but something about her had his inner beast pulling all the strings.

She moaned and nipped at his chin.

He slid the hem of her sweater up and over her head,

revealing beautiful, pale, satiny smooth skin—he'd never felt anything so soft—a lacy pink bra, and the best set of natural breasts he'd ever seen. She sat astride him and he stared—probably for a while, but damn, it wasn't every day a man got to disrobe the woman he'd been lusting over for weeks. But this was more. *She* was more—ripe, pink, lush, and overwhelming.

When her hands moved to cover her breasts, he realized his mistake. A blush ran from her chest right to her hairline. He blew out a breath. "God, Skye, I always thought you were gorgeous, but I was wrong. You're exquisite." Her breasts filled the cups, nearly spilling over; the dip of her waist fit his hands perfectly. No protruding bones, no sharp edges, just beautiful, soft, tempting curves.

He slid a strap off her shoulder with the tip of his finger. Her breath caught when his lips came in contact with the lacy edge. He traced it with his tongue and her hands fell from her breasts to his head. He smiled as she arched her back, pressing her nipple into his open mouth, and the taste of her had him craving more. With a flip of his wrist, he took care of the back closure and let the scrap of silk and lace fall. "So sweet." He switched breasts, drawing the other deep into his mouth.

Skye slid closer and rocked against his erection. If she didn't stop, he was going to embarrass himself.

His hands locked on her full hips, and when that didn't stop her, he flipped her onto her back. There was no way he was going to lose it before he got inside her. He'd waited too long. He'd been a walking hard-on ever since she stepped into his life.

She bounced into the pillows, her arms spread to catch herself. He took full advantage of her shock, yanked her sexy, clingy black pants off, and threw them over his shoulder. He'd wondered if she'd worn a thong ever since she bent over to look in the refrigerator, but he'd never suspected she was bare under there. He knelt beside her and groaned. "So beautiful." Pale skin from head to painted black-and-white polka-dot toenails, cut only by a small triangle of dark curls covering her mons. She snapped her legs together and did a modified hand jive.

God, she was sweet, and looked edible. "I don't know what to kiss first." He settled on her lips, the color of ripe berries, thinking he'd move south from there to be sure he didn't miss anything. Her breasts rose and fell with each breath.

He stretched out beside her, pulling her into his arms. She fit against him as if she were made for him. Her breasts pillowed against his chest, molding to him—real, soft, the tips of her pebbled nipples burning into his skin. He explored her mouth as his hands mapped the hills and valleys of her pliable body, listening for the change in her breathing. Watching, learning, discovering.

She tugged the button of his jeans and he brushed her hands away. When she made a second try, he caught her wrists in one hand and held them above her head, which did amazing things to her breasts. He rubbed his cheek against their softness.

He swallowed hard and prayed for strength and control. He was going to need both. He looked into her dark blue eyes—almost black with arousal. "Sugar, I'm a ladies-first kind of guy. But right now, the only way I have a prayer of making that happen is if you keep your hands to yourself for a while."

She licked her lips and his dick jumped in his jeans. God, what a mouth she had. "And if I don't?"

Her deep voice nearly did him in. He was screwed. "If you don't, I'll have to resort to desperate measures." He'd already recited the periodic table in his mind, and then added the atomic weights for good measure—it wasn't helping. "I'm good at tying knots."

Skye had never considered bondage a turn-on until that moment. She certainly wouldn't mind tying Logan up. Just the thought of it shot a surge of heat into her already overheated system.

She'd always known that there were some men, somewhere, who took foreplay seriously—she'd just never slept with any of them. Logan seemed to take it to the extreme—something she might appreciate later, but right now, not so much—especially if she wasn't allowed to join in on the fun.

He nibbled his way down the column of her neck and she slid her foot up his jean-clad leg, his razor stubble igniting her already oversensitive skin.

She might not be allowed to use her hands, but he'd never said she couldn't use the rest of her body. She held back a moan, tossed her leg over his hip, and groaned when she came into contact with his fly. "Oh God, yes."

His hands were everywhere, big, strong, long-fingered, and rough, as if he worked outside, but so gentle. They skidded over her body like a virtuoso's over ivory, hitting just the right notes to make the music come alive.

The tug on her breast drew the tension to her core as his hand squeezed her ass, then held her hip, pressing her back against the mattress. He overwhelmed her, controlled her, and felt almost too good. So big and broad, so freakin' beautiful. His skin was dark compared with hers. He was whipcord lean, muscular, and cut. He looked, smelled, and tasted like something out of a dream—but he was real and he was with her.

His knee slid between her legs, his tongue invaded her navel, and a hand brushed the inside of her thigh.

She sucked in a breath and squeezed her eyes shut— embarrassment mixing with intense pleasure as he kissed a path over her belly. Sparks of need shot through her. She never thought having Logan kiss her belly would be a turn-on. And she definitely had a belly. It had never bothered her before, but then she hadn't had anyone see her naked in . . . well, a long, long, long time.

She reached for him, but he'd already wedged himself between her thighs, which would not have been a problem if he still hadn't had his pants on.

Strong hands spread her legs, making room for his broad shoulders, gripping her hips, lifting, and then he sent her a sexy smile. "Dessert."

Her sputtered protest trailed off to a guttural moan. She'd known he had a talented tongue, but she had no idea he could do that with it. Her back arched, her toes curled, and she reached for his head, not sure whether it was to pull him away or hold him there forever. Pleasure so intense it skirted the edge of pain assaulted her, heat seared her, gathered, and then exploded.

He slipped a finger inside her, filling her, increasing the pressure, the pleasure, the intensity. She felt like a windup toy, wound past the breaking point. She couldn't think, she was incapable of words, of movement, of anything. As if his fingers, lips, and tongue weren't enough, the addition of his teeth sent her flying. It seemed to go on and on; she'd never survive. Her heart felt as if it were galloping right out of her chest; her throat was raw—the scream she'd heard must have been her own. Still, he didn't let up.

One orgasm built on another and all the while her body trembled, her muscles convulsed—her entire world seemed to collapse on itself and then splinter into a thousand shining pieces.

When she opened her eyes, all she saw was Logan's smiling face. If she could speak, she'd say something, but then he looked pretty pleased with himself—almost relieved, which was amazing, since all the pleasure had been hers. "I need a minute—or an hour. I'm not sure."

He grinned again, and she melted a little more and told herself that no guy was perfect—not even him. He had to have a fault.

He kissed her cheeks, her lips, and then her shoulder before pulling her into his arms. "I just want to hold you."

Her head rested on his chest and his heart beat a mad tattoo beneath her ear. She slid her leg over his, and felt nothing but Logan. She raised her head. "You lost your pants. When did that happen?"

He ran his hand down her back. "They were getting a little constricting."

She snuck a peek and swallowed hard. "I can imagine." Okay, that was a lie—she really couldn't imagine having something the size of that tucked into a pair of jeans. Hell, she couldn't imagine having something the size of that tucked into her. She stared. She couldn't help it. The more she stared, the bigger it seemed. Still, she'd come this far.

She walked her fingers over his abs, each muscle tensed beneath her fingertips. His heart rate spiked under her ear and she drew closer to get a better look. She wrapped her fingers around its girth. Hot, hard, and oh so smooth. It jumped in her grip.

She watched his face. Logan sucked a breath through clenched teeth. He looked as if he was in pain, but he didn't move to stop her.

A drop of liquid glistened on the sensitive head, so she licked it off and raised her gaze to his. "Tasty."

"Skye—" It sounded like half a plea, half a groan. She tightened her grip on his erection and slid her hand up to the top and back down while she traced the ridge with her tongue before opening her mouth and sucking on the head. Every one of his muscles within her line of vision delineated.

She moved between his legs, and smiled, nuzzling his dick. He smelled heavenly and tasted even better. She licked the length of him following the throbbing vein from base to tip.

"Stop."

Logan yanked the brown paper bag open. Chocolate and condoms fell out. She held back a laugh as he ripped open a condom and caught her watching. He looked almost embarrassed. "I didn't know which you'd be in the mood for."

She brushed his hand away before taking the head of his dick into her open mouth. She took as much as she could—in that position at least. His erection hit the back of her throat and the sound of his groan spurred her on. She added some suction and worked her hand in time with her mouth.

He quivered beneath her; his breath sounded as if it were being torn from his chest.

She moaned, loving the taste, the feel of him, the power she held, and then big hands lifted her off.

"Damn, Skye." He rolled on a condom and then pulled her onto his chest and kissed her, holding her close, so gentle but strong. His tongue tangled with hers and his hands grasped her hips, holding her still in his embrace.

When she reached between them and held him, he pressed against her opening—hot, hard, insistent. She took him in, inch by slow inch.

Logan watched Skye's eyes as she joined her body to his.

Her mouth formed an O and he clenched his teeth. She didn't blink, didn't break the connection they'd formed.

He watched with wonder, feeling everything. She was hot, wet, and, oh man, so tight. And the way she looked at him, so open, so beautiful, so much more than he'd ever imagined. His hands shook as he held her up. Keeping his hips on the mattress was a lesson in control. She was so small, lovely, delicate—he was scared to death he'd hurt her.

She eased onto him, her body opening to him, relaxing, drawing him in until she was fully seated. "God." She leaned in, chest to chest, and kissed him, never blinking, never breaking the connection as she rocked against him. "I was worried we wouldn't fit." She walked her hands up his chest and groaned when he slid out a little and then filled her again.

He sat, pulling her into his arms. "We fit just fine. Better than fine. You're perfect."

The look of shock on her face was one he'd never forget, but then she couldn't have been any more shocked than he was.

He'd had sex—a lot of it. He knew lust—they had plenty of that—he'd known desire, and he'd known the heat that came with compatibility, but he'd never known anything like this. He'd never had this need, this intense passion, this feeling of perfection. He'd never felt as connected to a lover as he felt at this moment. So good, so right, so much—it scared him.

He let Skye set the pace and let her experiment, using his shoulders for leverage, riding him right to the edge. She was stunningly open, real, totally immersed, focused, and completely uninhibited. He watched the way her eyes darkened, the radiant look of pleasure, the feel of her in his arms, and that sound she made when she found that one perfect spot.

Need reached up and grabbed him by the balls. He was so close, but he wanted her to go with him.

He rolled them over and changed the angle, her fabulous ass filling his hands as he held her.

After two slow, easy strokes, her legs were wrapped around his waist and her heels dug into his lower back, urging him on. She met him thrust for thrust, drawing him in and bucking beneath him. Her back arched and she wiggled that ass of hers, and damn if he didn't break out in a sweat, doing his best to hold back.

"Oh God, Logan. More. Harder. Faster."

He fought to keep himself in check, but she was having none of it. She dug her short nails into his ass and he completely lost the control he'd always prided himself on. He looked into her eyes and was powerless to fight it.

She went wild in his arms. "Oh God. Logan. That's it."

Her body grabbed on to his like a glove convulsing against him. She screamed his name, shuddered in his arms, and he followed her over. He came so hard, his vision blurred, and it didn't let up. He saw stars and Skye and felt something so deep it took his breath away and shot fear up his spine, making every hair on his body stand at attention. He looked into her eyes and felt something he'd never experienced, something so monumental he'd never forget, but so foreign it defied words. Euphoria? No, it was deeper, spiritual, almost reverent; it was more than that, though—so much more. It was addictive and scary, and mind-blowing. And the worst part of all was he saw the same wonder reflected in Skye's eyes. Their connection was so strong, so deep, so elemental, he had to look away or he'd be lost.

A shiver ripped through Skye when Logan looked away. It was as if a steel grate had come down and he'd closed up shop—hiding all the wonder and beauty she'd seen within him a second ago.

He rolled them over and questions raced through her mind. They were still joined, but he'd broken whatever other connection they'd had. Why? What happened? What was it?

There must have been a short circuit between her body and her brain, because her body never got the message that whatever they shared had just come to a screeching halt. Her blood still rushed through her ears, drowning out the sounds of heavy breathing, her heart still pounded as if searching for a way out of her chest, and aftershocks of cataclysmic proportions raced through her and into him.

Logan shuddered beneath her and she welcomed his reaction. It meant he was still with her—physically at least. She had no idea what he was thinking as her mind careened out of control. The only thing she knew was she felt the loss of something wonderful—as if she had the key to a priceless treasure—a treasure she beheld for only a moment, and lost in the blink of an eye.

She didn't know what to do or say. She didn't know

how to play this. She wanted to ask him what the hell just happened—other than the obvious.

Making love with Logan was unlike any sexual experience she'd ever had. And it was making love—until he pulled an emotional disappearing act anyway. Granted, she wasn't very experienced; she'd had only three boyfriends, all of whom quickly tired of her brothers' machinations. She couldn't blame them and it really never bothered her overly much—just enough to make her brothers' lives a living hell, but not enough to beg the guys to come back. Relationships seemed like too much work for too little payoff. She'd never really missed the sex, but then sex had never been anything like the sex she'd had with Logan. She had a feeling she'd miss it now—a lot.

Logan ran his hand over her hair. Great—she probably had bed head. Maybe she should have listened to Kelly after all.

"Skye," he whispered, "are you still awake?"

She was afraid to look at him. She didn't want to see that blank look on his face. "Yes, just comfortable. Sorry, am I crushing you?" The thought of sleep was laughable. She was physically and mentally exhausted, but she didn't think she'd be able to sleep anytime soon.

He chuckled and she lifted her head to brave a look. He wore a smile that didn't meet his eyes and looked a little frayed around the edges. He stroked her back, soothing, gentle, not letting on to the tension she saw around his mouth.

She needed to do something—anything—and the last thing she wanted to do was have the dreaded was-it-good-for-you discussion. "Are you hungry?"

"I'm a—"

"Guy. I know. You're always hungry."

He held her hips, and rocked into her, setting off a solar shower within her. "If not for food, then for you—sometimes both at the same time."

"God, Logan. Don't get me started again. You may not, but I need some recovery time. Besides, I'm hungry." Another lie. She'd been telling so many white lies lately; at this rate, she was going to need a nose job.

She might not be hungry, but she needed to cook. Cooking was the only thing that made everything better. It helped her level out, dispelling the emotion, and allowed her to see things as they were—without the aid of rose-colored glasses. And that was exactly what she needed now. Especially with Logan.

She slid off him, steeling herself against the pleasure. She sucked in a breath. Yes, her brain and body were so out of sync.

Logan grabbed her before she could scoot off the bed. He stared into her eyes as if he wanted to say something, and she feared she'd hear an apology, so she looked away.

She could handle a lot of things, but not an apology, not from him, not now—maybe not ever. "Come on. We have to discuss the tasting. I don't have much time, so I'll have to use the ingredients I have on hand. Although I'm sure if necessary, I can call a few of our suppliers in a pinch, but they won't be able to deliver. Would you be willing to pick up a few things? I don't have a car."

Logan watched her with concern in his eyes.

She looked around the room and saw that Pepperoni had taken her pants and pulled them up to the chair she liked to sleep on. Great.

"I'll use Pop's Jeep and get whatever you need." He

got out of bed and walked past, bare-assed, stopping only to give her a tap on the backside and a kiss on the cheek before heading to the bathroom. She yanked her pants out from under Pepperoni and gave the little girl a kiss before throwing the pants in the hamper. She pulled her sweater back over her head and tugged on a pair of paisley flannel sleep pants that clashed with her sweater. Oh well, he would be leaving soon anyway. In her experience, once guys got the goods, they didn't hang around long. She grabbed her chef's bible, and headed straight for her comfort zone.

CHAPTER 10

Logan stared at himself in the bathroom mirror after having the most incredible sex in his life, and wondered just what the hell had come over him. Temporary insanity was his only guess. He must have imagined it. He didn't feel things—ever. Okay, that wasn't true. He felt things for his dad and Nicki and his brothers, but whatever he thought he'd felt with Skye had to be imagined. When it came to women—he cared about them, he liked them, and he enjoyed everything about them, but he'd never met a woman he couldn't walk away from. Including Skye.

He turned on the cold water and splashed his face. He'd completely fucked things up with her. He'd freaked out and she'd caught him. She'd looked at him as if he'd hurt her, as if she wanted to be anywhere but with him. She'd looked ready to bolt, and probably would have if they hadn't been in her bed. She had nowhere to go.

He returned to the bedroom and pulled on his jeans. He heard Skye in the kitchen mumbling to herself—she always talked to herself without realizing it. He'd walked into the kitchen at the Crow's Nest on more than one occasion, thinking she was in the middle of a conversation only to find her alone. She was a piece of work all right.

He found himself smiling. When was the last time a woman made him smile? He couldn't remember. He didn't want to lose her—at least not yet. He just needed to figure out how to undo the damage he'd done.

Following the sound of smoky jazz, he found her dancing in front of the stove and stirring something that smelled incredible. His stomach growled.

She looked over her shoulder and caught him staring. "I hung up your T-shirt and sweater by the door. I didn't want Pepperoni to get them. She likes to drag clothing around."

"I've noticed." Skye pinked up again. "I didn't mention it before, but I have to tell you how much I appreciate your taste in lingerie. I also appreciate the fact you don't always wear it. Now, every time I look at you, I'm going to wonder what, if anything, you're wearing beneath your chef whites." He stepped behind her, wrapped his arms around her waist, and looked over her shoulder to see what she was making.

"I always wear underwear to work."

"Maybe we could change that."

She rolled her eyes and whisked the concoction over a double boiler.

"What's that?"

"Hollandaise sauce for lobster and spinach omelets." She shook a frying pan with spinach sautéing and tossed the contents a few times.

"Wow, that sure beats frozen pizza."

She shrugged. "I thought it would be a nice lunch entrée. You're my guinea pig."

"I'd be happy to eat whatever you put in front of me." He slipped his hand under the hem of her sweater and tucked his fingers in the waistband of her baggy flannel pants. No underwear. He swallowed and closed his eyes, remembering how he kissed every square inch of her stomach, how she came on his tongue, and how amazing she tasted. Just like that, his jeans got tight. "Did you put garlic in there?"

"No. No garlic."

"Good."

"If you ever want to eat, you're going to have to let me go. I can't think while you're touching me."

"Thinking is overrated." He should know—it wasn't helping him any. He just wanted to feel her against him, hold her in his arms, make her moan. "Give me a minute. I love touching you."

"You love eating more."

"That's debatable." He slid his hand out of her pants and right to her breasts—no bra. Thank God. He slid his teeth down the column of her neck and then soothed the skin with his tongue, sucking on the spot where her pulse thrummed beneath his lips.

Skye dropped the whisk, leaned against him, and let out a groan that he felt rumble between her perfect breasts. He was ready to suggest skipping the omelets entirely when she turned in his arms and gave him a shove. "I have a nice white wine in the fridge. Make yourself useful and open it. The corkscrew is in the drawer." She blew out a breath and picked up the whisk. "If I ruin this sauce, it's going to be all your fault."

"Yes, Chef."

She smiled at that. A smile was an improvement. He opened the wine, poured, and handed her a glass; then he

leaned against the counter and watched her do her thing.
The woman was amazing. She worked with an economy
of movement, precision, and finesse. She focused totally
on the task and fell into a rhythm. It was as if he and the
rest of the world had disappeared. He knew how it felt
to have that focus turned on him, and he wanted to feel
it again. Right after they ate.

She plated the omelets, drizzled hollandaise sauce
over them, and grabbed a towel, running it over the rim
of both plates before reaching into a bowl of freshly
chopped parsley to sprinkle it over the top. "Perfect."

He had to agree. She was.

"I'd serve this with a fruit salad of Asian pears, red
grapes, black mission figs, cantaloupe, and pink grape-
fruit. Hold on. I think I have some. You find silverware."
She buried her head in her overfilled refrigerator, cursed,
and then pulled a tub out and dished up two bowls of
fruit salad. She set the table and served.

Logan followed her and held her chair. "Thanks for
going to all this trouble." He sat beside her.

"It's no trouble. I really love to cook. It calms me. I'm
a mess if I don't get in the kitchen enough. *Bon appétit.*"

He dug in and shook his head. The omelet was amazing. He'd never been a big fan, but this was decadent.
"Man, I could get used to eating like this."

"You know where I work." She toyed with her food.
"I was thinking about the tasting tomorrow. I'd like to do
three dishes."

"Three?" She still hadn't taken a bite.

"I'd like to do a braised pork belly with mustard and
juniper berries, fried crisp, and served with sauerkraut
and currant jam. I have everything I need for that. I was
going to make it as a special appetizer this week. The

second is a duck confit rillette with crostini, cornichons, and dried cherries."

"What the hell is a cornichon?"

"They're small, tart pickles."

"If you say so." He looked from his empty plate to hers—she'd taken only a few bites. "Are you going to eat all that?"

"No." He thought she'd cut a piece off for him; instead, she passed him her plate and continued to nibble on her fruit and wrote notes.

"I thought you were hungry."

She was still looking at her notes. "Not as hungry as I thought." He watched her, amazed by the expressions crossing her face, and wondered what the hell was going through her mind.

Her eyes widened and then she smiled—the kind of smile that could steal a guy's breath if he allowed himself to feel. "How about butter poached lobster served with braised oxtail and potato gnocchi with shellfish butter?"

"Oxtail? Seriously?"

She looked up from her notes. "It's amazing. I braise it for hours covered in a consommé with garlic, onions, carrots, celery, and star anise. Then I roast it. You're going to love it."

"They're coming for the tasting at one o'clock—you don't have hours."

She waved away his objection. "I'll have plenty of time. How many are we expecting?"

"Five, I think."

"Good, I planned to braise it tomorrow anyway."

"You were planning to work tomorrow, beyond preparing the food for the tasting?"

She shrugged. "I was avoiding you, remember? And

you haven't been following me into the kitchen. Besides, what else am I going to do?"

"I don't know. Go out with Patrice and Rocki. I know they've wanted to get together with you."

"Only to grill me about you."

"Oh, so you've not only been avoiding me—you've been avoiding them too?"

"As if I could. Rocki has no qualms about coming into my kitchen. She stands by the fire extinguisher and stares at me until I talk to her." She looked up from the book she was writing in. "I'd rather keep this thing between us on the down low. I'm still not comfortable working together and, well, doing whatever we're doing."

"Dating."

She seemed to roll it around in her mind for a minute as if she wasn't sure she wanted to date him. "Are we dating other people or is this an exclusive thing?"

The thought of her dating someone else had his temper flashing like a short fuse on a pipe bomb. He looked at his hands and realized he'd bent his fork. He did his best to straighten it, then placed it carefully on the napkin, and rubbed his palms on his thighs. He watched her. "Do you want to date other people?"

"Do you?"

"I asked first." He held his breath.

"Logan, we're not in middle school."

"Fine. You want an answer?"

She swallowed hard and nodded when he leaned in.

"I don't want to date anyone else." He rose from his seat, pulled her right out of hers, and tossed her over his shoulder and headed back to bed. He laid her down, quickly stripped her bare, and then climbed on top of her. He held her chin and stared into her eyes. "I don't want you dating anyone but me. I want to be the only man who knows what you are or aren't wearing under your clothes. I want to be the only man who sees you naked, the only man you sleep with, and I want to do all of the above often. Do you have a problem with that?" The last came out on a gravelly growl.

She swallowed hard. "No. No problem. I just wanted to know the rules."

"Good." Need clawed at him. Man, he thought he'd needed her before, but it was nothing compared with this.

"Logan . . ."

He grunted like a caveman.

"Don't think you can pick me up and toss me on the bed and get your way every time we have a discussion." She yanked on the button of his jeans and his zipper slid down.

"I'm only concerned about this time."

She pushed his pants down to his thighs. "This time it's working for you."

"Thank God."

She laughed. "Don't let it go to your head."

"I'll keep that in mind." He grabbed a condom and rolled it on with shaking hands.

"Aren't you going to take off your pants?"

"No." He flipped her onto her hands and knees. He didn't want to tempt fate again and look into her eyes. No, this time he was playing it safe. He raised her hips to his and kissed her shoulder. He had one hand on her breasts, the other between her legs. She was hot and wet and ready. He drove into her in one smooth thrust, and that feeling nearly took his breath away. He was royally screwed.

*   *   *

Logan hadn't had to sneak into the apartment since he was sixteen. He took the back stairs—the ones farthest from Pop's room. He even avoided the squeaky top step. As soon as he opened the door, he heard his father's low laugh. "Foiled again, huh, Logan? When are you boys gonna learn you can't get one over on me?"

He switched on the light. "I don't know why I even bothered. I'm a grown man. I can come and go as I please."

"I assume you've been coming with Skye?"

"That's enough, Pop. My relationship with Skye is none of your business."

"Yes, it is." Pop dragged himself out of his Barcalounger and stretched. "She's my chef."

He dropped his keys on the counter. "I never said I wouldn't see her."

"No, but you said you'd slow the hell down. If this is slow, I can't imagine what fast is."

"Did you tuck in Nicki like I told you to?"

"Son, I've been tucking in Nicki for months. I don't need instructions from you."

"Fine. If you're through giving me a hard time, I'm going to take D.O.G. and go for a jog. We have a special tasting this afternoon and Skye might need me to run to a few suppliers."

"A tasting for what?"

"Foods of New York Tours. They're talking about starting a walking tour of Red Hook and someone in-house recommended the Crow's Nest. I guess Skye's food impressed the hell out of him."

"And you didn't think to mention this to me?"

"No. I figured I'd talk to Bree about it when she returns. It's a great way to attract new customers."

"I don't want new customers. Why the hell would I want a bunch of uptight city people at the Crow's Nest? We have too many of them coming over as it is."

"Oh, I don't know . . . to increase business, make more money, become a destination?"

"We're already a destination. We have a great customer base and we're doing well. I don't want that to change. I don't want to ruin a good thing. The Crow's Nest is a neighborhood joint. It's a place people come to see a friendly face and eat good food. It's a place to come for a beer after work or bring a date on a Saturday night. It's not a place to bring a freakin' tour group."

"Why not?"

"Because I own it and I said so."

"Well, sorry, Pop, but the tasting is on. It's way too late to cancel and besides, Skye's worked hard planning what to make."

"What's she making?"

"Three things that sound good. Braised oxtail and gnocchi, pork belly, and then something else that sounds interesting."

"What?"

"It's good. The woman can cook."

"Do you think my customers are going to eat oxtail and pork belly?"

"If Skye makes it, they will. Pop, this is important to her."

"Fine. But you're going to be the one to tell Bree that she's going to have a freakin' tour tromping in at all times."

"Bree will be fine with it." He hoped. He'd seen Bree with a mad-on and he certainly didn't want her to put him in her sights. Her aim was way too accurate.

"Yeah, well, if I were you, I'd start praying now." Pop walked right up to him and looked him up and down. "So, you and Skye are together now?"

"Yeah."

"Has she told you what she was running from yet?"

"No."

"So the lady keeps her cards close to her vest even with you two being together. It's a rough way to start a relationship. Secrets are never good."

"They're not always bad."

"Then why keep 'em?"

He shrugged—Pop didn't look all that concerned. "What do you know? Did you run a check on Skye?"

"Damn straight I did."

"What did you find out?"

"Nothing that I'll share with you. That's privileged information. If you want to know so badly, you're going to have to get it from her."

"I've tried. She said it's personal."

"And the fact that you're sleeping with her doesn't change things? Why do you think that is?"

Good question. "It's complicated, Pop."

"Relationships always are. Is she the only one keeping secrets?"

"I've been straight with her from the get-go." Except for the weirdness whenever he touched her. Yeah, the second time around he realized it wasn't only looking into her eyes that did it. He didn't know what the hell it was. All he knew was it freaked him out—just not enough to stay away from her. He didn't know what was wrong with him, but whatever it was, he wished it would go away.

Pop smiled at him like he knew something Logan didn't. "Oh, I see how it is."

"You see how what is?"

His smile just got wider and he rubbed his hands together. "Shit, boy, if you can't figure it out, I'm sure as hell not gonna be the one to tell you. You're smart—I know your IQ, remember? You'll put it together eventually."

"Give me a break, Pop. Will ya?"

"I am, son. Now you go ahead on your jog. I'm going to turn in. I'm gettin' too old for this shit."

"Yeah, so am I." He went and changed, got the dog out of Nicki's room, and took him for a five-mile run. It hadn't helped. Nothing took away the feeling that he was in way over his head this time.

Shit, one trip back home and now he was emotionally attached to a ten-year-old girl, the lover of a woman who had more secrets than the CIA, and the son of an ex-cop bar owner who was pissed as hell at him. He was triply screwed.

Skye came awake slowly and felt as if her head were on a hairy pillow—but Logan wasn't hairy. A snort had her opening her eyes and she realized she was using Pepperoni as a pillow and not Logan. "Sorry, sweetie." She pulled the sleepy puggle into her arms, avoided Pepperoni's mile-long tongue, or tried to anyway, and looked for Logan. He was nowhere to be found. She listened to the quiet of the morning. It didn't sound as if he was even in the apartment. He probably had to get home before Nicki awoke.

She stretched and hurt in places she didn't know she had, but couldn't erase the smile on her face. Logan had been insatiable and she'd learned that, with him, so was she. She felt great and would feel even better after taking a long soak in a hot tub.

She got out of bed carrying her chef's bible with her and looked over her schedule for the day. She had a plan, and her plan was going to take some time to make happen. She went straight to the kitchen to make coffee and clean up the mess she'd made, only to find it spotless. She did love a man who knew how to clean a kitchen. Okay, not loved—but liked a whole lot.

Logan had definitely made up for the weirdness after their first time. And by the fourth time, he looked as if he'd gotten over whatever it was that had bothered him—either that or she'd just been too exhausted to notice and too fulfilled to see straight. She'd curled up on top of him and slept like the dead.

By the time she'd bathed, dried her hair, and fed and walked Pepperoni, she was running late. She pulled her sweatshirt around her and shivered. It was time to go shopping for a coat—after her next paycheck. She ran into the kitchen of the Crow's Nest, started the coffee, and prepped vegetables.

An hour later she had the pork belly and oxtail braising, and the potatoes were almost ready to go into the vegetable mill to make gnocchi. She considered calling in one of her line chefs—Enrique had said he'd welcome more hours—but she wasn't in the mood to share her space. No, today, more than ever, she needed her kitchen all to herself. And making gnocchi was always relaxing. Besides—she looked over her notebook—there was nothing she couldn't handle on her own.

Logan lurked outside the kitchen listening to Skye talk to herself. She was a piece of work all right. He just hoped she wasn't pissed at him for leaving without saying good-bye. He'd thought about it, but she'd looked so cute curled up with the puppy, he didn't have the heart to wake her. He thought cleaning the kitchen would make up for any points he lost by not leaving a note—he'd tried to write one, but couldn't come up with anything that hadn't sounded trite.

He stepped inside the kitchen and waited for her to finish dropping what looked like dough into boiling water. "Good morning, beautiful."

She jumped and brought a floury hand to her chest. "You scared the crap out of me, Logan. Don't you know not to sneak up on people in a kitchen? We have sharp knives."

"Sorry." He pulled her hands away from her chest, ignoring the flour he was sure would dust his black sweatshirt, and brought them around his waist, then nuzzled her ear below her baseball cap. "I thought you'd hear the swinging doors. I came to ask if you needed me to make a supply run."

"No, I called and Dave is going to drop off a half-dozen lobsters. I was able to catch him before he left."

"Can I do anything to help?"

She looked into the pot and gave it a stir. "I need a bucket of ice."

"Ice." He was about to give her a kiss when she shoved a five-gallon bucket into his chest.

"Now. I'm going to have to pull these out in a minute and I need to drop them in ice water to stop them from becoming overcooked."

"I'm on it, but I want a rain check on the kiss." He didn't wait for her response; he just took the bucket and headed to the ice machine, wondering if she'd ever had sex in a restaurant kitchen. After all the sex they'd had last night and this morning, he should be sated. Hell, he should be incapacitated. He shouldn't want to take her on the worktable and run ice cubes all over her squirming body—at least not yet.

He might as well have disappeared after pouring the ice into a container of water. Her total focus was on the gnocchi she transferred from the ice water to a tub. She ran from the stove to the walk-in and back to stir whatever she had boiling.

He turned, not bothering to say good-bye—she was already talking to herself. Her complete focus was on her task. He didn't take it personally.

He stepped out of the kitchen, heading to the office to take care of the liquor order, when the sound of glass breaking made him take a detour. He cursed, grabbed the broom and a dustpan, and found Rocki practically hanging over the bar—her head and arms reaching over the service side, and her ass on the customer side. He'd recognize that ass anywhere—it was encased in black leggings, and her feet were hanging down.

"Shit."

One of her heels had fallen off and the other was hanging from her toes. At least the glass—make that glasses—she'd broken were behind the bar.

"Rocki, what the hell are you doing?"

She arched her back to peer at him through blond and pink bangs. "I was trying to get a glass."

He peered over. "Looks as if you got a few of them."

She blew the hair out of her eyes. "I was going for a soda."

He bent down and grabbed the stilts she called shoes. "You know, you could actually go behind the bar. That way you wouldn't drop your shoes or our glasses." He helped her down and handed over the heels. "I saved the shoes, but the glasses, I'm afraid, are a total loss."

Shaking his head, he grabbed the broom and dustpan, ducked under the pass-through, and cleaned up her mess. He'd been cleaning up after Rocki ever since he'd arrived. The woman was a walking disaster. He emptied the dustpan into the trash and washed his hands. "So, what can I get you?"

"Seltzer with lime."

He tossed a glass in the air and caught it. He'd already prepped the bar for the tasting, so he reached for the ice and poured, and then grabbed a lime and rolled it on the cutting board—knife in hand.

"So, you and Skye, huh? That certainly didn't take long."

He almost sliced his finger off. When he got the guts to look at Rocki, she didn't have to tell him; the jig was definitely up.

She brushed her bangs out of her eyes and shot him a don't-even-try-to-deny-it look.

Skye was going to be so pissed. If Rocki knew, it meant she'd alerted Patrice, who worked faster than the Associated Press. "Fuck."

"I should hope so, considering how long you were gone last night."

He shook his head. He didn't even want to ask.

"Nicki was worried about you. She called me to chat this morning. So, you got home at four and had words with Pete, and then took D.O.G. for a run? Like you didn't get enough exercise last night? Your stamina is impressive. But then I had a feeling you would be."

What was a guy supposed to say to that? He had no clue and cursed the fact that his ears were burning.

Rocki obviously relished his discomfort, if her cat-in-the-fishbowl smile was anything to go by. "When I told Patrice, we decided to give you a break—after all, Skye's a huge improvement over that Payton chick. It didn't take long for you to dump her when she got here."

"Look, Payton and I just didn't work out. She's not a bad person, she's just not the one for me."

"Yeah, it'd be like loving a mannequin with the personality of a Stepford Wife."

"Rocki, that's enough. This thing with Skye is—"

"Hot?"

He raised an eyebrow.

She leaned forward. "Just a tip: The next time you play with chocolate cake and whipped cream, you might want to clean up after yourselves. Simon said you went through a full can of Reddi-wip. Kinky."

Logan cringed. "We had help with the whipped cream."

Her mouth formed an O and her eyebrows disappeared beneath her bangs. "Intriguing."

"Not that kind of help. Damn, you've got a dirty mind. Let's just say Pop has a real gift when it comes to killing the mood."

"Coitus interruptus?"

"No. God, what kind of guy do you think I am?"

"The kind with a Y chromosome. Logan, women have to be in the mood; men just have to be breathing."

She had that right. Still, he didn't think he would have taken Skye on the bar. At least that was what he told himself, but after last night, he wasn't too sure. "So what are you doing here?"

She smiled at him—the kind of smile that made a man want to protect his privates. "I'm meeting Patrice."

He groaned. "No, give me a break, Rocki. Don't go

causing problems between me and Skye. She's still weirded out about the whole working-together thing."

"Yeah, about that." She placed her elbow on the bar to hold up her chin and then tapped hot pink nails against her cheek. "How did you two get together anyway? When she first started here, she didn't even like you."

He thought back to the first time he touched Skye and damned if he didn't have a shit-eating grin on his face. "Oh, she liked me all right. She just didn't want to. She still doesn't. So do me a favor, will ya? Just leave it alone."

There was a knock on the door. Rocki jumped off the stool and ran—her stilts tapping against the hardwood like a woodpecker—loud and annoying. She threw the lock and Patrice stepped in.

"Thank God for home day care." Patrice's eyes met his and she didn't even try to hide her you-got-trouble smile. "Heard you've been a busy boy, Logan. I'm just sorry I didn't get to meet your ex. It's a good thing Rocki filled me in. She texted me pictures and everything."

"Great. Thanks, Rocki."

"Don't mention it."

"So." Patrice tossed her purse on the bar. "Where is she?"

"Where is who?" Okay, so he was playing dumb. What else could he do?

Patrice shook her head. "It won't work. It doesn't even work for my husband and he's got skills. I take it Skye's in the kitchen?"

"Leave her alone, Patty, or I'll have to call Francis."

She smiled and all the hair on the back of his neck stood on end.

He wanted to bang his head against the bar—repeatedly. "Francis is on his way here now, isn't he?"

Patrice checked her watch. "He'll be here any minute."

The door swung open and Logan's refrigerator-sized friend stepped in.

"Francis." God, what else was going to happen? This was Skye's worst nightmare and it was quickly becoming his too.

"Hey, Logan." He shot him a she'd-tie-my-dick-in-a-knot-if-I-didn't-show look. The man was blushing like a schoolgirl on her first date. "I heard you and Skye—"

"Stop!" Logan slid under the pass-through. "Shit. It's like I've died and gone to hell."

Francis smacked his hands against his gargantuan thighs and shook his head. "Man, is Skye making you sleep on the couch already?"

Kitchen doors slapped shut. "No, but I might. What's going on here?"

"Skye." Every muscle in Logan's back and neck seized. He spun around feeling like a puppy that had been whipped, and its master had just come through the door with a new belt. Holy shit. He was acting like Francis.

CHAPTER 11

Skye looked from Rocki to Patrice to Francis, but her gaze didn't rest until it seared Logan's retinas. She didn't know what the hell was going on, but she knew it wasn't good. Especially since it appeared that everyone and their uncle knew she and Logan were sleeping together. Okay, not sleeping—she'd barely gotten any sleep, at least not enough to deal with this situation. She was going to kill him.

Francis sputtered and all the blood drained from his face.

Logan turned an alarming shade of red. She would have been worried about him had she not been mad enough to take up knife throwing, tie him to a wheel, and practice on him—blindfolded. She smiled to herself. She'd already fantasized about bondage—this put a whole new spin on it—literally.

Rocki and Patrice looked as if they'd both found a pair of Louboutin Lipsinka python point-toe pumps in their sizes mismarked for $12.95 instead of $1,295.00 and had a coupon for a free mani-pedi to boot.

Patrice smiled as if she was genuinely happy to see her. "Rocki and I came to help with the tasting. We thought we'd take you for a girls' night out when we're done. What do you say?"

Patrice might look harmless, but Skye didn't let that fool her. She'd known a lot of women who could pull it off.

Logan stood behind them with a pleading look on his face. He shook his head so vehemently, she wondered whether he might end up with a case of shaken-dumb-ass syndrome. "Sounds like fun, but I can't."

"Why not?"

Why not? Shit. She didn't think *because the two of you scare the crap out of me* would go over well. "I need to pick up a few things."

"What?"

"A coat. All I have are sweatshirts and it's getting cold. I even heard they're calling for an early snow."

Rocki turned to Patrice and pounded knuckles. "Score. It just so happens shopping is our favorite thing to do—especially when we don't have to use our own money. It's like getting to eat a pound of chocolate without the calories. We'll go with you."

Patrice nodded. "We'll hit all the best stores—then we can stop for dinner and drinks. It's about time we had a girls' night out. It's going to be great."

Logan cleared his throat. "No. Skye is going shopping with me. I need help buying Nicki clothes."

He stepped closer and she figured in this situation he was the least of the three evils. Better to deal with the devil you know—intimately.

Patrice flicked away his objection. "Better yet. This is

going to be great. I've noticed Nicki's outgrowing all her jeans and shirts. I think she takes after you, Logan—all long arms and legs."

Logan had started to say something, but Rocki cut him off. "No need to thank us. We love to shop for Nicki, don't we, Patrice?"

Rocki and Patrice had Logan cornered and sweating. He shot pleading looks toward Francis, who seemed powerless to do anything other than shake his head in sympathy.

"Face it, Logan, we love to shop for anyone." Rocki held out her hand, palm up.

Logan's grip on Skye's waist tightened. "What do you want?"

"Cash."

His gaze went from her to Rocki's open hand and back again. "Skye, can I speak with you in the kitchen?"

She was tempted to say no and leave him to the she-wolves. She might want to kill him, but she didn't want anyone else to have the pleasure. "Sure." She couldn't wait to hear what he had to say. "Let's go."

He kept his arm around her the whole way. He was either really brave or really stupid. They stepped in and she turned on him. "I can't believe you would—"

He cut her off with a kiss that had her eyes rolling back into her head. The man was definitely talented. He ended the kiss way too early for his own good and rested his forehead on hers. His eyes squeezed shut tight. "Before you say anything, listen to me."

That's why he kissed her? That was so not fair. Not fair, but effective.

"Nicki called Rocki this morning and ratted us out. I didn't say a word."

"I can't believe you're going to blame this on an innocent ten-year-old."

"It's true. Simon spilled the beans too."

"How did Simon find out?"

"Chocolate cake and whipped cream. Think about it."

"You didn't clean up the bar?"

"No, I was too busy being lectured by my father—then drinking. I completely forgot." He ran his hands up and down her arms. "Skye, don't freak out on me, but Pop knows too. He was waiting up for me when I got home this morning."

She banged her head against his chest. "Are you kidding me?"

"And since I'm already giving you the bad news, I might as well finish the job—"

"There's more?"

"Pop's not real happy with Foods of New York bringing the tour here."

"Why not?"

"Because he likes the Crow's Nest the way it is. He's not interested in attracting uptight city people. He says he has enough of them coming here already."

She looked around the kitchen. Her kitchen. "This is just great. Now my boss has two reasons to fire me."

"He's not going to fire you. He thinks you're amazing. I'm the one he's pissed at—if anyone's going to get fired, it'll be me."

"You're his son. I'm just an employee—and you said yourself you're out of here in a few weeks. God, I can't believe I was stupid enough to sleep with you. I knew this would happen. I told you. But noooo, you had to be Mr. Irresistible."

He stepped back. "Hey, you weren't complaining last night or this morning."

"I wasn't the talk of the restaurant or on the outs with my boss then either."

"You're still not."

"Right. Everyone out there knows what we did last night." She covered her face with her hands. "Oh God, a ten-year-old girl who I care about knows I've been ... that we've been ... It's just not right." Her eyes met his worried ones. "Is there anyone who doesn't know about my sex life?"

"What's done is done—it's not as if we have a *Men in Black* mind eraser."

"You're such a man. Did Francis and Simon give you a pat on the back? You're a stud, right? I fell right in line, didn't I?"

"Calm down, Skye. There's only one way to deal with this—"

"You're right. We won't see each other anymore outside of work."

"The hell we won't." His voice sounded gravelly, like an overfilled eighteen-wheeler with a new driver grinding the gears. He was six feet three of mad, alpha male marking his territory. "All we have to do is go about our business and we'll be old news in no time."

"Logan, you need to leave. I have too much to do to deal with drama."

She looked into his eyes and watched the steel grate descend, then turned her back on him.

"Fine. I'll leave, but this is not over. Not by a long shot. We'll talk after the tasting."

Not if she could help it. She was about to spell it out for him when the sound of hands slamming against the swinging doors stopped her, and his departure sent the doors creaking back and forth like a dead man hanging from the gallows.

Logan stood back and watched everyone from the tasting scarf down Skye's food. All three dishes were a hit. The only time he'd seen her since their fight was when he'd gone into the kitchen to get each dish to serve, but then he'd had Francis with him. She hadn't looked up at either of them.

He and Francis served, while Pop manned the bar and schmoozed with the people from Foods of New York Tours. From the look of his father, he'd never guess that Pop was anything but enthusiastic about the prospect of added business.

After the table was cleared, it had taken another hour to get all the information about payments, tour dates, and contractual obligations. Logan had explained that he was only the interim manager, and that Bree would be back in a couple of weeks.

He'd thought about what Pop had said and decided he'd get all the information, hand it over to Bree as soon as she came home, and let her make the decision. This was her restaurant, not his.

Skye was right—he was only there for a few more weeks. It wasn't as if he could hang out at the Crow's Nest for the rest of his life. He had to figure out what was next for him and Nicki. He had plenty of money saved, so it wasn't as if he had to make an immediate decision about their future, but he also couldn't just do nothing. He'd go crazy unless his doing nothing took place on a secluded beach with Skye.

Pop sat stoically, listening to the discussion and not saying a word. Logan didn't know whether that meant Pop was changing his mind or whether he waited for the group to leave so he could ream him. With his luck, it was probably the latter.

After he walked the group out, he returned and faced his father. "Well?"

Pete shook his head and stood, gathering the tablecloth. "Rocki, Patrice, and Francis left an hour ago while you were talking to the tasters. Is everything in the kitchen closed down?"

"Good question." Logan went in and all but the lights were turned off. There was an air of emptiness about the place. Skye had already rabbited—without even a goodbye. Great. He turned off the lights and found his father waiting for him at the bottom of the stairs.

"Skye looked pretty peeved. What happened? I know doing the tasting wouldn't send her into a tailspin. Not with her experience."

"Experience?"

"Yeah, boy. You might be sleeping with her, but you're definitely not knowledgeable about the woman. The sex may be amazing, but it's the other form of communication that keeps a relationship together. Talk to the woman. Find out what she's looking for and what she's running away from. Hell, son, I'd bet you dollars to Krispy Kremes you don't even know where she comes from."

He'd be right. Logan ran his hand through his hair. "You'd better get back to Nicki. I'll take D.O.G. for a walk and then go talk to Skye—that is, if she'll let me in. She's pissed that everyone in the restaurant knows about our sex life." He cut the lights and took the steps after his father.

Twenty minutes later he got a text from Francis about possible trouble. Patrice and Rocki had been in Skye's apartment since they'd left.

Skye unlocked the door to her apartment, more tired than she'd been in a long time. All she wanted to do was jump into a hot shower, wash the smell of food off her, and then go to bed. But first, she had to take Pepperoni out. She stepped inside and blinked. Patrice and Rocki had made themselves comfortable on her couch with her dog. "What are you two doing here?"

Patrice slid Pepperoni's head off her thigh, stood, and shoved a glass of champagne into Skye's hand. "We came to chat. Drink up." Patrice took a sip and gave Skye an encouraging smile. "This conversation has a three-drink minimum. I hope you don't mind us making ourselves at home. We took Pepperoni out—the poor thing peed like Austin Powers after coming out of cryogenic storage."

Rocki piped up, "Yeah, it was amazing. She took a power pee. Who knew something that small could pee so much?"

Skye drained her glass—the bubbles tickled her nose and the alcohol hit her empty stomach. This was a waking nightmare—one she'd thought she'd avoided by going out the back way. "How did you get in?"

Patrice refilled her glass and waved the keys in front of her face. "I have a set of keys, remember? But don't worry. I'll only use them in emergencies."

"And this constitutes an emergency?" Skye took another long drink of really good champagne. She had to admit Logan knew how to select wines.

Patrice shrugged and did a seventies Cher drag queen hair toss. "Definitely." She checked her watch. "It sure took you long enough to get here. We were bored, so we started without you. Great champagne."

"Logan brought it—it's from his vineyard." She'd been hoping to celebrate something with him, but now, no relationship, no reason to celebrate.

Patrice topped off her glass and Skye took another swig and plopped down on the couch. She knew them well enough to know they weren't leaving. "What's the deal? I know you came for more than the free champagne, and I'm not going shopping with you after three drinks—I don't drink and shop."

Rocki set the bottle in front of Patrice after filling her own glass. "What's wrong with you, Skye?"

"Shitty day."

Patrice ran her hand up and down the neck of the bottle. "I guess it's a good thing Logan brought a magnum, then, huh? We need information, girlfriend. We've had a bet going and you're the one who has to call the winner."

Patrice and Rocki sat at the edge of the couch like PTA moms vying for a seat on the fund-raising committee.

Skye set the glass on the coffee table and brought her cold hands to her heated face. "A bet? What kind of bet?"

Rocki covered Pepperoni's ears. "You've seen the goods. We want to know if everything Logan buys is magnum size."

Were they serious? She drained the glass, choked, and then wiped her mouth off with the sleeve of her sweatshirt. It was getting a little warm in there. She pulled one arm out. Okay, so maybe drinking three glasses of champagne in quick succession on an empty stomach wasn't the best idea. Things were getting a little fuzzy. "What goods? What are you talking about?"

Rocki sat forward. "Logan."

She smiled and her lips felt numb. She touched them to make sure they were still there. Should she tell them? It wasn't as if she and Logan were still seeing each other, and everyone knew they'd had sex. Besides guys always had sex-and-tell sessions; she'd heard her brothers on more than one occasion give a blow-by-blow of their dates—literally. Yuck. There was nothing worse than having to hear about her brothers' sex lives. "Logan's good at kissing. He has a talented tongue." She thought about all the things Logan had done to her with his tongue and then refocused her eyes and found Rocki and Patrice staring at her. "Do tongues have talent?" She shook her head. "No, I don't think so. But the man knows how to use his tongue and everything else for that matter."

Trying to watch Rocki was like trying to watch a TV with bad reception. "I knew it." She turned to Patrice. "But maybe four glasses was overkill. She's a lot smaller than we are. I think she's a real lightweight."

Skye leaned sideways and remembered she was in the middle of the couch. She caught herself just before she went all the way over.

Patrice knelt in front of her and put her hands on Skye's knees. "Skye, are you okay?"

"Who? Me?" She waved her hand—and it seemed really heavy, so she dropped it. "I'm fine." She leaned toward Patrice, trying to focus with the room spinning.

She held on to the arm of the couch so she didn't slide off. "So what if I just lost my only friend in New York? So what if I probably lost my job because I slept with him—the one guy who satisfies me in bed and the shower, and pretty much everywhere else too? So what if everyone I know in New York knows about the four times I've had sex in the last three years? Why wouldn't I be fine? After all it's over—I no longer have a friend, a lover, a job, and at the rate I'm going, I may never have another orgasm. I'm really going to miss them—a lot. So, yeah, Patrice. I'm fine. As a matter of fact, I'm just skippy." She went to rub her nose and realized her aim was off; then she hiccuped and covered her mouth with both hands.

Two sets of breasts came at her. She blinked and then she was lifted off the couch and onto the chair. Which was good because it was easier to sit on. She leaned against the side.

Patrice shook her head. "Why did you drink so much?"

"Hey. You're the ones who said it was a three-drink confersation." She reached for her glass to take another sip, but Rocki took it from her.

"Have you eaten?"

"No. Like I can eat with this thing with Logan hangin' over my head. He's there one minute—all there, like he can see into my soul kind of there. And then he's gone the next, like a cyborg or something. You know, like those guys who are great in bed but have no emotions. It's as if he's got an on/off switch—his shields come down."

Patrice looked over at Rocki. "Oh God, Logan's gonna kill us."

*   *   *

Logan walked into Skye's place with Francis and froze. Now he knew what kind of maniacal woman Francis was married to, and understood the I-pissed-her-off-once-but-I'll-never-do-it-again shoulder slump Francis assumed when Patrice gave him a certain look.

He heard more than saw Skye. Then he noticed the empty magnum of champagne and three glasses.

Both Rocki and Patrice wore twin expressions of shock.

"Don't worry," Skye muttered. "I snuck out of the kitchen. I told Logan it was over. I can't afford to lose my job just because he's Mr. Irresistabuble. I'm gonna miss him, though—his tongue and his . . . well, he's a talented man and just between you and you and me, when he went all caveman and took me to bed—I kinda liked it."

Rocki smiled right at him. "Wow, who'd have thought Logan had it in him? I guess there's some truth to the whole 'still waters run deep' thing. It's always the quiet ones who go alpha on us."

He stepped closer and saw the top of Skye's head leaning against the side of the chair, and she was shaking it, as if she was confused.

Skye giggled. "God, Patrice, you look like you just got caught with your skirt tucked into the back of your panty hose and discovered you're wearing a toilet paper train." She laughed so hard, she snorted.

Francis slammed the door. "Patrice. My God, girl, what have you and Rocki done to her?"

Logan stepped forward.

Skye jumped and whipped around. Her eyes widened as they met his. She teetered on the edge of the chair and went over.

He scrambled and caught her head in his hand just before it hit the corner of the coffee table.

She lay splayed between the chair and the table. Pepperoni jumped off the couch and onto her and licked her face.

"Logan?"

"Yeah, baby. It's me." He pushed the dog off and knelt beside her, still holding her head in his throbbing hand. If her head had hit that table, it would have cracked it open. As it was, she was going to have a hell of a bruise. He glared at Rocki and Patrice.

Skye gazed up at him. "The cyborg Logan or the real Logan?"

"What?" When he looked back at the coconspirators, wondering what the hell Skye was talking about, they'd already headed for the door, looking at everything but him. Dammit. They were no help.

"It's the real me. Come on, sugar. Let's get you on the couch." He lifted her into his arms and wasn't about to let go of her just yet. He sat with her in his lap and she snuggled closer, her head fitted in the crook of his neck. His heart hammered as if he'd just sprinted ten miles, and an adrenaline rush punched through his system. "Are you hurt?"

"Me? I'm just fine. I'm damn skippy. I'm gonna miss you, though."

"No, you're not. I'm not going anywhere." He kissed the top of her head and heard the door close. "What were you doing with Patrice and Rocki?"

"Having a three—no, make that forve-drink mini-mum confersation."

"I see. Did you eat anything today?"

"Nah, can't eat. I'm too worried about getting fired."

"You're not going to get fired." He kissed her and lifted her off his lap. "I'm going to get you something to eat."

"Oh, no. No food. I don't feel so good."

"Shit." He picked her up and ran to the bathroom.

CHAPTER 12

It isn't every day a man figures out he's in love — and Logan doubted many men realized it while holding their girlfriend's head over the toilet. Once he figured out it was love, and not the result of temporary insanity, he felt so sick, he had half a mind to join her.

He'd held her head, changed her out of clothes covered with regurgitated champagne, and forced aspirin and water down her throat. He'd cleaned the bathroom, washed her clothes, and heated up the soup he'd found in the refrigerator. There was nothing left to do to keep his mind off his dilemma. He was in love with Skye Sinclair and didn't know the first thing about how to handle it. Especially since he didn't think the feelings were reciprocated. Man, he should have run when he'd had the chance.

Logan sat back against the headboard of the bed watching Skye sleep curled around him. The puppy was snoring on his other side — out for the count too. The sight of Skye falling into the coffee table played on a continuous loop. If he'd been a split second slower, she'd be at the emergency room right now.

He shook his head, still not able to wrap his brain

around being in love. For a guy who never felt much when it came to women, he was making it up in spades when it came to what he felt about Skye.

There was always something different about her—he knew that from the first moment he saw her. He confirmed it at their first touch. He kept waiting for it to go away, or at least recede, but it had only gotten stronger. His dad was right—he'd figure it out soon enough . . . he hoped. He just wasn't sure how long it would take to come to grips with it. It had been a couple hours and he still felt a little sick.

He brushed his hand over Skye's hair, picked up Pepperoni, and left the bedroom. The dog's feet were running through the air before Logan ever set her on the floor. He watched Pepperoni run circles around the apartment, pulled out his phone, and called home. "Pop?" He shut the door to the newly cleaned bathroom to keep Pepperoni from going after the toilet paper— there were ribbons of the stuff draped around the bedroom. "I'm going to be a while. Skye's sick."

"Shit. What's the matter? Don't tell me it's food poisoning."

"No. Alcohol poisoning, maybe. From the sounds of it, Rocki and Patrice were trying to loosen her tongue—she drank too much champagne on an empty stomach. She was upset—she told me it was over between us and thought she was about to get fired."

"Fired? Why would I fire her? She's the best chef I've ever had."

"Because you're against the food tour, and you and everyone at the restaurant won't leave our relationship alone—that's why. She thinks that dating me is going to harm her career."

"So she pounded champagne? What the hell were Rocki and Patrice thinking? Skye's just a little bit of a thing."

"I don't think they took her size into consideration. She's sick as D.O.G. after he ate that whole bag of marsh-mallows—bag and all. I can't leave her like this, Pop. I want to make sure she's okay before I go. Can you put Nicki to bed for me? Tell her Skye's not feeling well and I want to keep an eye on her."

"Will do. Just be home to walk Nicki to school, okay?"

"I will."

"Do you want me to send over some soup or some-thing?"

"No, Skye's got a stocked refrigerator, but I don't think she's going to be eating anytime soon."

"That bad?"

"Oh, yeah."

"When she sobers up, be sure to tell her I'm not going to fire her. I'll tell her myself as soon as I can."

"Will do, Pop. Take care of Nicki, and I'll stop by in a while with Pepperoni to take D.O.G. out."

Logan paced the apartment for another hour and then peeked into the bedroom to check on Skye—she was still deathly pale, and out cold. "Time to wake up, sugar." He needed to get some more liquid in her. She was definitely going to be hungover—that was a given—but he didn't want her to be too hungover to work. She was already wigged-out enough. Having to call in sick might push her over the edge.

He sat on the bed and she rolled over onto him and cuddled close.

"Come on, Skye. You need to drink water and at least try to get some soup down."

She mumbled something, opened her beautiful blue

eyes, and took a few seconds to focus. "What are you doing here? And where are Rocki and Patrice?"

"I'm taking care of you. Your friends deserted you. Francis drove them home."

She scooted to a sitting position and then grabbed her head, as if holding on to it would keep it from exploding. He knew exactly how she felt. "God, I think I have the flu or something."

"Or something. Skye, you drank a ton of champagne. You don't have the flu; you're hungover." He handed her the bottle of water from the bedside table. "Drink this — slowly."

"I don't get hungover." She took a tentative sip and watched him.

"Well, you do now. I guess there's a first for everything." Today was full of firsts. It was the first time he'd wanted to hurt two women — Rocki and Patrice — for what they had done to Skye, the first time he freaked at the thought of someone he cared about getting hurt, and it was the first time he'd really taken care of a woman — well, aside from in the sexual sense.

In the past when Payton had gotten sick, he'd called her family's maid and asked her to stay. Heck, he'd even moved out of their bedroom one week when Payton had the flu, thinking she'd be more comfortable without him around. With Payton, it was the right thing to do, but that would never fly with Skye or him — not with the way he felt about her. No, if anyone was going to pick her up and run her to the john, it was going to be him. Sick and inexplicable, but true.

Skye closed her eyes because it hurt too much to look; then she must have fallen asleep again. When she opened her eyes the next time, she found Logan looking at her. "Why are you staring at me like that?"

"Maybe because even when you're green, you're still the most beautiful woman I've ever seen."

She laughed and her brain felt as if it were hemorrhaging. She pushed him away, or tried to. "God, don't make me laugh. It hurts."

"Champagne hangovers are the worst. Are you ready to sip a little chicken soup? I found it in the fridge along with ginger ale."

She rested her hand on her stomach and swallowed hard—not only no, but *hell no*. She might never eat again. "I'm not sure."

He held up a finger and then left the room. She thought about following him but didn't have the energy.

Logan returned a moment later with ginger ale. "Here—this might set better than the water. The more you drink, the better you'll feel."

She thought of all the champagne she drank. "It didn't work before."

He sat and wrapped an arm around her, pulling her to his chest, and she leaned against him—she was tired of holding herself up. "From the contents of your refrigerator, I wondered if you were a hangover aficionado. I had a friend who planned his hangovers. He made sure he was well stocked before he went out and got trashed. Sugar, you put that guy to shame."

"I can't imagine ever drinking again, no less planning to feel this way. I've never gotten drunk before."

"Today was the first time? So you always keep soup and ginger ale in the fridge?"

"Doesn't everyone? Chicken soup is comfort food

and ginger ale goes with everything, it settles the stomach, and what can I say—I love bubbles."

"I figured that out. When I brought you that magnum of champagne, I was hoping you'd share it with me, not drink it all by yourself."

"I didn't. Rocki and Patrice had it opened before I even got home." Little snippets of drunken memories flashed through her mind. She couldn't believe what she'd done, what she thought she might have said, the way she'd acted—

"What?"

She buried her face in his chest. "Oh God, I got drunk and I never get drunk."

"Yeah, we've covered that."

"But with Rocki and Patrice ... you don't understand—"

"Oh, sure, I do. They were on a fact-finding mission and got you trashed to get the goods. I heard all about it."

"You did?" She'd been mortified just remembering it herself, but it was nothing compared with the way she felt now.

"Yes. You said something about how you like it when I go all caveman on you. You told them that right before you fell off the chair." He lifted her chin, forcing her to look at him, and gave her a kiss and a sardonic smile. "Sugar, I'm glad you enjoy our sex life, but from now on, would you mind not sharing it with the dynamic duo? I'm never gonna live it down."

"Did I say anything else?" She knew she had; she just didn't know how much he'd heard.

"Something about a cyborg. Care to explain?"

"No." She remembered talking about his tongue and

his . . . "Oh God, shoot me now." She swallowed and coughed. She hadn't meant to say that out loud. She still wasn't positive she had. Maybe she just heard her own voice in her head.

Logan's gaze snapped back to hers. Yes, she continued to suffer from verbal diarrhea. She wished she'd known before drinking almost an entire bottle of champagne that, under the influence, she had very little ability to filter her thoughts.

"Sorry, I can't help you out there. The gun laws in the city are really strict. The only people who can get guns easily are criminals. I should know."

"I would think so, since your dad was a cop." She picked up a cracker from the sleeve he'd brought over and nibbled at the serrated edges—partly because it would keep her mouth too full to speak and partly because it tasted good right now.

Logan looked at everything in the room but at her. She wasn't sure if she was relieved or not. He took a deep breath. "That's not how I know. When I was a kid, I belonged to a gang—I was the youngest member of the Latin Kings. I had my first gun by the time I was in sixth grade. I never shot the damn thing—it scared the crap out of me. Guns were never my style. I specialized in building pipe bombs. If you're smart about it, pipe bombs allow you to be far away when they go boom."

"Boom?" Her stomach dipped just like the first and last time she'd gone on the Tower of Terror ride at Disney—only this was not a ride. Harrison had mentioned Logan's past, but she had no idea he'd been right about it. Nor did she think Logan had been that young. "You were blowing things up when you were Nicki's age? She's not allowed to play with matches and you were making bombs? What were you? Some kind of Unabomber savant? Did you know this stuff instinctively like Good Will Hunting knew calculus?"

"No." Logan wore that blasted fake smile—the same one she'd seen after the weirdness of their first time, the one that didn't meet his eyes, the one that gave her chills because of the emptiness she saw in him. "I got the basics from a book in the library and a few afternoons on the Internet gave me the rest of the information I'd needed. It was amazing what I could learn when I applied myself." He shook his head and stared into space, as if he were lost in the past. "I was a nerd back then, scrawny—a sitting duck. I learned quickly that knowledge was protection. I made sure I had a lot of knowledge the Latin Kings needed."

He didn't look at her, his gaze dropping to his feet. "Pop took me in when I was about twelve—after I was caught building bombs. He was my last chance before I ended up in juvie or jail." He fisted his big hands and then stretched them open, repeating the process over and over. "I'd spent the nine years before that bouncing from one foster family to another. I'd been dumped at a police station or hospital when I was about three, so apparently I had bonding issues. I probably still do—I guess it comes with the territory." He finally looked at her and in his eyes she saw fear, she saw embarrassment, and she saw hope.

When she'd met Logan, he'd looked no different from her brothers. Today she saw a man with a past she'd never suspected, maybe never believed—not really. She saw a man who had beaten the odds and had overcome more in his thirty years than most did in a lifetime. She saw a man with so many sides, he reminded her of a perfectly cut diamond—a brilliant being who refracted all the light around him and created beauty just by his presence.

"It's not that I don't appreciate this whole true-confessions thing. I just don't understand what you're going for." She looked into shocked eyes—yeah, well, join the club. This wasn't exactly what she'd been expecting either. "Why are you telling me this?"

"Because I care about you in ways I didn't know I could. Skye, I might have some issues, but when it comes to you and me, they don't seem to apply. I've been straight with you from the beginning and thought you deserved to know what you're getting into with me."

"But I'm not getting into anything with you. I told you why, and it has nothing to do with your past. We decided this afternoon that whatever this thing between us was is over, remember?"

"No, *we* haven't decided anything." Logan got that Cro-Magnon, alpha look in his deep-set eyes, the one that sent her heart racing, and had her thinking about running and squeezing her thighs together at the same time.

"Oh yes, we have." Her brain and body were completely out of sync—her brain said *run* and her treacherous body said *take me now*. She didn't know which was right. She was so disgusted with herself she felt like banging her head against a brick wall—she would have if her head hadn't already felt as though the devil had used it for kickball practice.

He took her face in his hands, forcing her to look at him. "You decided and you're wrong. You're not going to get fired. You're the best chef the Crow's Nest has ever had. Everyone cares about you—that's why they're sticking their noses into our lives. Things will calm down in a few days. Just give it a little time and we'll be fine."

She pushed against him to get some space, but his arms were locked around her like a vise. She opened her mouth to tell him she wanted to concentrate on her career. To tell him it had nothing to do with him, that it was her, and his kiss—a pleading, possessive, passionate, and mentally paralyzing kiss—anesthetized the space between her ears and sent shock waves through the rest of her body.

He held her in his arms and she felt the strongest man she knew shake. When he pulled away and stared into her eyes—there wasn't a trace of cyborg, just Logan—all of him. His gaze was so open, so honest, so full of an emotion she'd never seen before in the eyes of any other man. It took her breath away. No one had ever looked at her with such depth, with such surety, with such intensity.

"I know you're afraid. Hell, this thing between us scares me to death. But no matter how scary it is to feel the way I do about you, the thought of losing you is worse. Skye, I need you and I've never needed anyone. I feel things for you I've never felt for anyone. I want to spend the rest of my life with you, and I've never wanted to do that with anyone."

If Skye looked under the weather before, she looked like she had one foot in the grave now. Maybe it was a bad time to discuss this. He didn't know where his words were coming from, just that he needed to shut up because she was turning a pasty white, and it did not complement her coloring. Shit, he had no idea how to do any of this, because apparently he was doing it all wrong.

She was beginning to look oxygen deprived. Her mouth kept opening and closing like that of a fish out of water. Not really the reaction he'd been hoping for. Not that he'd planned this—which obviously was an error in judgment. "You might try breathing, sugar. You're beginning to turn blue—an improvement over the color you were a few hours ago, but it's still not optimal."

She took a deep breath and then blinked—several times. If he didn't know better, he'd think she was pulling a Payton, but that wasn't Skye. She looked as if she was questioning reality or wishing she'd wake from a nightmare—possibly both. "You want to spend the rest of your life with me?"

"That's the gist of it."

"That's like marriage."

Logan grinned. "That's what two people usually do when they love each other. Isn't it?"

"You can't love me. I'm difficult."

"I wouldn't say difficult. Challenging maybe."

She shook her head and then groaned and brought her hands to her face. "'Challenging' is just a polite way to say I'm a pain in the ass. I know I am. I've had plenty of people tell me."

He wasn't about to touch that one. She might be a pain in the ass on occasion, but he wanted her to be his pain in the ass. "I love you, Skye. I wouldn't change you even if I could." Although he might work on her tolerance for alcohol, but there was no need to tell her she was anything but perfect, and she was. She was perfect for him. "I fell half in love with you the first time I met you and you demanded to see the kitchen."

"I didn't even like you then."

"I know."

"No, you didn't."

"I did too. Ask Rocki and Francis. They had a theory as to why—"

"You can't love me. I'm your rebound girl." She crossed her arms and gave him one firm nod, as if that was all it would take to set the record straight. She looked inordinately pleased with her revelation.

"I hate to break it to you, Skye, but you're not my rebound girl." He wiped the sweat off his brow; things were going downhill fast and he had no idea how to stop this train wreck. "Don't you get it? I never loved Payton."

"Ever? Did you tell her you loved her?"

"No. You're the only woman I've ever loved."

"But you were engaged to her. You were going to marry a woman you didn't love?"

"She asked me to marry her. It seemed like a prudent business decision, and I didn't think I was capable of love—I had no idea what I was missing."

"You know, maybe you're mistaken about this whole love thing. You said yourself you know nothing about it."

"Nope. I've known in here—" He pounded his chest.

"Sounds like indigestion."

"I've known since the first time we made love. Maybe not in words, but I definitely knew something strange happened, something that changed everything, something that turned up the volume in my life, something that scared the shit out of me. It freaked me out."

"I was there, remember?" She took a deep breath and her hand went to her chest, as if she was trying unsuccessfully to slow her stampeding heart. Her eyes were dilated; her pulse point throbbed on her throat. "I caught that. I didn't know what it was, but it looked as if you wanted to run from the room screaming."

"I know. I'm sorry. I thought I was losing it. But then I think that pretty often where you're concerned."

"Thanks, I think."

"Don't mention it."

"God, Logan, I don't know what to do with this information. What do you want from me?"

Loving him back would be great, but it didn't look as if that was behind door number three. She hadn't said she loved him, but she hadn't said she didn't love him, so that meant it was a definite maybe. He could work with maybe. "Just keep an open mind and give us a chance."

She didn't look sold on the idea.

"My life is turned upside down, I'm waiting to hear about Nicki's paternity, and I just lost my job, my home. I know I don't look like a very good prospect right now, but think about it. I have some savings and there's a lot I can do. I could get back into brewing. There's a local brewer I could probably work for, or hell, I could start my own microbrewery."

"You want to brew beer?"

"Sure, I worked at a microbrewery while I was in school. I loved it. I'm good at it. I'd be brewing beer right now if I hadn't started dating Payton."

"So you went from brewing beer to wine because of a girl?"

Logan shrugged. "Pretty much. I met Payton and her family. Wine is fascinating and they gave me an internship. I did well. Payton was relatively low maintenance, and well, you know the rest."

"Is there anything you're not good at?"

"Talking you into giving us a chance, apparently."

"Logan." She put her hand on his. "It's not you. It's me."

And wasn't that just the kiss of death? The next thing she'd tell him was that he was nice and she just wanted to be friends. He cringed, because that was definitely every guy's worst nightmare phrase—especially after declaring his undying love.

She took a sip of ginger ale and then stared into her glass, watching the bubbles for a moment, as if she were trying to see the future in the bottom of her cup. "You just don't understand."

"Talk to me. Help me understand."

She reached over, set her glass on the bedside table, and moved to face him. Sitting with her legs crossed, she took his hand in hers and stared at them—his large and dark, hers small and so white. She took a deep breath and looked into his eyes. God, she had the most beautiful eyes he'd ever seen. "I just asserted my independence for the first time in my life, and I like it. I don't know if I want to give that up."

"You never told me that you ran away from a relationship."

She let out a laugh that was anything but funny. "More like six relationships. I'm the youngest of five. I'm the only daughter and my parents and brothers spent my entire life dictating how I should live it. They told me how to dress, how to act, and what job to do. I didn't grow up like you, Logan. I had every advantage. I was one of the privileged few. I was given everything. I just didn't want what they wanted me to want. I didn't want a life as a socialite and I certainly didn't want what they were willing to let me do with my life."

"Hold on, Skye. You've lost me. Back up."

"Okay." She looked away as if she was trying to organize her thoughts or get the courage to say what she needed to say.

Pinpricks of fear slid over his neck, his muscles tensed as if preparing for a deathblow.

"Have you ever heard of the Maxwell chain of restaurants?"

"Maxwell's? Of course. They're all over the West Coast. They carry Billingsly wines."

"I know. I ordered the wine. It's nice to meet you, Logan." She turned their hand-holding into a handshake. "I'm Skye Sinclair Maxwell—the youngest, lesser-known member of the Maxwell clan."

He sucked in a breath and pulled his hand out of hers so fast, you'd think she burned him, and maybe she had. What the hell? "You lied to me?" God, he was such a fool.

She reached for his hand again and held on tight, giving it a squeeze. "Not technically. Sinclair is my middle name. I just didn't mention my last name."

"And your family—"

She winced. "They have no clue where I am. That's why I couldn't tell you. When I found out who you were. I didn't want you to rat me out to my family. If you had known who I was, you would never have given me the job."

"That's not true." The look she shot him told him she didn't buy the line either. Chances were, she was right. But then, he had been desperate.

"You know my brothers."

And he knew Patrick Maxwell was going to kill him. Patrick might be a few inches shorter than him, but he was an ox who outweighed him by a good fifty pounds. He'd heard all about the Maxwell little sister. According to her brothers, she was off-limits. Hell, they joked about sending her to the nearest nunnery. "I play poker with Patrick and Colin at the club."

"I figured as much. And think about it—why would I

tell you? I wanted to get a job because of my expertise and not my family name."

"I don't understand why you came all the way out here. Why didn't you just work with them?"

"I want my own restaurant. Every one of my brothers was given their own restaurant when they turned thirty. I worked my ass off for years. I did everything they wanted me to. I paid my dues. The problem was they were too happy letting me run the business end of the restaurants to give me my own kitchen. I hate being a paper pusher, so I quit and came here. I was determined to get my own kitchen and make my way in the cooking world on my own without using my family name and that's just what I did."

"Your plan was to work in Red Hook?"

"No, I came to Manhattan, but I couldn't very well get a job in any of the trendy New York restaurants without revealing where I'd been working, could I? Especially since I didn't want to use my family as a reference."

"So you thought you'd slum it?"

"No. I just thought I'd have a better chance in one of the boroughs, and I was right. Okay, my best friend, Kelly, was right. I hadn't planned on running into you of all people."

"If you belong to the Napa Valley Country Club, how come I've never seen you there?"

"Because I avoid it whenever possible. Do I look like I'd fit in with the country-club set?" She spread her arms, the sweatshirt he'd pulled over her head after he'd cleaned her up slid off to one side, and he wanted to kiss the spot where her neck and shoulder met. He was such a sap.

He looked at her through new eyes—this explained

the shoes and the expensive lingerie. Still, he couldn't see her doing lunch with Payton and the society sisterhood. No, his Skye wasn't the type—hell, she shopped at thrift stores and seemed to enjoy it. "I can't see you lunching with the ladies, if that's what you're asking. That's not to say you wouldn't fit in just fine if that's what you wanted." Skye had grown up with everything he'd ever thought he wanted. She had the acceptance. She had the money. She belonged in that world. The weird thing was she resented it. She didn't seem happy to have any of the things he'd worked his entire life for.

"That's just it. I don't want any of it. I don't need to see and be seen. All I want—all I've ever wanted—was my own kitchen. Since I left, I realized just getting my own kitchen isn't enough. I want to make it on my own. I want to earn my own kitchen, not have it handed to me because my last name is Maxwell."

She crossed her arms and got that determined glint in her eyes that always half scared him and half turned him on. Aw, hell, there was no halfway about it. A determined Skye Sinclair—make that Maxwell—was a total turn-on.

"I have skills. I went to the California Culinary Academy in San Francisco. I did well. And as soon as I graduated, my family threw me in the business office. Sure, they'd let me play in the kitchens when it suited them. I have a knack for creating specials using seasonal food, but as soon as they had the recipes, they'd toss me back to deal with human resource issues, OSHA regulations, compliance, insurance, you name it. I'm good at the business end, but I'm better in the kitchen—not that they'd ever admit it."

It looked as if her head of steam had run out. She toyed with the blanket, picking the pills off the fabric, seemingly lost in thought, and let out a sigh. "Unfortunately, since I'm the only girl, the only sibling who has the ability to give birth, the only one without a penis, my brothers and my father decided I would eventually want to get married and have kids and wouldn't be able to handle my own restaurant. It was just a ridiculous excuse to keep me in the office because none of my brothers wanted to hire someone outside the family to keep the books. I felt trapped, so I quit. I had a fight with Paddy, packed my bags, took all the cash I had on hand—which wasn't much—and flew out the next day. I've been living on what I earn at the Crow's Nest. I haven't used any of my credit cards because I can't afford to have the sphincter police find me."

His head shot up. "The sphincter police?"

"My brothers."

"Shit, your family doesn't know where you are? They must be worried sick."

Skye shrugged. "Paddy told my parents I went on vacation."

"For a month?"

"That's his problem. He's probably starting to sweat about it right about now. He's going to have to fess up soon."

She was slumming it. She'd come here and thought she'd play with him, and then toss him into the bay when the excitement wore off. His face heated, blood roaring in his ears with the strength of a high tide during a full moon, pounding through his veins. Fear, anger, and hurt grew into one big throbbing force that knocked the wind out of him. "So what am I to you? A temporary fling? Did the debutante run away from home to play on the wrong side of the other bay?"

"No." Her face turned red and the pulse on her neck throbbed as fast as it did when they were making love. She looked about to blow her top or hit him. Instead she just crossed her arms and glared.

Good. Misery loved company, and he was plenty pissed himself, not to mention miserable and hurt. Shit, she had really done a number on him.

"This is no game. I'm not slumming it. And I'm not playing with you either. I quit my job, plain and simple. It's not my fault my brothers expect me to fall on my face and go running home crying when things don't work out. Don't you see why I have to make it? I can't go back to that."

He took a huge mental step back. He shut down his emotions, locked them in a box to deal with later, and separated himself. He looked at the facts, because right now, facts were all he could deal with. "You went from cooking at Maxwell's to cooking at the Crow's Nest— that's not really a lateral move."

"I only cooked when they needed me, which wasn't enough. They took all the credit for the dishes I created. It wasn't fair. I let them take advantage of me for years until I hit the breaking point. I quit and I don't regret it. I love what I'm doing now. The Crow's Nest isn't a five-hundred-seat restaurant, but that's just a difference in the number of staff. I've always thought I could handle my own kitchen, but now I know I can."

So, she accomplished what she wanted. She proved she could be successful on her own. Where the hell did that leave him? All those feelings he stuffed into the box exploded with the force of a pipe bomb. "Are you going back?" God, he hated how fucking pathetic he sounded. Even though he was pissed as hell, even though she'd lied to him, even though he felt as if she'd just filleted his heart, the thought of her leaving left him cold.

"To Maxwell's and my brothers? Hell, no."

He blew out a breath of relief, until he remembered she still seemed to want nothing to do with him. Oh sure, she liked the sex, but he wanted more than just a bed buddy. It surprised him how much more. But then today was the day for firsts, wasn't it? The first time he'd been taken in by a woman. Still, he had to ask. "So if you're not going back, and you're happy at the Crow's Nest, then what's the problem?"

"I don't have a problem."

"Yet you don't want to get involved with me."

Tears leaked from the corners of her eyes. He cringed. Real tears scared the crap out of him. He couldn't imagine Skye crying for effect or to get her own way. No, Skye wasn't a crier and she wasn't happy, as evidenced by the angry way she swiped at her tears.

"It's not that I don't want to get involved."

His get-real look had her scrambling.

"Okay, I didn't want to get involved with you or anyone for that matter. I didn't come here to get messed up in a relationship—I had other things on my mind. It's nothing personal, but a relationship wasn't even on my radar." She stared at the center of his chest and he thought for sure this was the end. Then she looked into his eyes. "It was the last thing I wanted. I couldn't help it, though. I am involved. Deeply involved. More involved than I've ever been with any man before. The thing is, Logan, I don't want to give up everything I achieved to have a relationship with you."

Relief washed over him and he drew in what felt like his first full breath since he'd found out who she was.

"Skye." He pulled her onto his lap, wrapped his arms around her, and felt whole for the first time in his life. He kissed her before forcing her to look at him. "I'm not asking you to give up a damn thing. God knows I want you to be happy. If you want to work, fine. If you want to stay at home, that would be fine too."

"But you're talking marriage—"

"Eventually, maybe. I want to be with you, but I have to stay here in Red Hook for Nicki's sake. I can't take her away from the only home she's ever known and all the people she loves."

"I wouldn't expect you to."

"So you're okay staying with me and Nicki in Red Hook?"

CHAPTER 13

"Whoa, I never said I'd stay with you and Nicki." Skye wiped the tears from her face, grabbed a tissue and blew her nose, and stared at Logan. He just asked her, all crying and snotty and hungover, to live with him. Maybe she was still drunk. Maybe she was dreaming, and if it was a dream, she wasn't sure whether this was a nightmare or not. God, why did everything have to be so confusing? "I mean, I care about you and Nicki, but as much as I love the Crow's Nest—"

"It's not exactly the kind of restaurant you want to spend your life working in."

"I don't know. It's not like I have a five-year plan. Hell, I don't have a five-minute plan." Well, except to never drink again, but that was more a lifetime thing. "Maybe the Crow's Nest isn't the be-all and end-all, but it's a great start."

"You could work in Manhattan."

"I could." But work wasn't what she was worried about. Work wasn't what was keeping her from jumping him, making love to him like a wild woman, and then running to the closest justice of the peace. Losing a job wouldn't break her heart, but buying into this whole relationship, labeling all the feelings she'd been avoiding since starting this thing with Logan, letting him in more than she already had, was a recipe for disaster. She needed a reality check, and so did he. It just sucked that the job fell on her. "Logan, what if Nicki isn't your daughter? Have you thought of that?"

He looked straight into her eyes and she caught her breath. He looked the same way when he'd told her he loved her. So open, so certain, so real and strong. "I love Nicki. She still needs a family and I want to give that to her. I want to be that for her. I want us to be her parents. It doesn't matter if I'm her biological parent or not."

Of course it mattered. He of all people should know how important it was to know where you came from and who your parents were, but that wasn't the point she was trying to make. "Is that what you told Payton?"

She could tell by the way his face blanched it was exactly what he'd told Payton. Knowing Logan, he'd even used the same words. "Skye, with you everything is different. I'm different. I never loved Payton."

And as much as she wanted to believe it, she wasn't sure he even knew what he was feeling. Logan certainly believed he did and talked a good game. Lord knew she wanted to believe him. She wanted to believe so much it scared her, so much she could easily ignore that voice in her head that told her this was all an illusion on both their parts. "I know things with us are different. We're attracted to each other. We're great together in the sack and out of it. We like each other and I adore Nicki. Maybe you're right. Maybe you love me. Maybe this thing between us will work out. But then maybe I'm just convenient."

She hadn't meant to give him a verbal low blow, but the way his breath rushed out as if he'd had the wind knocked out of him told her she might not have meant to, but did anyway.

He rose from the bed and paced. His hands clenched and released with every step. He crossed the room, turned, and stomped back again and then repeated the process. He stopped, ran his hands through his hair until it stood on end, and then faced her. "You think I'm with you because you're convenient?" His voice went low and gravelly, and made all the hair on her arms stand up. His eyes flared with anger so hot, she felt the burn in the pit of her stomach. A vein throbbed at his temple and it looked as if he were about to explode. "You." He pointed to her and back to himself. "Our timing. This relationship is anything but convenient. Look at us, Skye." He grabbed the back of his neck with both hands, either to loosen the tense muscles or to keep from strangling her—she wasn't sure which. "We're both practically homeless. Hell, you're hiding from your family. As for me, I don't even know who my birth parents are."

A picture of Logan as a little three-year-old boy dumped at a police station took up residence in her heart and mind. He must have been so scared, so totally alone. When she looked at him now, she knew that little boy was hiding inside of him and all she wanted to do was hold him and tell him she'd never leave him. She shook her head to dispel the image and tears spilled down her cheeks. She wiped them away, but they kept coming. Shit. She hated crying and the more she cried, the more nervous he looked, and more out of control she felt. She sniffled and hiccuped like a little kid trying not to bawl. She took three deep breaths, doing her best to get a grip, wiped her face, and reached for him, pulling him back onto the bed.

He sat and shook his head, his eyes closing as if he couldn't stand to look at her, as if it hurt. "Skye, I've lost my job, my home, and I might have a ten-year-old daughter who thinks of me as a brother. It's a mess no matter how you slice it. But that doesn't mean I don't love you." His eyes finally met hers and held. "The only thing in my life I'm sure of is that I love you."

Skye's lips trembled and she pressed them together until the trembling stopped. She didn't want to say this. She'd rather tell him anything but this, but she didn't have a choice. She had to be honest even if it hurt, and this one was a whopper of a hurt. "Look at this from my perspective. You were engaged to Payton and only broke up with her because she rejected Nicki. You want to get married—maybe you feel like Nicki needs a mom, or maybe you don't want to be alone. The thing is . . . I don't think I could take it if a while down the road you realize you never loved me at all. It would kill me to find out I'm nothing more than Payton's replacement."

He looked like a powder keg ready to go off. He did the whole caveman with a bad-boy twist to perfection. "You're not Payton's replacement." He grabbed her upper arms and turned her toward him.

She wished she could turn away, but he forced her to face him.

"I never wanted to marry her. Our engagement was a fucking business decision—one I'll never live down." He held her arms in his grip and gave her a shake. "I didn't know I was capable of feeling these things. . . ." A look of defeat crossed his face and sliced through her like her favorite knife through a tin can—jagged and painful. "I didn't know I was capable of feeling anything until I met you. I've never felt anything like what I feel for you. I never dreamed I'd fall in love. Ever. I don't need a wife or a mother figure for Nicki and I'm sure as hell not afraid of being alone." He released her arms and stared into her eyes. "Skye, I spent a lifetime alone—I survived just fine. The only thing I'm afraid of is losing you, because, God help me, I need you."

Skye wrapped her arms around his neck and when her lips touched his, her battle with self-restraint was lost. She'd never initiated a kiss, much less sex, but at that moment, all she wanted, all she could think of, all she needed, was Logan.

She pushed up his sweater, her hands sliding over his chest while she devoured his mouth—drowning in his taste, the feel of his tongue against hers. She was on top for once, in control, and Logan did nothing to take it from her. Not that he couldn't; he could move her around like a Barbie doll when he wanted to, but this time he sat back and let her love him.

She broke the kiss, straddled his hips, and rose to her knees to pull his shirt over his head before going for his button fly.

Logan stilled her hands.

She sat back on his lap and looked at him, really looked at him. He was still angry if the tick in his jaw was anything to go by. Something was definitely wrong. She snuck a peek at his prominent bulge, so it wasn't an equipment malfunction. "What's the matter?"

"I don't need a pity fuck." His placid expression seemed forced and his quiet, bored monotone amplified his indignation to a heart-shattering volume.

Her face flushed and stung, as if she'd just stepped

from a sauna into an ice storm. Icy needles pricked her flaming skin. Damn men and their freakin' fragile egos. She blew out a breath, dragged in more frigid air, and blew it out again. "Well, that's good, because this isn't a pity fuck." She got in his face. "Tell me something, Logan. What was it when you picked me up and threw me over your shoulder?"

Vacant eyes stared back at her, but she didn't look away. He shrugged one shoulder and the muscles in his neck twitched like a cat's tail before a strike. "I don't know. I needed you."

She wanted to touch him but drove her nails into her palms until her knuckles turned white. "So, it's okay for you to need me, but I can't need you?"

He looked like a kid who'd been expecting a beating and was given a lollipop instead. "You need me?"

So much it scared her. "Have you ever let anyone love you?" God, there was that look again, unsure as if searching for an angle, tentative, trepidatious.

"No one ever tried."

She didn't know what to say to that. A tear slid from her eye, and her throat slammed shut on all the words that raced through her mind. She leaned forward slowly and kissed his forehead. Her fingertips followed, smoothing the furrow between his brows. She kissed each eyelid as she traced his cheekbones.

His jaw clenched beneath her fingers and she ran her hands down his neck. Her tongue slid over the shell of his ear. "You need to relax. Trust me."

He blew out a breath, wrapped his hands around her waist, and dragged her closer. His mouth came down on hers, hard, demanding. She went with it—she didn't have much choice in the matter. His hands were everywhere as if grasping for control. His body tensed beneath hers, shaking, shaken.

She pulled her mouth away and nipped at his lower lip to get his attention. "It's my turn, remember?"

Her question was answered by a guttural groan as he ripped her sweatshirt over her head and dragged her pants down.

She yanked on his button fly and all the buttons popped—his erection sprang free. She slid off his lap and let him kick off his jeans before she went in for the kill and took him into her mouth.

She heard his sharp intake of breath, a muffled curse, and then his hand tangled in her hair. He didn't move, didn't breathe, as she slid farther down. Her hand gripped the base; her tongue traced the slit, and then swirled around the sensitive head. She squeezed her fist and drove her mouth down to meet it.

The breath he'd been holding whooshed out as she ran her other hand between his legs.

God, she loved the taste of him, the feel of power she held over him, the way he shook with his need to move. He vibrated beneath her, his dick jumped in her fist, and she took him deep until he hit the back of her throat.

He held her head in his hand, his fingers spread, but he didn't push, he didn't raise his hips, he didn't move. He stilled and gave up the cloak of control he'd always worn.

Skye had never been in this position before—not like this. She'd never known that control was such a complete turn-on. She'd never felt so powerful. Every groan, every twitch of his muscles, every intake of breath, was a sign. He was so close. She wanted him to lose it, but she wanted to watch his face when he did.

She sucked hard, moving off him, and released him

with a pop before she moved up his big body. Kissing him. Determined to remain in control. She drove him on further with her mouth and sank onto him. His hands were still buried in her hair as she lifted herself off and then dropped back down on him—her breath shot out as he hit her womb. Her fingers dug into his shoulders and she held his gaze. The look in his eyes sent her right into an orgasm so powerful it took her by surprise. It rolled over her and she had no choice but to go with it. She rode it out and every move she made intensified its power. Magnified it, and had her gasping for breath.

He gripped her hips, dragging her closer with her every thrust. Going so deep she swore he touched her heart, and when his hands tightened, holding her to him, she wiggled and he bucked beneath her. She'd never felt anything like that—she'd never felt so close, so immersed, so connected to anyone before.

She'd never felt so loved.

When his gaze locked on hers, her name flew from his lips and he came apart in her arms.

She followed him over, collapsing on top of him as little earthquakes shot through her. Tears rolled down her cheeks and onto him and she hid her face as she kissed the center of his chest, his heart pounding beneath her lips.

When she looked at him, she knew she was done for. She was helplessly, totally, and probably tragically in love with Logan Blaise.

Logan held Skye. He hadn't missed the tears she shed as they made love. He hadn't missed the look in her eyes— a look he'd never seen before. And he hadn't missed the fear that followed.

He'd have to be blind, deaf, and dumb to miss the way she dragged the sheet up over her body as if trying to protect herself from something—maybe from him.

She didn't speak as he held her, but her silence couldn't drown out the fight she seemed to be having with herself. Her body lay rigid against his and he did his best to soothe her, massaging tense muscles, working them one by one until they relaxed and sleep overtook her.

He watched her sleep and then rose to take Pepperoni out. He went home to grab D.O.G. and found a very sleepy Nicki wearing her Angry Birds nightgown sitting on the couch with her arm around the dog, waiting for him. "Hey, Nicki. What are you doing up so late? Your bedtime was an hour ago."

She stood and stretched as Pepperoni jumped on her skinny legs, trying to reach her face. She bent down to pet the pup and got a lick on the lips for her effort. "I knew you'd come home to take D.O.G. out and I wanted to find out how Skye is." She walked up to him and gave him a hug, resting her chin on his chest and looking up at him with eyes too old for her ten years. "I heard Pop on the phone with you."

"Shit."

"Logan, you'd better not say that in front of Bree when she gets home. She makes Pop and Storm put five dollars in the curse jar every time." She shook her head. "Bree said at the rate they're going, they'll have my college paid for in no time."

"I'm sorry." He took Pepperoni off her leash, peeled a five off his billfold, and stuck it in the jar. At least it was going to a good cause.

Pepperoni ran rings around D.O.G., biting on his ears and tail.

"Come here, Nicki. We need to talk."

Her eyes widened and she took a step back. "Am I in trouble?"

"No, kiddo. Nothing like that." He led her over to Pop's chair and sat, pulling her into his lap. "Nicki, Skye and I are dating—"

"Duh. Everyone knows that."

She leaned against him and rested her head on his chest. At least she wasn't scared anymore.

"Skye wasn't comfortable with everyone at the restaurant knowing we're seeing each other."

"Why? That's kinda dumb, isn't it?"

He agreed totally, but he couldn't very well cop to it. "We're working together, so it complicates things."

"How come?"

"Skye doesn't want everyone to think the only reason I hired her was because I liked her."

"Why would you hire someone you didn't like?"

Maybe he should have Nicki talk to Skye. She'd be much better than he was at pleading his case. "I like Wendy and Simon and Francis, but not the way I like Skye. Do you understand?"

She straightened up and looked at him just before rolling her eyes. "You don't just like Skye, Logan. You love her." Nicki looked so sure about it. As if it were the most obvious thing in the world.

"How'd you know?"

She shook her head as if asking the question made him too stupid to live. "'Cause you look at Skye the very same way Storm looks at Bree. And Skye looks at you the same way Bree looks at Storm. Skye tries to hide it, but she pretty much sucks at hiding stuff."

"Nicki. 'Sucks' is not a nice word to use."

"No, but it works, so I'm going with it. I'm not a baby, Logan. I know lots of things."

When the kid was right, she was right. She was also incredibly bright and she saw and heard everything. He couldn't very well lie about the way he felt about Skye, and he didn't want to ever lie to Nicki. "I do love Skye."

"And you didn't love Payton, but that was okay, 'cause she didn't love you either. She just liked you sometimes."

Wow. Was she psychic? "Skye went home after the tasting and Rocki and Patrice were there with a bottle of champagne opened. Skye hadn't eaten anything, and she's not much bigger than you. So when she drank, the alcohol hit her hard."

"My mom used to drink." Nicki didn't look at him; she just stared into space, as if she were watching a movie that only she could see. "She used to get mean whenever she drank, and she drank a lot. Sometimes she wouldn't eat just so she could get drunk faster. Is that what Skye did? Did she get mean?"

"No, honey. God, no. Skye made a mistake. It was an accident, and I can pretty much guarantee she'll never do it again. She's not feeling too good right now. And Skye didn't get mean. There's not a mean bone in her body."

"Really?"

"I swear." He held up his hand in what he thought might be the Boy Scout salute, but could very well have been the *Star Trek* Vulcan salute. He'd never been a Boy Scout, and he'd often wondered whether he was as emotionless as a Vulcan—until recently, anyway. "Skye's really embarrassed. Rocki and Patrice are both much bigger than she is, so they didn't know how hard it would hit her."

"They just wanted to get her to tell them all about

you. I heard them talking. They said they wanted all the gory details."

"Great. Has anyone ever told you it's not nice to eavesdrop on adults?"

"All the time, but if I didn't listen, I'd never know anything."

"Kids aren't supposed to know everything."

"No, but we do anyway. So we might as well know all the facts. It's scary when everyone hides stuff. I used to be scared all the time, Logan. I don't ever want to feel like that again."

Just the thought of Nicki being scared had guilt stabbing at him. Damn, it was all his fault. He should have kept in touch with Marisa; he should have made sure there were no consequences to their actions. He should never have slept with her in the first place, but he couldn't regret it. "I'm so sorry."

Nicki shrugged. "It's no big deal. No one knew about me and my mom. Mom just knew Pop took kids in like us, so she dumped me with him. But it's good, because I love him and you and Storm and Bree and Skye. No one here gets drunk and mean. No one hits. No one passes out. I hated when Momma would go to sleep and I couldn't wake her up. I thought she was dead." She shook her head, almost as if she was trying to erase the memories. That was something he was good at. He locked all the bad stuff away so he never had to think about it. But with Nicki around, things kept popping out of the box that had been sealed shut.

"There's always lots of food. I'm not hungry all the time anymore. And the best part is everyone here wants me around. You do too, don't you?"

"Nicki, I'd do anything to keep you forever. I'll always

love you and I'm always going to want you around. Same with Bree and Storm and Pop. You're one of us. You're my family. I'll always be here for you. That's a promise and I don't make promises I can't keep, so there's nothing to be afraid of. We won't let anyone or anything hurt you ever again. And if you have a problem, you come to me. I'll take care of whatever it is."

"Even if I did something bad?"

"Even then. We'll solve the problem, and then we'll deal with whatever you did. You might get punished, but you'll always be safe; you'll always be loved. Have you done something you need to tell me about?"

She thought about it and then smirked. "Nope, not lately. I've been on my best behavior so Bree and Storm will bring me a big present from New Zealand. Did you know New Zealand is on the other side of the world and their toilets flush in the opposite direction?"

"Yep. I did."

"You're real smart. I bet you never got into trouble when you were a kid."

"You're wrong there. I did a lot of stupid things when I was your age. I'm just lucky Pop set me straight."

"Storm says we're all really lucky. He's pretty smart too. I miss him and Bree. I wish they'd come home already, but I don't want you to leave."

He was in no rush for Bree and Storm to return—not that he didn't want them to. He just wasn't sure what the hell he was going to do when they got back. He wouldn't have the Crow's Nest to run, and he wasn't the idle sort. He had to make some plans.

She looked at him from under those dark lashes of hers, almost as if she were hiding. "Are you going to go back to California when they come home?"

"No. I'm afraid you're stuck with me, kiddo. I might have to go back to tie up some loose ends, but I'm moving back to Red Hook for good."

"You promise?"

"Yes. I promise." He gave her a kiss on the forehead and a pat on the tush. "Now you need to get to bed. Have you brushed your teeth?"

"Logan, I'm not a baby."

"I know, but you're growing up way too fast. I'd like you to stay a little kid for a while yet. There's no rush to grow up, you know. Now, jump into bed and I'll tuck you in before I take the dogs for a walk. I'm going to crash at Skye's place to make sure she's okay, but I'll be back in the morning to take you to school."

"You're going to bring D.O.G. back, though, right?"

"I sure will. He likes sleeping with you and your bear."

She jumped off his lap and ran to her bedroom and scooted under the covers. He grabbed the rainbow-colored bear that was almost as big as she was and tucked it in beside her. "G'night, Nicki. I love you." He gave her a kiss on the forehead and pushed her hair out of her eyes.

"Forever and always?"

"Forever and always."

"I love you too, Logan." She wrapped her skinny arms around his neck and kissed his cheek before curling around her teddy bear.

He hit the lights, made sure her night-light was on, and then tiptoed out just in time to catch Pop eavesdropping. Nicki had nothing on Pop—at least she came by it honestly. "Monkey see, monkey do."

Pop stood there in his boxers and T-shirt. "Are you calling me a monkey?"

"You've been called worse."

"Isn't that the truth?" He let out his shotgun laugh and Logan waved his hands to tell him to keep the volume down. "So, I heard you've figured out that you're in love with Skye, huh? It took you long enough. Still, I always knew you were smarter than Storm. It took him a hell of a lot longer to realize he was in love with Bree."

"Skye never hit me upside the head with a cast-iron skillet."

"Not yet, but don't let the fact that she's no bigger than a minute fool you. The girl's Irish. She may not be a redhead, and she might be tiny, but she's got a hell of a temper. She just hasn't aimed it at you yet."

"You might be right about that."

"So have you told her yet?"

He scrubbed his face with his hands and went to sit on the couch. From the looks of Pop, this might be a long talk. He was just glad Pepperoni already peed before they came over.

Pop took a seat on his chair and for once in his life was silent—never a good sign.

Logan blew out a breath. "Yes, I told her. I completely fucked it up."

Pop shot him that annoying smile of his. "That bad, huh? You need to talk to her, son."

"Oh, we talked. Did you know she's Skye Sinclair Maxwell, of the restaurant chain Maxwell's? Shit, Pop. I thought I fell for a chef, not a freakin' debutante whose family's fortune rivals Payton's."

"Skye is no Payton Billingsly, that's for damn sure.

And if you can't see that, maybe you're not as smart as you look."

"I know she's nothing like Payton, but that doesn't change the fact that she lied to me."

"She didn't lie for shits and giggles, son. She was just playing fast and loose with the truth. She had her reasons. Those brothers of hers are a lot for a girl to handle. They've kept her locked up for years."

"She told you?"

"Nah." He waved his hand. "I have sources all over the country. It didn't take me twenty-four hours to put all the pieces together. One of my buddies on the force knows a guy who knows a guy who works in the kitchen of Patrick's restaurant. He heard the whole thing. Skye quit, and when Patrick didn't want her to leave, she threatened to fillet him while she packed her knives. I told you she has one hell of a temper."

"And four overprotective brothers, who, I'm sure, are looking for her. They told her parents she was on vacation."

"I know that too. Looks like both you and Skye have a lot of unfinished business to settle. It might be a good thing to put your houses in order before you get in too deep."

"Before? Shit, Pop, I'm in so deep, I've gone under for the third time. I love her."

"Does she love you?"

"Nicki thinks she does."

A smile split Pop's wrinkled face. "Don't discount that—the kid has a way of reading people."

"I know. It's almost scary. Skye doesn't know what she feels, and she certainly doesn't trust that I know what I'm feeling. She thinks I'm on the rebound, or lonely. She thinks I see her as a replacement for Payton, or that I'm looking for a mother for my child. She'd believe anything other than the truth." He ran his hands through his hair and then shook his head. "I've never felt this way before, Pop. I never knew I could. I always thought that when it came to me, whatever part of the brain that deals with love had been surgically removed."

"Not removed, son, just locked away for self-protection. Skye just happened to have the key. Now all you have to do is wait and see if she wants to keep it. In the meantime, it wouldn't hurt to get your shit together. You need to figure out what the hell you want to do with your life and settle your accounts with Billingsly. I have a feeling this deal with you and Payton isn't as finished as you think it is."

"What's that supposed to mean? There was absolutely no ambiguity. I told her in no uncertain terms it was over. I never would have started something with Skye—"

Pop waved his hand and sent the dogs into a frenzy. "I know, but that's not what I'm talking about. You've had your hands full with your recent revelation. Falling up to your eyeballs in love sometimes slows a man's processing speed. Let me ask you this: Doesn't it strike you as odd that you haven't heard a word from your boss? If you've been fired, don't you think he would have said something?"

Maybe Pop was right about the whole processing-speed deal. "I hadn't thought of it. I'll call Walt tomorrow. But even if I have a job, I can't take Nicki away from here. She needs to be around her family. She's just beginning to get her feet under her."

"Remember what I said about Nicki. We don't know anything yet."

"A man knows his own child."

"Maybe, maybe not. I guess we'll find out soon enough."

"Not soon enough for me. Did you hear what she said about Marisa?"

"Yes. Marisa always had trouble holding her booze. She had all the signs of an alcoholic and an addict. I'll never forgive myself for not finding out about Nicki when I had the chance."

Logan looked up from staring at his hands and found Pop's face twisted into a grimace. "When was that?"

"Nicki was probably two when Marisa brought her into the bar. Marisa was looking for work and I showed her the door. She never said anything, but hell, son, I could do the math. I knew she spent time with you boys."

"You had no way of knowing."

"Don't change the fact that I should have asked. I should have listened to my instincts. I should have helped the girl out. I'll spend a long time in purgatory for that one. I'll regret it for the rest of my life, and believe me, son, regrets are a bitch."

"Tell me about it." Nicki went through hell and back because he hadn't cared enough about her mother. Marisa had been just like every other woman he'd been with. Every other woman but Skye.

CHAPTER 14

Skye awoke to find Logan hovering over her wearing a shit-eating grin and holding a Starbucks cup close to her nose. To say he was a sight for sore eyes was an understatement—she didn't know how anyone could look that good this early in the morning. But then so was the coffee.

"I brought you a red-eye."

Okay, maybe this whole love thing wasn't so bad after all. She could get used to having a gorgeous man waking her up with a cup of coffee every morning. She sat up in bed, the sheet pooling at her waist, and reached for the cup. She drank half of it—she couldn't remember ever being as thirsty as she was right then.

Logan wore a horny schoolboy smirk and stared at her bare breasts.

She tugged up the sheet and tucked it under her arms and smirked right back before draining her cup. It served him right. He should have brought her a venti instead of a tall.

"I called Harrison and asked him to take the early shift and do the prep work so you could sleep in."

"Thanks."

"How are you feeling?"

"Like I might just live if you have more coffee." She set her empty on the bedside table and reached for his.

He released his cup and she took a sip, congratulating herself on bogarting his coffee.

"That should prove my love. I've never let anyone swipe my coffee before." He pulled her onto his lap, and kissed her neck, breathing her in. "God, you smell good. All warm and sleepy. I want to crawl back in bed with you and spend the rest of the day making love."

"Too bad we have to work." She kissed him, hoping the coffee covered her morning breath. "Now let go of me so I can get a shower."

He groaned as she slid off his lap and walked naked to the bathroom. "Do you want something to eat?"

She looked at him over her shoulder. "Toast?"

He stood and adjusted the bulge in his pants. "Right. Another first. You're either brave or reckless."

"How can you screw up toast?"

She took a quick shower and then dressed in record time. When she left the bedroom, she saw Logan in her kitchen. He had his phone to his ear and talked while buttering a pile of toast. She walked up just in time to see him set it on a plate with eggs and petrified bacon. Her already queasy stomach clenched.

"Fine. I'll go to Portland, but I need to meet with you before that. I'll fly into San Francisco Thursday night. We'll go to the competition together and I'll catch a red-eye home from Portland on Sunday."

She took a slice of bacon and stuffed it in her mouth. It disintegrated. It wasn't burned, just really overcooked.

Still, it kept her from asking who he was talking to and what was going on. She reached for the silverware and grabbed a cup of coffee before sitting at the table and pulling her leg up under her.

"Just have a car meet me at the airport. I'll e-mail you my itinerary as soon as I make the reservation." He ended the call, let out a sigh, and grabbed his plate. "It looks as if I'm going to the American Wine Society Commercial Wine Competition this weekend."

"Oh."

"I can't get out of it. My appearance is expected—we have wines entered. It's a publicity thing. Do you think you could take Pepperoni and stay with Pop and Nicki while I'm gone?"

"Sure." All she wanted to know was who exactly he was meeting with in California before flying to Portland, but couldn't ask. She toyed with the runny eggs and watched him eat.

He looked up from his plate. "Not hungry?"

"Not really."

"I'd think you'd be starved. You haven't eaten anything worth mentioning since the day before yesterday."

Maybe this whole love thing didn't agree with her, but then it could be his cooking too. She wasn't a huge fan of eggs—especially if they were runny. Nor was she a fan of him leaving and spending the weekend with Payton. She never thought she'd be the jealous type, but then how would she know? She'd never been in love before. She wasn't sure if she liked it. She definitely didn't like the way she felt knowing he was going to be in close proximity to Perfect Payton. She couldn't compete. She didn't even want to try. But then the thought of losing something she just discovered was unappealing as well. She wished she could just keep Logan with her and forget the rest of the world existed.

She wished she'd never gotten involved with him. If she had just listened to her instincts, her heart would be safe—now it was anything but.

Logan reached across the table and took her plate. "I know I'm not the best cook, sugar. But at least eat the toast."

She took another bite of the overbuttered, barely toasted bread, washed it down with her coffee, and followed him into the kitchen, wrapped her arms around his waist, and leaned against his back. "I'm sorry. I appreciate the effort." The mess of a kitchen, however, was something she could have done without.

He turned in her arms and kissed her forehead. "I've already fed Pepperoni and took her out, so she'll be fine in her crate." He stepped away. "Let's go. I have travel plans to make. I'll catch Pepperoni." He corralled the puppy while she dragged on her sweatshirt. "Here." Logan tossed her his jacket. "Put this on. We need to get you a coat before I leave."

She set his jacket on the back of the chair. She had no intention of wearing it.

"It's getting too cold to be walking around in a sweatshirt. You'll freeze." He pulled her into his arms and kissed her, holding her chin in his hand so she had to look at him. "Don't get me wrong—I have no problem warming you up, but I don't want you catching pneumonia for my benefit. Besides, while I'm away, you'll be the chief dog walker. You need to keep warm and dry."

"I'm going to buy a coat with my next paycheck. I'm fine for now."

He didn't say anything, just gave her that annoying raised eyebrow—the one she'd always found so sexy until it was turned on her.

She slid out of his grasp. "I'll buy a coat when I'm good and ready."

Logan held the door open for her and mumbled under his breath—it sounded suspiciously like "my stubborn little pain in the ass."

She left his coat and walked out with her hands stuffed in the pockets of her hoodie. "Don't say I didn't warn you, 'cause I did."

Skye power walked down the alley and into the kitchen. She tossed her hoodie on the hook by the door, tied a clean apron around her waist, and didn't even notice Logan leave. Thankfully she was too busy to think of anything but work for several hours. Harrison had done a great job and had everything prepped for lunch. She even let him conduct the specials class—explaining the specials and how they were prepared to the servers.

Before she knew it, the lunch rush was over. She took a deep breath, pulled her baseball cap down lower, and thanked God she'd survived—barely. At least the kitchen staff hadn't heard about the champagne fiasco the day before. If they had, they'd hid it well. Still, knowing she'd had four eyewitnesses was enough to put her firmly on the wagon for the rest of her life.

When Pete stepped into the kitchen and looked at her, she swallowed back bile. "Skye, may I have a word with you in my office?"

All eyes went to her. She nodded, untied her apron, and set it on the worktable, wondering if Logan had been wrong about his assessment. If Pete wasn't going to fire her, why did they need to go to his office?

He held the swinging door open for her as she passed. "Come on, let me buy you a drink. I don't know about you, but I need coffee. Just don't tell Logan it's not decaf, okay? He's such a food Nazi."

"My lips are sealed."

"I can't live without the stuff. It's bad enough I'm not allowed to even drink a freakin' beer." He went behind the bar and grabbed the coffeepot.

Simon shook his head.

Pete turned to Simon and scowled. "Say a word to Logan and you're fired. You hear me?"

"Hey, I'm not your keeper, Pete. That's Logan's job." Simon caught her eye. "What would you like, Skye?"

"I'll take a Coke if you don't mind, please, Simon."

Simon shot her a smile and all she could think of was the chocolate cake and whipped cream mess she and Logan had left for him to clean up. She stood right in front of the barstool she'd occupied on that disastrous night. Her face burned at the thought that he and Pete were surely remembering one of her most humiliating life experiences. Simon filled a glass with ice and started pouring. "Are you feeling okay? Nothing personal, but you look a little under the weather."

"I'm fine, thanks." She took the soda and thought she'd feel a lot better if she still had a job after she spoke to Pete. She followed him back to the office and was surprised that Logan wasn't there. She hadn't seen him since he left the kitchen that morning.

Pete closed the door, which did nothing to alleviate her nerves. "Have a seat." He set his coffee on the desk, sat, and put his feet up, looking her over. "You've been busy this afternoon. The lunch crowd has really picked up since you've taken over the kitchen."

"The numbers look good and Harrison is doing a great job stepping up his game. He's a fast learner."

"That's good to know."

Maybe she should have kept her mouth shut about Harrison, but really, he deserved all the credit in the world. He was a fast learner and didn't need a babysitter—she appreciated that.

"I'll just get right down to it. I'm worried about you, Skye. You ran away from your home, your job, and your family, and it doesn't look as if you're any closer to dealing with the root of the problem than you were when you first walked in here. You need to stop hiding."

The breath she'd been holding flew from her lungs and heat seared her face. "Logan told you?"

"Logan didn't tell me anything I didn't already know, but I'm glad you told him. It was about time."

She didn't know what to say. The last thing she wanted to do was think about dealing with her family. The way Pete looked at her made her wonder if she'd have much of a choice.

"I think you're good for him. Hell, I think you're good for each other, but you both have things to finish before you get too serious."

Too serious? She was already in too deep to get out unscathed.

"Skye, how can you start something with Logan when you haven't closed the books on your past?"

"I did too close the books. I quit. That's as closed as it's gonna get, Pete."

"I know you quit. I heard all about it."

"You did?"

Pete nodded and tilted his head. "Skye, if you were any other employee, quitting would be sufficient. The fact is, you're not any other employee, and you and I both know that when you work with family, you're a hell of a lot more—and not always in a good way. You owe your parents a call at the very least."

She wondered if it would sound too immature and unprofessional if she said she'd waited to call her mother because she wanted Patrick to get in trouble first. For the kid who was voted most likely to remain a prick, Patrick was great at keeping his black light under a bushel.

Pete laughed out loud and then slapped his knee. "You're just giving that brother of yours enough rope to hang himself, aren't you?"

She shrugged and couldn't help but smile. "My best friend's been keeping an eye on things. Patrick has been calling her every day—something he didn't do when she made the mistake of dating him a while ago. If my mom gets really worried, she knows to call Kelly."

"Have you told Kelly about Logan?"

"Of course, she's my best friend." She rolled her eyes. "Kelly's already googled him. Why?"

"Just curious." Pete dropped his feet to the floor and held his coffee cup in both hands. "Skye, if you love Logan, you really need to get your life in order. Talk to your family. He has to close the books on his past too."

"But he lost his job. He was fired."

"Was he?"

"Payton said—"

Pete held up his hand like a traffic cop. "Payton wasn't his boss."

"Logan talked to someone this morning. Didn't he tell you? He's leaving for California Thursday for a meeting on Friday. Then he's going to a wine competition in Portland. He'll take the red-eye back on Sunday night. He's the one who requested the Friday meeting."

"With who?"

"I don't know."

"You didn't ask?"

"It's none of my business." She shrugged as if it didn't matter. From the look on Pete's face, he wasn't buying it either.

"Really? Would you say that if the meeting was with Payton?"

"I'm not stupid, Pete. He's going to the vineyard; chances are he's going to see Payton. I might not know her well, but I don't need to be her therapist to know that she can't be happy about canceling the wedding. She obviously wanted Logan to be her Mr. Billingsly and Payton has never been one to bow out of anything gracefully."

"Which might explain why no news of their breakup made the society pages."

"It hasn't?"

"Not that I've seen. I have each of my boys on Google Alert—I like to know what's going on in their lives. If I didn't know my son, if I hadn't watched him fall head over beer taps in love with you, I'd swear he was pulling the wool over all our eyes."

She shook her head. "Logan wouldn't do that."

"You're right, but still, I'm amazed you haven't checked it out."

"It never occurred to me. I've never been one to read the tabloids or the society pages. I've spent my life avoiding those people. Why would I want to read about them?"

"Because you're in love with Logan, and he's one of

those people—at least he played one on TV. Besides, you know Payton better than I do, and even I know she's not the warm fuzzy type."

"No, she isn't." But she was definitely the sneaky type.

"So you're just going to let him go?"

"Let him?" As if she had any say in the matter. "He's a grown man—he doesn't need my permission to do anything."

"Maybe not, but before he leaves, it would probably help if he knew how you felt. If you haven't figured it out yet, Skye, you better be quick about it."

"Okay, Dr. Phil."

Pete let out a laugh and stood. "You're doing a great job. I just thought I'd tell you in case you still thought I was going to fire you—I'm not, but I don't think you're going to be here forever either. The Crow's Nest is just a stepping-stone for you, and that's fine. Rex's mother died last week."

"Oh no. God, I'm so sorry. How's he doing?"

"He's hanging in. It's difficult, but she's in a better place and he's relieved that she's no longer suffering. He's still down there taking care of finalizing her estate, but he's already called to tell me he's going to come home eventually."

"And he'll want his apartment and his dog back." She would miss them both.

"The job is still yours if you want it, but I thought you should know that we'll be okay if you don't."

"Rex wants his job back?"

Pete nodded. "The job is yours if it's what you want, Skye. I'm just not sure it is. This would be a good time for you to think about what you want your future to look like, and whether or not you want that future to include Logan."

"I will." She stood and found herself enveloped in a hug. "I promise."

Skye unlocked the door to her apartment and answered her phone at the same time. "Kelly, what's up?"

"Paddy is freaking out and your mom's starting to ask questions. Are you ever coming home?"

"Not if I can help it." She stepped inside and dropped her bag. When she looked up, she noticed two boxes on the couch. Pepperoni ran over and jumped on her legs. She turned and found Logan in her kitchen cleaning up the mess he'd made at breakfast. "Look, I can't talk right now. I'll call you later."

"Why?"

"Because there's a strange man doing dishes in my kitchen."

"Strange because he's doing dishes, or strange as in a man you don't know?"

"The first one. Love you. Bye." She ended the call, shook her head, and took off her hoodie. "Logan, how did you get in here?"

"I used my key. How was your day, dear?"

"Does everyone have a key to my place?"

"Just me and Patrice as far as I know. I'm sure Rex still has his, but he's still in Florida. Why, is there a problem?"

"Yes, I'd like to be able to walk into my apartment and know no one else is here."

"Oh." He wiped his hands and closed the dishwasher. "Rough day, I take it?"

"No. Yes. Hell, I don't know. What are those boxes doing on my couch?"

"Waiting for you to open them."

He stepped out of the kitchen and drugged her with one of his kisses—one that lasted a while and had her tugging his shirt out of his pants. He pulled away and smiled. "Later. Open your presents first."

"I don't want to, because it'll just start a fight and I really don't feel like fighting right now."

"So don't fight me on this. They're presents—all you have to do is open them and say thank you."

"Why can't you just be nice and respect my wishes?"

"Because you're wrong and I'm leaving in a couple days. I need to know you'll be taken care of while I'm away and not catching your death of cold."

"So that makes it okay to disregard my wishes and become my personal shopper?" She walked over to the couch and lifted the top off the first box. It was a gorgeous wool coat. It felt like cashmere—but it was a brilliant dark blue—not a navy, but not a cobalt either. It was something in between and she loved it. She pulled it out of the box and held it close to her.

"I knew it—it matches your eyes exactly. Try it on."

He held it open for her and she stepped into it. It fit as if it were made for her. "How'd you know what size I wore?"

"I cheated—I checked your size before I left this morning. Then I talked to one of the women at the store. She said you'd need a petite. Do you like it?"

It was just the right length for her height. "That depends. How much do I owe you?"

"Nothing—it's a gift. You don't pay for gifts."

She took off the coat and set it on top of the box, not

sure exactly how to handle it. On one hand she was pissed he totally disregarded what she'd told him, and on the other hand she had to admit he picked out the perfect coat for her. She pulled the top off the second box and blinked at the white fur. "You bought me a fur coat?"

"Fake fur, but it feels really great."

It was so soft, she couldn't stop petting it. She lifted it out of the box and pulled it on. It was short and had a full hood. "Does it make me look like a big marshmallow?"

"No. You look gorgeous in both." He slid his hands inside the coat and pulled her against his hard chest before nuzzling her neck. "This is where you tell me you love them and thank me for thinking of you." He nipped at her ear, making it really hard to think.

"I do love them, and I thank you for thinking of me, even though I told you I wanted to buy my own coat, so I still want to pay you back."

"Which kills the whole gift thing, so no." He kissed the side of her neck.

She tilted her head to give him more room.

"Besides, you're doing me a huge favor babysitting Nicki, Pop, and D.O.G. You can think of it as a trade if it makes you feel better. That way we avoid the fight we don't want to have, and we can get back to where we were just a few minutes ago."

"Where was that?"

"On the way to bed. I've missed you."

"It's only been a few hours."

"I know. Being away from you for a long weekend is not going to be fun. We'd better take advantage of the time we have left."

"Good thing Harrison is scheduled to deal with dinner. I'm off for the rest of the day."

"Thank God." He lifted her off her feet and carried her to the bedroom.

"Hold on, let me take the coat off."

"No. I've spent the better part of three hours thinking about you wearing that coat and nothing else."

"You have a sick mind."

"Only when it comes to you."

She pulled off the coat and threw it on her bed while he unbuttoned her chef's whites.

He sucked in a breath when he found her wearing nothing but a red bra beneath them. He dropped to his knees and kissed her stomach as he pulled her pants down and caught the edge of her red panties in his teeth. "Maybe I'll let you leave these on too."

She laughed and ran her hands through his hair. "You're a nut."

He looked up at her. "But you love me."

"I do love you, which is probably why I let you get away with the whole coat thing." She screamed when she found herself lifted and unceremoniously tossed on the bed on top of the coat, which, she had to admit, felt incredible beneath her back.

Logan came down on her, kissing the breath that she had left right out of her. God she loved the way he kissed her—like he'd rather kiss her than do anything else, like his sole purpose in life was to please her with his mouth. His tongue dipped in and did a leisurely slide against hers in direct opposition to the urgency he displayed when he ripped away the scrap of satin that used to be her underwear.

Every muscle beneath her hands tensed, and without

ever removing his mouth from hers, he entered her in one swift thrust of his hips.

She wrapped her legs around his waist and held on as he lifted her hips and hit that perfect spot, shooting her into an orgasm so strong, she swore she saw stars.

His mouth loved her in time with his body. His hands were everywhere—always touching just the right spots, sending her higher and higher, harder and faster than he had before. She spun out of control—her mind racing, her body reacting to his every move.

He ripped his mouth from hers and stared into her eyes. The fierce possession she read in his expression scared her more than anything else she'd ever seen, and still, it sent her flying.

She took him with her, dragging him kicking and screaming over some cliff they hadn't scaled before.

He came with a curse and collapsed on her while her body still rolled through storms of sensation he'd sent swirling through every cell.

Logan knew he was probably crushing Skye, but he was unable to move. Hell, he couldn't even swallow. He'd kind of lost it when she told him she loved him. He knew he should say something, and he planned to say a hell of a lot if he was ever able to speak again—which might happen faster if she'd stop spasming around him. With every contraction of her muscles, incredibly, he got harder. He'd always thought he had a quick recovery time, but that was ridiculous.

He tried to put his weight on his forearms, which moved him deeper within her, and she tilted her hips, driving him even deeper still, and shot sparks that had him groaning.

He gathered the last of his energy and rolled them

over, grabbing her hips. He arched his back, and sent her flying. Watching Skye come apart on top of him was the most incredible thing he'd ever seen. "You're so beautiful, and you're all mine." He kissed her and pulled her to him, holding her tight, not wanting to let her go, not wanting to ever leave.

Skye lay curled against a snoozing Logan, wishing she could think of anything other than him leaving. When Pepperoni whined to go out, she didn't bother waking him, and slid out of bed so she could have a little time by herself to get her head together without his shoving his gorgeous nose into her thoughts the way he always did.

"Where do you think you're going?"

She pulled on a fresh pair of underwear and the clothes she'd picked up. "Go back to sleep, I'm just going to take Pepperoni out."

"Not alone, you're not. Besides, I need to walk D.O.G. anyway. What do you say to picking up a pizza for dinner? Maybe we can get a veggie pizza for Pop, or just order something from the Crow's Nest for him."

She didn't know how to say no to him. Besides, if things were going to fall apart when he went back to California, at least she could enjoy him while he was still here. "Sounds good, but hurry up. Pepperoni hasn't been out for a while."

They killed two birds with one stone by walking the dogs to Logan's favorite pizza place. Logan walked D.O.G. and carried the pizzas, taking a shorter route back. They turned a corner and Logan stopped in his tracks. "It's for sale."

"What?"

He pointed across the street to an ancient three-story

brick warehouse with arched windows and doors. It was gorgeous.

"I saw them putting the sign up a few days ago." She tugged on Pepperoni's leash and stopped when Logan didn't move. Drawing the hood of her new jacket up, she turned her back to the wind coming off the bay and shivered.

"It's perfect." He stared at the building and Skye could practically see his mind racing down some complicated track on warp speed.

"Perfect for what?"

"A microbrewery and restaurant. I was thinking about what I wanted to do when Storm and Bree come home. I need a job, so I started looking into opening my own microbrewery." He took her hand and pulled it into his pocket, warming it. "This place would be big enough for a microbrewery and a restaurant." He slid his arm around her and kissed her—his eyes sparkled and he had a weird smile on his face. "What do you say, Skye? Do you want to go into business with me? You can have a kitchen of your own and I can have my microbrewery. It'll be amazing."

Her stomach dipped like it was going down the big drop on Space Mountain. "Just like that?"

"Sure. We'll have to call and see what they want for the building and look into financing, but hey, we both have experience in the business and I have money saved. It should be enough for a down payment, and you have to admit we work really well together." His smile lost some of its brilliance. Maybe it had something to do with the way she backed out of his arms—or tried to. He held on, moving forward for each step back she took. "Think about it, Skye. We can build our own place and have a loft on the third floor—you, me, and Nicki. We'll be close to Pop's but not too close. I'll have my microbrewery, you'll have total control of the kitchen, and together we'll run the restaurant and bar. It's what we're doing now, but this will be ours. What do you think?"

She thought he was nuts, but she'd already told him that more than once. "Logan, you can't just say 'let's go into business' and expect it to happen."

"Why not?"

"Because we don't have a business plan or anything. We've only known each other a few weeks. This is huge. This is a big deal."

"So? This is just the first step, Skye. You want your own kitchen, don't you?"

"Of course I do."

"Do you think we work well together?"

"Yes."

"Has our relationship gotten in the way of our work?"

"No, but we haven't been together long enough to know if it will."

"Do you think it will?"

"No." She really didn't think they'd have a problem working together. She liked working with him and Lord knew she liked sleeping with him. The question was, if they stopped seeing each other, could they still work together? Would they want to?

"Are you willing to at least think about it?"

She shrugged and stared at the building. It was gorgeous—it would make an awesome restaurant with high ceilings, great light, exposed brick. . . . "I guess it couldn't hurt to look into what it would take. We'd have to build it out—that's expensive, and we'd need to get a liquor license."

"We'll talk to Pop. He knows how to get things done in Red Hook. And Bree is on the Revitalization Committee. Maybe she knows about some low-interest loans for rehabbing a building like this. They'll know all the people we'll need to talk to."

She tugged on Logan's arm to get him moving again. The pizza was getting cold. "Okay, but how are they going to feel when they find out you're planning to steal away their chef?"

By the look on Pete's face when Logan mentioned it to him, Skye didn't think Logan stealing Pete's chef would be a problem. She sat back, picked at her pizza, and listened to Pete, Nicki, and Logan tossing around ideas while shoving pizza down their throats at alarming rates. Logan never stopped touching her and kissing her—even in front of Nicki. She spent the entire time red-faced. After they ate and cleaned up the kitchen, she went to the door to grab her jacket. "Pepperoni, come on, girl. It's time for bed."

Logan came up behind her. "Why don't you wait until Nicki goes to bed and we can go together?"

"No, that's okay."

Nicki stepped beside her. "You're not going to tuck me into bed, Skye? You have to. How will you know what to do when Logan goes away and you're watchin' me and Pop?"

She looked from Logan to Nicki and knew she was doomed. They went through the entire bedtime routine including a tickle fight, which was two against one, and Skye and the mascara she'd brushed on before she left that evening came out the loser. She found herself sitting on the edge of Nicki's bed with Pepperoni and D.O.G. while Nicki and Logan put her backpack together for the next day, said her prayers, and then the entire crew exchanged hugs and good-night kisses. Skye even got talked into kissing D.O.G., who did his best to stick his big tongue in her mouth.

Logan gave the mutt a look and told him he didn't kiss boys, which sent Nicki into a fit of giggles. It took a while to get Nicki and D.O.G. settled. Finally, they snuck out of Nicki's room. Skye thought the worst was over until she and Logan found Pete waiting for them in the living room. She didn't think there was anything worse than getting caught at the bar with chocolate and whipped cream by her boss until she had to stand there while Logan told him he'd be home in time to wake Nicki for school the next day.

"You don't have to walk me home."

He raised his eyebrow and she wanted to smack him when he took it a step further and followed it up with a cocky-ass grin before pulling her into his arms. Sometimes it sucked that he was so much bigger than her. He had no problem moving her wherever he wanted her to go.

She smacked him. "Do you mind?"

"Not at all. I love it when you play hard to get. But you have to admit it would be ridiculous for us to walk to your place separately, since I'm spending the night with you."

"You weren't invited."

"Then it's a damn good thing I don't need an invitation. You're mine, I'm yours, and we're together."

"I'm going home."

"I'm right behind you."

"Great. Good night, Pete." She didn't wait for a response and just headed out the door, dragging Pepperoni with her.

Logan blasted down the stairs behind her and caught up. "What's the matter?"

"I can't believe you just told my boss you're coming home with me."

"He's my dad. And Skye, it's not like he doesn't know what we're doing. We're together and he seems fine with it. What's the problem?"

The problem was she wasn't used to having a sex life, much less one everyone knew about. "Look, I've never been anyone's anything before. I'm not sure what I'm supposed to do. I'm not comfortable with the entire world knowing about our sex life. You, on the other hand, seem to have no problem with it."

"I'm a guy. You're incredible. Why would I have a problem with everyone knowing we're together? I just don't get why you do."

She took off across the alley. "I don't know how to do this—whatever this is."

"It's a relationship, and it's not difficult, Skye. Just do what you've been doing. Love me. Let me love you. That seems to be working out just fine so far."

"Yeah, but until now, it's just been you and me. Now it's you, me, Pete, Nicki, Francis and Patrice ... oh, and Rocki—we can't forget her. And now you're going back to California, and I'm here. . . ."

"What does my trip have to do with us?"

She didn't know. She just couldn't let go of the feeling that something terrible would happen. "It's just that the world has a way of taking a wrecking ball to relationships, Logan. We just got together and now you're going back to your old life." Shit, she sounded pathetic.

"No, I'm not. I'm going back to finalize things, pack my stuff, and then go to the competition. I'll be home before you know it. I didn't have much of a life back there, Skye. I was just going through the motions—"

"You might have been, but you're going to have to deal with the fallout. Things happen, Logan. I know how Payton is."

"You're jealous?"

Was that what this was? She couldn't imagine it, but maybe she'd never had anything to be jealous of before. "I'm realistic." She let herself into the building and climbed the stairs, wishing they could just stop the conversation she'd never wanted to have in the first place. She shoved the key into the lock, opened it, and he caught the door behind her.

"Either you think I can't handle Payton or you don't trust me. Which is it?"

"Neither, both . . . I don't know." She turned to face him, expecting to find him pissed, but instead he looked almost pleased, which just made her angry. Then he wrapped his arms around her and all the anger seemed to go up in smoke. What was wrong with her? "It's as if right here, right now, we're in a perfect little bubble. Everything is wonderful because we're both away from our real lives—our real world. Now you're going back to yours. Don't you see that whatever you and Payton had together was just as real as what you and I have?"

"What I had with Payton was far from perfect and it wasn't even real—"

Skye put her fingers over his lips. "Listen to me. I'm just saying that when you go back, you might see things differently."

"The only difference is going to be that I'm going to miss you like crazy. I love you, Skye. When are you going to believe me? It doesn't matter what world I'm in—hell, if I were on Mars, I would still be in love with you. I've never loved Payton or anyone else, so you can just stop trying to get rid of me."

She let out a breath and looked up at him. Maybe she was being as crazy as he seemed to think she was. "Getting rid of you is the last thing I want to do. If it were up to me, I'd keep you here in our little bubble forever, but it isn't up to me. Reality is going to creep into our perfect little world eventually. All I'm saying is when you go back, if things change . . . if your feelings change—"

He unzipped her new coat and slid it off her shoulders. "It's not going to happen." He kissed her and walked her backward toward the bedroom. "If you went back to San Francisco, do you even for a minute believe you'd forget what we have together?"

"No, but then I wasn't engaged to someone like Payton either."

He actually laughed. "Skye, if you had been engaged to someone like Payton, you wouldn't be worried. Believe me when I say there's nothing Payton has or has ever had that could make me want her over you. Not in a million years."

CHAPTER 15

Logan had forgotten how long it took to fly from New York to San Francisco. It seemed like an eternity. He wished he could have talked Skye into going with him. He might have been more successful if Bree and Storm had suddenly appeared or even Slater, but he couldn't leave the restaurant without a chef and a manager even if Harrison could have handled the restaurant for a few days—maybe. Hell, he'd have been willing to let him try, but Skye wouldn't hear of it.

It hadn't helped that Nicki had been upset by his leaving. When she'd given him a picture she'd drawn so he wouldn't forget about her, he couldn't swallow the lump in his throat. He pulled it out of his breast pocket, opened it, and saw a damned good drawing of his girls. She didn't trust he'd come back, and neither, it seemed, did Skye. When Skye said good-bye to him, she looked as if she was afraid she'd never see him again.

He'd always thought that having someone miss him would feel good, but after seeing their faces through the back window of the cab as he pulled away, he would have given just about anything to ease their minds. It was all he could do not to grab the door handle on the cab and jump out, and he had to cross his arms to keep from doing just that. The farther away he drove, the deeper the cut. He'd felt as if someone had just scooped out his insides with a spoon—he was hollow, empty, and damned uncomfortable. He swallowed back a groan, rubbed the center of his chest, and tried to erase the eerily familiar feeling. One he'd had for as long as he could remember. One that had disappeared the moment Nicki and Skye had danced into his life. He'd never realized what it was before. He hadn't realized it until it slammed into his chest with the force of a meteor.

He was totally alone, completely solitary, desolate, and miserable. Even though he knew, with a certainty that kept him sane, that he would return to them in four days—ninety-six hours, give or take a few minutes—he'd never felt so scared. It was going to be the longest four days of his life.

The driver pulled up to his house at the vineyard and he got out, grabbed his bags, and waved away the offered help.

He walked up to the dark house wondering how he'd ever thought of this place as home. He took out his keys and watched the taillights of the limo until it disappeared over the hill. Again he tried to shake off the feeling that he should be anywhere but here. He told himself he was letting his imagination run away with him and let himself into the house.

He flipped on the lights and was tempted to reach for his shades—it was so white he was nearly blinded.

He looked around for any color—all he saw were different shades of white. The walls were white, the carpet was white—hell, even the leather furniture was white. It looked as cold as the Arctic and just as inviting. He stifled a shiver and tossed his keys on the chrome and glass table. There wasn't a speck of dust. Not a thing out of place. Everything looked the same as it had when he left—high ceilings, massive windows looking over the vineyard—although he couldn't see any part of it at that moment. Still, the vineyard was the only bit of color that came to mind when he thought of the house—not that he'd thought about it at all while he was gone. Looking out onto the vineyard might have helped. Unfortunately, on a moonless night, all he saw, all he felt, was deep, dense darkness. Everything was eerily still and quiet—something he used to find soothing. Now the quiet made him antsy; the hum of the refrigerator, the ticking of the world's loudest grandfather clock, and the buzz of a lightbulb seemed to echo in the huge, empty, cold house. He felt as if he were the only human on the planet. There were no cars going by, no planes overhead, no surf smashing against the shore a block away, no life, no laughter, no love—just emptiness.

He'd never realized how impersonal the house felt. Nothing there was his—not really. He supposed it was because Payton had decorated it in her taste, not his. But then, he wasn't sure what kind of taste he had. He'd never had a place of his own. He had a few apartments with roommates, but they were furnished in early Salvation Army. Now that he thought about it, that wasn't so bad.

As he looked around the house he'd spent the last several years living in, the only bit of him he saw was a few pictures of him and Payton together. He picked one off the shelf and hardly recognized the man staring back at him—a stranger. That guy wasn't him. He looked like a wax sculpture from Madame Tussauds. Everything was perfect, his clothes, his pose, hell, even his smile—perfectly fake. This wasn't the same man who tried to cook his girlfriend breakfast, or kissed Nicki good night. It wasn't the guy who held Skye's head over the toilet when she puked her guts up or went shopping for women's coats to make sure she didn't freeze to death. The guy in the picture never missed his girlfriend or anyone the way Logan missed Skye and Nicki, and he certainly never spent a sleepless night in a lonely bed after waking up reaching for the woman he loved and missing the way she curled up against him in her sleep. He'd never wanted a woman the way he wanted Skye—not only for sex, although, damn, the sex was great, but no, he wanted to be with her even when she was PMSing and spitting fire, or looking at him like if she blinked, he might disappear. The guy in the picture might have his arm around Payton, but he was alone. He didn't know how to love or be loved, but since he'd met Skye and Nicki, he knew how to do both in spades.

He checked his watch. It was too late to call Nicki—she was already asleep—but he could call Skye. He smiled for the first time that day, pulled his phone off his belt, and speed-dialed her.

"Hey, you called." She sounded sleepy and surprised—he heard a half smile in her voice, the sheets rustle as she stretched, and Pepperoni's piglike snore.

He pictured her in bed with her hair all messed up, warm and cozy, curled around the puppy instead of him. "I just wanted to tell you I got in safe. How'd it go tonight?"

"Okay. Nicki was a little down, but I made her favorite dinner and she perked up."

Logan groaned. "You let her eat peanut butter and bacon sandwiches for dinner?"

"With fries and gravy."

"That bad, huh?"

"She was pretty pathetic. You'd better FaceTime her tomorrow after school or her cholesterol level is going to go through the roof and I won't be held responsible."

He took a deep breath and felt something inside him uncoil and expand. "How are you doing?"

"Me?" She sounded surprised that he asked. When was she going to realize that he loved her more than he knew was possible? "I left the restaurant in Harrison's capable hands when Nicki came down the third time."

Shit, he knew leaving was a mistake. "I'm sorry, sugar."

"There's nothing to be sorry for. I wasn't having a great day either, so leaving wasn't a problem. I helped Nicki with her homework, I signed her agenda book, and we packed up her backpack, and then we popped popcorn and watched *Aladdin*. She says Aladdin reminds her of you. You're just missing the magic carpet. She loves you, you know."

"The feeling's mutual." He was surprised to feel his lips curl in a smile. He was no Aladdin, but hell, if Aladdin was who he reminded Nicki of, he'd start buying up Turkish carpets—they'd beat the shit out of the white wool he was walking around on.

"How was the flight?"

"Long. I'd forgotten how damn far away California is from Red Hook. Too far." He went into the kitchen, pulled Nicki's picture from his breast pocket, and rooted around the junk drawer until he found the magnets he'd bought a few years ago. Payton kept taking them off the damn refrigerator. When he'd asked her why, she'd said they were too pedestrian. He liked pedestrian. He smoothed out the crease in the middle of the picture and smiled at the drawing of Nicki and Skye holding a sign saying, "Come Home Soon. We Love You, Logan." He rubbed his chest and wondered if he was just hungry. Maybe that was what was bothering him. There hadn't been much to eat on the plane. He opened up the fridge and was surprised to see it filled with the foods that made up Payton's usual diet—celery, carrots, lettuce, and Greek yogurt. Until he'd met Skye, he'd never realized how nice it was to be with a woman who ate real food and cooked. There was nothing in the fridge he wanted, so he opened a bottle of water and took a sip. "Is Pop behaving himself?"

"No. He tried to sneak down to the bar, but I called Francis and Simon and threatened their lives if they let him drink. For some strange reason I get the distinct feeling that Francis is afraid of me."

He couldn't help but laugh. "Frankie's been well trained by Patrice. I think he's afraid of anything that vaguely resembles a female. Even Pepperoni makes him break out in a cold sweat."

"Good to know. I'll have to ask her how she pulled that one off for future reference. So, what are you doing?"

"Me? I'm going to bed."

She sighed the kind of sigh that made his dick jump. "I wish I was there, or better yet, you were here."

"We can still go to bed together. How do you feel about phone sex?"

"Right now, I'm totally open to it. I miss you."

"Really?" Well, damn, that was a pleasant surprise. "Okay then, why don't you start by telling me what you're wearing?" Her laughter spilled over him as he headed toward his bedroom. He took a swig of water, hit the lights, and choked when he saw Payton posing on his bed wearing a sheer black gown. He blinked and shook his head. Too-thin spaghetti straps threatened to snap under the weight of what he used to think were a magnificently matched pair of double Ds. Tiny buttons ran from the V of her bosom to the O of her navel and disappeared under a layer of sheer netting. She knelt and the skirt fell open, revealing a barely there G-string. Three months ago he'd have dived into the alphabet. But now the memory of Skye's slightly mismatched B/C cups were more to his liking. After all, variety was the spice of life.

He dragged in a breath and coughed again. "I have to go."

"Are you okay?"

"I'm fine. I'll call you tomorrow."

"Logan, what's the matter?"

"I have an unexpected visitor."

"Is Payton there?"

"Yes."

"In your bedroom?"

"Yes, but not for long. I have to go. I'll call you tomorrow. Don't worry about it. I can handle her. You just get some sleep."

"Right, like that's going to happen. Call me when you're through. I'm suddenly wide-awake."

No doubt. Damn it. He didn't need this. Logan ended the call and shoved the phone in his pocket. He squared his shoulders as she shimmied to the edge of the bed, confusion marring her brow. "Get the hell out of my bed and put on some clothes."

Her hands went to her hips, and her face flashed red

under what was left of her war paint. "Who were you talking to?"

"None of your fucking business." He clenched his fists to keep from picking her up and throwing her out. "Get dressed and get out. Now."

She scurried off the bed and went toe-to-toe with him. "This is my home." Her cloying perfume made him step back and breathe through his mouth.

"No, this is my home. You and I are no longer living together. I thought I made that clear in New York when I told you we were finished. What part of that conversation didn't you understand?"

He didn't bother to wait for her answer—he just turned, walked out, slammed the door behind him, and headed straight to the wet bar. His hand shook as he grabbed one of her precious Baccarat crystal tumblers and the decanter she made him pour his tequila in. The damn set had set him back over two grand. Maybe he'd take them with him, but then what the hell would he do with them? He'd be just as happy drinking out of a jelly jar.

The door slammed open and she stomped out in those ridiculous heels she called slippers. The slap of her pedicured foot against the shoe hit him like the zap of a Taser and only added to the mad he had building. "You wouldn't dare throw me out." She'd pulled on a sheer black robe that hid nothing, and tied it so tightly around her, he was surprised she didn't cut off her circulation.

He looked her up and down and shook his head. What had he ever seen in her? He preferred Skye in her ripped sweatshirt and yoga pants, though he had to admit she would look great in Payton's getup. "I'm not going to get into this with you, Payton. I want you to pack your things and get the hell out of my life."

She went from spoiled brat to charity case in the blink of an eye. "Where am I supposed to go?" He really couldn't believe he'd ever fallen for her theatrics.

"I ceased to care when you told me you wanted nothing to do with my daughter."

"You can't mean that."

"I can and I do. I've moved on. You need to too." He took a sip of great tequila and listened to her labored breathing. Her face morphed from shocked to embarrassed to conniving so quickly, he almost missed it before she gathered her composure and hit the serene button. It was fascinating.

"Logan." Her voice took on a low, sexy, Kathleen Turner quality. "We're engaged."

"The sex kitten act isn't working. Payton, we were engaged and now we're not. You never loved me. I never loved you. The whole engagement was a disaster in the making. It's a good thing we called it off when we did."

"You can't just dump me. Without me, you're nothing."

From sex kitten to Leona Helmsley—the Queen of Mean—in less than two seconds flat. His hand tightened around the tumbler. He was glad it had some weight to it—if it hadn't, he would have crushed the damn thing in his fist. He took a deep breath; every muscle in his entire body vibrated. "If I'm such a nobody, why in the hell are you trying so hard to get me back?" His mind raced and then he saw the look on her face—the look that told him she'd been caught red-handed. "You haven't canceled the wedding."

"Why would I? I've decided to take you back. When you were in that dump you call a restaurant, you weren't thinking straight. Now that you're home, things will return to normal. You'll see. We'll have a fabulous wedding and wonderful life."

"I already have a wonderful life—one that does not include you. We're not right for each other, Payton. The only thing I want from you is for you to leave."

"You can't mean that. I'm the best thing that ever happened to you. I even pulled some strings and got Vicki into one of the best prep schools in the area. It took some doing, of course. . . ."

He couldn't help it; he laughed. "My daughter's name is Nicki, not that you really need to know that."

"Don't you dare laugh at me."

"Listen and listen good, Payton. I have a meeting tomorrow morning with your father. Either you tell him we're through or I will. It's up to you."

"He'll fire you."

"I really don't care. I have to resign my position regardless. I have a family to think about now, and I won't move Nicki away from the only home she's ever known. I'm moving back to Red Hook permanently. It's my home. It's where I belong. I'm happy there." He shook his head and actually felt sorry for her. The anger left him just as quickly as it hit. He was sick and tired of this thing he'd thought of as a life before he knew better. "Look, Payton, I'm tired. I have nothing else to say to you, so I'm going to sleep in the guest room. I'll pack my things in the morning and leave. You can stay for as long as you want—your father owns the place anyway. Have a nice life."

"You're not getting rid of me that easily, Logan Blaise. We're going to be at the competition together. And don't even think about embarrassing me."

"I have no interest in embarrassing you. You do a good enough job of it all by yourself. I just want to get through this weekend and go home where I belong. Do us both a favor and stay the hell away from me. I'm going to talk to your father in the morning, so if you want to be the one to tell him the news of our breakup, I suggest you get dressed and take a run over to his house. Explanations like these are better when done in person. Good night."

Logan grabbed his bag and headed to the other end of the house. He stepped into the first guest room, closed and locked the door, then shook the handle for good measure and considered using the dresser as a barricade. Taking a deep breath, he hit speed dial and called Skye.

"What happened?"

Thank God she answered. He hadn't exactly said good-bye and didn't say he loved her because he didn't want Payton to know who he was talking to. The fact that Skye answered on the first ring meant she was either worried or pissed. Either way, playing it straight was his only option. "Payton hasn't told anyone about the breakup. She's decided to take me back." There was silence on the end of the line and his stomach dropped. "Sugar, are you there?"

"I'm here." Her voice sounded distant and empty. He broke out into a cold sweat and remembered the bleak look on her face when he left. That desperate gnawing started in the pit of his stomach, the one he used to get whenever the social worker showed up. It had always meant the end was near and disaster was barreling toward him at warp speed.

"I told her I wasn't interested."

"Okay."

"I warned her about the meeting I have tomorrow morning with her father. I'll tell him about our breakup then if she doesn't get off her ass and do it first."

"Payton left?"

"I doubt it. I took my bags and locked myself in the guest room."

"You're staying with her?"

"No. I'm staying in the guest room and talking to you." He sat on the edge of the king-sized bed and stared into the empty fireplace wishing she wasn't on the other side of the country, wishing he could hold her, and have her hold him. "It's just you and me, sugar. Now, where were we?"

He heard her breath catch and then a quick sniffle—damn, he'd made her cry again. That was going to stop right now. He forced his face into a smile, hoping it would reach his voice. "Oh, right. I remember. You were just about to tell me what you're wearing."

Skye looked over her kitchen. She had three line cooks running like mad, her chef de cuisine was backed up, and one prep cook worked on dinner—and Rocki was in everyone's way. "What do you want, Rocki? And what can I do to get you to leave?"

"You can agree to have a drink with me and Patrice."

"That's so not happening." Skye grabbed Rocki's arm and dragged her out of the kitchen and into her office. "I'm never drinking with you two again."

Rocki crossed her arms, snapped her gum, and tapped the pointed toe of the hooker heels she wore. She was dressed as a hotter, prettier version of the Wicked Witch of the West—minus the green face paint. Okay, she had green eye shadow, so it was close enough. Maybe Rocki was trying out her Halloween costume a little early. Still, the girl could pull just about anything off.

In flats, Rocki stood eight or nine inches taller than Skye; with her heels today, Rocki had a good foot on her. "Look, I have to deal with tall people all the time—you glaring at me from on high is not going to sway me. I'm having a bad day. I'm not the kind of company you're looking for."

Rocki rolled her eyes, threw herself into the chair opposite Skye's desk, and tossed her black-and-white-striped-legging-covered leg over the arm of her chair. "We're not doing this for us, Skye. We're your best friends and we're doing this for you. We know you're going through Logan withdrawal and we thought we could help."

Skye collapsed on her desk chair hoping a house would land on Rocki, and tugged on her neck to relieve the stress that was crawling up her spine toward her aching head. After the sleepless night she'd had, she doubted anything would help—except if maybe Logan came home, and it didn't sound as if that was going to happen.

She learned a little too late that phone sex only made her miss Logan even more than she had already and made her hornier than she'd ever been before.

Rocki preened into a compact mirror, spiking her blond hair, and then fixed her bright red lipstick. She looked over the top of the compact at Skye and smiled. "You can drink a Coke if you want. We promise not to serve you any alcohol ever again." She frowned for a second and then waved her hand. Her nails were painted a fluorescent green to match her eye shadow. Skye didn't know anyone could pull that off, but Rocki somehow made it work. "Sorry about getting you drunk by the way. We had no idea what a lightweight you are."

"Okay, I'll join you in a while. Just let me get through this lunch rush. I'll be out as soon as I can."

Rocki tilted her head and stared at her. "He really loves you, you know. It's been written all over his face since the first day you walked in here. I don't think you have anything to worry about."

"Right." She just shook her head and went back to the kitchen. If she started to think about Logan sharing a house with Perfect Payton, she'd make herself sick. They didn't know Payton the way she did, and they didn't know that Payton was still living in Logan's house—or was it technically Payton's house? She really didn't know. She pulled the bill of her baseball cap down, walked into the kitchen, and checked the computer screen. "I need an allergy carry." She took the dish for the person with an onion allergy, wiped the rim with her towel, and drizzled hollandaise sauce over the lobster omelet, and tossed some parsley on it. "Where are those potatoes for the onion allergy?"

"Right here." Harrison slid them onto the shelf separating the front of the kitchen from the stoves.

She took the plate and eyed her sous chef. "You followed them?"

"I made them myself. No onions. Promise."

She hated stepping out of the kitchen when she was supposed to be in charge. Following this dish had been her job—a job she'd handed over to Harrison while she took a get-rid-of-Rocki break. "Thanks, Harrison."

She turned and grabbed Wendy. "I have an allergy carry to table ten. Can you take it out?"

"Sure." Wendy placed a cloth napkin on her arm and set the dish on it before giving Skye a once-over. "You hanging in there, Skye?"

"Of course. Why wouldn't I be?"

"Because Logan's gone and you look as if you didn't get any sleep." She tilted her head and then patted Skye's arm with her free hand. "When Jeff left me, it took a good week before I could sleep without him. It'll get easier in a few days."

God, did everyone know she and Logan were sleeping together? Dumb question, obviously. "Wendy, Logan didn't leave. He went out of town on business. He'll be back Monday morning."

She must have spoken a little too loudly because everyone in the entire kitchen stopped what they were doing and stared. She turned back to Wendy, who was doing a great imitation of a whipped puppy. Damn.

"Sure, Skye. I didn't mean to suggest—"

"I'm sorry." She tried to rub away the throbbing of the headache taking root in her temples. "I know. I'm just—"

"Worried. It's understandable. I'd be worried too if my hottie of a boyfriend flew off to the other side of the country to spend the weekend hanging around his ex."

"I'm not worried and Logan is not hanging around his ex." *He's just sleeping under the same roof with the barracuda.* "He's just packing his things to move home and then going to a wine competition or something."

"Okay, sure. Sorry I mentioned it."

Skye blew out a breath and looked around—everyone was staring.

"Chef?" Harrison, God bless him. "Could you give me a hand back here?"

"Sure."

She turned and followed him into the walk-in. "What do you need?"

Harrison turned around and leaned against one of the tubs. "Nothing. I just thought you could use a minute to cool off. Wendy didn't mean anything by that comment. She's still getting over Jeff taking off, and well, when you're in her situation, you see problems where there are none. You know?"

"Yes, I do. I didn't mean to overreact."

He smiled and gave her a hug. "You've just been a little off your game since Logan left." He placed his hands on her shoulders and held her arms so he could look her over. "Why don't you take Rocki up on that drink? I've got everything handled here. I'll call you if I need you."

"Are you giving me a time-out?"

"No, I'm just giving you a break. You look like you need one."

"Fine. I'll go, but only because I know you can handle the kitchen. Thanks for all the great work you're doing. You've really stepped up—I've told Pete that you're my rock back here."

"You have?"

"Harrison, of course I have. Why wouldn't I?"

He turned red. "I don't know. I always thought that Rex and I worked well together, but the small changes you've made to the line have really made a big difference. Now things run much more smoothly. Don't get me wrong. Rex was great.... I just didn't feel like I could take on more responsibility with him around. With you things are different."

"Except when I haven't gotten enough sleep, huh?"

Harrison shrugged again. "We all have bad days. Go ahead and let off some steam with Rocki and Patrice. I'll cover the kitchen for a few hours; then you're on your own."

"You talked me into it. Thanks." She untied her apron, took off her jacket, thankful she had thrown a shirt on underneath her chef's whites today, and headed to the front of the house. She spotted Rocki and Patrice in a booth and stopped by the bar. Simon was busy, so she went through the pass-through, poured herself a Coke, and asked Wendy to bring over a few appetizers. Even without alcohol, she needed some food to ensure that she kept her mouth shut. "How's it going?" She slid in beside Rocki, who sipped her wine. "I hope you're hungry. Food is on the way."

Patrice smirked and nudged Rocki across the table. "I told you befriending the chef came with perks." She tossed her hair over her shoulder and gave Skye the once-over. "You look like hell, girlfriend. It's a good thing we showed up when we did. Now spill, what's wrong?"

Skye forced a smile — it took some doing and from the looks on Rocki's and Patrice's faces, she didn't do a very good sales job. "Nothing's wrong. Why?"

Both Patrice and Rocki laughed, but Patrice didn't look happy. "Okay, sure. You look like roadkill, but nothing is bothering you. Come on, Skye. I didn't get a sitter and come all the way down here for my health. Rocki and I came for yours." She unrolled her napkin and set her silverware on the table. She placed her napkin in her lap and then speared Skye with her razor-sharp gaze. "Pete said you needed a few strong shoulders to lean on. He's worried about you. Now why don't you stop wasting my child-free time and just tell us what the hell happened?"

"Pete called you?" God, she must look worse than she'd thought.

Rocki nodded and snapped her gum.

Patrice reached across the table. "Swallow it or spit it out, Rocki. You sound like a cow chewing cud."

"How would you know? You've never seen a cow except for those commercials with the talking cows from California."

Patrice shrugged. "True, but believe me, girlfriend, the way you chew gum is not attractive and it's beyond annoying." Patrice reached into her purse and pulled out a tissue. "Now do us both a favor and spit it out so we can move on."

Rocki lost the gum and then stuck her tongue out at Patrice, who rolled her eyes.

"I think you've been hanging around my girls too much—their behavior is starting to wear off on you."

"Just because you're the only one at this table who has children doesn't mean you can treat me like one."

Patrice ignored her and zeroed in on Skye. "You might as well just put it all out on the table so we deal with it."

"There's nothing to deal with. Logan went to his house last night and found Payton in his bed."

"What?" Rocki planted her elbows on the table. "He dumped her after she showed up here, didn't he?"

"Yes, he did." Skye closed her eyes and rubbed her aching forehead. "You know that and I know that, but apparently it was news to Payton. She thought she had the option of taking him back and never told anyone the wedding was off. For all I know, she's still planning the society bash of the year."

Patrice held up her hands. "Hold on. How do you know this?"

"Because Logan was on the phone with me when he

walked into his bedroom. He started choking and said he had to go, that he had an unexpected visitor—Payton— and that she was in his bed waiting for him." Skye left out the whole phone sex thing—Rocki and Patrice already knew more about her sex life than they needed to.

"So what happened?" Patrice asked.

Skye tried to shrug off the worry, the fifteen minutes of hell she'd gone through imagining the worst, the stabbing pain she'd felt, the complete and utter sense of impotence that crushed her like an anvil—making it difficult to breathe. "I gather they had words. Logan told Payton it was over and said he had a meeting with her father this morning and would tell him the wedding was canceled if she didn't get off her ass and tell him herself. Then he took his bags, went to the guest room, and locked the door."

Rocki thunked herself on the forehead with the heel of her palm and groaned. "He stayed with her?"

"Technically, yes. But he called me when it was over. He sounded pissed, then sad, then . . . I don't know. . . . He sounded so alone. He tried to hide it, but I could tell he was upset—like a kid at a slumber party who's scared to stay but too afraid to admit it."

Both women nodded. Patrice grabbed Skye's hand, and Rocki's arm came around her in a half hug. Skye wasn't used to whatever this was. She supposed if she had to label it, she'd call it support. She and Kelly were close, but Kelly was the only one she knew who would hug her. It was strange but nice.

Rocki gave her a squeeze. "You know you don't have anything to worry about, right?"

"No, I really don't." She shook her head and wanted to die when tears burned her eyes. God, she was tired.

The two stared at her with their mouths hanging open.

"I'm not stupid. I know Payton, and believe me, she's not going to let this go. She's got him there for the weekend and knowing Payton, she's going to make the most of it."

Rocki's arm tightened around her. "But Logan doesn't love Payton. When I talked to him, it didn't even sound as if he liked her. And after what she said about Nicki, there's no way—"

Skye's head pounded harder. "There's nothing I can do but wait and see. It's not a fun position to be in, believe me. I feel as though I can't control a damn thing."

Patrice's eyes widened and she tugged on Skye's hand to get her attention. "That's not true. Have you called him today?"

"No." She'd wanted to. She must have reached for her phone a hundred times, but didn't. "This is something Logan needs to deal with on his own. I don't want to sound like I'm desperate." God, and she felt desperate and scared, and, well, a little bit lost.

Patrice shook her head, her hair swinging back and forth like she was auditioning to be the new Breck Girl. "Logan needs you. He needs to know you're there for him."

Rocki nodded while taking a drink of her wine—it was a miracle she didn't spill it.

"I'm here for him. Logan knows that."

"He might know it here"—Rocki pointed to her head—"but he doesn't trust it, not in his heart, where it counts, Skye." Rocki blew out a breath, as if she was trying to collect herself. As if she were fighting her demons and Logan's single-handedly. "You don't understand what

Pete's boys are like. They don't fall in love easily—Logan especially. He's lost everyone he's ever loved except Pete and his brothers. He's still that traumatized three-year-old inside—total abandonment affects a person for the rest of his life. Even big, strong, gorgeous guys like him. When they open themselves up to loving someone, it scares the crap out of them. Logan might logically know you're here waiting for him, but the traumatized boy inside needs to hear it and hear it often."

Patrice sat back and crossed her arms. "You see, Skye, this is why I put up with Rocki. She knows her shit and I can't agree with her more. I've always known that he and the boys didn't grow up with the support system some of us had. I'm going to let you in on a little secret—you are both sworn to secrecy. Okay?"

Skye and Rocki nodded.

"When we were kids, I had a bit of a crush on Logan. I was really shy back then—I know, it's amazing but true—and I never said anything, but believe you me, I watched him. I spent more time studying that boy than anyone. Wanna know what I learned about Logan?" She paused dramatically for effect and raised her perfectly shaped eyebrows. "Logan was always there for his brothers—he was always the one everyone turned to. He was the voice of reason and got Slater and Storm out of more scrapes than you could imagine. But he never once turned to anyone—it was as if he didn't trust anyone to be there for him—not even Pete. It was one thing for him to love and care for his brothers and Pete, but he never seemed to believe anyone had his back. It was as if he was never willing to test it—he never asked for a damn thing, so he wouldn't be disappointed. In all the years I've known him, he's never once asked anyone for help, advice, anything. He still doesn't. He's never really needed anyone. No one but you. Skye, he's trusting you—you can't let him down now."

"I'm not letting him down. I'm just not going to call him every five minutes like a desperate, jealous, crazy woman."

She looked from Rocki to Patrice and took a sip of her drink.

Wendy saved her from having to say anything more when she delivered their food. She set down a basket of wings and a plate of cheesy nachos. "Ladies, this is supposed to be a happy get-together. You look like you've stopped in on your way to a funeral." She didn't wait for a response, which was good, because Skye didn't trust herself not to fly off the handle.

Patrice grabbed a chip and shoved it into the pile of guacamole. "She's right, you know. You do look as if something or someone just died."

"I don't know. I just have a really bad feeling about this whole thing. And unfortunately, my feelings are almost always right."

Rocki ripped a piece of meat off a chicken wing and covered her mouth with her napkin. "So, tell Logan."

"I did. I sounded pathetic, but I told him and he still left."

Patrice smiled at Rocki. "It sounds as if Logan isn't the only one with abandonment issues."

"I don't have issues."

"Girlfriend, you're a woman; you have more issues than *Good Housekeeping*. It's just our makeup. We can't help it. You'll feel better once you call him. Now go on, run back to your office, or hell, go home if you need to, and call the man. You're not going to get any more work done until you do."

Skye felt herself smile—the first real smile since Logan left. Who knew all it would take was a get-out-of-girl-jail-free card. "Okay, I will. Thanks for coming over to try to cheer me up."

Rocki gave her another hug. "Not that it worked, but hey, we had to try."

"And I appreciate it."

Patrice got out of the booth and wrapped her arms around her. "You'll call us and tell us how it goes, won't you?"

"Yes. But don't worry. I'm probably just overreacting." She stepped out of Patrice's grasp and hightailed it out of the bar. She didn't even bother grabbing her coat, and headed home for a few minutes.

CHAPTER 16

Logan had a sleepless night in a strange bed. The few times he did drift off, he'd woken up reaching for Skye. He stood in the kitchen, drinking coffee and staring at the only thing in the room that helped his state of mind—the picture Nicki had drawn for him. Even with that, it took him three cups before his brain began functioning.

Pushing himself away from the counter, he took his coffee and walked around the house looking for stuff to pack. Except for a few things in his office and his bedroom, he didn't see much he wanted. "Less to move."

"Did you say something?"

Shit. He spun around and found Payton eyeing him like a ripe peach on a hot summer day. He didn't think she'd be up this early. "Just talking to myself."

Payton still wore her ridiculous negligee—it lost something in the light of day, or maybe it was the expression on her face. The one she couldn't quite replace with her model smile. The one that cracked a little at the edges. The one with a slight worry line between her brows that no amount of Botox could erase. She tried to hide her tension, but it showed in her straight back and the way she bit her lower lip.

He needed to get the hell out of there. "What do you want, Payton?"

"I want you." She moved toward him, rolling her hips, flashing thighs, allowing the robe to slip off her shoulder. Man, she was working it. "I know I've been . . ."

A bitch? He bit the inside of his cheek to keep from saying it.

"I was shocked, but I've reconsidered, and I'm ready to compromise." The honeyed tone of her voice scratched his consciousness like the pen of a lie detector against cheap paper with too many highs and lows.

"What you said goes well beyond shocked. You expected me to abandon my daughter."

"I'm sorry."

Her face got that look, the one that would have every man reaching for a hankie—he'd seen it before. It was like clouds before the storm of tears. He really, really hated tears—at least the fake ones. One, two, three. Right on cue. Her face shattered like a windshield on the wrong side of a driving range.

"Not interested." He picked up a box of tissues and passed it to her before continuing to pack. "I have a meeting with your father, and I want to finish packing my things beforehand. It won't take long."

He knew that when Payton didn't get what she wanted, she behaved like a brat. It was a bad sign that she followed him. He was too tired to deal with her, but knew the relationship wouldn't be truly over until it got ugly.

"While I finish in here, why don't you shower?" With

any luck, he'd be out of the house before she spent her allotted hour and a half putting herself together.

She crossed her arms and spread her legs as if she was preparing for a fight. If she was going for intimidating, she missed the mark by a long New York block. He wasn't in the mood to argue. He looked at his dive watch. "I guess if you want to spend the day in that getup, it's your choice, but I have someone coming over to pick up my car and sign paperwork."

Her face morphed from pissed to surprised. "Why?"

He shrugged. "I'm selling the Jag. I need something more practical. Maybe I'll get an SUV." The thought of piling Skye, Nicki, and the dogs into a big rig and taking a road trip brought a smile to his face. The classic two-seater had to go. Besides it was worth upwards of a hundred grand—a good chunk to add to the down payment for the warehouse he wanted.

"You? Practical?"

"I'm a family man now. I don't need a 'fifty-six Jag Roadster where I'm going. I need something big enough for Nicki and D.O.G. Besides, the Jag wouldn't last a day in Red Hook." Red Hook was a lot safer than it used to be, but he wasn't stupid—usually. Lately he'd wondered about his IQ—especially when it came to Payton.

"There's no need to do that."

"If you want to buy it, it'll cost you a hundred and ten grand. I'll need a check before I leave. If not, I'm going to sell it to the dealer. He has a few people interested." He grabbed a couple of boxes from the garage and tossed one on the floor of his office—he'd been hoping to lose her. He'd never been that lucky. He packed up his desktop computer, the awards he'd won for his wine, his framed diploma from Stanford, and all his tax and banking records—those he'd definitely need.

Payton stood just inside the door clutching the tissue box he'd given her and sniffling. "You're really going to leave? What about your job? Your life here? Me?"

"What about it? Think about our time together, Payton. Were you happy? Did I make you happy?"

"We were good together."

"I'll take that as a no. We didn't make each other happy; we just didn't make each other miserable—until lately. Marriage would have been a mistake. I think we've both wasted enough time trying to make something unworkable work. We were roommates with benefits. Nothing more. I want more. Hell, I even want more for you. I'm just as much at fault for perpetuating this relationship. I thought this was all I was capable of. I was wrong. Wrong about a lot of things. It wouldn't have been fair to either of us, and it wouldn't have lasted."

Payton's shoulders fell, and she pulled the see-through robe around her—as if trying to hide behind a clear window. It didn't work; spidering cracks appeared and grew, marring her usually flawless veneer.

He looked away, not interested in watching her dissolve. She'd shake it off eventually, plaster herself back together, and move on. Instead, he searched his office for anything else that was his. Everything left—most of the contents—was just things. Things Payton had put on the shelves. Things he didn't even like. Things that reminded him of living a lie. Even the books were ones he'd never read. He was into horror, legal thrillers, and suspense, not highbrow literary fiction. He wondered if Payton read—but not enough to ask her—which he supposed was a sad commentary on their relationship. Sure, they lived together, they had shared a bed, but that was about all they'd ever shared. He'd wasted years with the woman, and would have wasted a lifetime if he hadn't run into Skye.

He pictured Skye curled up with a dog-eared romance and warmth filled him, making him aware of the coldness of his surroundings. When Skye wasn't talking to herself or driving him crazy, she had her nose buried either in a romance or in her chef's bible. He doubted she'd ever fill his office with books neither of them would read just to impress someone with her literary taste. No, she'd have piles of romances lying all over the house.

He taped the boxes he'd filled and set them by the front door before heading to the bedroom—Payton followed him like a hacking cough after a bad cold.

He tossed a box on the unmade bed and opened his top dresser drawer. A collection of watches on black velvet sparkled in the morning light. He wore a nice dive watch he'd bought himself. He'd never worn the others unless Payton insisted. He didn't like them. They were too flashy, too expensive, too ostentatious. None of the watches looked like something a guy like him would wear. One would think Payton would know that. Hell, maybe she did and just didn't give a shit.

He was just about to close the drawer when something dull and black caught his eye. "What's this?" He slid his hand into the back and touched the worn leather of his old biker wallet—still sporting its heavy chain. Memories long relegated to his mental lockbox containing the past leaked out and slid over him like the first gulp of morning coffee—hot, strong, and satisfying. "Damn, I'd forgotten I saved this."

He looked up and found Payton's face screwed up

into a disgusted twist. Obviously she'd never been told not to make horrible faces for fear they'd stay that way.

"My father bought it for me before I left for Stanford." He wasn't sure why he was talking to her at all, but what the hell, she was there. Maybe she'd finally take the hint that they weren't right for each other.

The worn leather was smooth and curved as if it had molded to his ass. He flipped it open to find a picture of his family at Louis Valentino Jr. Park. They'd climbed out on the painted toylike alphabet blocks spelling out "Red Hook" at the water's edge. He sat on the "E" between Storm and Slater. Pop stood behind embracing them. He laughed. Man, they looked like a bunch of juvenile delinquents. No wonder Pop was always bugging them to get their hair cut.

He'd looked like the troublemaker he was, but he'd looked happy. He saw something in the eyes of the kid he'd been that he hadn't seen in any of the pictures of him and Payton. He looked at himself in the mirror and was relieved to see that spark of life, of happiness, of belonging, he'd lost for so long.

Pop had told him to never forget where he came from, and for years he'd tried to do just the opposite. Hell, he'd hidden it the same way someone would hide a criminal record. He'd done exactly what Pop had told him not to do. He'd forgotten who he was. He'd been as big a fake as Payton. He tossed the wallet in the box and left the watches—slamming the drawer. From now on, he'd be himself, whoever the hell that was.

He looked up and was surprised to see Payton still staring at him. "I'll leave the watches you bought me as gifts."

"You don't have to do that."

"Yes, I do. Give them away or sell them. I don't care."

She sucked in a breath, lost her balance as if he'd hit her, and took a step back to keep from falling. "Why?" Her voice was quiet; there was no guile, no artfulness, no wiles, no Payton—not the Payton he knew.

"Because, Payton, these watches . . ." He opened the drawer. "They're not me. I'm not the person you thought you were marrying. I pretended to be someone I'm not, and you helped. You gave me the twenty-four-karat gold bond—but what I've learned is that no matter how good the gold plate, the brass always ends up showing through."

It didn't take long to dig through the rest of his clothes. He tossed his tux on the bed—something he needed for this weekend—and two suits just in case he had to meet with bankers for a loan for the microbrewery or if he ever talked Skye into marrying him.

He skipped all the flashy shirts and ties Payton had bought him. He grabbed his belts, a few pairs of shoes, and smiled when he found his old motorcycle boots. Payton had hated them and his bike. He'd caved and sold his bike, but he refused to get rid of the boots—they'd even had a huge fight when he found them in a pile of clothes she was giving to Goodwill—that had been one for the record books.

He pushed all the clothes to the middle and checked out the edges—places he knew Payton would shove the things she didn't want him to wear. He laughed out loud when he found his leather biker jacket—that was a keeper. He'd saved for months to buy the darn thing and even now, he still liked it. He found his Rangers jersey. Pop had taken him and his brothers to a hockey game and sprang for them. Pop had never been one to buy much or take them out at night. Taking them to the game had been a big deal because it meant taking a night off. He grabbed the jersey signed by Mike Richter and Adam Graves—his two favorite players—and folded it. He'd wanted to have it framed and put in his office, but Payton nixed the idea. He stuffed his jersey in the box, taped it up, and carried it, his hanging bag, and a leather suitcase to the front door with the others.

The last twelve years of his life fit into a handful of boxes and two bags; the first twelve fit into a beat-up duffel bag and a photo album. What did that say about him?

Logan stepped into Walt's study and looked through dim light and wisps of sweet, cherry-flavored pipe smoke. The study was the only comfortable room in the house. It was a room filled with large, heavy, worn leather and oak furniture he didn't have to worry he'd break. It invited him to sit a spell, put his feet up, and relax, watch a game, or talk business over a bottle of wine or scotch.

"Logan, glad to have you back, son." Walt Billingsly wrapped beefy arms around Logan and pounded him on the back. "I was beginning to wonder if I'd ever see you again. You've been missed around here."

"Thanks, it's good to see you too." Logan took a step back and realized Walt was the only person in the state he would miss. He looked like the aging linebacker he was—big, not so lean, but still in good enough shape to inflict serious damage.

"All ready to go?"

"Yes. But there are a few things we need to talk about."

"Okay." Walt went back around his desk and then emptied his pipe into the ashtray.

Logan did his best not to fidget. He wasn't normally a fidgety person, but he'd never had to drop a bomb quite like this one. He'd much prefer dealing with explosives. Walt had a type A personality with a short temper, and an even shorter fuse. Most things didn't bother him, but Logan never knew what would act as an accelerant. Chances were that dumping his precious daughter and breaking her heart would probably do the trick.

"Sir, I really appreciate you giving me a leave of absence, but I'm afraid I have to tender my resignation."

Walt was in the process of filling his pipe. He stopped and looked up. His smile fell and hung there like a tattered flag on a windless day. "Why?"

"I recently found out that I have a daughter. She's ten and her home is in Red Hook."

"Red Hook? Where in the hell is Red Hook? I thought you were from New York."

"Brooklyn. I'm from Red Hook, Brooklyn."

Walt backed up and sat in his squeaky desk chair. "And how does Payton feel about this?"

"We've called off the engagement." Logan sat and scrubbed his face with his hands. "Payton didn't take the news well."

Walt held the arms of his chair in his viselike grip. He blew out a breath and seemed to be fighting his temper. "I'm sure it was a shock, but something she'll overcome. There's no need to call off the wedding."

Logan didn't want to discuss Payton or her reaction. "Walt, since I've been away, I've taken some time to think about my life, Payton, our future. I've realized that with or without Nicki, the marriage would never have lasted."

"Have you talked to Payton about this?"

"Yes, when she visited me."

"The wedding?"

"Is off. I thought she would have told you."

"Logan, I know Payton is a little spoiled and Lord knows, she can be difficult—"

"Payton and I don't love each other, Walt. We never have. After all that's happened at home, having Nicki, I want more—for me and for Payton. Payton deserves to be loved. We both do. I'm just not the man for her."

"But your relationship with Payton has nothing to do with business."

"I appreciate the opportunity you've given me. But I need to think of Nicki now. I can't take her away from her home. I'm sorry."

"Logan, you need to think about this. This is your future and the future of your daughter we're talking about. Take some time. Take all the time you need. You have a hell of a future with Billingsly Vineyards with or without Payton. This is business. I've invested a lot in you. I've groomed you to take over. I saw something in you even before you and Payton started seeing each other. You have the drive to succeed. You work hard, no matter what that work is. That's rare. You've earned my respect and my trust. You've built yourself a good, stable life here. Do you just want to throw it all away because you've broken up with my daughter? What are you going to do?"

"I'm thinking of opening a microbrewery—maybe a restaurant too. I've enjoyed running my dad's place. I have no firm plans, just an idea and a location so far." He pushed himself out of the chair.

Walt stood, walked around his desk, and leaned on it.

"I'm sorry to lose you as a future son-in-law, but I'll be sorrier to lose you as an employee. You are the best I've seen. You need to think about this and not make some knee-jerk reaction to a lovers' quarrel."

"I have thought about it, Walt. Nicki needs the stability of her family, and they're all in Red Hook."

"Kids move all the time. They're resilient. She'd have a much better life here in the Wine Country than she'd have in Brooklyn. She'd have all the opportunity she could ever want. We'll see to it. Think about it, Logan. Think about what you want. More money? You have the house. . . . What will you be able to offer your daughter if you leave here?"

Logan fought his temper. There were a lot of things he could do.

"All I'm asking is that you let this marinate for a little while. We have a lot to offer you and your daughter. This is a business, Logan. Whatever happens between you and Payton, you need to know that there will always be a place for you at Billingsly Vineyards. Don't forget that."

"Thank you."

"I just want to ask you one favor. Can we keep your breakup under wraps until after the competition? I have a feeling we're going to bring home awards, and I don't want the story to turn into something for the society pages instead of what it should be—a story of our success."

"That's fine. I'll let you deal with the announcement. I'm heading home right after the competition. I've already packed my things to be shipped home and sold the Jag. I'm ready to go whenever you are."

Logan's phone vibrated and he glanced at it. Skye. He let it go to voice mail and turned to follow Walt out.

The door flew open, almost hitting Walt. Payton walked in, wearing her debutante-on-a-mission look. Maybe she was going to the club—he never understood the subtle competition between the women with whom she socialized—the way she spoke about them, he wondered if they even liked one another. Payton stepped into her father's arms and kissed his cheek. "Daddy? Are you ready to go?"

Logan skirted the two of them. "I'll wait outside. Walt, we'll leave whenever you're ready."

Payton pulled away from her father. "Good, I put my bags next to yours, Logan. Be a dear and make sure Jeffrey loads them in the limo."

Shit. "Why?" He supposed an emergency trip to Tahiti was too much to ask for.

"Because I'm coming with you." She shot him a twisted I-got-you-by-the-short-hairs grin.

"That's not a good idea."

"I'm the PR person. It's my job." Payton put her hands on her hips. "Right, Daddy?"

Walt folded like a protein into a tertiary structure.

Logan had that same sinking feeling in his gut that he always got just before disaster struck. "Since when?"

"Since I came back from college."

"Payton, I lived with you, remember? I know you've never worked."

"I'm working now. Isn't that right, Daddy?"

Walt patted her shoulder. "I had Arleen book a suite. We can order a cot if you two can't share a bed. It will be fine, Logan." He gave Payton a look Logan had only ever seen when Walt dealt with problem employees, a look that put them on notice. One look, and whatever happened never happened again. A look Logan was willing to bet Payton had never seen before.

"Fine? I don't think so. I'll call the hotel and get my own room."

Payton's smile was back.

"Payton, behave," Walt said.

She flipped her hair over her shoulder and her smile only got wider. "All the rooms are sold out—even in the neighboring hotels. It looks like you'll have to rough it."

She clutched his arm and brought her lips to his ear. "But then, you always liked it a little rough. Didn't you, Logan?"

Skye ended the call without leaving a message and tossed the phone beside her on the bed. She hated leaving messages—especially when she had no real reason to call. She'd sound like a sap if she told Logan she'd just wanted to hear his voice.

"Skye," Nicki yelled over D.O.G.'s and Pepperoni's barks, "some guy is here."

Shit. She jumped off the bed and ran into the living room, where she found Nicki with a strange man wearing a black leather jacket and worn jeans. "Nicki, didn't I tell you you're not supposed to answer the door without an adult?" She pulled Nicki behind her and looked up— way up. Damn, this guy was tall. Tall, and broad, with longish, curly chestnut brown hair. The curls hung in messy ringlets. His hazel eyes were so warm, she considered losing a layer of clothing.

Nicki squirmed. "I didn't answer the door. He has his own key."

"Can I help you?" The man looked big, tall, and dangerous—not in a run-for-your-life kind of way. No, he looked dangerous in a hold-on-to-your-panties kind of way. Not that she was interested, but damn, she wasn't blind either.

D.O.G. planted his front paws on the guy's chest and licked his chin, while Pepperoni used his jean-clad thigh as a scratching post, vying for attention.

"I'm looking for my father, Pete Calahan. I'm Slater Shaw." He had a deep voice with a hint of Brooklyn, and a smile that would make any sane woman's knees weak, confirming the fact that she was certifiable.

Logan had described his brother Slater as a pocket-protector-carrying computer nerd. Skye might not be drooling over him, but this guy was no computer nerd. "Welcome home. We weren't expecting you, were we? Pete's out for the afternoon. I'm Skye Maxwell—chef turned babysitter." She released Nicki, who jumped in front of her like she had springs for legs.

"Slater! You're here. I'm Nicki, your sister."

If it was possible, his smile brightened, and his head bobbed in time with Nicki's bounce, either confirming her statement or trying to follow her. "I've heard a lot about you, Nicki. I thought it was about time I came home to meet my little sister. You're even prettier than they said you were."

Nicki pinked up and Slater shot Skye a sideways glance and winked. "Where's Logan?"

Nicki stopped jumping and dug her foot into the carpet. "He's in California with Payton, but he loves Skye, so he's coming back. He promised."

Slater's gaze bounced from her to Nicki and back again.

Skye felt her face flash hot and put her hands on Nicki's shoulders, wishing she could put one over her big mouth. "Nicki."

Nicki leaned toward Slater. "Skye's weird about people knowing they love each other, 'cause they work together. I think it's dumb, but whatever—"

Skye gave Nicki's shoulders a squeeze. "Nicoletta, that's enough."

Nicki leaned toward Slater again. "See what I mean?"

Slater looked like he was holding back a laugh. "Nobody tells me anything. I guess I've missed all the news. It's a good thing I've got you around, Nicki, or I'd be clueless. Last time I talked to Logan, he was engaged."

Nicki shook her head. "Not anymore. He dumped Payton, but that was okay 'cause she didn't love him. But he loves Skye and she loves Logan, so it's all good."

Skye wanted the earth to open up and swallow her whole. "So, Slater. Since you're here, I guess I can pack my things and head back to my place once Pete comes home."

He tossed his bag down. "There's no rush. Let me take you ladies out to dinner. It'll give us a chance to get to know each other."

"Can we go for pizza?" Nicki asked.

"If that's okay with Skye, it's okay with me. I haven't had a good pizza since the last time I was home."

Skye just wanted to go back to her place and worry in private. "Thanks for the invitation, but I think I'll let you, Nicki, and Pete have some family time. You don't need me getting in the way."

"Skye, you're never in the way." Nicki grabbed her hand. "You have to come. You're practically family."

"Sure she is." The rumble of Pete's low voice sounded behind them.

They turned to find him standing inside the door. Pete's gaze landed on Slater and stuck. "Damn, boy, I wasn't expecting you home for a few more weeks." He wrapped Slater in a hug and then held him at arm's length. "You need a haircut, but you look good. I'm glad you're home."

Pete looked from Slater to Nicki and back again and seemed to pale before Skye's eyes. "Pete, are you okay?"

"Pop?" Slater must have seen the same thing.

Slater grabbed Pete's arm and Pete fought him off. "I'm fine. I'm not a damn invalid. Leave me alone."

Slater held his hands up as Pete lumbered over to his favorite chair and sat. "I'm just a little tired. I was out too long."

"Hey, Nicki." Slater bent down to her level. "Maybe we should get the pizza to go and bring it home. What do you think?"

Skye looked at Pete—he really did look pale. "How about I fix dinner? I'll throw together something Pete can eat that won't blow his diet."

Nicki groaned. "Healthy food again?"

Slater was still eye to eye with her and had his big hands wrapped around Nicki's little waist. "Healthy food is good stuff, Nicki. How do you expect to get as big and beautiful as Skye if you don't eat right?"

Nicki shrugged. "I'm almost as big as Skye, and I'm only ten and three-quarters. All that healthy eating didn't help her grow very tall."

Skye rolled her eyes, and gave Nicki's shoulder a squeeze. "That's just genetics, kiddo. There was nothing I could do to change that. My grandmother was only four foot eleven. Unfortunately, I take after her. My mother even named me after her."

"I guess it's a good thing her name wasn't Bertha or something horrible, then, huh? I don't know how my mom came up with my name."

Skye looked at Slater, and then at Pete—both of them avoided her gaze. Skye was on her own with this one. "'Nicoletta' is a beautiful name, and 'Nicki' is a cool nickname—they both suit you. I'm sure your mom took one look at you and knew it would be the perfect name for her perfect baby."

"You think I'm perfect?"

"Yes, I do, a perfect angel sometimes, a perfect devil others, but no matter what part of you shows, you're always loved. Face it, kid, you're lovable."

"Not everyone thinks so," Nicki mumbled, looking at Skye and wearing an expression she'd never seen on someone so young. Nicki looked world-weary.

Skye found it hard to swallow past the lump in her throat. Nicki had to miss her mother, she had to be worried sick about her, and she had to be waiting. She was probably half hoping for and half dreading her mother's return. And every day that her mom didn't show, she had to lose a little of the hope she'd held for so long.

Nicki dug her sneaker into the carpet. "Can I go to my room until dinner?"

Skye pulled her into another hug and kissed her forehead. "Sure, sweetie. I'll call you when it's ready."

They watched as Nicki didn't skip, didn't bounce—heck, she didn't even walk; she moped across the living room and disappeared down the hall.

"How long has it been?" Slater asked.

"How long has what been?" Skye wasn't sure whether

she should go to Nicki. She wanted to, and not for the first time, she wished Logan were there. He always knew what to say and do when it came to his little girl. Skye was still new to all this.

"How long has it been since she was dumped?"

Pete hauled himself out of the chair and rubbed his chest. "Almost six months."

Slater nodded to Skye as if it all made perfect sense. "It takes at least a year to either stop running for the door or away from it every time someone knocks."

He must have seen her look of confusion, so he continued. "It takes a couple years to stop waiting for the case manager to show up and tell you to pack your bags."

"How long do you think it'll take for her to believe that we love her?" Her voice was almost a whisper.

Skye watched Slater; his eyes held that same quality Logan's did. Strength, depth, with a scary twist of total desolation.

"I don't know. Maybe it's the day after you finally figure out what the fuck you did to make your real parents stop loving you. When I figure it out, I'll let you know."

And just like Logan's, Slater's shields rolled down, closing himself off to her, to Pete, to everyone.

"I'm going to talk to her. Okay, Pop?"

"Sure, son. It might be good for both of you."

Slater picked up his bag and headed down the hall, walking the same walk Nicki had, the same plod of his feet, the same angle of his head, the same slow, purposeful gait. He looked like a giant, lighter-skinned, male version of Nicki.

Pete stared after Slater and then, as if his legs couldn't hold him up any longer, collapsed into his chair. Thank

God he hadn't moved. He covered his face with his hands and cursed.

"Pete, what's the matter? Are you okay?" Skye knelt beside the chair before she even registered moving.

"Yeah, I'm fine."

Pete wasn't a very good liar. Something was definitely wrong, but she didn't think it was his heart.

CHAPTER 17

Logan walked from the limo to the club with Payton and Walt. He had a part to play. The same part he'd played for years. It fit like an itchy wool sweater—it looked fine, but looks didn't make it any less irritating.

He held the door for Payton, who stuck to him like gum to the bottom of a favorite shoe, reminding him with every step that something was wrong. Dead wrong. No amount of rationalization would make him feel less guilty. He'd never cheated on anyone—until today. At least that's what it felt like. Everything he did felt as if he were betraying Skye. Every step he took was like another shovel of dirt—digging himself deeper and deeper into a hole he feared he might never be able to escape.

They were seated in the main dining room of the country club—the club for which he'd worked so hard for acceptance and realized that admittance as a fake didn't equal acceptance at all. If the people surrounding him knew him—the real him, the one behind the facade—most wouldn't give him the time of day. He'd become a cardboard copy of every other person in the room.

Halfway through the meal, his phone vibrated and he knew it was Skye, the same way he knew she wouldn't understand any of this. Hell, he wasn't sure he did anymore.

Payton's chair was too close, her perfume too strong. She'd been force-feeding him bites of her food, and making it impossible to ignore her without being rude. She slid her nails over his thigh, and his muscles jumped beneath her claws. He caught her hand, gave it a punishing squeeze, and leaned in to whisper in her ear. "That's enough, Payton. I'm not putting up with this. Leave me the fuck alone."

He pushed his chair away. "Excuse me."

Walt leaned forward. "Logan, you gave me your word."

"I know."

"This competition is important, not only to the future of Billingsly wines, but if you remember your contract, it's important to your future income."

"I realize that. If it weren't, I wouldn't be here." Logan stood and adjusted his tie. His eyes landed on Skye's brother Patrick, who dined with a woman who stared right back, shooting virtual daggers at him. He didn't even know her. It made no sense. He was sure that Patrick knew nothing about his relationship with Skye. Patrick didn't even know where Skye was, so why was Patrick's date looking as if she'd like to fry his entrails in hot oil?

Logan stepped away from the table and headed to the men's room. He needed to at least text Skye. Tell her he loved her. Let her know he was thinking of her. Missing her. He might have to play the part of Payton's fiancé a little longer, but then they were through, and he didn't want Skye to worry.

He stood in the small sitting room just outside the

restrooms and sent Skye a text. "Having lunch b4 leaving 4 competition. All packed, sold my car, can't wait to get home. I miss u like crazy. I love u, L."

"Was that your fiancée, Payton Billingsly, with you?"

He looked up from his phone, a stupid smile still on his face, and stared into the eyes of Patrick Maxwell's lunch companion. "Have we met?"

"Not formally, no. But unlike you, I don't conspire with the enemy. And you, Logan Blaise, are a lying, cheating sack of shit in an overpriced suit."

"What? Look, lady, I don't know who you are or what the hell your problem is—"

"My problem is that my best friend is in Red Hook taking care of your family while you're here playing slap-the-salami under the table with your supposed ex-fiancée."

Logan's heart thudded like a flat tire and then stopped. "You're Kelly?" Shit. "Hold on." He grabbed her arm, and the look on her face had him release her immediately. "It's not what it looks like."

She stepped closer so he could see the image on her phone. "Pictures don't lie. Here's a message from Skye." He didn't even see the hand coming until it slapped his face so hard, he was sure it left a handprint. The sting made his eyes water and his jaw ache.

She brought the hand that slapped him to her chest, then shook it out before balling it into a fist.

Oh God. Skye thought he was back with Payton. He held up his hands. "Wait a minute. Kelly, you don't understand."

"Go to hell, asshole. One word and I'll sic her big brother Patrick on you." She turned to walk away and nearly collided with Payton and Walt.

Payton skirted Kelly and wrapped herself around Logan's arm. "You two know each other?"

"Just by a mutual acquaintance." Kelly's gaze met his and he knew just how a feeder mouse felt when it was dropped into a python's cage. He wasn't sure how long she'd toy with him before she went in for the kill. What Kelly didn't know was that if Skye thought he and Payton were really back together, the deed was as good as done. Kelly's misinformation just might have killed any dream of a life with Skye. He watched Kelly walk away, still stunned by what she had just done.

Walt stepped forward. "We have a plane to catch, Logan."

"I just need a minute. Then we can go." Logan didn't even look at Walt. He shook off Payton and followed Kelly. He needed to explain.

"Kelly, wait. Please."

She stopped just before entering the dining room. "Forget it, cretin. You and Payton deserve each other."

Before he could speak, Kelly slipped through the door and any chance he might have had was gone.

"Logan." Payton slid her arm though his and hung on like industrial-strength Velcro. "We have to go. Daddy's not too happy." She pressed herself tighter against him. "What was that all about anyway? And why is the side of your face so red?"

"It's nothing that concerns you, Payton. Leave it alone."

When the walls of the hole he'd dug himself into collapsed around him, drowning him in dirt, making it impossible to breathe, he was still too stunned to react.

"Logan, let's go." Walt urged him forward and he followed without protest.

*   *   *

Skye was in the kitchen dealing with the beginning of a typical Friday night rush. The tritone of her phone announced a text. She tossed a towel over her shoulder and reached for her cell. A picture and a text popped up from Kelly.

Skye clicked the arrow to expand the picture to full size and her breath caught. It was a picture of Logan and Payton together dining at the club. Payton was pressed against his side with her hand in his lap, while Logan whispered in her ear. The caption said, "Should I hit him?"

Pain battered Skye with the force of a kick to the stomach, all the air in her chest rushed out, and her mouth filled with saliva. She felt physically ill, off-balance, and it sounded as if a thousand flies buzzed in her ears. She gripped the edge of the counter.

"Skye, are you all right?"

Harrison stood beside her looking at her phone—the picture. Logan and his fiancée. She pressed the kill button. "I'm fine, but I need a minute." Her voice sounded so normal, almost bored. Her world crashed down around her feet and her voice was calm and steady. Amazing. "I'll be in my office." She took a deep breath and walked blindly through the kitchen. Her phone rang out with texts. She silenced it, stepped into her office beside the kitchen, and shut the door.

She'd known this was going to happen.

The vision of Logan and Payton flashed before her eyes. Her face heated, her ears burned, and she covered her mouth, trying to hold in the sob that somehow made it through her closed throat.

Anger bubbled inside her with a rage she'd never experienced.

Should she let Kelly hit him? She wished she could be there to do it herself, but if she couldn't, Kelly was second-best—Kelly was bigger and took stick fighting. A slap from Kelly would probably leave a mark. Good. She'd never wanted to hurt someone before. She did now.

Skye pulled up the text. "Hell, yes!" She shook so hard with anger, she had a difficult time texting. "Go 4 it. Give him a msg for me. Tell him he's a lying, cheating sack of shit in an overpriced suit." She took a breath, wiped the tears trailing down her cheeks, and hit Send.

She was in full meltdown when the phone vibrated in her hand. She glanced at it.

"Consider it done. Off to slap the shit out of him. He just left the table."

A minute later she received a text from Logan. She didn't bother reading it. She cleared the entire conversation. She couldn't believe how stupid she'd been.

The next text was a picture of Logan's shocked face with a red handprint on his right cheek. She laughed through her tears and texted back:

"Thx 4 delivering the msg. I lov u."

"Anything 4 u. I'm here w/Paddy. Should I have him break Logan's legs? They haven't left yet."

"NO!!! Don't tell Paddy."

"Ok. U hanging in there?"

"I'm fine."

"U lie."

"Going back to work. :(Don't worry. I'm fine."

She didn't have much of a choice; she had a kitchen to

run. She'd fall apart after her shift. Besides, she had the rest of her life to cry.

Skye dried her face, took a deep breath, and moved. One foot in front of the other, one dish at a time, one minute ticked into the next. The night seemed interminable.

Harrison kept shooting her strange looks; she ignored them. She ignored everything but her job. That was the one concrete thing she knew she could handle. Everything else in her life could fall apart, but as long as she was in the kitchen, she kept her sanity.

When Skye heard the crack of gum behind her, she cringed. There was only one person who could crack gum loud enough to rattle the windows. She pulled a burger off the shelf and measured out a serving of fries before tossing a pickle on the side. "Rocki, it's not a good time."

"So I hear. Logan's burning up my phone with text messages."

Anger, hot, strong, and violent, shot through Skye and she turned so quick, Rocki had to step back. "Get out. I'm working. I'm not dealing with this now. Leave. Now."

Rocki sucked in air and choked—probably on her gum. She coughed and then swallowed. When she stopped choking, she wiped her eyes. "Okay, we'll talk later. I'll call Patrice."

Skye held on to her temper by a quickly fraying thread. "Don't bother. Just leave while you still can."

"God, Skye, you don't have to shoot the messenger." Rocki held up her hands, holding her phone in one—its text screen shining toward Skye. "Logan's worried about you. He said you have the wrong idea, but he didn't go into details about what the wrong idea was. So, are you gonna tell me or what?"

"No."

Harrison stepped in between them. "Rocki, don't you have a set to play?"

Rocki looked from Harrison to Skye. "Fine, you don't have to ask me twice." She stepped toward the doors. "Okay, you do. I'm leaving. Skye, you know where I am if you need anything."

Skye watched Rocki strut through the kitchen on her ridiculous heels.

Harrison put his hand on her shoulder. "You okay, Chef?"

"I'm fine, thanks."

"Patrice will be here in about twenty minutes if I know those two. Things are under control if you want to skip out the back way. I suggest you don't answer your door tonight."

She didn't even try to smile; she was afraid her face would crack. Tension radiated through her—even her eyelids twitched. Not a good sign. "I might just take you up on that."

Harrison walked her to the back door and held her coat for her. "I don't know what happened, but call me if you need a shoulder to cry on. You know when I get off work."

She slid into the coat and the vision of rolling around naked on the bed and making love to Logan with the soft fur coat beneath her skin flashed on her mental Jumbotron. Pain hit her again, quick and sharp and deep—like a punch to the heart. "Thanks, but I'm fine." Maybe if she said it often enough, she would be.

He just nodded and didn't look as if he believed her. She didn't blame him.

She stepped out into the cold alley, and her phone rang again. This time it was Kelly. "Hey, thanks for slapping Logan for me."

"It was the least I could do."

"No, only best friends smack the shit out of cheating lovers. I hope I never have to return the favor."

"What are you going to do?"

Skye unlocked the door and headed up the stairs fumbling with her keys. "I'm going to call Rex, the old cook, and see if he can be back before opening on Tuesday." There, she said it out loud—she was leaving. She had to.

She let herself into the apartment, tossed her keys on the table, and shrugged out of her coat. Pepperoni was still at Pete's, which was just as well. She didn't feel like taking a midnight stroll.

"You're going to quit? I thought you loved working there."

"I do. I mean, I did. But, Kelly, I can't be here and work with Logan. I just can't." She couldn't imagine ever being able to see him without completely falling apart, and she didn't fall apart. It wasn't her MO.

"Are you even sure he'll be back? If he and Payton are still engaged—"

"Of course he's coming back. Nicki's here. Logan would never leave Nicki."

"But he'd cheat on you? He'd leave you?"

"You saw it with your own eyes. You tell me."

"He did say it wasn't what it looked like. Maybe you should talk to him."

"Kelly, I saw the picture. What did she do, tie him to the chair and force him to whisper sweet nothings in her ear? I really don't want to hear anything more from him ever again."

"I don't know. Talk to him. Get the whole story. It will give you closure."

"Has closure ever helped you?"

"We're not talking about me. Don't you want to know why he'd do this?"

"I know why. Look at that woman—she's supermodel material and I'm the Pillsbury Dough Girl."

"You're beautiful."

"I'm short and fifteen pounds overweight, which, at my height, makes me practically obese."

"You're being ridiculous."

"No, I'm finally being realistic. It's about time I got a shot of reality. At least Logan got his too."

"I have a bad feeling about this, Skye."

"Probably the same one I've had since the beginning. I knew it was a mistake and I did it anyway. It serves me right. I'll never make that mistake again. Lesson learned: Never fall in love with a man you can't imagine living without, because you'll surely have to learn."

"What are you going to do?"

"I don't know, Kell. I didn't think anything short of being hit by a bus could hurt this bad. I'll probably cry myself to sleep and get up and go to work tomorrow morning. Being in the kitchen always helps me forget what a disaster I've made out of my life. Then I'll get the hell out of Red Hook before he comes back on Monday. Let me go so I can call Rex. I'll talk to you soon. Love you."

"Skye, think about what I said. Call me if you want to talk more. I'm always here for you."

Skye couldn't say anything, so she stood there with

tears streaming down her face and nodding before she was able to croak out the word, "Bye." Skye ended the call, curled up in a ball on the couch, and fell apart. The worst part was that the only shoulder she'd ever wanted to cry on belonged to the one man who built her up only to turn around and tear her down. And still, even after he'd shattered her heart, she still wanted him, she still missed him, she still loved him.

Skye had only quit one job before, and she didn't know how to quit without building up a head of steam.

She was out of steam, out of tears—she checked her watch: four p.m.—and out of time. She had to get this over with.

Every time she walked past her computer on her way to the walk-in freezer, she refreshed the screen. She was OCD-ing like a sadist with a new bullwhip. She stared at the picture of Logan receiving a congratulatory kiss from his beautiful fiancée—the caption below the photo was *Logan Blaise—a Double Winner*. Payton's engagement ring caught the light at the same time the camera caught their kiss.

If there was a possibility that the nightmare of the last day was a misunderstanding, the pictures, tweets, Facebook postings, and video feed coming out of the competition put a bullet through the heart of her last hope.

The blogs were all over the fairy-tale story of Logan's success and his and Payton's upcoming New Year's Eve wedding.

She didn't know why she was glued to her computer—it was like some sick masochistic fascination. And every picture, every interview, every mention of Logan and

Payton together, just shattered what was left of her already broken heart.

She shut down the computer, took off her apron, and walked out onto the floor. She did her deep-breathing exercises on her way to the office and knocked.

"Come in."

Slater sat at Logan's desk. His hair shone in the overhead lighting, and his hazel eyes seemed to see right through her. "I was looking for you last night. Rocki said you ducked out the back. I even went up to your place—you didn't answer the door. Logan was concerned about you."

The last thing she wanted to do was discuss Logan. "I went to sleep early. Is Pete around? I need to talk to him."

"He's upstairs—Nicki just got home from Francis and Patrice's place." He clicked something on his computer—a computer that looked like a spaceship. Neon green lights shot through the keyboard and around the edges. It was the biggest laptop she'd ever seen. It must have had a twenty-inch screen. Alienware—she'd never heard of that brand but wouldn't mind taking it for a spin. Then again, maybe not. She'd already spent enough time looking at pictures of the love of her life with his fiancée.

Slater's fingers flew over the keyboard at unbelievable speeds. He scanned the screen, hit a few more keys, and then looked at her again. "I can see you have something to discuss. Come on, I'll take you up."

She got a sudden chill; she wasn't sure if it was from the glacial look in his eyes or the room's frigid temperature. "You don't have to. I know the way."

He leaned back in the worn desk chair—the look in his eyes belying his relaxed pose. "You do realize I'm managing the place while Logan's away. If there's something you need to discuss with Pop that has anything to do with the restaurant, I need to be there."

Too damn bad. "I'd prefer to speak to Pete alone."

Slater saved his work and shut the lid with the finality of slamming a door. He stood. "No."

"What are you, some kind of self-appointed bodyguard? Pete doesn't need protection from me."

"I don't know what's going on with you and Logan. I really don't care. All I know is that Logan is strung tighter than a nuclear power plant's IT guy who just discovered they were being attacked by the Fukushima virus."

"Fukushima virus?"

"Take my word for it: It's bad. I don't know what the hell is wrong, but I know it has something to do with you. So forgive me if I don't want to let you run roughshod over my father too."

"Run roughshod over your father? As if. And as for Logan, I'm hardly the cause of whatever it is that's bothering him. Maybe it's his guilty conscience. I'm not the one cheating."

"Logan doesn't cheat. Ever."

"Right. That's why he's kissing his ex on camera. Look, I'm not here to get into a pissing contest with you, Slater. I don't have the right equipment. And I'm not gonna stand here and listen to you sing your cheating brother's praises. I quit. I'm leaving after my shift tonight."

Slater's mouth dropped open and Skye wanted to stick the stapler in it. Instead, she held up her hand to stop whatever was about to come out. "Don't worry. I've already spoken to Rex—the chef I replaced—and he'll be here before opening on Tuesday. The kitchen is covered. I'm finished. And you and your sainted brother can both go to hell."

Rocki burst through the door like a neon-colored cyclone. "Skye—there's a table that wants to compliment the chef. They sound like they know you. I don't know what you've got goin' on, sister, but they are four of the hottest guys I've ever seen in one place—well, maybe except onstage in *Magic Mike*. Those guys were hot, but then they were wearing a lot less then the men asking for you. So I'll gladly wait to make a more informed decision at a later date. I wonder if they dance."

"What guys?" Skye and Slater asked in stereo, which was just too weird for words. Slater puffed up like Barney on steroids. Why should he care if there was an entire football team waiting for her?

Rocki blew her pink streak out of her eyes and grabbed Skye's hand. "I figured you and Logan must be through for you to call your posse—"

"My posse?"

"Please tell me you'll share. I'll give you first dibs and everything. No pressure, but the ginger with the earring is definitely my type."

Rocki tugged on Skye's hand and dragged her through the door. She stepped out onto the floor and a table of men stood at attention. Her gaze landed on Paddy.

"Hey, squirt, you've put together an amazing menu. The food was excellent. You've done us all proud."

His worried eyes locked on hers, he opened his arms, and it was as if the dam broke. She'd been holding it together all day. Through the morning prep, the lunch rush, the dinner prep, and all the times she checked the Internet for updates on Logan. She'd been stuffing all the tears, putting emotions on a back burner. But one word of praise from her big brother shattered her composure. She ran for him blubbering like a baby.

Paddy wrapped his arms around her and picked her up, leaving her feet dangling. "We're here now. It's going to be okay."

She looked over Paddy's shoulder and saw the rest of her brothers looking nervously from her to one another.

Kier shrugged to Colin, and Reilly looked like he expected their father to come after him for pulling her hair.

"What . . . what are you doing here?"

Paddy set her down but didn't let her go. "Kelly said you needed us. I sent out a code red and we jumped on the next plane."

"Who's taking care of your restaurants?"

"Our sous chefs."

"But you never leave—not all of you."

Kier gave her his you're-in-danger-of-getting-a-smack-on-the-ass look. "You never needed us before. When we get a code red, we come to fix the problem." He thrust out his chest and scanned the room, his blue eyes flashing, looking almost purple in the bar lighting, and landed on someone.

Skye followed his gaze and saw it was locked squarely on Slater.

Slater's gaze shot from Kier—the ginger Rocki had talked about—to Rocki and back again. His bearing went from confused to street fighter in a nanosecond.

Pete and Francis flanked Slater.

Reilly and Colin stood on either side of Kier. Shit. All they needed were cowboy hats, six-shooters, and some cheesy piano music and they'd have their own spaghetti western. This was so not good.

Skye stepped out of Paddy's arms, wiped her tears, and went straight to Pete and grabbed his hand, tugging him forward. "Pete Calahan, this is my family."

He leaned in and whispered. "Your brothers?"

She nodded. "Patrick's the big one—you heard about him. Kier is the ginger with the earring—our rebel without a clause. A lawyer turned chef—"

Rocki actually swooned. "He's a lawyer and can cook too? Yum." She stepped closer to Kier, gave him the seal of approval, and flashed the bright white Rocki special. "Hi. How are you with torts?"

Slater took a step forward. "Can it, Rocki. Pretty boy's not here for a quickie. He's come to rescue the little princess who's been slumming it and playing us for the last month. Little Ginger's here to take her back to the castle. Isn't that right, Skye?"

Colin stepped in front of Kier—either to shield him or to get first dibs on Slater.

She pushed Slater back a step for his own protection and because if someone got to hit him, she'd take the first swing. He stepped back willingly, obviously, since she'd have as much chance of pushing him around as she would pushing a freakin' mountain. She was surprised he moved. "Slater, leave Rocki out of this. I don't know where you came up with this princess crap or what kind of castle you think I'm from, but you know nothing about me. I don't care if you don't like me, but I don't want trouble, so I strongly suggest you keep your mouth shut. You see my brother Colin over there? The big guy in the red shirt? He's a seventh-degree black belt in tae kwon do. He can turn you into a pretzel if he wanted to. So be a good boy and back off."

She turned to Reilly, who looked happy enough to

just stand back and watch the proceedings—Reilly was so laid-back, sometimes she wondered if he wasn't adopted. "Reilly, would you please throw some water on these guys or take them out back and let them beat the crap out of each other? I don't care what they do as long as they don't do it in here. I've had enough."

She didn't wait for a response before ignoring the lot of them and focusing on Pete. "Pete, I'm sorry, but I'm leaving. I talked to Rex last night and he's on his way home. I tried to tell you earlier. I went into the office to talk to you but ran into Slater instead. I'm not his favorite person, obviously."

Pete pulled her aside. "Skye, I can see you're upset, but I don't understand. What the hell happened? Yesterday afternoon everything was fine. What changed?"

Slater let out a laugh that was more menacing than funny. "She's not leaving, Pop—she's running. She probably found out Logan's not as rich as he looks. You know princesses expect a pedigree and Logan doesn't have one."

Her head whipped back to Slater. The man could go from Dr. Jekyll to Mr. Jackass with a chip the size of Mount Rushmore on his shoulder in under a minute—she wouldn't have believed it if she hadn't seen it with her own eyes.

Pete speared him a warning look that had Slater taking a full step back. After seeing that look, she had no problem imagining Pete as the tough detective he was purported to be. "That's enough out of you, boy. Skye's brothers are our guests. If you can't be nice, go upstairs and check on Nicki."

Slater gave him a curt nod, and shot her another disapproving glare. "Your psycho fantasies aside, my brother is no cheater." He looked back at his father and shrugged. "I'll be at the end of the bar if you need me, Pop."

"Fine, just don't cause any trouble, and I mean it, Slater. I don't know what bug flew up your ass, but it ends here. Do I make myself clear?"

Red stripes sharpened Slater's cheekbones like war paint against his pale skin. His hazel eyes flashed over the crowd, then settled on Pete. "Yes, sir."

Skye leaned into Pete. "Military?"

"Navy."

"I hope he's better at following orders than at conversation."

Pete cracked a smile. "Let me get a drink—not a word, young lady."

"I'm not saying anything. While you're back there, pour me one of whatever you're having. I could use something—anything but champagne, that is."

"Go on back to the office. I'll bring the drinks and we'll talk about whatever it is that's got everyone in an uproar, okay?"

She nodded and took a step forward. All her brothers moved in unison. She turned. "I'm fine. Just do me a favor—sit down and behave yourselves. You too, Rocki." She smiled up at Francis. "Feed them dessert."

Francis clapped her shoulder. "Sure, Skye. I'll babysit the boys."

CHAPTER 18

Skye finished packing and had everything ready to leave. The limo was waiting to take her and her brothers to the airport. The only thing she hadn't done was say good-bye to Nicki. She checked her watch. She couldn't put it off any longer. She packed up Pepperoni's toys and food, put her on her leash, and let the dog pull her across the alley.

Letting herself into Pete's apartment, Skye took Pepperoni off her leash. When she stood, she saw the second-to-last man she ever wanted to see.

Slater tossed the book he'd been reading on the coffee table and stood, forcing her to look up. If he'd stayed seated, they would have been almost the same height.

She waved him off. "Give it up, Slater. I don't intimidate easily, and I'm not in the mood. I'm here to drop off Pepperoni and say good-bye to Nicki. Where is she?"

"She went to her room after dinner. She's been there all night."

"Is she asleep?"

Slater shrugged.

"Did you tuck her in?"

He looked confused.

"You know, put her to bed, pull the covers over her and her teddy bear. Hugs and kisses, prayers . . ."

He stared as if she'd asked him if he had a spare tampon she could borrow.

"I take that as a no." She ignored the answering glare and turned down the hall to Nicki's room and knocked on the door. D.O.G. and Pepperoni circled each other in the narrow space and pushed her into the wall. "Nicki, it's Skye. Can I come in?"

There was no answer.

She opened the door and peeked in. It took a moment for her eyes to adjust to the darkness. The shadow of Nicki sitting holding her teddy bear under one arm and her iPad to her chest became clear. She didn't move, she only stared into space—small, lost, dejected, alone.

The dogs ran in. D.O.G. leaped on the bed and it took three tries for Pepperoni to make the jump. The dogs nudged Nicki. D.O.G. whined and licked her face. Pepperoni stood on Nicki's lap, rested her paws on Nicki's shoulders, and gave her kisses. Nicki didn't move. She didn't pet them. She didn't even blink.

"Hey, Nicki. Are you okay?"

"I'm fine." Nicki looked at her—or rather through her. Her voice was flat—like a computer-generated voice that told you to press one for Spanish. It was low, steady, emotionless, vacant.

She knew.

Skye's heartbeat slowed. She looked around the perfect pink room with the canopy bed. A perfect room for a little girl with a less than perfect life. And now Skye was going to make it worse. She'd never intended to hurt Nicki, but that was exactly what she was doing. Guilt rested like a two-ton anvil around her neck, pulling her down. She thought she'd sunk as low as humanly possible into the depths of depression. She was wrong. "Nicki, Rex is coming back, and I'm going to have to leave. I wanted to say good-bye."

"Sure. Bye." Nicki tossed her iPad on the bed, wrapped her arm around D.O.G., and sank into the bedding, turning her back to Skye.

"I'm sorry, sweetie. I don't want to leave."

"Then don't."

Pepperoni rested her head on Nicki's hip and whined. Staring at Skye with those bulging, expressive, worried eyes.

"I can't stay, but it has nothing to do with you." Her heart beat hard. So hard it felt as if her blood had turned to sludge—too thick to flow.

"You're a grown-up. You can do whatever you want."

Every word hit Skye like a three-inch nail shot out of a pneumatic nail gun.

"You just don't want to stay—not bad enough."

She stepped back with each hit.

"You love Logan, but not enough."

Pain—hot and sharp—radiated through her, starting at her head and not stopping until even the soles of her feet burned.

"That's okay. Me and Logan, we're used to not enough, so go ahead and leave."

"I'm sorry." Skye held back a sob. She released the grip on the chair that had been holding her up and backed out of the room. She closed the door and slumped against the wall. The steel bands that had wrapped around her when she looked at that first picture of Logan cinched tighter with every hit. Nicki's dismissal was the final crank.

Slater stood there, arms crossed. His smile looked more like a sneer chiseled in granite, his eyes dull and lifeless and shuttered. "I guess she told you, huh?"

She covered her mouth with her hand, but still the sob escaped.

He stared through her just like Nicki had, just like Logan had. "You know the way out, right, princess? Go ahead, run away."

She dropped her hand and stared up at him. "For your information, I'm not a princess."

Slater laughed. "Yeah, I know your type—you're the princess who likes to slum it with us bad boys until it gets a little too hard, a little too dirty, or a little too serious, and then you go running back to Daddy and your nice castle with your servants and rich boys you can lead around by the nose. Was Logan your little fling on the dark side before settling down with a well-heeled, pedigreed pooch? If this is how you treat Logan, he's better off with Payton."

He hadn't just rammed the knife through her heart; he twisted it like spaghetti on a fork. "You're a sick, cruel, small, small man."

The corner of his mouth turned up in a twisted smile. "Yeah, but at least I don't hurt innocent little girls. If I'm so fuckin' cruel, what's that make you?"

Skye burst into tears. She couldn't take it anymore. She didn't care what she looked like. She had to get out of there.

Slater's laughter chased her out the door and down the steps.

Skye flew through the outer door; the sharp cold wind slapped her wet face. The limo waited by the curb, the door opened, and she launched herself inside.

Her brothers piled in behind her, shooting worried looks at one another.

Skye pulled the sweatshirt around her and curled into a ball. Sure, she was running. Just not fast enough to leave behind the anger, guilt, betrayal, and loss. Not fast enough to evade the pain. Not strong enough to dodge the tears. Not good enough to win Logan's heart.

Not good enough totally sucked.

Paddy reached over and pulled her into a hug. "It's gonna be all right, squirt. We just need to get you home where you belong."

Skye shook her head, burrowed into her brother's jacket, and released the torrent of grief she'd been holding at bay for the last few days.

It wasn't going to be all right.

It was never going to be all right.

Home was in the rearview mirror, slipping farther and farther away.

She was leaving Red Hook, she was leaving Nicki, she was leaving Logan, but most of all, she was leaving her heart.

If there were a Biggest Loser for relationships, Logan would win hands down.

He looked around the ballroom crowded with ten-top tables and people dressed as if they were walking the red carpet instead of gathering to judge wines and give awards. Awards that could make or break a vineyard. Awards that would be heralded and talked about by wine snobs around the world.

He had nothing against wine snobs—hell, he was one. But winning all the awards in front of him wasn't worth losing the one person who brought him love, happiness, and total fulfillment. Nothing was worth losing Skye.

A camera flash momentarily blinded him.

"Payton, give Logan a kiss for the Web site." The blurry photographer's voice sounded across the table. "We missed the congratulatory kiss."

"No." Coming here, doing his duty, wasn't worth losing Skye. He tugged the tail of his bow tie and stood. "I'm sorry, I have a family emergency. I have to go."

Payton pushed away from the table, wrapping her arm around his waist. "Not now," she said through her fake cover-girl smile. "Don't you dare embarrass me."

He leaned in and whispered in her ear through clenched teeth. "Not everything is about you. I have to go. If you don't want to cause a scene, I suggest you say good-bye and smile."

"I'm coming with you." She grabbed the joke of a purse and slid the chain over her shoulder.

He couldn't deal with this. He may have won best in show and best red, but he was the biggest loser on the face of the earth. He was whipped, weary, worried, and pissed. He should have put his foot down. Hell, he should never have come in the first place. His wines would have won whether he'd been there or not.

"Walt, I've got to go. Alone. Now." God, he hoped he wasn't too late.

Walt stood beside Payton and put his beefy hand on her shoulder. "That's enough, Payton. Let him go." He gave Logan an apologetic grin. "Good luck, Logan. I wish you the best. Let me know if you need anything—letters of recommendation, help with funding—anything.

You'll always have a place at Billingsly. You have a safe trip back, keep in touch, and think about what I said, my friend."

He reached around Payton and shook her father's hand. "I will, and I expect you to hold up your side of the bargain."

Walt gave him a firm shake and a nod. "You can count on it."

Logan left the room without a backward glance and started running as soon as he hit the hall. He had his jacket off before he reached the elevator and within three minutes he had his bags and was headed to the airport. "I'll give you an extra hundred if you get me to the terminal in a half hour."

He made the last flight out and was in a cab at Newark by a quarter to six the next morning. He pulled up to Skye's place just before seven and used his key to get in. Pepperoni ran out of the bedroom and did a full-body wag. "Shh, calm down. I'll take you out in a minute."

He put his bags down, tossed his jacket on the back of the chair, and headed toward the bedroom. He heard a huge snore. A man's snore. "Just what the fuck is going on here?" He walked through the bedroom door, pushing it open harder than necessary so it bounced off the doorstop.

A big, naked man shot up in bed.

"Rex?"

Rex pulled the sheet over him. "Shit, Logan. What the hell are you doing here?"

"Where is she?"

"Who?"

"Skye, damn it. Where is she?"

"She's gone, man. She called Friday night, said I got my job back and needed to start Tuesday. I drove straight from Florida and got in about two this morning. She left the keys on the table like she said she would. Pepperoni was having a sleepover with Nicki. I came home and fell into bed. The apartment's spotless and the refrigerator is stocked. She even put clean sheets on the bed. Nice girl, that Skye."

Pepperoni chased her tail at Logan's feet, spinning crazy circles at high speeds.

He looked around the room—she'd taken everything, her clothes, her books, her warmth, even her scent. There wasn't one sign that she'd ever stepped foot in here. Not one sign that everything they shared here, everything he'd felt, everything he dreamed and based his future on, ever existed.

All the energy drained from Logan's body like water out of a tub, leaving him empty.

Hollow.

Alone.

Numb.

He stumbled back and sat on the chair that Skye used to use as a clothes rack and stared at Rex without seeing him. "She left? I missed her?"

"I guess. She said something about having to leave. Slater dropped Pepperoni off about an hour ago, after her morning constitutional." Rex dragged the sheet around him and got up. "Hey, man. Are you okay? You don't look too good. You want I should make you something to eat? You look real pale."

Logan just stared into Pepperoni's eyes. "She left? She's just gone?"

"Dude, like I said, Skye called Friday night, said she

was leaving, and that Pepperoni was at Pete's. That's all I know. Maybe Pete knows more."

He pushed himself out of the chair and fought for breath as he escaped the bedroom.

"Logan, are you gonna be okay?"

Fuck no. But he didn't say that. "Yeah, I'm good. Just tired. I caught the red-eye. I'm sorry I woke you." He took the keys to the apartment off his ring and put them on the table.

"No problem. And hey, if you talk to Skye, tell her thanks for taking care of Pepperoni."

Logan had a feeling he wouldn't be talking to Skye anytime soon. He'd called, texted, and e-mailed her a hundred times between the time he'd gotten smacked by Kelly and when he was told to turn off all his electronic devices on the plane. When he got her voice mail, he left messages until her mailbox was full.

A few minutes later he found himself sitting at his desk. He didn't remember coming in. He just blinked and there he was, staring at a registered letter addressed to him. Nicki's paternity test.

Logan took a deep breath, broke the seal, slit the envelope open, and stared at it until the results blurred. His eyes burned. His throat constricted and pressure crushed his chest, making it almost impossible to breathe.

Negative.

The paper slid out of his numb fingers and crashed like a wrecking ball through whatever was left of his world.

Logan climbed the stairs to the apartment wondering what the hell he was going to do with his life. All he knew was that he needed to be there for Nicki. No matter what that test said, he loved her. He'd promised he'd always be there for her, and he always kept his promises.

He put on his game face and when he opened the door was attacked by D.O.G. "Hey, boy, where's Nicki?"

"Right here." Nicki was curled up on the couch in her pink nightgown.

"Hey, kiddo, what are you doing?" Something was wrong. Nicki's face was pale and drawn. The look in her eyes was one he'd seen in his own. One he'd seen in his brothers', and in the eyes of other kids in foster care. It was the look of loss, fear, rejection, and hopelessness. On top of that, she looked sick.

"Nicki? Are you okay?" He felt her forehead. Not that he knew what he was doing, but her forehead didn't feel any hotter than his—he didn't think she had a fever. He sat beside her and she climbed on his lap. "What's the matter, baby?"

"Skye left." Nicki's eyes filled, then overflowed. "I'm sorry, Logan. I didn't mean to make her leave. I was as good as I know how to be. I tried, I really did—"

"Oh, baby, no. Skye didn't leave because of you. She loves you. You didn't do anything wrong. I'm the reason Skye left. I'm the one who screwed up." He thought that would have helped, but it seemed to make things worse. He'd seen Nicki cry when she fell and hurt herself, but he'd never seen her cry like this. Like her heart was breaking. He felt like the biggest bastard on the face of the earth.

Her little body was racked with sobs. He was afraid she was going to make herself sick. "Nicki, calm down. It's okay."

"No." She fought for control, hiccuping, trying to catch her breath. "I . . . I was so mean to her."

He held her and rocked her and rubbed her back. Powerless to make things better, which really sucked because he caused the whole damn thing.

She wiped her face on her sleeve, hiccuped a few times, and took a deep breath. "Skye came to say goodbye and I told her to go like I didn't care. Logan, I just didn't want her to leave."

"I know, Nicki. I know and Skye knows. It'll be okay."

"No, it won't. I was mean. I told her to leave. I told her we didn't need her. And Slater . . ."

"What about Slater?"

"He called her names and made her cry."

He'd deal with Slater later. "Nicki, I know Skye loves you, and she understands. You can call her and tell her you're sorry. How's that sound?"

"Did you?" Her tears slowed, and she stopped gasping, just hiccuping every once in a while.

"Yes. She's not answering her phone. I didn't mean to, but I think I hurt her pretty bad."

"Did you leave her a message?"

"About a hundred of them. She won't talk to me."

Nicki rubbed her wet face on his shirt and rested her head on his chest. "How are you supposed to make up if she won't talk to you?"

"Good question. I don't know. I just don't know."

He ran his hand over her hair and down her back until she quieted. Her hold on him relaxed, and the next time he looked down, she was asleep. He knew he should put her back in bed; the poor kid probably didn't get much sleep last night. A guilty conscience and sleep usually didn't mix well.

He held Nicki close, knowing that somewhere out there was the man who fathered her and had the ability to take her away from him. But for now, he'd hold her, listen to her deep, even breaths, watch her sleep, and memorize her face. He studied the way her nose was pointed at the very tip and the little divot above her Cupid's bow top lip, her mouth that smiled bright enough to light a room, her strong chin that quivered when she cried, or could rise to a haughty angle, and her large almond-shaped eyes that could shoot daggers at him one minute and melt his heart the next. He could watch her for the rest of his life and never tire of seeing her. She was still so little, so innocent, so intelligent, and she wasn't his.

He wiped away the wetness on his cheek and realized he'd been crying. He couldn't remember ever crying before. Maybe it was because he'd needed a heart to cry, and he hadn't had one until Nicki and Skye had given him theirs. Now that he'd lost them both, he wasn't sure he wanted his heart. Before, he didn't feel much, which wasn't so bad; at least then he'd never felt this kind of pain.

He must have nodded off, because the next thing he knew, Pop was standing over them. Looking like the worried grandfather and father he was. Logan had no idea how Pop knew about the results of the test—the envelope had been sealed. What did it matter? He and his brothers stopped questioning Pop's methods of information extraction years ago. It was a waste of time. Pop knew, and like always, Pop had known he wouldn't take the news well.

Pop didn't say anything. He didn't need to. He just gave his shoulder a squeeze and damned if Logan didn't feel his eyes sting again. Shit, he'd never felt as devastated as he did when he'd opened that envelope and seen the results. Pop had warned him. Pop had told him there was a chance Nicki wasn't his, but he hadn't listened. He didn't think it was possible to love someone so much. He thought their connection was a genetic thing. A man knows his child—well, apparently not. He picked up Nicki and carried her to bed. She didn't stir when he laid her down. He tucked her in with her bear, and tiptoed out, closing the door behind him.

Pop was in the kitchen pouring coffee. He turned and handed Logan a cup. "You're home a day early."

"Not early enough. Skye's gone." He took a sip and tried to wake up. He hadn't slept since before he left.

Pop set his coffee down and gave him a look he must have given to hundreds of criminals he'd arrested. It was the kind of look that made him want to run for cover—if he were fifteen years younger, he would have. Pop stepped forward, got right up in his face, and Logan did what any sane man would do when his dad tossed him in the center of the ring—he puffed out his chest and backed up. "Do you want to explain to me what the hell you were doing with Payton, when your girlfriend was living under my roof, covering for you at the restaurant, and taking care of Nicki? Because right now, son, I don't know what to believe. Unless all those photographs of you and Payton together are fakes, it looks to me like I raised a good-for-nothing, low-life, cheating son of a bitch."

Logan's face heated and felt as if it were scalded.

Pop's expression morphed from pissed to disgusted and landed firmly in the land of disappointment. Logan hadn't seen that look since he first moved in, since the day Pop caught him with the Latin Kings. He never forgot the embarrassment, the shame, the humiliation, and he'd sworn he'd never feel that way again. He'd been wrong.

"I didn't cheat. I flew back to California, went to my house, and found Payton in my bed. She never told anyone we'd called off the wedding. She decided to take me back."

"Lucky you. So you just went along with it? Did you jump right back into bed with her?"

"No. What the hell do you think I am?"

Pop shook his head and ran his hand through his hair. "When Skye showed me those pictures, I couldn't blame the girl for leaving. You broke her heart."

"I slept in the guest room. Skye knows that. We were on the phone when I discovered Payton hadn't moved out."

"So what the hell were those pictures of you kissing Payton?"

"Friday, I met with Walt, tendered my resignation, and told him the wedding was off. Walt asked me not to say anything about the breakup until after the awards. He had a feeling we were going to win, and he wanted the news to be about the wine, not about Payton and me. I agreed as a favor to him. He's going to announce our breakup in the next few days."

"So you just pretended to still be engaged without telling your girlfriend? Did you ever think that she wouldn't know you were pretending? Did you ever think how it would look to her? How she'd feel? Skye thinks you and Payton are back together."

"I was going to call her and explain everything, but Skye's friend Kelly saw Payton and me having lunch with Walt at the club before we flew to Portland. She told Skye before I could; then she slapped me."

Pop laughed. "I think I'm gonna like this girl, Kelly. Sounds like Skye's going to do all right. Skye's brothers came all the way out here to get her. It's a good thing you were on the other side of the country or I have a feeling I'd be visiting you in the hospital. Not that I don't think you belong there myself."

"I didn't cheat on Skye."

"Oh, you cheated all right, you just didn't sleep with your ex. How would you feel if you saw Skye plastered all over some guy, kissing him in public? You know, Logan, you're living proof that a high IQ is not a good measure of intelligence, because, son, you just pulled the stupidest stunt I've ever seen."

CHAPTER 19

Pete slid behind the bar and stood beside his bottle of Macallan 18. He scanned the floor looking for Bree and smiled when he realized she must still be in the office. She and Storm had been back for a week and she was already on his case. He loved his daughter-in-law, but the girl was a total pain in the ass when it came to his not drinking. He poured a scotch and took a swig while he watched Logan in the mirror's reflection. Logan didn't handle rejection well—even when he deserved it. He'd retreated into the same damn shell in which he'd spent his entire life. Someone had to do something and it looked as if, like usual, it fell on him. He looked at the drink in hand and wished he'd poured a double. Logan sat at a booth, just like he did every night, staring into his glass.

Francis caught his eye and took a seat in front of him at the bar. "He's looking over the plans for the warehouse."

"I'm not blind, Francis. I got a bum ticker, but my eyes are just fine."

Francis scratched the frost off his beer mug. "He won't

talk to me about it. I've tried, man. You need to do something."

"He hasn't spoken much to anyone except Nicki."

They watched Logan get rid of the woman trying to get his attention. He either blew off or completely ignored every woman who went after him.

Francis shook his head. "He's got girls fallin' all over him."

"Not the one he wants, and he's too busy licking his self-inflicted wounds to do anything to correct the situation."

"Someone has to talk to him."

"Storm tried to get him out of his funk and it almost ended in a fistfight and Slater's still recovering from the 'talk' Logan had with him about the way he'd treated Skye before she ran off." Pete shook his head. "My boys have come a long way, but when emotions are involved, I wonder if they've changed at all since the day I took them in. One major emotional hit and they land right back where they started."

Francis took a sip of his beer and nodded. "Yeah, and Logan's had a double whammy. Man, it was like he lost Skye and Nicki in one day. He loves that little girl. Speaking of which, have you said anything to Slater yet?"

"No, I didn't want to rub any salt in Logan's wounds. Besides, it's important for Slater and Nicki to get to know each other better."

"Slater's got to be blind not to see the resemblance. I don't know how we didn't see it from the beginning."

"I know, when you see the two of them together, the similarities are striking, but until I did, I never put it together. I must be getting old. Hell, I feel fuckin' ancient."

He sat on the stool beside Francis, where he could keep an eye on Logan.

"What are you gonna do about Logan?"

"I don't know. I thought if I gave the boy some time, he'd get off his ass and do something, try to get Skye back, but it's been two weeks and I'm not a patient man. If Logan doesn't do something soon, it'll be too late to reverse the damage."

"I looked at those plans of his. Don't you think it's interesting that they include a restaurant and microbrewery? Maybe he's planning to do some kind of grand gesture. It's not as if he's sitting on his ass doing nothing."

"I received an interesting call the other day."

Francis's big bushy eyebrows rose. "Heavy breathing?"

"No such luck. Skye's friend Kelly called me. It seems as if Skye's in pretty bad shape. Kelly's worried and she blames herself, since she's the one who told Skye Logan was cheating on her."

"Why the hell did she do that?"

"Because he was or it looked as if he was. She's a good friend."

"So why doesn't she just tell Skye it was a mistake?"

"She did but it didn't seem to make much of a difference, since Logan has done nothing to get her back. The boy's his own worst enemy. He wouldn't say shit if he had a mouth full of it. What the hell does he expect? Skye to come running back to him after what he did?"

"I don't know, Pete. I'd think he was giving up if I hadn't seen the architectural drawings. He wouldn't be planning a restaurant if he didn't want Skye involved, would he?"

Pete slicked his hair back and then cracked his knuckles. "For all we know, he could have spoken to the architect before his life hit the skids. But even if he didn't, even if he's planning this whole thing, he's still not going to get Skye back until he gets off his ass and goes to see her. And the longer he waits, the harder it's going to be."

"So what are you gonna do?"

Pete looked at Francis. "Why does everyone look at me to do something?"

"Because you're the only one Logan won't try to beat the crap out of if you try to talk to him about Skye."

"Have you tried?"

Francis shook his head. "Nah, I know I can take him, but shit, Patrice would kill me if I hurt the guy. I'd be sleeping on the couch for the rest of my life. Logan's happiness is just not worth that much to me."

"Once again it falls to me. What the hell are you boys going to do when I'm gone?"

Francis gave him a horrified look. "Maybe if you'd stop ignoring your doctor's instructions, we won't have to find out for a good long while. I for one would appreciate it."

"One scotch once in a while isn't going to kill me. You boys and your damn problems might, though." He slid off his stool, finished his drink, and went to deal with Logan.

Logan stared at the preliminary drawings of the microbrewery and restaurant until his eyes crossed. A part of him wanted to rip them to shreds and shoot them all over the Crow's Nest like confetti after a New Year's Eve bash. The other part wanted to hold on to them to remind him of what it felt like to be so close to having everything and lose it all because of one bad move and a reliable condom.

He was just about to roll up the plans when Pop hefted himself into the booth across from him. His father had taken off more weight, but there was still only an inch of space between his gut and the table. "It's not a good time, Pop."

"It's never going to be unless you do something to change it. You've been miserable since Skye left."

"What the hell am I supposed to do? I've called her, texted her, and e-mailed her. I've done everything but hire a skywriter to fly over her apartment building and write 'forgive me or at least answer your phone.'" He ran his hands through his hair and didn't even care if it was standing straight up. "Sometimes no message is a message in and of itself. Skye wants nothing to do with me."

"Do you even know where she lives?"

"Of course I know where she lives. I'm in love with her." He didn't mention that it had taken him two hours on the Internet to figure it out. He went on Google Earth to check out the building—it was nice. Real nice. Maybe Slater had a point when he talked about pedigree, but he'd sooner die than admit it. He made a fist and looked at his bruised knuckles. His hand was a little swollen, but it still looked a damn sight better than Slater's face.

"You're just going to give up?"

"What do you expect me to do?"

Pop's eyes flashed and he leaned forward until he just about covered the table. "I expected you to adjust your drawers over a week ago, get on a plane, and bang on her door until she opened it. I expected you to do what every man who loves a woman has to do eventually—I expected you to beg. When you didn't, I decided to take matters into my own hands."

There weren't many times Logan lost his temper—okay, so he'd lost it when he saw Slater and heard what he'd said to Skye, but other than that, he couldn't remember the last time he had the urge to pummel someone. And never his father. Not Pop. But he did now. Instead, he rolled the plans up so tightly the paper squeaked. "What did you do?" he asked through clenched teeth. It sounded more like an accusation than anything that deserved a question mark at the end.

Pop's smile was like adding black powder to a bonfire. "I'm kicking you out." He pressed an envelope to Logan's chest. "Here's a ticket. I won't allow you to sit here and wallow in self-pity. I didn't raise you to run away like a whipped puppy. Don't come back until you've talked to Skye in person." He looked at his watch. "If you want to pack a bag, you better get a move on. You've got to be at the airport in under two hours."

"What am I supposed to say to her?"

"Hell, son. Do you want me to write you a freakin' speech? How the hell do I know? If you want advice on groveling, talk to Francis. He's the one with all the experience, and hey, it must work, since he and Patrice have been together for years." He tapped the plans. "Oh, and you might want to take these with you. If you need to resort to bribery, these plans might just do the trick."

Skye stood in front of her refrigerator filled with food and healthy ingredients. Nicki would hate it. God, she missed that little girl, but she couldn't think about Nicki now. Every time she did, she just felt worse. She turned her attention back to the food in her fridge, knowing she should eat something, but she couldn't muster any interest. She hadn't cooked since she'd been home. She hadn't watched TV. She hadn't checked her e-mail. She hadn't read a book. She hadn't answered the phone—she wasn't even sure where she put it. The only thing she'd done was sleep and stare into space and replay every memory of Logan and Nicki ad nauseam.

She grabbed her coffee and shuffled through the living room. She'd always thought her home so beautiful, but now it didn't feel like home. She and Kelly had spent months decorating, searching the stores for the perfect couch, the drapes, that stupid table she thought she'd use as a desk. Only she never did. She always worked so much that table became nothing more than a convenient place to leave her purse and briefcase. It was the same place she'd dumped them when she got home almost two weeks ago. She hadn't even charged her phone. What was the point?

A knock at the door had her double-timing it back to bed. Her brothers and Kelly took turns stopping by every day to harass her. She'd hoped they'd eventually get the message and stop. It looked as if today wasn't her lucky day. No surprise there. They'd spend an hour with her. An hour filled with uncomfortable silence or even more uncomfortable conversation, and a good amount of staring. They'd try to ply her with to-go boxes filled with the daily specials that only ended up in the garbage.

She looked around her pristine bedroom and missed the dog toys she was used to stepping over and the fact she no longer had to put all her lingerie out of puggle reach. Shit, she missed everything and everyone from her old life—and it was just that—a life. She certainly didn't have a life now. She didn't have much of a life before she went to Red Hook. And the future wasn't looking promising.

Today she decided to sleep through the visit. She put her coffee on the bedside table, slipped back into bed, and drew the covers over her head.

The knocking stopped; the front door swung open; someone came in and slammed the door.

She knew it was one of the sphincter police by the heavy footfalls across the hardwood floor of her living room. Kelly didn't stomp like an elephant or slam doors.

The elephant stopped beside her bed. "Your coffee is still steaming."

Shit, it was Paddy.

"I know you're awake. Time to get up." He ripped the covers off.

She shot right up in bed. "It's a damn good thing I wear clothes to bed or you'd be getting an eyeful." She cringed when she saw his face. "What?"

"Here." He dropped a beautifully wrapped package on the bed.

"This is a new one. So far you guys have brought me chocolate, flowers, Oprah books, and at least a dozen chick flicks. Hell, Kier even brought me a DVD of *Magic Mike*."

"I know. He still hasn't lived that one down. He was pulling it out of the Redbox when one of his old girl-friends ran into him. He followed her all the way down the produce aisle trying to explain that he hadn't rented it for himself." He picked up her coffee and took a sip.

"Help yourself."

"You weren't drinking it. You were sleeping, remember? The present isn't for you. It's Mom's birthday."

"You bought her a present from me?"

"Of course."

Her big brother actually went shopping? She couldn't believe it. "Oh God, maybe I took a wrong turn at depressed and went straight to delusional."

"Good to see you still have your snarky sense of humor. Kelly bought it and wrapped it. We're expected at the club in an hour and a half. You're going if I have to pick you up out of bed and carry you."

She got up on her knees and planted her hands on her hips. "You wouldn't dare."

"Watch me. Mom and Dad have been asking questions, and the four of us have run out of excuses. Either you come, or Mom is going to kill us all. You know how she is about her birthday."

"Oh, come on, Paddy. Tell her I'm sick or something." Shit, she was actually whining. She was beginning to sound like Nicki.

He set her coffee down, sat on the edge of her bed, rested his elbows on his knees, and scrubbed his face. "No, Skye, I can't. And unless you want Mom to see you looking like a rougher version of that bag lady we saw pushing her shopping cart down your block in New York, I suggest you do whatever you need to do to transform yourself back into my little sister."

The bravado she'd had a minute before deflated. She scooted closer to Paddy, took his big hand in hers, and earned a suspicious quirk of his brow. "I can't go to the club tonight. I just can't." She hated that she was never more than a blink away from tears.

"It's been two weeks. You've hidden out and we've all been covering for you. We don't even know what's going on. Kelly only told me you fell for some guy and he broke your heart. But I have to tell you, squirt. It's getting old. I've known you your whole life and I've never seen you like this. What do I have to do to get my little sister back? Just tell me. I swear, I'll do it."

"I wish I knew. I don't know how to get past it. Every morning I wake up thinking that maybe it'll stop hurting. It hasn't."

"Skye, sitting around here isn't working. You have to try something else. If you don't want to come back to work, that's fine. If you do, that's fine too. If you want your own kitchen, you can have mine. Just don't do this anymore."

"Do you think I enjoy being miserable? I go to sleep thinking about him. I dream about him. I wake up reaching for him—then I remember what happened and it's like it's happening all over again."

"Who is this son of a bitch? I'll kill him."

"No, you won't." But then the way Paddy looked, she was beginning to wonder. "It doesn't matter. He just didn't love me—not enough."

"You quit and moved to New York because of this guy?"

"What? No. I quit for all the reasons I told you. I wanted my own kitchen. That's why I went to New York. I thought I'd get a job where no one knew me. I even used Mom's maiden name so no one would connect me to Maxwell's. I walk into the Crow's Nest and who do I end up working for? Logan Blaise. It's a small world."

"The winemaker? What was he doing in Red Hook?"

"He grew up there. His father owns the Crow's Nest, and Logan was helping out while Pete recovered from a heart attack."

"So Logan Blaise did this to you? But until about two weeks ago he was engaged to Payton Billingsly."

"They broke up again?"

"I don't know about again. I heard about it after we came back."

"It doesn't matter. Logan told me he'd broken up with Payton before we started seeing each other. Maybe the breakup was a lie, or maybe I was his rebound relationship. I don't know. He swore I wasn't. I thought things were good, but then he flew back to go to a wine competition and he and Payton got back together. He said he loved me, Paddy. He made me believe him and then he cheated on me. I had to find out from Kelly."

"How did Kelly know and why didn't you tell me?"

"Because she's my best friend and you were being a real ass. Anyway, Kelly saw Logan and Payton together at the club and smacked him for me. I couldn't stay at the Crow's Nest and work with him, so I found a replacement chef and left with you before he got back."

"You were together for a few weeks and you got in that deep?"

Skye couldn't help it—she rolled her eyes. "How long does it take? Paddy, I love him so much, I don't know how not to. Believe me, I've tried." She wiped her eyes on the worn sleeve of her thrift store Pratt sweatshirt. God, she was sick of crying, and sick of herself. "It's as if he ripped out my heart and somehow I'm still alive. I loved him, his little girl, Nicki—I even loved the dogs, his father, and all his friends. When I was with Logan, I felt so alive. I don't know how to explain it. It was as if my universe expanded. And when he left, when he got back together with Payton, everything was just gone. I've tried, but I don't know how to get over him. I'm hoping I just haven't figured it out yet."

"I can tell you one thing, squirt. You're not going to

do it lying in bed crying. You just have to get up and get on with your life. You go to work, you go home, you go through the motions until you're not going through the motions anymore."

"How long does that take?"

"I don't know. I'll let you know if I ever figure it out."

Where had she heard that before? Oh right, from Slater. Coming from Slater, it made sense, but not Paddy. Paddy was always the one to dump the women he went out with. He was married to his kitchen; no one else could compete. "You were in love?"

"Do you think I have no heart?"

"No, I just don't remember you ever getting attached enough to anyone to end up hurt and I can't remember you ever getting dumped."

"It's not something I publicize and nothing personal, but a guy doesn't cry on his little sister's shoulder. We just go on. It gets easier. Eventually. Now get up and get yourself together. If we're late, I'm going to blame it on you, and you know how Mom and Dad are when it comes to punctuality."

Skye stared at the tablecloth while polite party chatter played on around her like country-club Muzak. She twisted her napkin around her hand until it turned red and throbbed.

Payton sat two tables away having dinner with three of her girlfriends, laughing and snickering and looking like Malibu Barbies.

Paddy kicked Skye under the table and she had half a mind to gouge him with her heel.

"What?" she whispered. When she looked up, every-one was staring at her. Colin's eyes were round, Kier tugged on his collar as if he were trying to loosen a noose, and Reilly was just . . . looking down the server's blouse. Typical. Both he and her father were oblivious to the tension growing like Mount Vesuvius during an active period. When her eyes met her mother's—she knew she was in trouble.

Mary Margaret Maxwell looked at each of her sons in turn, calmly placed her napkin to the side of her plate, and stood.

All five men scrambled to their feet.

She took her purse. "Excuse me, I need to powder my nose. Skye, will you join me?"

"Yes, ma'am." Skye would rather attend a hanging than sit there listening to Payton chortle. Her mother's lecture—the one she knew she'd have to sit through eventually—was a cheap price to pay.

She followed her mother out of the dining room, hearing snippets of the same conversation at every table they passed. The same conversation she'd heard every time she'd come to the club, the same people she saw, dressed in the same style clothing. It seemed the only one who didn't fit in was her. It was as if she'd landed here from another planet—the planet Red Hook.

Her mother entered the restroom before her, did a stall check, and then locked the door. The click of the lock sent a shiver up Skye's spine. When she looked back, Mary Margaret stared at her with her hands on her hips and an I-mean-business twist to her lips. "Out with it. Where have you been for the last month? And don't you dare tell me the islands, because you look as pale as an albino Eskimo."

"Paddy told you—"

"Oh, not you too." Her mother opened her purse,

pulled out a makeup bag, and took out her lipstick, doing a quick touch-up while she eyed her reflection. "I used to think it was great that you kids couldn't lie your way out of a coffin. Now I'm not so sure." She replaced the lipstick cap with a click and turned. "Sometimes a mother doesn't want to know the truth. But I look at you, and I know you've had your heart broken. I know that whoever it was took away your reason to breathe. I know you feel broken inside. What I don't know is why I've been kept in the dark."

Skye didn't realize she'd been crying until her mother took three tissues out of the box and placed them in her hand. "I'm sorry. I didn't mean for any of this to happen. God, Mom, I couldn't take it anymore—working in the back when I wanted to cook, cooking only when the guys let me. I quit and took off for New York. I got a job at a great little place, and I made the mistake of falling for the owner's son."

"What's so wrong with that—except for quitting without discussing it with me and your father first?"

Skye blew her nose, then reached for more tissues. This was going to be a half-a-box confession. "Do you know Logan Blaise?"

"Wasn't he the man engaged to the Billingsly girl? He works with her father, right?"

"He's the one, Mom." She dabbed at her eyes, but it only made it worse. Now she looked like an addict jones'n' for a fix. "He said that he and Payton had called off the engagement."

"That was a couple of weeks ago."

"Right." She laughed but it sounded more like a sob. "He told me that over a month ago. Then he came back for a wine competition and the next thing I know, there are pictures of Logan and Payton Velcro'd together all over the Internet. God, Mom, how could I be so stupid?"

Her mother sat on the settee and smoothed her skirt. "Have you talked to him?"

"No. Why would I want to listen to any more of Logan's lies? Didn't you hear a word I said?"

Her mother sat there perfectly composed as if her daughter hadn't just had her heart smashed, as if she hadn't just gone through twelve tissues crying over losing the love of her life, as if her world hadn't just fallen apart.

"I heard every word you said, dear. I only ask because Pete Calahan told me that Logan's been as miserable as you. Only he hasn't been sitting around wallowing—he's been doing something with his time." She held her hand out to check her nails. "Of course, I can't condone violence, but Pete assured me that Slater got no more than he deserved and lived to tell about it."

"You spoke to Pete?"

"Do you think I've raised four boys and your father without knowing exactly what my children were doing and where they were doing it every day of their lives? Do you actually think I didn't know where you were within forty-eight hours of your disappearance? Honestly, dear, give me some credit."

Skye almost walked into the wall and realized she'd been pacing. She turned and faced her mother, who, she was beginning to realize, might be a stranger. "Why didn't you say anything?"

"Because I enjoy making your brothers suffer. They've been squirming like nuns at a Chippendales show for over a month."

"What did Pete tell you?" God, she hoped he didn't

mention the chocolate cake incident and the champagne incident. She'd had two incidents in her whole life and Logan caused both of them. That had to mean something.

"Pete only told me that you're a hell of a cook and that you were safe and happy. He gave me his word that he'd keep an eye on you." She lifted her chin to her I'm-the-queen-of-all-things angle. "Unlike some people I know, he didn't want me to worry."

Really? Skye couldn't believe her mother would pull this kind of shit. She wasn't a teenager anymore. Come to think of it, her mother didn't pull that when she was a teenager—this was a first. "Mother, I'm thirty years old. I don't have to tell you my every move."

"And I'm your mother. It's my job to know you. I have a PhD in Skye Sinclair Maxwell. I've known for quite a while you were unhappy with your work and I waited patiently for you to do something about it. I have to say, it took you long enough. You're a smart, strong, incredible woman, Skye. And the only one who doesn't know that is you. You've let your brothers push you around your whole life. I had to stop playing referee for your own good. It was past time you learned to stand up for yourself and push back. So now you've finally taken a stand. You've finally left the safe life you've been living. You've finally opened yourself up and let someone get close to you. But at the first sign of trouble, what do you do? You run home and hide your head under your duvet. If you want Logan Blaise, don't you think you should fight for him?"

"But, Mom, he doesn't want me."

"How would you know? From what I hear, you haven't even turned on your phone. How is he supposed to communicate with you? Telepathically? If you love this man, get your head out of the sand and go get him."

"You make it sound so easy."

"I never said that. Do you think your father just fell in line? I not only had Payton Billingsly's mother to fight off; I had every other debutante in our social circle after him. If I had acted like you, you would never have been born."

"You fought Payton's mother for Dad?"

"Well, I wouldn't call it a fight, but there was an unfortunate incident with a bottle of red wine. It was such a shame about her dress, but I had to make sure that no amount of club soda would remove that stain."

"Mother!" God, Skye looked in the mirror and shocked herself. She looked like that person in Edvard Munch's *The Scream*—only paler.

Her mom smiled a terribly wicked smile. Who knew she'd been such a devious debutante? If Skye's brothers ever found out their mother was always one step ahead of them, they'd leave skid marks, and not on pavement.

"Skye, if you really love Logan Blaise, you need to decide how far you're willing to go to win him back. You need to decide if you're willing to spend the rest of your life wondering if you could have worked things out. If you're asking my advice, I'd suggest you give him the opportunity to explain his actions and beg for forgiveness. You have to give him the opportunity to get down on his knees and grovel. It's only fair."

"How do you know he's going to grovel?"

"Because if you love him, he has to be a very special young man. And trust me, dear, if a man isn't willing to beg and grovel, then he's not worth the effort. My makeup is on the counter. Splash your face and put yourself back together. You wouldn't want Payton to see you at less than your best and we have a birthday party to finish." Her mother stood and hugged her. "I love you, Skye. You've always been a precious gift. All you have to do is believe it, and believe in yourself."

"You have to say that. You're my mother."

"No, I don't, and I wouldn't because I'm your mother."

Skye looked into her mother's eyes and she saw love, she saw determination, and she saw truth.

Logan couldn't believe Pop had been in touch with Skye's mother the entire time Skye had worked at the Crow's Nest. The two of them sounded uncomfortably chummy. Still, Pop had been able to tell him exactly when and where to find Skye, so he wouldn't spend hours standing outside Skye's apartment being harassed by the doorman.

Unfortunately, nothing Pop had said helped Logan deal with his nerves. He refrained from drinking on the plane and chose to sweat it out. And sweat he did. By the time he got to his hotel room, he was anxious, sick to his stomach, and in desperate need of a shower.

Luckily, the ticket Pop foisted upon him gave him plenty of time. He had checked into his hotel with an hour to spare, which he spent pacing, trying to figure out what to say to Skye, and imagining worst-case scenarios.

By the time Logan pulled his rental car into the club parking lot and handed the keys off to the parking attendant, he was in full Francis mode: scared shitless and not afraid to show it.

"The Jag in the shop, Mr. Blaise?"

"No, Joey, I sold it."

The poor kid looked like he was about to cry. He nodded, swallowed hard, and handed Logan the ticket.

Logan patted Joey's back, pulled a couple twenties off his billfold, and handed it to the kid. "This is for your car fund. But just remember, in the end, a ride is just a ride."

"Thanks, Mr. Blaise." It didn't look as if Joey believed him, and Logan figured he wouldn't have either if someone had told him the same thing a few months ago. He hoped Joey would figure it out before he got to be Logan's age. He nodded to the doorman, took a deep breath, and straightened his tie.

The maître d' met him at the entrance to the dining room. "Would you like a table, Mr. Blaise, or are you joining Ms. Billingsly?"

Shit, of course Payton would be here to witness his demise. "Neither. I'm meeting someone else. Don't worry—I'll find my party."

"Certainly, sir."

Logan figured if this whole adventure went south, he could kiss his membership good-bye and then realized he couldn't care less—he might as well dump the club anyway. He stepped inside and scanned the room, praying Payton wouldn't spot him.

His eyes locked on Skye and the upside-down feeling, the echoing emptiness, the jumbled confusion he'd accepted as his new normal, instantly disappeared. It was as if his whole world righted itself. The millstone he'd had strapped to his chest vanished and he breathed freely for the first time in weeks. His facial muscles reconfigured and tugged his mouth into a natural smile. He froze, afraid to move, or blink or make a sound, for fear she'd disappear.

Skye stood over what looked like a chocolate birthday cake, removing the candles and licking the frosting off the ends. As if she could feel his gaze, she looked up—she smiled, and just as quickly that smile disappeared. All the color drained from her face.

"Logan!" Payton's voice rang through the restaurant. Shit.

He didn't take his eyes off Skye until Payton blocked his view. "I knew you'd come back." She reached over to kiss him and he caught her shoulders.

"Payton, I'm not here to see you. I'm meeting someone else. Excuse me."

Payton's mouth dropped open.

Logan took full advantage of her shock and stepped around her, leaving her standing in the middle of the dining room.

"But, Logan." Her whine followed him across the room, each "But, Logan" increased in volume, and then it changed to "Logan, come back here!"

By the time he made it to Skye's table, every one of her family members stared at him. Patrick, Colin, and her other two brothers stood with hands fisted at their sides. Anger radiated from them in waves that crashed on Logan with the force of a tsunami.

Jack Maxwell, Skye's father, placed his napkin beside his plate. "What's going on here?" He stood and their eyes met. "Who the hell are you?"

"Logan Blaise, sir." He held his hand out and after a nudge from his wife, Mr. Maxwell gave it a crushing shake; Logan blew out a relieved breath—he didn't think it was broken. The pain in his hand was nothing compared with the pain he'd seen in Skye's eyes when Payton screamed his name. "I'm sorry to interrupt, but I need to borrow Skye for a moment."

All four of Skye's brothers surrounded her. Patrick was their mouthpiece. "Over my dead body."

Skye couldn't see Logan. Her brothers were acting like human shields. She poked Paddy in the kidneys—hard. "That can be arranged, Paddy. Go sit down. That goes for all of you." When they didn't move, she went up on her tiptoes and whispered in Paddy's ear. "I'm warning you, Paddy. The next thing I poke you with will have a serrated edge."

The guys scattered—Kier and Colin knocked into Logan's shoulders on their way to their seats—it was amazing he stayed on his feet. Paddy was smart to leave well enough alone. She'd deal with Colin and Kier later. She crossed her arms to hide her shaking hands and stared straight at Logan's tie tack. "What do you want, Logan?"

He reached over and tipped up her chin so she had no choice but to look him in the eye. Shit. That was so not fair. His touch shot off fireworks through her body. Her face flushed and her pulse skittered beneath his fingertips. He slid his hand around and under her hair, running his fingers over the back of her neck.

She raised her gaze from his nervous smile to his dark brown eyes and let out a string of silent curses. His eyes were so open, so full of love, so honest and true. Logan—her Logan—not a cyborg in sight.

He looked like crap. Like he hadn't slept in weeks. Like he'd lost weight. He looked like she probably did.

He stepped closer. Her crossed arms brushed his chest and his scent wrapped around her like a warm blanket. "Skye, it's you I want. You're the one I love. You're the one I need. You're the one I can't seem to live without. What I've been doing since you left can't be considered living. I love you, Skye. I can explain everything. Please, sugar, I'm begging you. Just give me another chance. I'll spend the rest of my life trying to deserve you."

Her legs didn't seem to want to hold her up anymore and she sank onto the chair. "But you were with Payton. I saw you. Kelly even asked you if Payton was your fiancée. You told me it was over."

Logan went to his knees and took her hands in his. "It was. I swear. My boss just asked that we not announce the breakup until after the competition. If we won, he wanted the story to be about the wine. Skye, you have to believe me. I didn't know Payton was going with us. Honest to God, if I had known, I never would have agreed. I don't think Payton's dad realized what she would do. Hell, even I was surprised."

"You kissed her. I saw it."

"I know that's how it looked. I'm sorry. But technically, she kissed me on camera. I couldn't very well push her away."

"So if some guy just came up and kissed me senseless, you'd be fine with that?"

"No, I'd have to kill him."

"And I'm supposed to just trust you're telling me the truth?"

"I fully expect you to make me grovel for a long, long, long time. Patrice even offered to give you tips on how to torture me."

"Wow, you must be really desperate. That woman has moments of pure evil genius." If Logan were a dog, he'd win the national championship for begging, hands down.

"Skye, you make my life worth living. Please come

back home. Marry me. Make a family with me—a real family of our own. I made an offer on that property. Just say the word and we can make our dreams come true."

"What about Nicki?" The tortured, raw look in his eyes stole her breath and she had the urge to wrap her arms around him.

"The test came back negative. I love her and I always want her in my life. We'll see about the rest."

"Is Slater her father?" She remembered watching them walk away—remembered thinking that Nicki looked like a miniature female version of Slater.

Logan shrugged, closed his eyes, and squeezed her hand. When he opened his eyes again, they looked glassy, filled with pain.

"I'm sorry. I know how much you love her."

"That hasn't changed. She might not be my daughter, but she'll always be my kid. I gotta tell you, though, in one day, I thought I lost both of you. God, Skye. I don't ever want to feel that bad again. Please don't give up on us. Please don't give up on me. Marry me."

Skye looked over at her mother.

Mary Margaret Maxwell gave Skye a thumbs-up. "Well, dear, he certainly has the begging and groveling part down. I think he shows promise."

Jack turned to his wife. "Mary Margaret, what is going on?"

"Shush, Jack. Logan's proposing to your daughter." She looked over at her sons. "And I'll not have you wearing out your knuckles on your future brother-in-law. He's got too pretty a face."

Skye looked at Logan and the background faded and blurred—only Logan's face remained crisp and clear and solid. "Do you want a piece of chocolate cake?"

Logan looked over at her brothers and then back at Skye. "Is that a yes?"

She nodded and couldn't hide the stupid grin on her face. She threw her arms around him, gave him a kiss that she intended to be chaste, but the moment his arms came around her, she didn't care that she was in the middle of the dining room at the club, she didn't care that her parents were three feet away, she didn't care that the sphincter police were probably sharpening their knives.

"I'll take that as a yes." Logan rose to his feet and signaled the waiter. "Can we get two pieces of chocolate cake to go?"

Skye didn't bother hiding her grin before turning to the waiter. "And don't forget the whipped cream."

EPILOGUE

Logan sat on a hard plastic chair and watched Nicki inspect a litter of puppies—what she was looking for was a mystery. She'd repeatedly told him she knew what she was doing. He figured it wouldn't hurt to let her take the lead—after all, this was new to him. He didn't think she could do any worse than he would.

The lady who set them up in the adoption room said the puppies wouldn't be large—she said they were a beagle mix—but the size of their paws had him questioning her knowledge. Apparently the whole litter had been found in a box beside a Dumpster. They were cute as hell—all ten of them. They had big brown eyes, a short coat, white with brown spots, long brown ears, and feet too big for their little bodies.

Nicki stood beside his chair, leaning against him. "You see that one pushing all the others around?"

Logan nodded. "Reminds me of Francis."

She laughed and nudged him. "Mr. Francis is like a big teddy bear, but this puppy—he's too aggressive. He's out."

"How do you know?"

"I read about what to look for when adopting a puppy on Yahoo. I've done research."

He was glad one of them had.

Nicki pulled a squeaky toy out of her pocket, and tossed it. Two of the puppies ran away; the others went to play. "Those two are too skittish."

"Okay. Three down, seven to go."

Then she sat on the floor and let the puppies crawl all over her. She picked them up one by one. After holding every one of them several times, she stopped and smiled and pushed herself to her feet while holding a puppy in her arms. "I found him!"

"Him?"

"D.O.G. needs a boy to play with. And look at this one—he's chubby and cuddly and he doesn't have a problem lying in my arms with his belly up."

"Why would he have a problem lying on his back?"

"The article said that when you pick out a puppy, if it struggles when you hold them like this, they're either too timid or too aggressive. Look at this little guy—he loves to cuddle and he likes being touched. He played with the toy and he didn't spook earlier when I clapped. Besides, he loves me."

"That's not much of a test, Nicki. Everyone loves you."

Nicki held the puppy to her chest. "I know. It's something I have to learn to live with. But this little one—he's special, just like Skye."

The attendant knocked on the door and stepped in. "Have you made a decision?"

Nicki held the puppy tighter and he burrowed into her neck. "We'd like to adopt this one."

"Okay. You've already filled out the application and

everything is in order, so all you have to do is pay the adoption fee and you can take your puppy home."

Two hours later they parked Pop's Jeep in front of the Crow's Nest.

"Logan, tie the ribbon around his neck in a big bow."

"Do I have to? He's going to look like a sissy."

"No, he's not. He's going to look like a present, silly. It's blue. He'd look like a sissy if the ribbon were pink."

Logan reached over the seat back at an awkward angle, tied the big blue ribbon around the puppy's neck, and did his best to make a bow that didn't look like crap. He had to admit, the kid had picked well. For a pup, he was nice and calm. They'd walked all over PetSmart filling up a grocery cart, buying bowls, toys, collars, leashes, puppy food, and even a sweater, until the little guy planted his butt on the linoleum floor and refused to walk any farther. Logan picked him up and the pup fell asleep in his arms—which made it a little difficult to pay the bill, but they'd managed.

Nicki unbuckled her seat belt and bounced with the puppy in her arms. "Come on. Skye's probably wondering what happened to us."

"Okay, let's go. I'll come back later and get the rest of the stuff."

Skye stood in Pete's kitchen, picked up the frying pan, and gave the string beans she sautéed in garlic and olive oil a toss. She turned the heat down and counted the plates she'd need to set the table and placed them on the counter.

Nicki and Logan had been gone for hours, and before they pulled their disappearing act, they'd been whispering behind her back. She didn't know what they were up to. "Pete, when did you say Logan and Nicki would be back?"

Pete looked up from his paper and smirked at Bree and Storm. "I didn't."

"I can see you, you know. What's going on?" The three of them eyed her like some kind of science experiment.

Bree strolled into the kitchen and stole a string bean out of the pan. "Don't worry. It's not as if Logan's going to do anything stupid like teach Nicki how to drive."

Skye opened the oven to check the standing rib roast. It was almost done. "I should hope not. Nicki's only ten. She's not even tall enough to reach the pedals and see over the dash—heck, she's not even old enough to sit in the front seat. Why would he teach her to drive?"

"I have no clue, but that didn't stop Storm." Bree rolled her eyes and shot Storm a disapproving glare.

He came into the kitchen and wrapped Bree in a bear hug. "You're never going to let me live that down, are you?"

"Nope, I plan on holding that stunt over your head for the rest of your life. I'm going to get as much mileage out of that as humanly possible." She kissed his cheek and returned her attention to Skye. "Logan's the responsible one. I don't think you have anything to worry about."

Still, Logan and Nicki had been gone all afternoon— she missed them. She'd been home a little over a week and this was the first time she and Logan had been apart for more than an hour. They'd moved into Bree's old one-bedroom apartment over the bar, across the hall from Pete's, and planned to stay until they finished renovating the warehouse. The plans were done, and the construction had begun, but it would still be months before they'd be able to move into their loft above the brewpub they were opening.

"How is the construction coming?"

Skye shrugged. "Good, I guess. Right now, it just looks like a big mess to me. Rocki is having a great time supervising the construction workers. She's forever running over there delivering lunch, coffee, and God only knows what else. She has a new fascination for men in tool belts."

Slater, who had been sitting on the couch behind his ever present laptop, grumbled something.

Skye pulled the potatoes off the stove and dumped them into a colander to mash. She gave Bree a knowing look and the two of them tried not to laugh at Slater. When she returned, he'd apologized to her for being an ass. He was still sporting the bruises from his discussion with Logan. He'd been great ever since. Whenever Rocki was around, Slater seemed incapable of keeping his eyes off her, and Rocki didn't seem to realize Slater even existed. Every other man, sure, but to Rocki, Slater seemed invisible. "Storm, Slater, would you two put a few leaves in the table? Rocki, Francis, Patrice, and the girls should be here any minute."

Slater put his laptop on the coffee table and shot off the couch. "Rocki's coming to dinner? Why?"

"Because she's practically a part of the family, and I thought it might be nice for you two to get to know each other better." Men were so clueless.

Slater shrugged and Bree pushed Storm out of the kitchen to help.

There was a commotion in the hall, but Skye didn't bother looking—she was too busy taking the canapés out of the oven.

Bree slid beside her and took the tray from her. "I'll deal with this. I think you're needed in the living room."

"I am?"

Just then Nicki ran into the kitchen. "Skye. Close your eyes and follow me."

"How am I supposed to follow you with my eyes closed?"

Nicki grabbed her hand. "I'll lead you. Just keep your eyes closed or you'll ruin everything."

Skye gave Nicki a hug. "Okay. Just don't let me run into a wall."

"I promise."

Skye closed her eyes and let Nicki lead her into the living room. "You better make this quick, Nicki. I have to mash the potatoes. Bree, can you take the roast out of the oven to rest?"

"Sure thing."

Skye heard the door open and the sound of Logan whispering to Nicki. She couldn't keep the smile from her face. She'd been wearing it ever since they'd gotten engaged. She shifted her engagement ring on her finger. It still felt weird—weird but good.

Logan stepped closer—even with her eyes closed, she knew it was him.

He pulled her into his arms, standing behind her, and kissed her temple. "Okay, open your eyes."

"Surprise!" Nicki yelled, and bounced on the balls of her feet.

Skye was looking at Nicki's bouncing, so it took her a second before she saw the little puppy wearing a big bow that was almost as big as he was, sitting at Nicki's feet. "You bought another puppy?"

Logan tightened his hold around her waist. "He's for

you. You've been missing Pepperoni so much, we thought you'd like to have a puppy of your own. Do you like him?"

Nicki picked the puppy up and held him out to her. "He's so small."

"Let's hope he stays that way. The lady at the SPCA said he was a beagle mix, but I have my doubts. Look at the size of those paws."

Skye held him close, and the little guy nuzzled her neck, and she rubbed her chin against his bony head. Yeah, she was in love. She drank in his puppy scent and did her best to blink away the tears, but that wasn't working too well.

Nicki's face crumbled. "You don't like your present?"

"No, I love him." She stepped out of Logan's embrace and pulled Nicki into a hug. "He's precious and perfect and sweet. Just like you."

"But he's a puppy."

"He certainly is. Nicki. This is the best present I've ever been given. Thank you."

"I picked him out just for you. I researched it and everything, so he's going to be the best dog ever—next to D.O.G., that is."

Francis, Patrice, Rocki, and the girls all piled into the apartment and the volume rose, but it didn't seem to bother the puppy, who was happy to watch the proceedings from the comfort of Skye's arms. "I've never seen such a cuddly dog—not that I've had much experience, but the only time Pepperoni was cuddly was when she was half-asleep."

Nicki smiled up at her when D.O.G. gave the puppy a cursory sniff. "Now we can walk our dogs together all the time."

"We sure can."

"What are you going to call him?"

"I don't know. Let me get dinner on the table and then we can discuss it. Maybe something will come to us. Will you hold him for me?"

"Sure. I'll puppy sit." Nicki took the pup and ran off to play with the dogs and Francis and Patrice's girls in her room.

Skye turned to Logan, who still wore a worried look. "Thank you. I love the puppy."

He pulled her into his arms and kissed her. "Well, that's a relief. Nicki has a way of getting her own way, and she was sure you were miserable without Pepperoni."

"I wouldn't say I was miserable, but I did miss my little puggle. I've never had a puppy before, though, so I don't know how to train one."

"Yeah, that makes two of us. But it's okay. I bought a bunch of books and signed us up for puppy school. We start next week."

"What do we do until then?"

"I guess we just have to wing it. Remember, as long as we're together, there's nothing we can't handle."

She kissed him again and pulled away. "You're definitely right. But at the moment, I have a dinner to finish preparing. Boys," she said a bit louder than her normal speaking voice, "you're on dish duty, so get the table set. Dinner is in ten minutes."

There was a bunch of grumbling, but one look from Bree and they all became very quiet.

Francis and Rocki handed the utensils and the glasses across the breakfast bar while she made decadent mashed garlic potatoes with heavy cream, butter, and sour cream. The finished product was well worth the calories. She made a skinny version for Pete—she figured she'd mix them half-and-half, so hopefully he wouldn't notice.

Everyone piled around the table. Logan poured wine for the adults, and ginger ale for Pete and the kids.

Skye watched as Pete switched glasses with Bree when Logan wasn't looking. Pete gave Bree a wink that made Skye think there was an interesting story behind the switch.

Skye looked at the table loaded with food and all the people she'd grown to love. She couldn't believe how much love could be contained in one place. She was humbled to be a part of this loud, crazy, loving family, and she wouldn't have traded them for the world. She looked at the kids, caught Nicki's eye, and blew her a kiss.

Pete held up his glass. "Here's to our growing family."

Logan held up his glass and cleared his throat before turning to her. "I have known many, and liked not a few, but loved only one, and this toast is to you, Skye. I love you." He reached over and kissed her. Rocki and Patrice sighed, the guys rolled their eyes, and Skye kissed him until she heard gagging noises coming from the kids.

"I love you too."

"I fell in love with you the first time I saw you. Skye, you're the one."

Read on for an excerpt from the first
Bad Boys of Red Hook novel,

BACK TO YOU

Available now from Signet Eclipse

Mug in hand, Bree waited for the coffee to brew. She looked away from the pot when Storm walked through the front door, wearing running shorts and a sweat-stained T-shirt. The sight of him stole all the oxygen from the room, maybe the whole building.

"Morning, Breezy."

"Morning."

Storm lifted the hem of his shirt and wiped his face, baring his washboard abs and revealing the treasure trail of dark hair disappearing into the waistband of his shorts. Rounding the breakfast bar, he set two bags of what smelled like bagels and all the fixings on the counter, then grabbed a water from the fridge. As he downed the entire bottle, his Adam's apple bobbed with each gulp.

"Coffee?" She cleared her throat, hardly recognizing her own voice. She grabbed another mug and, without waiting for the machine to finish, poured two cups.

Flashbacks, like grainy sex tapes of the last night she'd seen Storm before he'd left, ran through her mind. Every. Humiliating. Moment. She took a slow, deep breath.

Storm stared at her.

She raised her chin and stared right back. He'd changed—physically at least. He was broader and more muscled. His tall, skinny frame had filled out in manhood, and the angles of his face had sharpened. His nose was narrow and a little crooked, probably the result of all the fights he'd gotten into as a kid. His square jaw was more defined, and his neck was corded with muscle. He was solid, heavy, dangerous, and so full of charged energy, he seemed to barely kept it in check.

Needing something to do, Bree opened the bags and peeked in. "Thanks for picking up breakfast."

"Anything to keep you away from a frying pan."

She winged her eyebrow as she snatched the first salt bagel she saw, ripped a piece off, and stuffed it in her mouth.

"I didn't know what you and Nicki liked, so I got a little of everything—just to be safe." He pulled his shirt off and dragged it across his neck and chest. "I'll just grab a quick shower."

She stared at his six-pack. Why couldn't it be a keg?

"Hello? Breezy? Did you hear me?"

"Uh, yeah." She handed him his coffee and watched him walk to Pete's room. Wasn't she just chock-full of inspired repartee? She wasn't out to impress him or anything, but sheesh, she'd sounded like a member of the dim-bulb club.

Nicki padded out of her room in her Hello Kitty nightgown. "He's still here?"

"Shh. He might hear you."

Nicki smiled as she climbed onto the barstool. "I can live with that."

"What, that Storm is here or that he might hear you?"

"Both, actually. I bet Pop will be happy to see him." Nicki tilted her head to one side. "How come Storm's been gone so long?"

Bree closed her eyes and rubbed the spot on her temple that throbbed with every beat of her heart. God, she was in no mood for twenty questions. "I'm not sure." She knew why Storm had left, but not why he stayed away. "I guess you'll just have to ask him."

Bree poured a glass of orange juice and slid it across the bar. "How did you sleep?"

"Fine after you took Storm down. Man, that was epic. You were like Wonder Woman with a frying pan instead of the rope."

"Yeah, that's me. Wonder Woman with her frying pan of truth." Bree arranged the bagels on a plate and grabbed another for the whitefish and lox. There must have been seventy-five dollars' worth of lox, not to mention the schmear. She handed the plates to Nicki. "Why don't you set the table so we can eat? We need to get down to the hospital, and I'm already running late."

Nicki walked around the table, placing the napkins on top of the plates.

No matter how many times Bree corrected her, she couldn't break Nicki of the habit. "Food goes on the plate. Napkins belong under the fork or on your lap."

Nicki stopped. "When you sit down, the first thing you do is put your napkin in your lap. What's it matter if the napkin's under the fork or on the plate?"

Bree sighed. What was the point? They'd had the discussion thirty times. It never changed the way Nicki set the table, and it only served to remind her of Nicki's first dinner at Pete's, the day Bree fell in love with the little scamp.

Pete had asked Bree to come because Nicki seemed uncomfortable alone with him. The poor thing had just been abandoned by the only parent she'd ever known. She was hurt, scared, and thrown into the care of a big bear of a man.

Nicki had spent the meal hunched over her plate, guarding her food. She'd even hidden some in her napkin for later. Bree's heart broke every time she thought about it. She placed her hands on Nicki's shoulders.

"What?" Nicki gave her that look—a little confused, a little shy, and still, even after almost three months, a little scared.

Bree pulled her close and held her, resting her chin on the top of Nicki's head. She loved Nicki as much as she imagined any mother loved her child. She'd always wanted a family—a traditional family like the one she had before her father died. She remembered what it was like when she had two loving parents and then what her life was like after her father had died. She was afraid of being the same kind of single parent her mother had turned into—smothering, obsessive. Bree wouldn't do that to a child. No, unless Bree found a man and was happily married, she'd never have a child of her own. Many single women had children and were fabulous parents, but the deep fear of becoming like her mother was enough to make her not want to take the chance. "I love you, Nicki."

Nicki snuggled in. "For always and forever?"

Bree held her tighter. "For always and forever. No matter what."

"Even if I never put the napkin in the right place?"

Bree felt a smile tug on the corners of her mouth. The little brat was testing her. "Even then. I love you for who you are, not what you do." She kissed the top of Nicki's head and looked up to find Storm leaning against the doorjamb. The curious look in his eye had Bree hugging Nicki tighter. She wasn't sure what Storm was curious about, but then, she didn't know Storm Decker—not anymore and maybe not ever.

It was an affront to all womankind that Storm could take a five-minute shower and come out looking edible when it took Bree an hour just to come out looking not scary.

Bree kissed the top of Nicki's head again, released the little rascal, and then reached for a bagel for Nicki. Cutting it in half, Bree stopped just short of slicing her hand. The damn man made her nervous.

"Good morning, Nicki." Storm sat at the head of the table while Nicki piled her bagel with lox. He took up more room than any man should—all spread out, as if he didn't have a care in the world.

"That's Pop's chair."

"Yeah, well, you're sitting in mine."

Nicki snorted. "Doesn't have your name on it."

Bree watched as Nicki sized up Storm. He looked loose and comfortable, as if his father weren't in the hospital; as if he hadn't been away for more than a third of his life; as if he ate breakfast with her and Nicki every day.

Storm set his coffee on the table and sat straighter in his chair. "What grade are you in?"

Holding her bagel with both hands, Nicki continued to eye him. "I'm going into fifth grade." She took a big bite of her bagel and struggled to keep it in her mouth.

Bree stopped herself from telling Nicki to take human bites. The girl didn't eat food; she inhaled it.

"So that makes you how old?" Storm asked, either not noticing Nicki's lack of table manners, or ignoring them.

Bree pushed Nicki's juice toward her. "Ten."

When Nicki finally swallowed, she shook her head. "Ten and a half."

Bree snuck glances at Storm as she fixed what was left of her bagel. Licking the remnants of schmear off the side of her finger, she lifted the bagel to her mouth to lick what had escaped.

She caught Storm staring. She remembered that look; no matter how many times she'd tried to forget it, it returned to her in her dreams. It was the same look she'd seen in his eyes right before he'd shut down and run away from her all those years ago, leaving her naked and needy. Fidgeting in her chair, she crossed her legs before wiping her fingers on her napkin, and tried to erase it from her inner hard drive.

Bree saw Nicki goggling at Storm. God only knew what would come out of Nicki's mouth next. The girl was not only perceptive, but she said whatever went through her mind. "Nicki, why don't you run and get dressed. Don't forget to wash your face and brush your teeth. You can take the rest of your bagel with you and eat it on the way to the hospital."

Nicki looked at her plate.

"I'll wrap up the leftovers so when we come back, you can make another bagel to bring down to the restaurant if you want."

"Okay." Nicki rose, still looking longingly at her half-eaten bagel, and then swiped her tongue across the schmear.

Bree cringed—as if anyone else would eat it. "Just

leave it. I'll put it in a sandwich bag for you. And don't forget to bring a sweater. It's always chilly in the hospital."

Nicki did the patented teenaged eye roll and headed to her room, muttering, "Bree, I'm not a baby."

Storm turned the full wattage of his smile up a few degrees and aimed it at Bree. "The kid's still protective of her food after three months? I'm surprised she didn't spit in her juice."

"Like you never backwashed your Coke. At least she doesn't hunch over her plate anymore." She picked up Nicki's bagel. "Are you going to eat anything?"

"I guess I should. She didn't lick anything else, did she?"

"You should be safe. She's had all her shots."

He fixed a monster bagel while Bree made another for Nicki and grabbed a juice box.

"Where'd Pop find Nicki?"

Bree shrugged and pulled out a few sandwich bags. "You need to talk to Pete about that. All I know is one day Nicki was here. Pete said he'd known her mom years ago and that she couldn't care for Nicki anymore, so she signed over all parental rights and left Nicki with him."

"Who's her mother?"

Bree stashed the food in the fridge. "I don't know, but it doesn't matter. Right now, it's more important for Nicki to know she has a real home where she's loved and wanted."

Storm's straight dark brows drew together as if he didn't believe her. Well, that was his problem. She didn't owe him anything, but she owed Pete her life. Pete had been her father's lifelong friend and partner on the force. He'd taken her under his wing after her dad's death, loving her and supporting her like a surrogate father. Pete gave her a safe place to escape her mother, he gave her guidance, and eventually he gave her a job and a home. She'd do anything to protect Nicki and Pete.

At the thought of Pete, she realized Storm was going to have one hell of a shock when he saw him.

Bree stopped what she was doing. "Storm, Pete's changed a lot. He's aged. He's not the same big guy you saw six years ago."

"People don't change that much."

"They do after open-heart surgery."

ALSO AVAILABLE

FROM

Robin Kaye

BACK TO YOU
Bad Boys of Red Hook

Storm Decker's childhood was bleak until an ex-cop took him in and became like a father to him. Now Pop has suddenly fallen ill, and Storm is called home. Breanna Collins never expected to see Storm again after he left town, breaking her heart. She hopes he'll see through his painful memories to the changes in their hometown. But unless she can remind him of all the reasons to stay, she knows he'll never give their romance the second chance it deserves…

Praise for the novels of Robin Kaye:

"A treat to read."
—*New York Times* bestselling author Eloisa James

"Charm[s] readers with her wit and style."
—*Booklist*

Available wherever books are sold or at
penguin.com

facebook.com/LoveAlwaysBooks

ALSO AVAILABLE

FROM

Robin Kaye

HOMETOWN GIRL

AN EXCLUSIVE DOWNLOADABLE PENGUIN
SPECIAL FROM SIGNET ECLIPSE

Elyse Fitzgerald is on a blind date from hell in Brooklyn's
historic waterfront neighborhood of Red Hook when she
stumbles into a childhood friend—and longtime crush.
She knows Simon would never be interested in his little
sister's friend, even though she's all grown up. So it's a
lucky break that he doesn't recognize her…

Simon Sprague is an artist who picks up bartending shifts
at a local family-owned pub. To the artistic Simon, the
women he usually meets at work are uninspiring. Except
for the dark-eyed goddess who just walked into his bar.
He feels an instant connection with her, and the
mysterious woman seems to know him. Quick on his feet,
Simon goes along with the ride…but will he lose his heart
to a hometown girl along the way?

Available wherever e-books are sold or at
penguin.com

facebook.com/LoveAlwaysBooks

LOVE
ROMANCE
NOVELS?

For news on all your favorite romance authors, sneak peeks into the newest releases, book giveaways, and much more—

"Like" Love Always on Facebook!
 **LoveAlwaysBooks**

Penguin Group (USA) Online

What will you be reading tomorrow?

Tom Clancy, Patricia Cornwell, W.E.B. Griffin,
Nora Roberts, William Gibson, Catherine Coulter,
Stephen King, Dean Koontz, Ken Follett, Nick Hornby,
Khaled Hosseini, Kathryn Stockett, Clive Cussler,
John Sandford, Terry McMillan, Sue Monk Kidd,
Amy Tan, J. R. Ward, Laurell K. Hamilton,
Charlaine Harris, Christine Feehan...

You'll find them all at
penguin.com
facebook.com/PenguinGroupUSA
twitter.com/PenguinUSA

*Read excerpts and newsletters, find tour schedules
and reading group guides, and enter contests.*

Subscribe to Penguin Group (USA) newsletters
and get an exclusive inside look
at exciting new titles and the authors you love
long before everyone else does.

PENGUIN GROUP (USA)
us.penguingroup.com

S0151